W9-CAB-530

MORPHEUS ROAD
the light

PENDRAGON

**JOURNAL OF AN ADVENTURE
THROUGH TIME AND SPACE**

MORPHEUS ROAD

the light

D. J. MACHALE

Aladdin

New York London Toronto Sydney

ALADDIN
An imprint of Simon & Schuster Children's Publishing Division
1230 Avenue of the Americas, New York, NY 10020
First Aladdin hardcover edition April 2010
Copyright © 2010 by D. J. MacHale
All rights reserved, including the right of reproduction
in whole or in part in any form.
ALADDIN is a trademark of Simon & Schuster, Inc.,
and related logo is a registered trademark of Simon & Schuster, Inc.
For information about special discounts for bulk purchases,
please contact Simon & Schuster Special Sales at 1-866-506-1949
or business@simonandschuster.com.
The Simon & Schuster Speakers Bureau can bring authors to your live event.
For more information or to book an event contact
the Simon & Schuster Speakers Bureau at 1-866-248-3049
or visit our website at www.simonspeakers.com.
Designed by Sammy Yuen Jr.
The text of this book was set in Apollo MT.
Manufactured in the United States of America
0210 FFG
2 4 6 8 10 9 7 5 3 1
Library of Congress Cataloging-in-Publication Data
MacHale, D.J.
The light / D.J. MacHale. — 1st Aladdin hardcover ed.
p. cm. — (Morpheus Road ; bk. 1)
Summary: Sixteen-year-old Marshall Seaver is expecting a boring summer when his best friend goes away, but instead he finds himself haunted—and hunted—by ghosts that want something from him which he cannot decipher.
ISBN 978-1-4169-6516-9 (hardcover)
[1. Horror stories. 2. Ghosts—Fiction. 3. Supernatural—Fiction.
4. Death—Fiction.] I. Title.
PZ7.M177535Li 2010
[Fic]—dc22
2009040624

For Donna

Foreword

I love scary stories.

Always did. I think it started when I was a toddler and my mother read me the Dr. Seuss story *What Was I Scared Of?* I moved on to reading ghost stories like *The Children of Green Knowe* by L. M. Boston and Shirley Jackson's *The Haunting of Hill House*. Most Saturdays my friend Frank and I would go to the horror matinee at the local theater where they showed bizarre fright films from Italy and England and Eastern Europe and who knew where else? I had nightmares for years after seeing a film called *Black Sabbath*. (In hindsight I wished I had skipped that one.) I don't think I've seen any of those films since, but they definitely left an impression.

Once I started writing for young people, my natural inclination steered me toward telling tales of the supernatural. For years I made a TV show called *Are You Afraid of the Dark?*

Between the ninety-one episodes of that show and the spinoff books and games and short stories, I think I've explored just about every scary convention that exists . . . and some that I made up.

When I try to figure out what it is about supernatural stories that intrigues me, I don't think it's for the obvious reasons. Sure, I think it's cool when your palms start sweating because you don't know what might be lurking around the corner, and it's a rush when something unexpectedly jumps out at you, but that's only part of it. I think the great thing about supernatural stories is that they are so full of possibility. As a storyteller, you aren't restricted by the laws of nature. Anything can happen. Being somebody who likes to put twists into my stories, having a bottomless toolbox of surprises to dig into is a wonderful thing. The only limit is your own imagination. How great is that?

But the other aspect of spooky tales I like is that, like any good story, it's really about the characters. Whatever the boogeyman happens to be, the story is really about characters the reader can relate to as they try to understand why they are being tormented by supernatural doings. Since all stories are about dealing with conflict, it's a lot of fun putting characters into situations where the conflict is something you don't normally encounter in real life (at least I don't, anyway).

That brings us to Morpheus Road: *The Light*. It's going to be a trilogy, but I don't want to reveal where the next two Morpheus Road books will take us. That's all part of the mystery of what is about to happen to Marshall Seaver. You'll learn right along with him. For those of you who have read my Pendragon series, you know that I like to take you on a journey that is always surprising. Just when you think you know where you're going, you don't. Sometimes you'll guess right, other times not, and when you hit the end, it isn't.

Yeah, you'll find all that stuff here.

Though the story is different, I'm fortunate that my cast of supporting players continues to remain the same, and I'd like to acknowledge them.

I am very grateful to all my good friends at Simon & Schuster Children's Publishing for giving me the opportunity to explore stories that don't involve Bobby Pendragon. They've put their faith in me with not only Morpheus Road, but two other new book series, and for that I am very thankful.

Liesa Abrams was the final editor on the Pendragon series, and I'm thrilled that she has stayed with me for this new adventure. Her insight and guidance has proved invaluable in shaping Marsh's story. (And she even introduced me to the Goon graphic novels. Thanks, Liesa.)

Richard Curtis has forgotten more about the publishing business than I'll ever know, and I am grateful to him for his sage guidance during every step of the process. And he's a terrific guy . . . for a Mets fan.

Peter Nelson and Mark Wetzstein continue to have my back on all things contractual. One of these days I may actually read one of those contracts. (Doubt it.)

The girls I call "my two blondes" make this all worthwhile. My wife, Evangeline, continues to be the first reader of every word that I write and always keeps me honest. My daughter, Keaton, continues to amaze and inspire me with her imagination. She is almost old enough to be reading my books, though I think I'll hold off on letting her read Morpheus Road for a while. I don't want her having a *Black Sabbath* incident. Thanks, ladies, I love you both.

Finally, to all of you Pendragon readers who have decided to give this new story a shot, I thank you and hope you enjoy it. If not for you, this book would not exist. Hobey ho to you all.

When I finished making *Are You Afraid of the Dark?* I took a long break from writing about the supernatural. I hung out with castaways on a tropical island for *Flight 29 Down* and traveled across time and space to create massive battles for Pendragon. When I decided to take a trip back into the supernatural world and started to write *The Light*, I had some doubts. I felt a little bit like a gunslinger who had hung up his shootin' irons for a long time. I had to dust them off, strap them on, and hope that I still knew how to shoot.

The answer came quickly. The guns were loaded and shot true. I knew it as soon as the bodies started falling. And as everybody knows, you can't have ghosts without bodies.

It was good to be back in the saddle.

I love scary stories.

See you in Trouble Town.

—D. J. MacHale

Prologue

I believe in ghosts.

Simple as that. I believe in ghosts.

Maybe that doesn't come across as very dramatic. After all, lots of people believe in ghosts. You always hear stories about some guy who felt a "presence" or glimpsed a fleeting, unexplainable phenomenon. There are mediums who claim they can make contact with the great beyond and receive messages to let the living know that all is well. Or not. Then there are those people who operate on a more philosophical level . . . the spiritual types who believe that the energy of the human soul is so powerful, it must continue on after death to some other plane of existence. Of course, there are millions of people who love getting scared by ghost stories. They may not believe, but they sure have fun pretending.

I'm not like any of those people. At least not anymore. A little over a week ago you could have put me in the category of somebody who didn't necessarily believe in anything supernatural, though I did like horror movies. But that was then. Before last week. A week is like . . . nothing. How many particular weeks can anybody really remember? A week can fly by like any other. Or it can change your life. You tend to remember those weeks.

I remember last week.

It was the week the haunting began.

Or maybe I should call it the hunting because that's what it was. I was being hunted. And haunted. It wasn't a good week.

My name is Marshall Seaver. People call me Marsh. I live in a small town in Connecticut called Stony Brook. It's a suburb of New York City where moms drive oversize silver trucks to Starbucks and most kids play soccer whether they want to or not. It's the kind of place where kids are trained from birth to compete. In everything. School, sports, friend- ships, clothes . . . you know, everything. I'm not sure what the point is other than to win bragging rights. Luckily, my parents didn't buy into that program. They said I should set my own priorities. I liked that. Though it puts pressure on me to figure out what those priorities are.

I guess you'd call us middle class. We've only got one car and it's almost as old as I am. I can't believe it's still running, because we drove it into the ground. My parents liked to travel. That was one of *their* priorities. Whenever they had two days off, we'd hit the road, headed for some national monument or backwater town that served awesome gumbo or had historical significance or maybe just sounded differ- ent. I complained a lot about how boring it was, but to be honest, I didn't hate it. Bumping around in the back of a car wasn't great, but the adventure of it all made it worthwhile. It's kind of cool to see things for real instead of on TV. I miss those trips.

Other than that, my life is pretty usual. Unlike a lot of people in this town, I've never been inside a country club. Most of my clothes come from Target. I ride my bike to school. We don't live in a monster-size house, but it's plenty big enough for the three of us.

That is, when there were still three of us.

Things have changed. Not that long ago I thought I had a pretty good handle on what normal was. I was wrong. Nothing about my life is normal anymore. The events that unfolded over the last week weren't just about me, either. Many lives were touched and not all for the better. As I look back, I can't help but wonder what might have happened if different decisions had been made. Different paths taken. So many innocent choices added to a butterfly effect that fed the nightmare. Or created it. I guess it goes without saying that I'm still alive. Not everyone was so lucky. That's the harsh thing about ghost stories. Somebody has to die. No death, no ghost. I survived the week and that gives me a feeling of guilt I'll carry forever. Or at least for as long as I live. I hope that's a good long time, but there are no guarantees because this story isn't done.

The hunt is still on.

My story may sound like a fantasy, and maybe some of it is. But many things happened over that week that can't be ignored or explained away as having sprung from an overly imaginative mind. People died. Lives were changed. That was no dream. After what I saw and experienced, there's one other bit of reality I have to accept.

I believe in ghosts.

After you hear my story, I think you will too.

1

Cooper Foley was in trouble. Again.

"What were you thinking?" I screamed at him. "Counterfeit tickets? Really?"

"Easy, Ralph," Coop replied calmly. "I didn't know they were bogus."

Cooper always called me Ralph.

"Even so," I argued. "It's illegal to scalp *real* tickets."

"No, it's not," he corrected. "Not if you sell them at face value."

"Did you sell them at face value?"

He smiled. "No."

I wanted to smack him.

Cooper and I were making the long walk to school on the last day of the year before summer vacation. He was my best friend. Okay, my only friend. My only *good* friend, anyway. I think the main reason we got along so well was because we were completely different. I worry. Cooper doesn't. I think things through. Cooper doesn't. I freeze in social situations. Cooper doesn't. I hate playing sports. Cooper doesn't. I worry about what people think of me. Cooper doesn't.

I think we stayed friends because there was never any competition between us. We had plenty of fights over the years, but they always ended up in a wrestling match that lasted about eight seconds. No punches were ever thrown in anger. As we walked along on that hot June day, I was ready to plot out all the exciting adventures we'd be sharing that summer. Instead I found out that Cooper was in trouble. Again.

"What's going to happen?" I asked.

Cooper shrugged as if he didn't really care. "Nothing. I got spanked, that's all. Nobody thinks I printed out a bunch of phony Yankees tickets. And for the record, I didn't."

"Then who did?"

He gave me a sly smile. "Can't tell you that, Ralph. I'd have to kill you."

Coop was changing . . . and not for the better. Though he was always a wild guy, he never got into serious trouble. With him it was about being a goof in class or skateboarding without a helmet. The thing was, he always made the teachers laugh and didn't need a helmet because he never crashed. Ever. Once when we were around ten, we snuck into the private stable of some uber-rich Wall Street guy. I was so scared, I wanted to puke. In fact, I did. All over my pants. Not Coop. He hopped on the back of a prize thoroughbred and rode it, bareback, out of the stable and across the huge lawn, shouting, "Yippiekiyay!" He didn't get in trouble, either. I, on the other hand, caught hell for ruining my pants. Cooper lived a charmed life. He never puked on his pants.

That is, until we got to high school. That's when he started pushing things. He got into fights. Real fights. He'd skip school. His parents started coming down on him for his grades, which made it pretty tense around the Foley house. They grounded him . . . he snuck out. We'd go for weeks without seeing each other because he started hanging around with some older guys. They smelled like bad news, so I didn't go anywhere near them. I'd bet anything they had something to do with the counterfeit tickets Coop was busted for selling.

None of this was like Coop. At least not the Coop I knew. Yeah, he liked to have fun and push some limits, but he wasn't a bad guy. Or maybe I was just naive.

"It's okay, Ralph," he assured me. "It was dumb. I get it. I'm not going there again."

I'd heard that promise before.

"C'mon!" he said. "Tomorrow the gun goes off on summer. What's the plan? I know you've got a plan."

My mood changed instantly. Coop had that ability. When he got psyched up about something, he brought everyone else right along with him. He was right. I had a plan. I'd been looking forward to this summer for months.

"It's gonna be great," I said with excitement. "The rocket kits finally came in. We can set up shop and build 'em at my house . . . wait'll you see the new plasma Dad got from work . . . hello, Yankees in high def . . . then we can head up to the reservoir and camp for a couple of days and launch 'em."

Cooper gave me a blank stare. "Okay," he said with absolutely no enthusiasm.

Undaunted, I pressed on. "Oh! And the Jansens said I could take their Hobie Cat out whenever I wanted. I'm thinking we can race the ferry out to Captain's Island like we did last summer. Remember that?"

Cooper barely reacted. No, I take that back. Each time I mentioned something I thought was cool, he winced like I was nailing him with poison darts.

"What?" I asked, confused. "Doesn't that sound great?"

"Uhh . . . yeah," he muttered awkwardly. "But I was kinda thinking more like we should hang out at the beach."

"No problem," I said. "We'll do that, too."

"A lot?" he asked.

"Yeah, sure, if you want. But there's so much more we can do."

Coop gave me a sly smile. "Not that involves girls in bikinis."

Couldn't argue with that.

He added, "I'm thinking the beach at the Point will be our base of operations. Or maybe our *entire* operation. Why not? We've only got a couple of months."

"But . . . really? That's all you want to do? Hang out at the beach?"

"No! I'm all for the rocket thing," he exclaimed. "Let's get that on the schedule for, oh . . . sometime in late August."

"You're killing me," I said.

I was disappointed in Coop. He hated being bored and so did I. He was always looking for different things to do and coming up with new adventures that kept us moving. That was his job. Trolling for girls at the beach was okay by me, but I didn't want it to be our sole focus. Besides, the girls I liked had more interesting things to do than spend every waking moment sitting around at the beach comparing tans.

"Aw, c'mon, Ralph!" Coop said. "What's better than sitting on a blanket in the warm sand next to three or four or eight girls wearing little more than underwear?"

"And talking about . . . what? Reality TV? Perez Hilton?"

"Okay, now *you're* killing *me*!" he said. "Who *cares* what we talk about?"

I guess I did. Unfortunately. Truth was, I needed help in the girl department. Whenever I was around somebody I liked, I got self-conscious. I'm not sure why, either. I think I'm okay-looking and wasn't hit too hard by the acne stick. I've got blond hair and brown eyes, which I've heard more than once is a pretty good combination. I think part of my trouble is that I get nervous and start talking too much about things I'm interested in, and most girls don't care about graphic novels or wartime history. At least not the ones I've met. Coop may have had high hopes for a stellar summer at the beach, but I couldn't see myself starting up a casual conversation about the Battle of Bull Run with a bunch of near-naked girls. They'd crucify me.

Besides, I liked building rockets.

"C'mon, Ralph!" Cooper said. "What's wrong with messing around a little? That's what summer's for. It's in the rule book."

"There's nothing wrong with it," I shot back. "But there's other stuff too. You always liked doing stupid stuff like building rockets."

"I liked Power Rangers too . . . when I was six." He put his arm around my shoulder and said, "We are looking at what could be the most awesome summer of our lives, and all we have to do is . . . uh-oh."

He spotted something over my shoulder.

"Trouble Town," he whispered.

The courtyard in front of school was packed, but the crowd parted magically to reveal a stunning girl walking toward us. She had long, shiny black hair that fell to her shoulders and dark skin that was the product of an early season tan. Judging from her short shorts, she didn't mind showing off her long legs. She was hot, and she knew it. Her dark eyes were focused on Coop. My mouth went dry. Something was about to happen. She walked right up to us, locked eyes with Cooper, and snarled a simple, succinct, and venomous "Idiot," then blew past us without breaking stride.

"I love you too, Agnes," Coop called to her.

Whenever Cooper gave a girl a hard time, he called her Agnes. With guys it was Richard. In this case the Agnes was Sydney Foley. Cooper's older sister. She and Coop didn't like each other much, which was too bad because I wouldn't have minded hanging out with her. I didn't have the same trouble making conversation with her like I did with other girls. That's because when I was with her, I couldn't speak at all. Seriously. My tongue would swell up and my throat would close. I guess you would call her intimidating. She and Coop had the same dark hair and blue eyes, but that's where the similarity ended. The girl was cold. I mean icy. She was a year ahead of us in school and light-years ahead academically. I think she'll have a shot at class valedictorian. She always had a boyfriend but never anyone for long. I guess she got bored easily. Sydney Foley was definitely out of my league . . . if I were to be in a league. Still, I would have welcomed the chance to hang out with her a little, and if it just so happened to be on one of those days that Coop made me go to the beach and she just so happened to be there in a bikini, maybe I'd have to think twice about being so critical of Coop's summer plans.

"I guess she found out about the scalping thing," I said weakly.

"Yeah. Dinner tonight's gonna be a real party," he lamented. "I'll get lectured by my parents about straightening up and being responsible while she stares through me with those undead vampire eyes. Yeesh."

I didn't think Sydney's eyes looked undead at all, but I could see where getting stared at would be unnerving. But that's just a guess. Sydney barely knew I existed.

Coop shrugged it off and broke out a big, winning smile.

"But it's cool. Tonight I pay the price and tomorrow . . . summer!"

He gave me a double okay sign. That was his way of saying not to worry and that it's all good.

"You know what?" he added. "I say we load up on frozen pizzas, head to your house, and build us some rockets."

I had to smile. "You're a piece of work, you know that?"

He gave me a friendly shove and said, "Absolutely. It's all part of the Foley mystique."

Coop had done it again . . . he made things right. As we strode into school, I had new hope that the vacation might turn out to be decent after all, especially if I got the old Coop back.

The last day of school was pretty much a blow-off. You're supposed to go to classes, but exams are over and teachers don't care what you do. Most everybody hangs out and gets their yearbooks signed with "See you this summer!"—which seems like a lame thing to write, but who am I to judge? I didn't buy a yearbook, so I headed right for the art department. That's where I hung out when I wasn't in class. The art rooms were a refuge for those who didn't fit into a particular clique . . . which I guess meant we were our own clique. But since we didn't run with each other outside of school, it was a limited social circle.

The art department wasn't just a hideout. I liked to draw. I'm pretty good, too. Whatever talent I have I got from my mom. There were a bunch of sketches in my cubby that I'd been procrastinating about bringing home because my bedroom was already a mess of paper and half-finished drawings. Bringing home more would probably make Dad's head explode, but I couldn't leave anything at school over the summer, so it was time to clear out.

I'd been working on an idea that was slow to form. I wanted to create my own superhero graphic novel. That sounds fairly cool and a no-brainer except for one thing . . . it's a no-brainer. Meaning: Superheroes have been done to death. Pretty much every superpower has already been explored. Besides, I didn't like the whole tights-and-cape thing. For a while I monkeyed around with a character I considered to be the "true" Superman. My theory was that if Superman was powerful because he came from a planet with heavier gravity than Earth, then why the heck *d* ' he have huge muscles if he never had to strain to do any ug? In reality he should look like a skinny wimp. But creating a superhero that looked like limp lettuce didn't seem promising, so I scrapped it.

What popped out of my head instead was something I hadn't planned on or set out to do. I kept coming back to a character I called "Gravedigger." He wasn't a superhero at all. In fact, he looked more like a super*villain*. He was more or less a skeleton with a thin covering of powder white skin. His fingers were abnormally long and spiderlike. His eyes were hollow. He wore a dark cloak and a broad-brimmed black hat. Very creepy. I hadn't even come up with any stories about him. I simply sketched him in various settings . . . skulking through an ancient graveyard, lurking through the ruins of an old church, cowering around dark alleys. (I'm good at depicting skulk, lurk, and cower.) His signature weapon was a sharp, lethal-looking, double-edged pick like you use to crack rocks in a mine. Or gouge out the earth to dig a grave.

Whenever I tried to draw something else and use a bright color like blue or red, my hand automatically went back to the blacks and grays. I don't want to say that Gravedigger was drawing himself, but the ideas came easily and I sketched hundreds of incarnations of the guy. I didn't even know what the point was. Who was he? Was he evil? Was he the living dead? Did he need to eat a potato and get a little sun? I didn't know. Gravedigger pretty much represented all the work I had done that year and it was time to move him home, so I began the long process of stacking the pages.

"You are obsessed with death," came a soft, flat voice over my shoulder.

I turned quickly to see Tyler Frano, a student teacher in the art department. The guy was shorter than me by at least a foot . . . not quite Munchkin-like but in that ballpark. He always dressed in black because he said it hid the streaks of sketching charcoal that got on his clothes. I think it was more because he was an art poser and wearing black made him look the part. He had no personality that I could sense and always spoke in a dull monotone. He was creepy but harmless. I think.

"I'm not obsessed with death," I said defensively. "I'm developing a character."

"It's all you ever draw," he countered. "That's bordering on obsession."

"Well, maybe, yeah, but . . . it has nothing to do with death."

Frano gave me a skeptical look. "Or perhaps you have no significant life experiences to draw upon for inspiration."

The guy was starting to piss me off. "No, I have choices," I said. "I just choose to develop *this* character."

"Good luck with that," he said with a superior sneer and walked off to do whatever student teachers do on the last day of school.

The guy was all wrong. I had plenty of inspiration. And I wasn't obsessed with death. I glanced through a few of the Gravedigger sketches, trying to imagine what Frano saw in them. Okay, my character looked skeletal. Okay, he hung around cemeteries. Okay, I called him Gravedigger. Okay, he was all that I drew. So what? Did that constitute an obsession with death?

I quickly jammed the sketches into a portfolio, zipped it up, and got out of there. I was sick of hanging around the art department. Vacation couldn't come fast enough.

At 2:05 it did. Summer. I love the feeling of stepping out of school on the last day of the year, because the next day of school was as far away as it could get. I think I was especially psyched about this summer because it held so much possibility. I even had some money to spend. I had been lucky enough to land a part-time job with a small company that made trophies and awards. In a town like Stony Brook, where so many kids went to sports camp, there was a huge need for all sorts of trophies. It wasn't exactly exciting work, but building and engraving the awards made me feel like I was using my artistic talent in some small way. Better still, I could work as much as I wanted because the regular engraver had quit. He was a kid a few years older than me named Mark Dimond. Since Mark left, there was plenty of work for me. I planned on putting in at least a few hours a day to keep the cash flowing. Thank you, Mark.

So the summer was shaping up nicely. I had money coming in from a job that didn't suck, lots of projects to work on, and truth be told, I wasn't going to mind putting in a little time at the beach. I figured that as long as Cooper kept his promise and didn't do anything else that was dumb or criminal, the two of us were set for a summer to remember.

2

Later that same day I rode my bike over to Cooper's house to begin the festivities. As I approached, I saw that Sydney's boyfriend, Mikey Russo, was sitting on the porch steps. Mikey was an idiot. There's no better word to describe him. He was a big guy who the girls loved because of his looks, but as soon as he opened his mouth, it was clear that he cowered at the sight of fire. He was going to be a senior, but I had no idea how he kept passing. My guess was that he threatened to injure any teacher who didn't give him at least a D. What made even less sense was that Sydney, who was a brain, hung out with him. It had to have been a physical thing because I doubted they had much to talk about. It was a doomed relationship, just like all of Sydney's relationships.

Mikey sat on the top stair, looking at the ground, probably thinking deep thoughts . . . like planning the number of squats he'd be doing later at the gym. I dropped my bike and started up the stairs while doing my best to look invisible. I didn't get far. Mikey held his hand out to stop me.

"No," he commanded.

"No what?"

"Nobody goes inside until Sydney's done."

"Done doing what?"

"Done telling your weasel pal how it's gonna be," he growled.

This was the most Mikey and I had spoken in, well, ever. I was one of those wallpaper guys who never entered his sphere of consciousness, which was fine by me. The most interaction we ever had was when I had to leap out of his way or get bulldozed. I was less than nothing to him, and I was stuck.

"Marsh!" came the voice of my savior, Mrs. Foley. She pushed open the screen door and leaned out. "Would you please talk to Cooper?"

Mikey quickly jumped to his feet and faced her. With an impossibly polite voice he said, "You're right, Mrs. Foley. I was just saying the same thing. Cooper needs a good talking-to."

Weasel. Mikey turned his back to Mrs. Foley and gave me a look that was so intense, it made my forehead burn. "Tell Cooper to be smart and do what he's told." His voice was polite, but his glare was scary.

Mrs. Foley held the screen door open for me. "Thank you, Mikey, we'll handle this," she said as if he were two years old, which he was. At least mentally. It must have made her sick to think Sydney was hanging around with that goon.

When I passed Mikey, he whispered something quietly so that Mrs. Foley couldn't hear.

"Tell him I'll hurt him," he snarled.

The madness in his eyes told me it wasn't an idle threat. I leaped up the stairs, two at a time, because I didn't like having my back turned on the guy. Mrs. Foley was waiting for me inside.

"What's going on, Mrs. F.?" I asked.

"Cooper is being Cooper," she said, exasperated. "Would you please get him to see reason?"

It wasn't an unusual request. I'd heard it a lot lately.

"What's he being unreasonable about?" I asked.

She took a tired breath and said, "I'm sure you know about the tickets."

I nodded.

"Such a mess. We decided to take Cooper out of the situation for a while and get him away from, you know, *influences*." She whispered the word "influences" like it was a four-letter word that should never be spoken aloud.

"How are you going to do that?" I asked.

"We want to take him up to the cottage for the summer."

The Foleys had a great house on Thistledown Lake, a few hours north of Stony Brook. It was the kind of place where you could swim and canoe and hike and water-ski and just hang out. I had visited the Foleys up there a couple of times and had a blast.

"Are you talking about the *whole* summer?" I asked.

"Absolutely. He needs to clear his head and that won't happen down here. Not with all that's going on."

It was a good idea . . . that I totally hated. If Coop took off, the stellar summer I was planning would turn into a two-month bore. I wanted things to cool off for him but not at the expense of summer. Before I could try and talk her out of the idea, I heard an angry shout come from upstairs.

"Why?" came the anguished cry. "Why is it always about you?"

Sydney. I looked to Mrs. Foley. She gave me an embarrassed shrug. From the bottom of the stairs I looked up to see Coop's sister on her way down.

"Get over yourself for once and just go!" she barked over her shoulder.

The first thing I saw were her legs. They didn't stop moving. I pressed my back against the wall as she blew past me. I don't think she even knew I was there. Her eyes were straight ahead, her body language tense.

"What did he say?" Mrs. Foley asked sheepishly.

"Who cares?" Sydney spat back. She hit the bottom of the stairs and didn't break stride as she pushed open the screen door to make a dramatic exit.

Mrs. Foley gave me a helpless look.

"I'll talk to him," I said, and ran up the stairs.

I found Cooper lying on his back on the floor of his bedroom, tossing a football into the air.

"What the heck?" I asked.

"Can you believe it? They want me to get out of town like some mob guy who has to lay low until the heat dies down."

Coop was genuinely angry. That didn't happen very often.

"Maybe you could just go for a week or two," I offered.

"No. They're talking the whole summer."

My stomach sank.

"That lake is death, Ralph," he added. "What'll I do up there? Fish? That gets old after eight seconds. The place is great if you're six or sixty. For everybody else . . . torture."

I was in the weird position of trying to talk him into doing something I didn't want him to do. I chose to duck the issue.

"What's Sydney's problem?" I asked.

"Who knows? My parents aren't even making her go. She gets to be on her own for the whole summer while I'm sentenced to two months at Camp Kumbaya."

He sat up and threw the football into his chair angrily.

I wasn't used to seeing Cooper like that. Even when things were going badly, he always laughed it off and figured a way to make the best of it. Not this time. He wasn't giving any double okay signs.

"Mikey the Mauler's downstairs," I said. "He threatened to hurt you. What's that all about?"

"Nothing," Coop said dismissively. "Forget it."

"Did he give you the fake tickets?"

"No!" Coop barked. "Let it go, all right? It's none of your business."

He jumped up and went for his window. His escape route. We used to climb out and crawl across the roof whenever we wanted to sneak out of the house.

"It *is* my business!" I shouted back. "You did something stupid, and now you're going to have to take off for a couple of months to get away from the mess, and *poof!* There goes summer."

Coop slammed the window shut so hard, it made me jump. "That makes it your business?" he asked. "Because I'm ruining your summer?"

"That's not what I meant."

"Yeah, you did. Gee, sorry, Marsh. I should have thought it through before doing anything that might spoil your fun. How inconsiderate of me."

Cooper never called me Marsh. He was ticked.

But so was I. "Don't go there," I shot back. "I know this isn't about me, but it's not just about you, either. The stuff you do has fallout."

"Fallout? I'll give you fallout. The cops threatened to throw me in juvie unless I told them where I got the fake tickets . . . so I gave up a couple of guys. And you know what? I don't care because those dirtballs set me up. But now I'm looking over my shoulder in case they find out I ratted and come after me. That's fallout. So I'm sorry if I messed up your plans to pretend like we're still twelve, but you know, things happen."

"That's cold."

"Move on, Marsh. We're not kids anymore."

"I know that."

"But hey, who am I to judge? Do whatever you want. I'm sure there are plenty of guys who want to hang out with you and watch cartoons. I'm not your only friend."

He paused and then added, "Or am I?"

That was it. He was upset and scared and I felt bad for him, but he had pushed it too far.

"Have a good summer," I said, and walked out of the room.

I heard a crash as Cooper threw his football at the wall. I couldn't believe it. My best friend had turned on me. Sure, he was upset and scared, but it wasn't my fault he chose to walk on the dark side.

I stormed down the stairs, passing Mrs. Foley.

"Will he go?" she asked.

"Probably," I answered, trying not to show my anger. "He's just got to get his head around it."

Mrs. Foley looked relieved. That made exactly one of us.

"Thanks, Marsh. Maybe you can come up and visit?"

"Yeah, maybe," I answered, and walked out the door.

I had no intention of going up to that lake. Coop had made it pretty clear that we were headed in two different directions. He was on his own . . . and so was I. I pounded down the porch steps and was nearly at the bottom when Mikey appeared from nowhere and gave me a shove that literally launched me off my feet and sent me sprawling into a bush.

"What was that for?" I shouted as I scrambled to sit up. As angry as I was, there was no way I'd jump up and push the guy back. That would have been suicide.

"You hang with that weasel, you pay the price," he growled.

"Mikey!" Sydney called from the street, where she sat in her VW Beetle.

I didn't think she saw what happened, so I got up fast. I didn't want her to see me looking like some little kid who had just gotten shoved by the big bad bully . . . which is exactly what I was.

"Let's go," she commanded.

Mikey followed her instructions like an obedient dog. As he backed away he pointed a threatening finger at me as if to say, "Remember what I said."

My excellent summer had suddenly taken an incredibly rotten turn.

3

In only a few short hours I had gone from thinking there were too many exciting adventures to fit into a single vacation to wishing I could magically make school start again the next day.

I rode my bike home and did the one thing that always helped when things weren't going well. I read. Books were my refuge. Getting lost in a solid adventure story was the best way I knew of to turn off reality. There was nothing like a trip to Tralfamador or Middle Earth to help escape real life. I went to my bedroom and tried to get lost in the pages of one of my favorites: *The Hitchhiker's Guide to the Galaxy*. It wasn't working. I was still too caught up with Cooper's drama. I tossed down the book and grabbed a sketch pad to do a little drawing and clear my head.

My hand instinctively started tracing the lines of Gravedigger's face. I got as far as the sunken eyes and had to force myself to stop. I needed to come up with something else to draw. Tyler Frano was wrong. I was an artist. I had all kinds of inspiration to call on. It was in my blood.

My mom was an artist. Actually, she was a photographer, but the images she created were works of art. She was a freelancer who traveled all over the world on assignment for magazines like *National Geographic* and *Smithsonian*. Mom loved to shoot ancient structures like churches and old villages. I'm no expert, but I think she was good. She could take something that looked like a crumbling pile of rocks and, by using light and the perfect angle, create a stunning picture that made you feel as if you were stepping back through time to see the building in its original glory. It was like she had a third eye that saw possibility where most people saw, well, a pile of old rocks.

I had prints of some of her photos hanging in my bedroom. One made the Great Wall of China look like a living serpent, snaking across misty green hills. Another was a black-and-white image of a doll's face taken through the window of a long-abandoned shop in a California ghost town. It was creepy and sad at the same time. I often wondered who the doll belonged to. Besides her photos, I had one whole shelf of stuff Mom had picked up on her travels and sent back to me. There wasn't anything cheesy like: *My parents went to Jamaica and all I got was this lousy T-shirt*. There were hand-carved jade elephants from Indonesia; a marionette from Germany; a voodoo doll from New Orleans; a flute from Chile; and one item I had no clue about.

It was a golden ball about the size of a plum. I think it might have been made of glass, but it was hard to tell because the entire surface was painted with odd designs that could have been some strange alphabet or just random doodles. The thing had weight but wasn't heavy. It had absolutely no useful purpose as far as I could tell. I didn't even know where it came from or when I had gotten it.

As I did so many times, I sat and let my eyes wander over Mom's stuff until I came to one particular photo. It was a spectacular shot of an abandoned, centuries-old temple. The place looked like it had been built in the year one, but my mom captured the warm light of sunset on its surface in such a way that it looked timeless. It was a great picture.

I hated it.

"Dinner!" came a call from downstairs.

Seven o'clock. I could set my watch by when Dad had dinner on the table. I wasn't hungry but didn't feel like sitting in my room by myself, searching for inspiration. There would be plenty of time for that over the next two months.

Dad made spaghetti. His specialty. Pasta in boiling water and a jar of sauce. Real fancy stuff. I didn't eat much. I kept playing the events of the day over and over in my head.

"So?" Dad asked, pulling me into the moment. "Vegas?"

With all that had been going on, I'd totally forgotten. Dad was a marketing guy for a home electronics company. It's how we got the sweet plasma TV. He was headed to Las Vegas for a weeklong convention and wanted me to go with him. I hadn't thought much about it because I was expecting to be kicking off summer with Cooper.

"I don't know . . . ," I replied.

"C'mon! It'll be great. While I'm working, you can check out all the new tech stuff. Then we'll catch some shows at night. You know, Cirque du Olé."

"Cirque du Soleil."

"Yeah, that. We'll stay on a couple days and do some fishing. Maybe see Hoover Dam. L-D-I!"

That meant "Let's do it." Dad was a goof. He often spoke in acronyms like "L-D-I" or "I am O-O-H" ("out of here").

Maybe that came from working the BlackBerry too much. Or maybe he was just a goof.

"They're kind of relying on me at work," I said. It was a lie. They weren't relying on me at all.

"Work? You sound like some old guy. C'mon! It's summer! L-I-U!"

That meant "lighten up." Or "live it up." I wasn't sure which.

As I think back, I wonder what would have happened if I had made a different decision. What if I had gone with him? Would things have played out differently? Or was everything that happened inevitable?

"I really don't want to go, Dad."

He was ready to jump in with another reason to tempt me to go, but turned serious instead. "I hate leaving you home alone."

"I know, but it's cool. Really. You know that."

Dad frowned. "I do. I'm just worried about you, Marsh."

"Dad! I'll be fine! Seriously. You know I won't throw parties or trash the house."

"I know. I almost wish you would."

"Uhh . . . what?"

He got up and started clearing the dinner plates. Something was bugging him.

He finally said, "We never talk about Mom anymore."

"Whoa. Change of subject."

"Not really. Mom was always the one who got us going. She came up with the ideas and the adventures. Right? You used to love going on trips. That's what we did. But we haven't gone anywhere since, well, since Mom planned the last one. With her gone, it's like we're not . . . we're not . . . things are just different."

"Well . . . yeah."

"But it's not right."

"Is that why you want me to go to Vegas? You're trying to come up with an adventure like Mom used to do?"

"No. Maybe. I don't know. I'm just afraid that . . . I don't know how to say this, Marsh . . . I see you closing into yourself."

"Huh?"

Once Dad found the words, he couldn't stop. "Don't get mad. It's just that I wish you'd get out more. Make more friends. Join a team. I think it's great how you're so into your books and your comics and your drawings. That's all great. But it's so . . . solitary."

He really caught me off guard. I wasn't expecting any of that. "I've got friends," I said defensively.

"You've got Coop, and he's entering the Witness Protection Program. Where does that leave you? What are you going to do the rest of the summer?"

"I've got plenty to do," I shot back.

"I'm sure you do and that's great—I just want you to get out a little bit and have some fun. That's all I'm saying. It's what Mom would have wanted."

"Mom never would have said anything like that," I said, my anger building.

"Probably not. She was much smarter than me. But she knew what she wanted for you and it wasn't to live a life inside your head."

"Where do you get that stuff? Are you reading psychology books or something?"

"No. Okay, maybe a few. I'm feeling my way along here. You're a smart guy, Marsh. I'm really proud of you. But you need people in your life. You need to get out. Go to parties. Chase girls. You know . . . do normal stuff."

I jumped out of my chair. "You think I'm not normal?"

"No! I didn't mean it like that. C'mon, you know what I'm saying."

"I have no idea what you're saying, but I think you better stop saying it before you say something even dumber than you already have."

I blasted out of there and headed back to my bedroom. I'd never spoken like that to my dad, but then again, he'd never spoken to me like that either. Where did he get off saying I wasn't normal? Things were different. He didn't need to point that out. I was dealing with it. Okay, maybe I spent a lot of time alone, but that was my personality. I wasn't a big-group kind of guy. I stormed into my bedroom and stood there, not sure of what to do with my anger. Scream? Punch the wall? Throw myself on the bed and kick my legs like a little girl? My eye caught the photo on the wall. Mom's photo. The temple. It brought back a flood of memories that only made me feel worse.

It could have happened yesterday. That's how vivid the moment was. But it was nearly two years before. I was in my bedroom, playing Jenga with Cooper. It was a game for five-year-olds, but we always made it more interesting by balancing a glass of water on top or playing for Cokes. It was way more fun when something was at stake. Except that Cooper would always make me laugh at a critical moment and I'd end up knocking over the tower and owing him. It was one of those great memories not so much because of what it was, but because it was the final moment before things would change. If I had a time machine, I'd pick that moment to go back to . . . and stay there.

Dad came into the room. His face was gray. I remember that. He usually bounced in with a loud "Hello, girls!" or something equally goofy. Not that time. His eyes were red. I knew instantly that he'd been crying. I don't know how or why, but as soon as I saw him, I knew what I would hear. I didn't yet know the details, but something bad had happened and I was pretty sure of what it was.

"Maybe you should head home, Cooper," Dad said, his voice cracking.

Coop moved to get up, but I pushed him down.

"Stay," I said, and looked to Dad. "What happened?"

Coop's eyes were so wide, it was almost comical. For once, and maybe for the last time, he was speechless.

Dad sat down on the floor, facing me. He didn't have to talk because for some reason I knew what he was going to say. All he could offer were details, and I wasn't so sure I wanted them.

"Mom had a bad accident," he said. Everything after that was white noise.

Mom had been on assignment in one of those Eastern European countries that changes its name every two weeks. "Somethingistan" or whatever. She was there to do a study of ancient buildings. It happened in a city where she was shooting a centuries-old temple. It was an earthquake. A serious one. The temple was destroyed. Dozens of people were killed.

It was a wrong-place, wrong-time event . . . that killed my mom and changed our lives.

When I first got the news, I was angry. I had the whole "Why her?" thing going on. (Though to be honest, it was more of a "Why me?" thing.) I had no choice but to accept it. Or try to. I still get angry sometimes and this was one of those times. It didn't help that I was already pissed off at Cooper. At that moment I was pissed at Mom, too. I wanted to hit something. Or someone. I needed to release the pressure or I was going to scream.

I should have screamed.

I looked to the picture on my bedroom wall. The temple. It was the last photo she ever took. She would soon die inside of it. When I look at it, which I do most every day, I can't help but think that it didn't matter how many centuries it stood—it was moments away from crumbling to dust, along with my mom. What seemed so strong was actually very fragile.

It's a beautiful photo.

I hate it.

I reached for the shelf that had all of Mom's mementos and grabbed the small, golden ball with the odd markings. It was exactly what I needed. I spun, cocked my arm, and whipped the golden orb across the room, nailing the photo of the temple. It was exactly the release I needed . . . and one I instantly regretted. When the golden sphere hit the picture, it shattered, along with the glass over the photo. Tiny bits of glass flew everywhere. It was like a small explosion. At that same moment I felt a sharp rumble as if a heavy truck was rolling by outside, shaking the house. It was so short, I figured my loss of control and release of pent-up energy had thrown off my equilibrium somehow.

When the ball broke, it splattered deep red liquid all over the photo and wall. The spray reached beyond the black frame, staining the wall with dark, red-brown juice. I couldn't get my mind around what I was seeing. The ball seemed ancient. How could it be filled with liquid? I walked to the photo, transfixed by the sight of red rivers drooling down the wall. Was it colored water? Or juice? I reached up and gingerly touched a glistening rivulet. I rubbed my fingers together, smearing it around and wiping it back onto the wall. It was thick. It smelled like steak.

It was blood.

"Dad!" I screamed, and ran out of the room. "Dad, c'mere!"

I stood on top of the stairs as Dad hurried up. "What?"

I ran back into my room with my dad right behind me. "I threw this thing and when it hit the wall, it shattered and spewed . . ."

I looked to the bloodied wall to see . . . it wasn't bloody anymore. The photo and the wall around it were completely clean. I felt dizzy. How could that have happened?

"What did you throw?" Dad asked, confused.

Only a few seconds before, the wall had been splattered with what I thought was blood. There was no way it could have run down and left no trace. At least not that fast. The floor was covered with broken glass and shattered pieces from the golden ball. I hurried over and picked up two of the larger pieces of the destroyed ball. I felt the inside for traces of liquid. It was bone-dry.

"Was it Mom's?" Dad asked.

I couldn't think straight. "Uh, yeah. I threw it at the picture."

"You what? Marsh!"

"It was . . . I mean . . . I shouldn't have. I know. I was mad. But when it broke, there was red stuff inside. Like blood."

He hurried to the wall and touched the photo where there was a small gouge from the impact. He ran his finger over it like it was a wound. A wound I had caused. He didn't have to say anything. I knew what he was thinking. I wasn't normal.

All I could say was "Sorry."

Dad nodded. "I am too."

"Was it valuable?" I asked.

Dad shrugged. "I don't know, your mom was always collecting things. Listen, Marsh, I didn't mean to get you so angry. I just . . . I want things to be good for you."

"But I'm okay, Dad. Really."

He gave me a small, sad smile that said he didn't believe

me. He didn't push it, though, and neither did I. He bent over to clean up the remains of the shattered globe and the glass from the picture.

I wasn't mad at him anymore. I knew he was just as upset about Mom as I was, and when you're upset, you say things you don't mean. We usually handled it well. Sometimes we didn't. That was a fact of our new life. There was nothing to do but help him clean up.

The storm had passed, at least for the moment. I was left with a mess to sweep away, a damaged picture, and the mystery of what had happened to the blood that was no longer splattered all over my bedroom wall.

4

Cooper and I didn't talk to each other again before his family left for the lake. A couple of times I thought about giving him a call to settle things, but didn't. I figured it was better if we both took some time to cool off.

I tried to stop thinking about the broken globe and the blood. Whether it was valuable or not, it was one more piece of Mom that was now gone, thanks to me. I couldn't come up with any logical answers or explanations for what had happened, so I pushed the whole event out of my head.

All the fun things I had planned to do didn't seem like much fun anymore, so I spent most of my time those first few days either reading or picking up hours at work. As long as I was going to be bored, I figured I might as well make some bucks. Not that I had anywhere to spend it. I actually started to think that Dad was right. I should get out a little more and make some friends. I might have done it too . . . if I knew how.

I'd only been out of school for three days, and the summer had already become deadly monotonous. That changed when a visitor came to see me at work. I was hunched over my engraving machine, etching out a sailing trophy for the local yacht club, when I heard a familiar singsong voice call out to me.

"Hello, Marshmallow!"

I looked up to see Ennis Mobley step into my tiny workplace.

"Ennis! Hey!" I jumped up and hugged the guy.

Ennis was a guy my mom used to work with, but he was more like family. I think he was around forty years old, though I'm not the best judge. He was from Jamaica, which accounted for his singsong voice. Mom always hired Ennis whenever she went somewhere on assignment. He would help with the gear and travel arrangements and basically free Mom up to focus on taking pictures instead of sweating logistics. Ennis was with her when the earthquake hit. As I heard it, he was nearly killed himself. He was able to salvage most of Mom's gear, which is how I got the film with the picture of the temple. More important, Ennis worked hard to cut through the red tape and transport Mom's body back home quickly. We owed him for that in a big way.

He was almost as torn up about Mom's death as Dad and I were. I want to say that when I think about him, the first thing that comes to mind is his quick smile and easy laugh. It isn't. I picture him standing over my mother's grave at the funeral, crying. He put a small bouquet of flowers, which he told me came from a tree called *lignum vitae*, on her casket. He said it produced wood that was so strong, it was called the "wood of life." He loved my mom. We all did.

Since the funeral, he'd send an e-mail to check in every

once in a while, but we hardly ever saw him in person . . . which is why it was a total surprise when he showed up at the trophy shop.

"How are you, Marshmallow?" he asked.

He had called me that ever since I was little. It was cuter when I was little.

"I'm good. What are you doing here?" I asked.

"Visiting you, my friend. My, you've grown."

I shrugged. What are you supposed to say when somebody comments on your growth curve?

"Have you seen Dad?" I asked.

"No. I do not have the time. I am leaving on assignment to Pakistan this evening. It is you I came to see."

That was odd. It wasn't my birthday or anything. Ennis seemed nervous, shifting his weight from foot to foot while his eyes darted around, as if looking for something.

"Are you all right, Marsh?" he asked. Ennis's speech was normally kind of loopy. He stretched out his vowels in a way that made it sound like he was singing. Now his words were clipped and short.

"Uh, yeah. Fine. Why?"

"And your father? How is he?"

"He's fine too."

"I worry about you two," Ennis said, deadly serious.

"We're okay. I mean, we both miss Mom a lot. But what can you do?"

He looked me square in the eye as if trying to figure out if I was hiding something. It was weird.

"Good, good," he finally said, satisfied that I was telling the truth. "Here, take this."

He reached into his shirt pocket and pulled out a business card. It only had his name and a phone number.

"That is my cell phone. Call me if you need me. Anytime. Promise me that."

"Okay, sure, but . . . you're giving me the creeps, Ennis. What's going on?"

"Nothing, nothing, Marsh. I am being an overly cautious fool."

"About what?"

He seemed to relax a little. I think maybe he finally believed there was nothing wrong with us.

"You are my friends," he said, sounding more like himself. "My family. I want you to know that if you need anything, I am there for you."

"O . . . kay. That's cool. Same here. Is there anything *you* need?"

"No, Marshmallow, I am fine. Especially now that I know you are too. Please give my best to your father. I will come for a longer visit when I return from Asia."

He grabbed me and gave me a hug. It wasn't one of those quick handshake-style hugs either. I'm not sure how to describe this, but Ennis held me tight, as if he wanted to protect me or something.

"You sure everything's all right?" I asked.

Ennis let go and backed away. "Yes, absolutely. Do not lose my card. And call me."

"Yeah. Sure."

"Good." He turned serious again. "Take care of yourself, Marsh. I will see you in a few weeks."

That was it. He turned and left quickly. I didn't know what to think of his visit. Ennis was always an open book. That book had suddenly turned into a mystery. There was definitely something going on that he didn't want to explain.

I told Dad about it that night. He didn't know anything more about it than I did.

"It was strange," I said. "It was like he was expecting me to say something horrible had happened to us."

"Maybe he was just checking up," Dad offered. "The guy's a worrier."

"Yeah, maybe. But why now?"

Dad shrugged. "You're asking me like there's a chance I might have an answer."

I liked it when Dad talked to me like an equal instead of a little boy. In spite of our occasional blowups, we got along pretty well. I don't think most parents would leave their teenage kid home alone when they went off on business, but Dad trusted me. Before every trip he'd load up the kitchen with junk food . . . the kind of stuff he'd never let me eat when he was around. I think he did it out of guilt, thinking it would make being alone a little special. That was fine by me.

The worst *I* had to worry about was that something might happen to him and he wouldn't come home. I tried not to go there. Traveling was part of his job, and we both had to deal with it. Other than the paranoia, I actually kind of liked it when he left me alone for a few days. It meant no cleaning up; lights out whenever I wanted; no restriction on music volume or song selection; and best of all, 360 on the plasma. Being alone had its advantages.

The only real responsibility I had besides not burning down the house was to feed our cat, Winston, and scoop out her litter box. Pretty simple.

The next day he left for Vegas.

It was the day the nightmare began.

I went into work to engrave a bunch of brass plates to go on trophies for a football camp. I finished up and was ready to head home when my boss, Mr. Santoro, checked my work and pointed out that "receiver" is spelled with an *ei*, not *ie*. You know, *i* before *e* except after *c*. Oops. Tack on another hour to redo a dozen plates. Idiot. I was going to stop at Garden Poultry for a sandwich and fries on the way home, but I was too beat. Instead I rode my bike straight home, opened up a can of clam chowder, and downed half a bag of Doritos. I finished my gourmet meal, topped it off with a can of vintage, sparkling Dr Pepper, dumped everything in the sink, and began my first night at home alone.

I was psyched. There were so many options. None of them involved washing the dishes. I could start to build one of the model rockets. I could spread out my sketches and work on the graphic novel. I could kick a little Call of Duty butt. I could go through our DVD collection and watch any movie I wanted. Twice. I could go online and spend all night on Hulu. The future was in my hands. It was a feeling of complete power and freedom. So what did I do?

I turned on the TV and fell asleep in about six minutes.

Actually, I didn't fall completely asleep. I was watching a show on the Discovery Channel about sharks and kind of drifted off. But not all the way. That's happened to me before. You're asleep but not. You're kind of aware of your surroundings, but you aren't conscious enough to move. It's like being paralyzed. For some reason whenever that happens, it always seems like there are other people in the room. Of course, there aren't. It's all part of the dream. Still, it's scary to be lying there, unprotected, wondering who is walking around your living room . . . and what they might do to you.

My eyes were closed. I knew I was on the couch. The sounds from the TV were unintelligible . . . and so were the voices I heard in the room. I sensed movement. Somebody was hurrying around. Did Dad come home? Did he forget something?

I tried to call out, "Dad?"

Didn't work.

There were more voices. Whispers. Who could it be? How did they get in the house? Did I forget to lock the door?

None of their words made sense. Were they planning something? I couldn't think clearly. I willed my hand to reach down and pull up the comforter at my feet. I thought that having a blanket over me would protect me. No go. I couldn't move.

None of this was real, of course. It was a half-dream. But it was still unnerving.

The voices grew louder, more urgent, as if they were running out of time. It sounded like gibberish. It *was* gibberish. I knew that. It was a dream, right? That's what I told myself and it calmed me down. That is, until I heard a single word break through the haze—a word that was as plain and clear as if someone had leaned over and spoken directly into my ear.

"Morpheus."

It was enough to shock me awake. I didn't sit up fast, breathing hard and in a sweat like you see in every movie about nightmares. I simply rocketed back to consciousness. I instantly understood that nobody was in the room. Nobody had spoken in my ear. The sharks on TV were still going for the chum. All was well. As nightmares go, it was uneventful. There were no monsters. No chasing. No falling. There was only a word.

Morpheus.

Where did I come up with that? Was it something from TV that I yanked into my dream? Or was it something I had heard once that got stuck somewhere in my subconscious? Either way it meant nothing to me. In a few seconds I had gone from a state of semiconscious panic to realizing absolutely nothing had happened except that I had done a pretty good job of scaring myself.

I should have gone to bed, but I was wired and it was still early. Turning in at nine thirty was beyond pathetic, so I decided to listen to some music. With the house empty it was the perfect chance to play a little air drums without fear of being caught and looking like a dork.

When playing air drums, you've got to go with the rock classics. They have the best solos. My current favorite was a song called "(I Know) I'm Losing You" by the Faces and a raspy-voiced singer named Rod Stewart. The drum solo is awesome. Dad had the song on his iPod and I had a dock with speakers in my bedroom, so the stage was set.

We live in an old three-story house with narrow hallways and inside doors that don't close all the way. Or lock. Not even the bathroom. I hated that. The yard is decent-size, but the neighbors aren't far away, so I had to be careful about playing the music too loud. I didn't want somebody pounding on the door to tell me to keep it down, or calling the police. So I shut my windows tight, pulled down the shades, and pushed the bedroom door closed as best as I could to muffle the concert. I put my desk chair in the center of the room, cranked the volume as loud as I thought safe, grabbed a couple of chopsticks, and a few short seconds later I was performing for a crowd of thousands. Or one, actually. Winston was stretched out on my bed, looking bored. I guess she didn't go for classic rock.

Music filled the room. I'd listened to the song so many times that I knew every note. Every drumbeat. Every twitch in Rod Stewart's quirky voice.

This time I heard something different.

A minute after the song began, there was another sound. It was a beat that drifted under the music. I'd never heard it before. How was that possible? I listened for a few seconds until I realized it might not be part of the song. I quickly reached over and hit pause. The music stopped instantly. The room went quiet. Whatever the sound was, I couldn't hear it anymore. With a shrug I hit play and picked up my performance. In a few seconds I heard the sound again.

What was it? I hit pause again and listened. Nothing. I was worried that maybe I was bothering the neighbors and somebody was downstairs pounding on my door. I figured if that was the case, they'd keep pounding. I listened for a few more seconds, but there was nothing.

When I hit play again, I heard nothing but Rod Stewart and the familiar music. Excellent. I was back in the zone. I closed my eyes and was preparing for the big solo when the rogue beat came back. I quickly punched off the music, expecting to hear the same nothing as each time before.

This time the sound didn't go away.

What I heard came from the other side of my bedroom door. It sounded as if someone was pounding on the wall. I froze. The pounding stopped and I distinctly heard the sound of somebody standing up. It was as if they had been sitting on the floor and their back brushed against the door as they got up. I then heard an exhale and the sound of footsteps walking away.

This was no half-asleep dream. Somebody was in the house.

What should I do? There was no phone in my bedroom, so I couldn't call the police. My cell phone was downstairs. The room was on the second floor, so I couldn't go out the window. I was trapped, and whoever was in the house knew I was there. It wasn't like I was being quiet. I looked to the cat. Winston lay on her side with her eyes at half-mast as if about to fall asleep. She hadn't budged. She wasn't even on alert. Why didn't the sound bother her? She must have heard it. She's a cat! Cats hear grass growing!

I sat there for a few seconds, fighting panic. My mind sped to a million explanations. Was Dad home? Was it a neighbor checking up on me? Did Ennis come back? Then, of course, there were the bad possibilities. Burglars. But that didn't make sense. Why would a thief break into a house when somebody was obviously home blasting music?

I couldn't just sit there. I had to find out who it was. Looking around my room, I found something I could use to defend myself. Since the house was so old, most of the doors didn't stay open on their own, so my mom used heavy, old-fashioned clothes irons as doorstops. One sat on the floor inside my room. I grabbed it. It had to be at least five pounds. If somebody jumped me, they were going to get a face full of steel. I crept slowly toward my door, trying not to step on a squeaky floorboard. I got closer to the door, reached for the knob, grabbed it, raised the iron . . . and yanked the door open.

If somebody had been there, they would have lost teeth. The dark, empty hallway loomed ahead of me. I wished I had left a few lights on before going into my room, but I hadn't expected to confront an unwanted invader. I kept the heavy iron high, ready to swing. I left my room and walked slowly down the hall, making my way toward the overhead light switch. Whoever was in the house could easily be hiding in a dark corner. I needed to see. A few agonizing seconds later I reached the switch and flipped it on, lighting up the entire upstairs hallway. There were no intruders. No concerned neighbors. No boogeyman.

Things were making less sense. I had definitely heard somebody pound on the wall and walk away. But that was all. I didn't hear anybody go down the stairs. If somebody was in the house, they would still be on the second floor. They couldn't just disappear. Since the other rooms were dark, the person was either hiding and playing with my head or they were up to no good. I crept into Dad's room and flipped on his light to see . . . nothing. Nothing strange, anyway. I even went into his closet and swung the iron around behind his hanging clothes in case somebody was hiding back there.

I searched the guest bedroom, then the bathroom. The thought hit me that I was doing the same dumb thing that people do in horror movies. They always go to investigate. It makes you want to scream out, "Don't look in the basement! Get the hell out of there, fool!" But that was because you knew it was a horror movie and something nasty was going to happen. This was reality. The odds of a serial killer in a hockey mask and a chainsaw finding his way into my house were pretty slim. My common sense told me that there had to be an innocent, logical explanation for what I had heard, and I needed to find it.

I searched the entire house, turning on every light. It was nerve-racking, but I did it. I went through every room. Every closet. Even the basement and attic. I found that every window and door was locked. Nothing was broken or out of place. Everything was as it should be. As it became clear that nobody else was in the house, I started questioning what it was I had heard. It was a really old home. There were always strange noises going on. The faintest breeze would make the old wood creak and crackle. Was it possible that my imagination had taken some innocent house sounds and created something that wasn't there? It was starting to seem that way.

I was in the living room, ready to accept that I was being paranoid, when I began to sense a new, odd sound. It was like a steady drone. At first I thought it was something electronic wreaking havoc with my eardrums. I stuck my pinkie into my ear and shook it, trying to get rid of the strange sound. It didn't help.

I soon realized it wasn't a sound at all. In fact, it was just the opposite. What I was hearing was . . . nothing. The house was old and full of random sounds. Heck, the whole world is old and full of random sounds. But all those sounds had suddenly stopped. There was no sound at all. Absolutely nothing. For a second I feared that I had gone deaf. I snapped my fingers and heard that clearly enough. There wasn't anything wrong with my ears. I stood stock-still in the middle of the living room, desperately trying to pick up any sound that would tell me that the world hadn't stopped turning.

What I heard was the sound of a dripping faucet. It was the kind of sound that would normally get lost amid every other sound in the world. But not then. It was faint but unmistakable. It was a steady *drip . . . drip . . . drip* that seemed to be coming from the downstairs bathroom. I had to check it out. I was drawn to it because it was the only sound that existed. I crept through the living room and down the small hallway toward the bathroom to see that the door was closed. I had inspected the room a few minutes earlier and the faucet hadn't been dripping . . . but it sure sounded as though it had started. I raised the heavy iron again, just in case I had missed something. Or someone. Slowly I pushed the door open.

Sure enough, the sink faucet was dripping. It was a steady *plip . . . plip . . . plip* sound that bounced into the standing water in the sink and echoed through the otherwise silent house. I tightened up both valves and the dripping stopped. Silence had returned. But not for long.

Another dripping sound came from somewhere else. I walked from the bathroom and listened. It was coming from the kitchen. What was going on? Had the plumbing in the house suddenly gone wacky? More important, why was it the only sound I could hear? I moved across the living room. The only other sound was the squeak of my sneakers on the wooden floor. The dripping sound grew louder. I crossed through the dining room to the swinging door that led to the kitchen. As I pushed the door open, the dripping sound grew even louder. I was all set to walk in and turn it off, but when I stepped through the door and looked to the sink, I saw that the faucet wasn't dripping.

Huh? I still heard the sound, but the sink was dry. I looked around quickly. Where was it coming from? There were no other faucets. It was like the dripping was just . . . there. It grew impossibly loud, like it was a sound effect and somebody was slowly turning up the volume. The gentle dripping sound had become an incessant, booming echo that bounced off the walls. I was desperate to stop it but didn't know how.

I was a second away from running out of the room when the sound stopped. Just like that. It was like I had hit the pause button on the iPod. The room fell deathly silent. I was in a vacuum again.

I'm not sure what made me look back to the sink . . . and the window above it. The empty window. It was night. There was nothing to see on the outside but blackness . . .

. . . and a pale white face that hovered there, staring in at me.

It was such a shock that I stumbled backward as if I had been pushed. The sounds of the house suddenly rushed back. The ticking of a clock, the buzz from the refrigerator, the hum of a fluorescent light, the far-off sound of Rod Stewart's voice . . . the house was alive again. I hit my back on the edge of a counter, twisted, and nearly fell down. The weight of the heavy iron in my hand yanked me toward the floor. I grabbed the counter with my other hand and managed to stop my fall. Once I got my balance, I was ready to run out of the room. I didn't want any part of whoever was out there. I had only seen it for a fleeting instant, but that was enough. It was a man with skin that was so white, it seemed transparent. His dark eyes were abnormally large, and in the split second I saw him I knew they were looking at me. I wanted to get out of there and find a closet to hide in.

I took a step to run but stopped. This was my house. I was in charge. Running away was not acceptable. I stood up straight, held my breath, and forced myself to look back at the window. Slowly, I turned around to see . . .

The face was gone. I could breathe again. Whoever it was didn't want any part of me. But who was it? Why was he creeping around my house? I had to know. I grabbed the iron and ran for the back door. There was a creep lurking around in my yard, peering in at me, and he wasn't going to get away with it. I threw open the door and jumped outside, screaming, "Hey! Who are you?"

I stood outside the kitchen door, breathing hard, ready for I-didn't-know-what. The heavy iron was up and poised to strike. I looked to the window where the guy had been. The wind was blowing hard, knocking around the branches of a bush next to the house. It scraped against the window like it was scratching to get in. A flash of white caught my attention. I think I screamed with surprise. I heard a steady flapping sound and looked to see a white, plastic grocery bag caught on a branch, fluttering in the wind.

I had found my lurker.

It wasn't a face outside the window—it was a grocery bag caught on a branch. A gust of wind kicked up, tearing it from the bush. It whipped away on the breeze and disappeared into the neighbor's yard . . . maybe to peer into their window.

Once my heart stopped pounding, I went back inside and closed the door, double-checking to make sure it was locked. Everything was normal. Even the sounds. It sure seemed as though I had been terrorized by my own overactive imagination. What else could it have been? I figured my ears must have been ringing because I was playing the music so loud, which is why my hearing was messed up. And our house was old. Who knew what kind of shape the ancient plumbing was in? That could explain the pounding and the dripping. It wasn't a monster—it was old pipes.

The intruder at the window was the easiest of all to explain away. It was a plastic shopping bag from Trader Joe's. Nothing sinister about it.

Though I was certain that nothing strange had happened, I left all the house lights on anyway. Why not? Dad wasn't around to tell me to put them out. I went upstairs, took off my clothes, and crawled into bed. Winston hadn't even moved. It gave me more confidence that nothing strange had happened.

It would be a while before I could power down enough to sleep. Adrenaline takes time to get out of your system. I had really done a number on myself. I figured I had better get a grip or it was going to be a long week. I don't know how many hours went by before I finally calmed down enough to nod off.

The last thing I remember before my eyes closed was a sound.

Somewhere in the house, a faucet was dripping.

5

I woke up before the alarm.

Usually I'm knocked out until the buzzer shakes me awake, but not that morning. I felt a slight breeze on my face that gently brought me back to consciousness. It was kind of nice. Definitely better than any alarm sound. I lay on my back, enjoying the feeling as it rustled my hair. I stretched, feeling pretty good considering I had only gotten a few hours of sleep. The weird events of the night before were more or less forgotten. I thought about how I had to get up, eat something, and get to work. I was actually looking forward to it, seeing as I didn't have anything else going on.

I felt the breeze again. It made me think that an alarm clock that blew warm air across your face would be a cool invention. I filed it under "things to do but probably never will" and reached over my head to pull the window shut.

My hand hit glass. The window wasn't open. Huh? I

sat up straight and looked to the other window. It was shut tight. My bedroom door was closed too. Where was the breeze coming from?

Brraaaannngggggg!

The alarm went off. The *real* alarm. I was definitely awake after that. I hammered it off and sat there wondering why our house had suddenly sprung a wind leak. I decided not to stress and to tell Dad about it when he got home.

My breakfast was a healthy combination of raspberry-filled Pop-Tarts and chocolate milk. I fed Winston, got out the Ovaltine, and stirred up a king-size glass. It wasn't until I was sitting at the kitchen counter, chewing on the raw Pop-Tart (I never bother to toast them), that I looked to the window over the sink and remembered what had happened the night before. It was already a bright morning. Warm summer sun streamed in. The idea that a mysterious creeper who hated classic rock was lurking around outside seemed kind of silly. I listened. There was no dripping water. All the normal sounds of the house were there, just as they should be. I laughed, remembering how terrified I had been as I searched every dark corner with a heavy iron, ready for action. I felt pretty silly about the whole thing.

I was reaching for my glass of chocolate milk when Winston suddenly jumped up onto the counter.

"Whoa!" I shouted, and pulled back quickly. My sudden move startled the cat and she shot past me, knocking over the container of Ovaltine. Brown chocolate powder spread all over the white tiles of the counter.

"Winston!" I yelled, as if that would have done anything. It wasn't like she was going to come back and clean up. I was ticked. The Ovaltine was supposed to last me for the week. I hated to trash it, but the idea of shoveling it all back into the container to be used again kind of grossed me out. It was officially garbage. I pulled the trash can from under the sink and grabbed a sponge.

As I was about to turn away from the sink, I felt another short, soft breeze. I wasn't imagining it—the air had definitely moved. But the window wasn't open. None of the windows were open. I went into the living room to check the thermostat. Maybe during my frantic house search the night before I had accidentally turned on the air-conditioning. Those stray puffs of air must have been coming from the air ducts built into the floor and the ceiling.

When I checked the thermostat, I saw that everything was turned off. Still, I knew it had to be something else that was equally simple, so I shrugged it off and went back into the kitchen to scrape up the Ovaltine. I was about to start wiping up the powder when the puff of wind returned. This time it not only blew my hair, it blew some of the chocolate powder across the counter. I froze in midswipe and leaned down so that my face was on counter level. Several impossible puffs of air from nowhere blew the chocolate around like a mini storm in a desert. I couldn't take my eyes off it. It was like some odd air vortex was spreading the powder across the countertop.

After a few seconds the brown powder was spread out over the white tiles. For a second I actually thought it was a cool phcnomenon. I was debating about whether or not to clean it up or leave it to show Dad . . . when the breeze returned and I watched the impossible happen. The powder moved, but instead of spreading out randomly, a pattern began to emerge. While much of the brown chocolate blew to the side, some of it remained in place. Slowly, very slowly, the powder that was left behind formed a swirl. Then another. And a third. They were all the same size, about four inches in diameter and connected in the center. It was a simple pattern, but there was no way a random puff of air could have formed it.

I had no idea of what I was seeing, or how it could be happening. I wasn't scared—I was dumbfounded. I tried to think of a logical explanation, but nothing came to me.

Bang bang bang!

Somebody was pounding on the door. I think I jumped a few inches. Was it the intruder from the night before? It didn't matter that it was a bright, sunny day—I flew right back into terror mode.

Ding dong!

The doorbell. That calmed me down. Intruders didn't ring doorbells. Unless they were particularly polite intruders. Still, I didn't take any chances. I grabbed the first weapon I could find. It happened to be a small fire extinguisher. I figured if there was trouble, I could squirt the guy in the eyes and then bean him on the head. Gripping the red cylinder, I hurried for the living room. I didn't want to open the door without knowing who it was, so I first peeked out of the front window over the couch. It wasn't an intruder, but the guy standing there was definitely a surprise . . . and not a good one. I dropped the fire extinguisher and opened the door to greet Mikey Russo, Sydney Foley's goon boyfriend.

"Where is he?" Russo snarled.

He was angry. Or at least excited. Something was up. It made me want to go back and grab the fire extinguisher. Instead I went outside and joined him on the porch. I didn't want this guy in my house.

"Where's who?" I asked.

Russo was edgy. He glanced around to see if anybody was watching, then gave me a shove that nearly knocked me off my feet. I stumbled back a few steps and hit the wall.

"Stop doing that!" I yelled. "What is your problem?"

"Where's Foley?" he demanded to know.

I knew exactly where Cooper was . . . at the lake house

with his parents. But if this creep was looking for him, I saw no need to tell him that.

"I don't know. Ask your girlfriend," I said dismissively, and backed toward the door.

Russo grabbed my arm and yanked me forward, getting right in my face. He was strong and stood a couple of inches taller than me. I felt like a rag doll. "You tell him to keep his freakin' mouth shut or he's gonna get hurt," he growled.

I suddenly understood what this was all about. Unfortunately, my mouth started working before my brain did.

"Ohhhh . . . ," I said knowingly. "*You* gave him the counterfeit tickets!"

Bad move. Russo shoved me so violently, I thought I would break through the screen door when I hit it.

"He *told* you that?" Russo asked, his face red with rage.

"No, *you* just told me," I countered, trying to keep my voice calm. "I knew Coop was in trouble for scalping counterfeit tickets, but he wouldn't tell me where he got them. If you're so worried about him talking, then he must have gotten them from you."

Russo's eyes turned scary. The guy had a temper, and it looked like I was a second away from paying the price for stoking it.

"I'll get my dad," I said, pointing inside the house. "Maybe he knows where Coop went."

There was no way Mikey Russo could know that my dad was on a trip. At least that's what I was counting on. He hesitated. I could sense the wheels turning in that simple brain. He was calculating his next move. He glanced inside, looking for my dad. I felt his anger rise. He was ready to pound me but knew he was going to have to back down in case Dad was there. The frustration was killing him, poor guy. He wasn't used to thinking so much. He let go of my arm and backed away.

"Tell Foley what I said," he demanded, pointing at me.

"Right," I replied. "'Keep his freakin' mouth shut.' Do I have to drop the *g* in freaking?"

Russo gave me an odd look as if he didn't get what I meant. Idiot.

"Just do it," he commanded, then turned and ran off the porch.

I had come dangerously close to being pounded, but at least one mystery was solved: Mikey Russo was the guy who gave the fake tickets to Coop. For all I knew, Russo had been poking around the house the night before, looking for him. I wouldn't put it past him. Thug. But why didn't he know where Cooper was? Didn't he talk to Sydney? Maybe Sydney was protecting Cooper. She didn't like her brother much, but maybe her heart wasn't cold enough to actually rat him out.

I went back inside, making sure to lock the door in case Russo changed his mind and decided to charge back and injure me. No sooner had I twisted the lock than I remembered the other mystery. The one that wasn't solved. I ran for the kitchen.

The Ovaltine powder was all over the counter and the floor. The three-ring design was gone. Winston had walked through the chocolate and left kitty footprints everywhere . . . across the counter, on the floor, and into the dining room. I stood staring at the counter, trying to make out the remains of the design. There was nothing. Any sign that it had been there was gone. I questioned whether I had seen it or not. It's easier to think something like that was a trick of the imagination than to believe there were inexplicable forces at work. I stood still, trying to feel for rogue gusts of wind. There was nothing. I stood still for a solid five minutes, waiting. I didn't feel even the hint of a breeze. Whatever the event was, it was over and all there was to show for it was a messy kitchen. There was nothing for me to do but clean it up.

Later that morning at work I had trouble focusing and ruined three silver bowls in about ten minutes. Engraving was easy, but you had to concentrate and be precise. Unfortunately, I couldn't and wasn't. Silver bowls weren't cheap. Mistakes got tossed, which didn't make Mr. Santoro too happy. I think I had ruined two bowls the whole time I had worked there. That morning I trashed five. It had to be a record.

"Take a break," Mr. Santoro said, holding back his anger. "Go for a walk. Clear your head."

"Okay, sorry," I said lamely, and went out to Stony Brook Avenue. I grabbed a Coke from the Garden Poultry deli and sat down on a bench in the pocket park next door. My mind wasn't in the moment. All I could think about was the swirling design that appeared in Ovaltine on my kitchen counter . . . and the bag face at the window. I had to force myself to stop obsessing. It wasn't like it was getting me anywhere.

I turned my thoughts to Cooper. Mikey Russo wasn't balanced. If he thought Cooper was going to turn him in to the police, he would hurt him. It wouldn't matter that he was Sydney's brother—Coop would be in trouble.

I didn't want to deal with any of it. Summer wasn't supposed to be so stressful.

My cell phone rang. Only two people called me on the cell. Dad and Cooper. I was hoping it would be Coop so I could tell him about Russo. Besides, I didn't want to deal with my dad. I wouldn't know what to tell him when he asked how things were going.

"Hello?" I said, hoping to hear Coop's happy voice saying, "Hey, Ralph!"

"Is this Marshall Seaver?" came the monotone voice of a guy I didn't recognize.

"Yeah."

"This is Mr. Frano."

I had no idea who Mr. Frano was. My silence must have made him realize that.

"From school," he added.

Oh. Right. Him. I never thought of Frano as "Mr. Frano." The guy wasn't that much older than I was. The fact that he was calling my cell seemed almost as impossible as the mysterious wind that created a pattern in chocolate on my kitchen counter. Almost.

"Oh, hi," I said.

Frano spoke in his usual flat, emotionless voice. Over the phone it sounded even stranger because you didn't have the visual of the black-wearing art poser.

"I discovered another one of your sketches here," he said, sounding annoyed. "I have to clean out the room, so if you want it, I suggest you come by today or else it'll be tossed."

I was a second away from saying, "Trash it." It wasn't like I needed to save every last sketch I had ever done, but with all that was going on, the idea of going on a simple, mindless mission appealed to me.

"Don't," I said. "I'll be there."

"Fine," Frano said, and hung up without so much as a "Good-bye." Creep.

It wasn't until I was halfway back to work that I realized how strange it was that Frano had called me on the cell phone. How did he get my number?

I put in another hour of work (without ruining a single bowl, I'm relieved to say) and asked Mr. Santoro for some extra time at lunch to do my chore. He had no problem with it. Mr. Santoro was a good guy, though I think he was just as happy to see me gone and not destroying any more expensive bowls.

I rode my bike over to Davis Gregory High, which was actually pretty close to my house. It was odd to see the parking lot completely empty. It made sense since summer school hadn't started yet, but it was still weird because normally it was jammed. Walking through the empty corridors was just as strange. It was a big school with a lot of students. Even when most everybody was inside a classroom, you could feel the energy of the people in the building.

Not that day. The place was empty. It felt dead.

I walked to the far end of the sprawling complex where the gym, music department, and art department were located. I didn't pass a single person. It made me wonder what Frano was doing there all by himself.

"Hello?" I called when I stepped into the art room. "Mr. Frano?"

No answer. I figured he had gone out for lunch. Assuming he ate like a normal person. The room was shut down for the summer. Chairs were up on worktables, supplies were out of sight, and the art cubbies were empty. I thought I was too late to salvage my sketch and was about to leave when I spotted something on a worktable across the room. A single chair was on the floor, and a large piece of white drawing paper was on the table. I made my way across the room to see that the table was set up as if somebody had been working there. Charcoal pencils lay next to the paper, along with a gum eraser. I recognized the sketch. Sort of. It was one of mine. Gravedigger. The sketch was a big close-up of his face and shoulders, but there were no facial features, only the familiar outline of his skull-like head topped off by the wide-brimmed black hat. I had shaded in his dark suit, but the face had no detail. Oddly, I had no memory of having done the sketch. I guess that wasn't so strange. I had done hundreds of sketches of the G-man. No way I could remember every last one . . . especially the ones that weren't finished. Still, this one wasn't coming close to ringing any bells.

Something felt off. There were plenty of details in the sketch, just not in the face. That was the exact opposite of the way I usually worked. I liked to draw the features first, then frame them with the contours of his face. Why had I done this one backward? I'm not sure why, but I sat down to finish the job.

I was reaching for one of the charcoal pencils when I was suddenly tickled by another puff of air. The pencil rolled a few inches away from my fingers. My hand hung there.

A second later, a dark shadow leaped at me. I jumped sideways in surprise and looked to see . . .

. . . Winston, my cat, standing on the worktable across from me. Though it took a second for me to register that it was her, there was no mistake. Winston was a uniquely colored tortoiseshell tabby. That alone wasn't proof, but the cat had on Winston's purple collar and I.D. tag. I saw her name engraved in white letters. It was definitely Winston. What the heck was she doing there? How did she get into the school?

"Winny?" I called tentatively. "C'mere."

Cats don't normally do what you tell them, but Winston was more like a dog. When you asked her to come, her tail would go up with a happy flip and she'd prance over to get a scratch on the head. I expected her to run to me and jump onto my lap. She didn't. With a short meow Winston jumped off the table and ran for the door.

"Hey!" I shouted. "Winny!" I got up and chased after her. The surprise of seeing her made me forget about the moving charcoal pencil. All I could think to do was catch her and get her home. Winston trotted out of the art room and along the corridor just fast enough to stay ahead of me. She must have gotten out of the yard and somehow wandered over to the school. Our house was only a few hundred yards away. It wasn't impossible . . . unless you figured in the whole coincidence of it. Then again, I didn't know what she normally did during the day. For all I knew, she hung around at school all the time and was just as surprised to see me as I was to see her.

"Winston!" I shouted. "C'mere! Stop! Sit!" No amount of yelling got through. Every few feet she'd glance back to see if I was still following . . . like it was a game. Whenever she hit an intersection of corridors, she'd sit down with her tail wrapped around her paws. I'd approach her slowly while softly whispering, "Stay there . . . that's good . . . don't move . . . good kitty . . ." But as I was about to grab her, she'd bounce back to her feet and scamper off. Brat. It was making me nuts.

The school was one of those old-fashioned brick structures that probably started out as one building, but as it grew and new wings were added, it became a sprawling mass of interconnected modules. I had gotten lost in the labyrinth more than once. Apparently that wasn't a problem for Winston. She seemed to know exactly where she was going. How odd was that? My cat knew her way around my school better than I did.

She led me deep into the wing that housed the athletic department. The place was an odd mix of the old and the new. The gym was new, but the locker rooms were crusty old. The weight room was modern, but the pool looked like something my grandfather used to swim in.

The door to the boys' locker room was slightly open and Winston scampered for it.

"No!" I shouted. I was afraid she'd find a locker to hide in and I'd never get her. Of course, she didn't listen and shot inside.

There was an outside exit door across the corridor from

the locker room door. I was about ten yards away when I felt a rush of air. Instantly the locker room door closed and the door to the outside blew open. I stopped short. Doors didn't do that on their own. My logical mind raced for answers. I guess it was possible that Winston had somehow nudged the locker room door closed and maybe the gust of wind had kicked open the door to outside. But gusts of wind happened *outside* of buildings.

The exit called to me. I really wanted to get the hell out of there, but I had to find my cat. So I turned away from the outside door and entered the locker room.

The place was dark and musty smelling. Nothing new there. It was always dark and musty smelling.

"Winston?" I called out.

I saw my cat trot straight past a line of lockers, headed for the showers. That was good. If she went in there, she'd be trapped. I didn't hurry after her. I didn't want her changing her little kitty mind and hiding somewhere else. A few seconds later she skittered around the tile wall and disappeared into the large shower room.

"Gotcha," I said to myself.

I had to be cagey. Cats were fast. If she felt trapped, she could easily turn back and shoot past me. I had to hope that she'd stop in the dead end of the showers and end this dumb game of cat and mouse where ironically, I was the cat. I walked slowly toward the entrance to the showers.

"Winny!" I called in a friendly, singsong voice. "Time to go home."

Before stepping into the shower room, I heard a sound come from inside. It was the soft but unmistakable *creaking* sound of a door opening. That was impossible. There were no doors in the shower. I entered the dark space and waited for my eyes to adjust. Once I could make out detail, I looked around the floor of the shower. Winston wasn't there. How could that be?

When my eyes adjusted further, I saw the answer. There was another door in the shower room. When it was closed, you might not even realize it was a door. I had no idea it was there, and I'd taken more than one shower in there. It was covered with the same tiles as the rest of the shower and looked like part of the wall. But it was definitely a door because it was now open. It had swung out a few inches, plenty of room for a naughty cat to squeeze through. I hoped it was a janitor's closet or a storage area for towels . . . a perfect kitty trap. I walked to the door on alert in case Winston suddenly shot out. When I reached the opening, I knelt down and put my hand near the floor.

"C'mon, Winny! Let's go. Who wants a treat?"

Winston didn't take the bait. She was a cat, not a moron. I was going to have to go in after her. I got down on my knees and crawled toward the door, thinking it would be smart to be ready to grab her in case she bolted. I got to the door, reached out, and carefully pulled it open wider. I kept low. No way that cat was getting around me.

Turned out I didn't have to worry. What lay beyond that door wasn't a closet. I was staring into what I can best describe as another world.

And Winston was long gone.

6

I had stepped back through time.

At least that's what it seemed like. What lay beyond the hidden shower door was an old, abandoned gymnasium. The place looked like it hadn't seen action for decades. It wasn't much bigger than the size of the basketball court. It was old-school (literally) with an indoor track that circled above. Dusty shafts of light came in through cloudy windows near the high ceiling. Wooden retractable bleachers were closed against the wall. The basketball backboards were white instead of glass. The thick climbing ropes were still hanging, but the bottoms were looped up and tied to the safety railing of the track above.

It wasn't a gym anymore. It was a big storage closet full of somebody else's history. I saw a bunch of ancient gym equipment like antique parallel bars and an old-school pommel horse. There were twisted piles of old wooden classroom desks and chairs that rose like elaborate sculptures toward the high ceiling. Leaning against one wall was a stack of huge glass windows in peeling wooden frames that I'm guessing were taken from one of the school buildings during a renovation. There looked to be a dozen of them, each twenty feet high and four feet across. There were also tons of cardboard boxes full of who-knew-what stacked everywhere.

My first thought was, *Whoa, cool.* My second thought was, *No way I'm going to find my cat in this mess.*

"Winny!" I called out. "C'mon!" I made a kissing sound. Cats love that. Usually. Not this time. I decided to make my way to the far side and walk back to try and coax Winston toward the shower. Walking across the gym floor was like moving through a maze. There was so much stuff piled up that I was afraid to bump into something and start an avalanche of junk.

"Winston! C'mon, let's go!" I shouted, hoping she'd sense my anger and run out from wherever she was hiding. Yeah, right.

I moved past the tall stack of windows, scanning the floor, hoping to see a little black shadow dart by. This wasn't like Winston. She always came when I called her. I thought maybe she was freaked by this strange place and was hiding somewhere in fear. But what did I know? I wasn't a kitty psychiatrist.

When I reached the far wall, I stopped and listened in case she was on the move. I didn't hear a thing. Literally. Something felt off. It was the sound.

Or the lack of sound.

The place had gone deadly silent . . . like my house the night before. The creaks and groans of the old gym were gone. I stood there, afraid to move, wishing I could hear something. Anything. Finally, I did, and it didn't make me feel any better. It was a dripping sound. Hollow, wet *kerplunks* echoed through the big gymnasium. It was steady. Incessant. Impossible. Just like the night before.

The sound was coming from my left. I turned slowly toward it.

There was no leaking faucet. What I saw was something far worse. Splattered across the yellowed wall not five feet from me was a spray of something wet and red. It looked exactly like the explosion of blood that had erupted from the golden glass ball I had destroyed in my room. Only there was a lot more blood. It ran down the wall and dripped into a red pool that was slowly growing on the gym floor. I watched in stunned wonder as the thick red liquid drooled from what looked like a gaping, vicious wound.

Cat or no cat, I didn't want to be there anymore. I turned and started running back through the gym but didn't get far.

Someone was blocking my way.

He stood between me and the door to the shower. Between me and escape. He was on the far side of the gym, still as a statue, his hollow eyes focused on me. I stood perfectly still, not believing what I was seeing. It was impossible. It had to be a dream, but that was just as impossible because I wasn't asleep.

Standing alone, silently staring at me, was Gravedigger. My creation. In the flesh. On his shoulder was his gleaming silver pick, his bony white fingers wrapped around the handle. His black hat was pulled down low over empty eyes, but I knew he was watching me.

The sight jolted me. I didn't stop to think or analyze how impossible it was that a character from my imagination had suddenly appeared in front of me. All I knew was what my gut told me, and at that moment it was screaming that the guy was trouble. I jumped to my right and slammed into a pile of chairs. I stumbled and fell to the floor as the tower of chairs came crashing down on top of me. I had to throw my arms up to keep from getting hammered. The chairs hit the floor around me, one after the other, bouncing and twisting every which way.

I heard a snapping sound, like the crack of a whip. I looked up to see that the climbing ropes had come to life. They pulled away from the rail and were slashing through the air like angry snakes. I watched, transfixed, until one caught the top edge of the stack of tall windows. The rope went taut . . . and pulled over the entire stack. I was in the wrong place. The heavy pile of glass windows toppled directly toward me. If I didn't get out of there, I'd be shredded. I scrambled away on my knees and slammed into a chair. One of the legs jabbed into my side. Pain shot through my rib cage. I didn't care. I had to get out from under the falling glass. The windows loomed over my head, arcing toward the floor. In seconds I would be hamburger. I pushed off the floor, shifting balance to my legs. I coiled and sprang forward with my arms outstretched like a superhero taking off. I sailed over a pile of chairs and landed on an empty spot of basketball court on the far side. My hands hit, and I tucked my chin to my chest and rolled forward. It wasn't graceful. I twisted sideways and slammed into another stack of chairs, toppling them down on top of me. It hurt like hell, but at least I was out from under the falling windows.

I heard more than saw what happened behind me. The heavy stack of glass hit the floor and exploded. Bits of glass flew everywhere, filling the air with a storm of sharp, shiny fragments. I glanced back in time to see a wave of broken glass headed my way. I ducked quickly and covered my face before I got sliced. I felt the sting through my clothes as I was pelted by the glass, but I didn't dare budge. After a couple of seconds I cautiously peeked over my arm to see the carnage. The four climbing ropes were hanging straight down, swinging gently, no longer animated.

My adrenaline was spiked, but I forced myself to stay calm, think clearly, and figure a way to get out of there. Dust filled the air. I wanted to cough but didn't for fear of breathing in tiny bits of glass. Cautiously I peered around a fallen desk to see what Gravedigger was up to.

He was gone. Or maybe he was moving through the junk, winding his way closer to me with his pick held high. I stood slowly and felt the sharp pain in my side where the leg of the chair had jabbed me. I didn't let it stop me. It was the least of my worries. I was almost to my feet when I heard a crackling sound. Quickly I ducked back down and covered up. If something else was going to land on my head, I wanted to be ready for it.

Nothing was moving, yet the crackling sound continued. It seemed to be coming from below. I looked to the floor and the shattered windows. Broken glass was everywhere. Thousands of tiny, sparkling bits covered the wooden gym floor. It looked like the aftermath of a hailstorm. The crackling sound continued . . . and I felt a soft breeze on my face. I wanted to scream but held it in. From the corner of my eye, I caught movement. Next to the pile of broken frames the tiny bits of glass were moving as if being pushed around by the breeze . . . like the chocolate on my counter.

I started to shiver. I think I was probably in shock. I wanted to run in the worst way but couldn't take my eyes off the moving glass. The tiny bits were being blown about randomly, away from a central spot. It only took a few seconds to realize what was unfolding before me.

As more glass moved, a pattern emerged. It was the triple swirl design I had seen on my kitchen counter. That was the last straw. I couldn't take it anymore. I didn't care if I ran into the figment of my imagination or knocked over more chairs or even if I got my cat out. I didn't want to be in that haunted gym for another second, so I took off, sprinting toward the door, ready to bulldoze over the dark figure if he was stupid enough to get in my way. I blew through the door into the shower room, sprinted past the lockers, and jumped out into the corridor. I should have run out of the building. The exit was right there. But I wasn't thinking— I was reacting. I was out of my mind. I sprinted through the empty corridors all the way back to the art room. Once there I realized I didn't want to be there, either, so I put my head down and kept running. A second before I reached the door, a figure dressed in black stepped out in front of me.

"Ahhh!" I screamed. It was too late to stop. I slammed into him, knocking him into the wall.

"Seaver!" the guy yelled in surprise. "What are you doing?"

Hearing the voice brought me back down. I focused on the guy. It wasn't Gravedigger. It was Frano. I bent over, leaning on my knees, gulping air.

"What are you doing here?" he asked, seething.

I took a few more breaths to try and calm down. When I looked at the pasty-looking art geek, the truth hit me.

"What is your deal?" I snapped at him.

"Excuse me?"

"Don't do that. Don't pretend like you don't know. I'm not an idiot."

"Don't know what?" he asked.

"Seriously?" I shot back. "I know that was you back there. What were you thinking? It would be funny to get me down here and dress up like Gravedigger to freak me out? That's like . . . so juvenile. Those windows could have killed me! That would have been real funny, wouldn't it!"

Frano gave me the same blank stare he always gave. You could never tell if he was excited or asleep. "I have no idea what you're talking about," he declared with no emotion.

"Oh, please. Then why did you call me to come pick up my artwork? It's only one piece and it isn't even finished. You just wanted to set me up for a little prank."

Frano frowned, which for him was a major show of emotion.

"I didn't call you," he said flatly.

"Yes, you did!"

"You're saying I called you to come here and pick up some artwork?" he asked.

"Don't go there!" I yelled. "Don't pretend like you didn't call. I can . . . I can check!" I pulled out my cell phone and fought my shaking hands to scroll through the list of incoming calls. I didn't get many, so I figured it would be easy to spot Frano's. I went through the list once. Then again. There were only two numbers . . . Dad's and Cooper's.

"It's gotta be here," I said, desperately searching through other folders on the phone.

"Mr. Seaver, I don't know what you are up to here, or why you're even in the building, but I promise you I didn't call you to pick up any artwork. Why would I? It's all been cleared out. Every last piece."

"Every last piece?" I repeated. "Then what's this?"

I blew past him and charged into the art room. He followed right behind.

"You are not supposed to be in this school," Frano whined. "Please leave before you get yourself into trouble."

I ran for the table with the unfinished sketch of Gravedigger and declared, "Explain that!" I stared right at Frano while pointing to the sketch on the table. He looked puzzled.

"All right, I suppose I missed one," he said.

"Yeah, tell me about it. I am *so* going to report you to somebody."

"Didn't you say it wasn't finished?" he asked.

"Yeah, it's probably one I threw away and you pulled it

out to . . ." I looked down at the sketch as the words caught in my throat.

The sketch was finished. Gravedigger's face was there in full detail. More detail than I think I'd ever done with one of his drawings. His skeletal mouth was twisted into an evil sneer while his sunken eyes seemed to stare at me from the page.

"What exactly is your issue here, Mr. Seaver?" Frano asked.

I swept the sketch off the table and crushed it into a ball.

"I know you did this," I said to him. "I don't know why, but you better not mess with me again or you're going to be in huge trouble."

I threw the crumpled paper at him and ran out of the room. I didn't want to see it, ever again.

7

I was in no shape to go back to work.

My house was only a few blocks from school, so I rode straight there. I didn't even call Mr. Santoro to tell him I wouldn't be back. There were too many other things banging around in my head to worry about being responsible. I wanted to be home. Home was safe. Home was sane. I felt sure that as soon as I got there, I'd calm down and start to piece things together.

When I got to the house, I locked the door and ran around the entire downstairs, pulling shades and closing blinds. I didn't want anybody looking inside and I didn't want to be able to look out, either. When I thought back to the face that appeared at the kitchen window, it gave me the sweats. It may have been a shopping bag, or not. I didn't know and I wasn't taking any chances. Either way I didn't want any more faces or bags or whatever peering in at me.

I ran up to my room, planning to lock myself in and sit in a corner with a blanket over my head. I had to think. I had to figure this out. I sprinted up the stairs and down the hall to my bedroom. The door was closed. When I pulled it open, any hope of figuring out a sane, logical explanation for what had happened at school was destroyed.

Lying on my bed, fast asleep, was Winston. There was no way for a cat to get in or out of that bedroom. Or the house for that matter. The cat I saw at school couldn't have been Winston. But it was. It had Winston's tags. My legs turned to rubber. I sat down on the floor, staring at my contented little kitty. She didn't even budge. Somehow until that moment, I had been able to convince myself that there were logical explanations for everything I had seen and heard. The sounds; the artwork; the rogue breezes; the symbol; the cell phone; even what I thought was my Gravedigger character come to life . . . I felt certain that with enough reasoning I could find innocent solutions to everything.

Except for the cat.

That was definitely Winston at the school, but there was no way for her to have gotten out of the house. Seeing her lying on that bed made me realize that whatever the explanations were for what was happening, I wasn't going to like them.

So much was happening that defied the rules of the world that I started to wonder if the problem was me. Maybe I was going crazy and imagining things. Why not? Gravedigger existed in my head. Frano might have been right. I might have been obsessed. It wasn't a happy solution. But accepting that everything existed only in my mind was easier to buy than any other explanation I could come up with. Because I couldn't come up with any. What did "going crazy" mean anyway? Was I going to be committed to some institution and live in a rubber room? And if I had suddenly gone out of my mind, why then? Things kind of sucked since Mom died, but that was a few years before. Why would I suddenly start getting all nutty now? Was I going to have to lie on a couch and talk to some psychiatrist guy in a beard while he nodded knowingly and took notes? I didn't feel crazy, though I wasn't sure what crazy was supposed to feel like.

I really wished Dad was home. I needed to hear a normal, strong voice. I went downstairs and used the kitchen phone to call his cell. After three rings I was afraid I'd get his voice mail. On the fourth he answered.

"Hey, you!" he exclaimed brightly. "H-T-H are you?"

Hearing his voice was the best thing that had happened to me all day. Dad was talking loud because he was on the convention floor. The background noise was a dead giveaway.

"I'm okay," I said, lying. You can't start a conversation with: "I'm going out of my mind. H-T-H are *you*?"

"This place is nuts!" Dad yelled.

I wanted to say, "Don't get me started," but decided against it.

"Business is great," he continued, sounding genuinely excited. He then called out to somebody. "Can't now, I'm talking to my son." He focused back on me and said, "What's going on? Any problems?"

I wanted to say, "Yeah. I'm imagining things and it nearly got me shredded," but couldn't get the words out. Thinking about what I would say and how I would say it made it all seem so . . . silly. As much as I wanted to talk to him and hear him tell me how everything was going to be okay, I couldn't. There was nothing he could do about it anyway. Not from a few thousand miles away. I wanted him to get on the next plane and get home ASAP . . . as he would put it. But that wouldn't have been fair. Whatever problems

I was having, they would have to wait until he finished his trip. It would give me time to come up with a way to tell him I was going crazy without sounding like I was going crazy.

"No problems," I said. "Just wanted to say hi."

"I'm proud of you, Marsh!" Dad yelled into the phone. "I'm sorry I have to be away so much."

"It's cool, Dad. This way I don't get sick of you."

He laughed. "Gotta run. Call me later, okay?"

"Yup," I said. "Later."

"G-N, kiddo," he said, and the line went dead.

"G'night, Dad."

I was so incredibly alone. I wondered if any of this would have happened if Dad hadn't gone on the trip. Does your mind hold off on turning wacky until you're at your most vulnerable?

I felt something touch my ankle and nearly screamed. As it was, I jumped back and nearly trampled Winston. She had rubbed up against me, probably to ask for dinner.

"Was that you at school today?" I asked the cat.

Winston chirped an answer, though I think it was, "Shut up and feed me, nutboy."

I scooped her litter box and gave her food and water. I didn't have much of an appetite but put a frozen pizza in the oven anyway. Even lunatics had to eat. While the pizza cooked, I did my best not to look at the window over the sink. A reappearance of Trader Joe would have dropped me off the deep end, so I kept my eyes on the oven. The room started getting dark earlier than normal because a storm was headed in. It made me want to be there even less, so as soon as the pizza was done, I threw it onto a plate and brought it up to my room with a can of Coke. I sat on the floor to eat, but the pizza tasted like nothing. I didn't know what I was supposed to do next. My mind was everywhere and nowhere.

I glanced up at the photo of the temple and flashed back to the sight of it covered in blood. That pretty much killed what little appetite I had. I pushed the pizza away and sat there listening for odd sounds. Or for no sounds.

It wasn't long before the storm arrived and rain started to fall. It pounded on the roof, filling the room with white, wet noise. It made me nervous. I wanted to be able to hear in case something was out there.

Something? What did I think was there? Gravedigger? I kept running the events of the past twenty-four hours over and over in my mind to try and make sense of it. I must have sat there on the floor staring at nothing for a couple of hours with nothing to show for it but a sore butt. It had grown totally dark. Dark was bad. I went around the house and turned on every light. Dad was going to get a surprise when he saw the electric bill, but I didn't care. I thought about playing a little 360 but figured it would only wind me up. I was better off sleeping. At least when I was asleep my mind couldn't play tricks on me. Or so I hoped. Before hitting bed, I took a shower. We had a big, glass-walled stall that took up most of the bathroom. I liked to run the hot water and let it fill up with steam to pretend I was in a sauna. It didn't matter that it was summer and eighty degrees outside; for some reason being in a warm cloud was relaxing.

Since Dad wasn't around to yell at me for using all the hot water, I took my time. It was great. Being in that steamy enclosure was like being in my own private world. For the first time in a day, I relaxed. Nothing strange had happened since my trip to school. It made me think that whatever I was going through might just be over. I decided to stay there in my safe, warm cocoon until the hot water ran out, but that wasn't meant to be.

I saw it before I felt it.

The steam that filled the shower started to swirl. Small

white clouds moved past my face. It made no sense until I felt a faint puff of air. My back stiffened as I instantly went on full alert. Whatever it was had returned. I was suddenly feeling vulnerable. Like *Psycho* vulnerable. I was standing butt naked in a shower stall, facing the tiled wall with my back to the glass. If something was out there behind me, there was nothing I could do about it. I didn't move. Where would I go? Several seconds went by. I felt a breath of wind on my wet back and got the shivers. It didn't matter that hot water was rushing down on me. The goose bumps were up. I heard a squeaking sound, like somebody's finger was sliding across wet glass. I knew I had to turn and see. Looking around, I found the only thing I could use to defend myself. It was a wooden back-scrubber brush hanging from the shower knob. I reached out cautiously and clutched it. It was ridiculous. What did I plan on doing? Give somebody a good brushing? Still, it gave me the slight bit of confidence I needed to turn around. I moved slowly, first turning my head to get a look over my shoulder (I wasn't in any hurry to face an intruder naked).

My heart thumped. My eyes traveled across the steamed-up glass until they came upon the impossible. It was the symbol. The triple swirl. It was somehow drawn on the glass by wiping away the moisture that had collected there. The sight made me jump. My back hit the tiled wall. Was I imagining this? Was this something my mind had created? In that moment I actually hoped I was crazy, because the idea that some entity was in that bathroom drawing symbols on the shower glass was far worse. I had to know. I tentatively reached toward the swirls. Though it had to have been a hundred degrees in that shower, my hand was shaking. My fingers touched the glass and wiped through the interconnected circles. It was real. Or at least my mind was telling me it was real. As my fingers slid across the wet glass, a realization came to me that nearly made my head explode. The moisture was on the *inside* of the shower. If something had actually made this symbol, it wasn't out in the bathroom. It was in the shower with me.

I cranked off the water, yanked the shower door open, leaped out of the stall, and ran soaking wet out of the bathroom and down the hall into my room. I threw on sweats and flip-flops, not bothering to dry off. Once dressed, I stood there, still wet, not knowing what to do. Should I run? Scream? Go for the heavy iron again? I grabbed my cell phone, thinking I should call the police. But what would I tell them? And what could they do besides think I was crazy . . . and they would be right. I thought about calling Dad, but he couldn't help—he was on the other side of the country.

There was only one other person I could think of to call. Cooper. I had no idea what I would tell him, but I knew I wouldn't have to worry about it like I did with Dad. We were best friends. Who cared if we had an argument? Our friendship was stronger than that. I was ready to tell him everything and sound like a lunatic. I didn't care. Maybe he'd come home with his parents. The lake was only a few hours away. I could hold out that long. Yeah, that sounded good. The Foleys would come over and together we'd all figure this out. I didn't know how we'd do that, but I definitely wanted to try. For sure I didn't want to be alone.

I punched in Cooper's number and got back an automated voice that said: "The number you are trying to reach is temporarily out of service. Please try again later." I quickly hit end and tried again. Maybe I had dialed the number wrong. No go. I got the same message. Damn! Cooper's parents must have killed his cell phone as part of his summer exile. I didn't have any other numbers for them. I wanted to scream.

My eye caught something on the table near my bed. It was a business card. Ennis Mobley's card. I had completely forgotten about his odd visit. He was worried about me and wanted to know if anything was wrong. Back then everything was fine. That had changed. Dramatically. I wondered if what was happening had anything to do with Ennis's concern. I couldn't imagine what kind of connection there might be, or how he could predict that I was about to go off the deep end, but at that moment I didn't care. He said to call if I needed help and I definitely needed help.

Ennis's number had a 212 area code. That was New York City. He said he was leaving for Pakistan and didn't give me a foreign contact number. I had to hope that his calls were being forwarded. What did I have to lose? I punched in his number and waited. There was a series of beeps. Beeps were good. It sounded like I was going to be forwarded to wherever he was. What time was it in Pakistan? I didn't know and didn't care. I also didn't know what he could do to help me from so far away, but if there was any connection between his concern for us and what was happening to me, I wanted to know. Was it possible that he had predicted this? Whatever "this" was?

The beeping was replaced by a harsh sound I had never heard over a phone before. There was static along with some shrill shrieks that cut through me like fingernails on a chalkboard. I had to hold the phone away from my ear because it was making my hair stand on end. I was about to hang up and try again when I heard a faint voice through all the noise.

"Hello?" I said.

I figured it was a bad connection and checked the bars on my phone. My reception was solid. Whatever was wrong was happening on the other end. The voice was still there, but I could barely make it out.

"Hello?" I said again.

The voice came somewhat clearer. ". . . make the journey . . . ," I thought I heard. It was a man's voice. That much

I could make out. It didn't sound like a recording, either.

"Can you hear me?" I said. "Ennis?"

". . . the source . . . ," I heard.

"Who is this?" I demanded to know.

The static grew less, but the shrill squeals continued. The man's voice seemed to grow out of them.

". . . search is over . . . journey will begin . . ."

"What journey? Who is this?"

Suddenly the static stopped. The squealing stopped. I thought the phone had gone dead. It hadn't. I heard a deep, booming man's voice clearly say, "The journey along the Morpheus Road."

I snapped the phone shut. *Morpheus Road.* It was the word from my dream the night before. A dream. Was it possible I was still dreaming? Was that the answer to what was happening? Was this all a dream? Was I still lying on the couch in my living room, missing a TV show about sharks?

I heard music. It was so faint, I thought it might be coming from next door. Or maybe it was the TV and it would wake me up from this nightmare. It sounded like a music box. Or something the ice cream guy plays from his truck when he trolls the neighborhood. It was odd but not threatening in the least. If anything, it was strangely compelling. I walked in a daze to my bedroom door. When I opened it, the music got louder. It was coming from inside the house. As far as I knew, there was nothing we owned that would play music like that. I stood in the doorway, listening. It only took a few seconds to recognize the tune. It was a Christmas carol. "Santa Claus Is Comin' to Town." As strange as it was, the music was soothing. It made me think of holidays when I was little. It reminded me of Mom. I remembered coming out of that same room on so many Christmas mornings, carefully making my way down the stairs in the dark, wondering if Santa Claus had paid a visit and what he might have left under the tree. The music was calling me to the magic.

I walked slowly along the upstairs hallway, headed for the stairs. The house was dark. Had I turned out the lights? It didn't matter. It only added to the familiar sensation of a predawn Christmas morning. As I crept down the stairs, the music grew louder. The song played over and over again. I had a brief thought that if it was a wind-up music box, it must have a pretty huge spring to be playing for so long. Looking to the bottom of the stairs, I saw a warm glow of flickering light coming from the living room.

I questioned what was happening but wasn't scared because I was experiencing one of my favorite memories of childhood. I was being swept along in a kind of euphoria. I loved Christmas morning. What could be better? It made me think of hot cocoa and candy canes and parents who would ooh and aah when I opened every gift from Santa as if it were the first time they'd seen it. Sure I was confused. I knew it couldn't be real, but part of me wanted to pretend it was. If only for a little while.

As I moved down the stairs, I focused on the mysterious glow of dancing light that came from the living room. I knew what I'd see when I hit the bottom and turned the corner. The music continued. Did I have a music box like that when I was a baby? Maybe. It sounded so familiar. So comforting. So inviting. I reached the ground floor and walked the last few steps that would take me to the living room. The anticipation was way greater than anything I had ever experienced on mornings of Christmas past. I hoped the payoff would be just as good. When I turned the corner to look into the living room . . .

I wasn't disappointed. It was everything I hoped it would be. A fully decorated tree stood in the corner where it always had. It was lit with multicolored lights that created a magical aura in the dark room. A fire crackled in the fireplace, where three stockings were hung with care . . . each stuffed with presents. The tree was surrounded by stacks of gifts wrapped in colorful Christmas wrapping. Santa had worked overtime. The tree looked like every other tree we ever had, only better. Glass bulbs of gold, red, blue, and green hung from every branch, reflecting the colored light. A silver garland of beads was draped perfectly from top to bottom. Santa Claus had definitely come to town. As much as I was lost in this perfect dream, I knew that what I was seeing was impossible. It had to be in my head, but at that moment I didn't care. It all looked so real. So perfect. I wanted to touch it, but feared I would break the spell. Still, I couldn't resist. I stepped up to the tree and reached out to one of the golden glass ornaments. I expected my fingers to travel through it as if it were an illusion.

They didn't. The glass was solid. Was that possible? Could this be real after all? Maybe it had all been there when I got home and I just hadn't seen it. But then who would have done it? Was it Cooper? Or maybe Santa Claus himself. Why not? That made about as much sense as anything else I'd seen. I accepted that everything had been happening in my head. Feeling the solid ornament made me realize I had to deal with the possibility that it was actually there.

I then sensed the music changing. The music box sped up. The song twisted out of tune. I looked to the ornament I was touching to see that it had transformed. Or had it always looked like that? It was no longer a simple, round golden ball. Markings appeared on its surface. Strangely familiar markings. It had become the golden orb I smashed against my bedroom wall. I pulled my hand away and looked at my fingers to see they were wet. And red. They were covered with blood. My mind couldn't accept it. Was I bleeding? No way. I hadn't cut myself. Yet blood dripped from my fingers.

I looked back to the gold ball to see red streaks where my fingers had touched it. Was the ornament bleeding? I took a step back to see that none of the ornaments on the tree were the same. I was looking at a tree that was now loaded with dozens of the strange, golden orbs.

I backed away, my mind racing to make sense of what I was seeing. No sooner had I stepped back than the bloody ornament fell off the tree on its own, seemingly in slow motion. I watched the blood-streaked golden ball plummet to the floor, where it hit a package wrapped with green Santa paper. The glass bulb exploded the same as when it hit the photo on my wall. Blood splattered everywhere, even on me. I felt the warm wetness on my arms. I wanted to turn away and run, but I was mesmerized by the sight.

One by one, the other balls began dropping off the tree. They released, fell, and exploded to create multiple bursts of blood. The sticky redness splashed over all the presents like a holiday slaughterhouse. The music twisted further. Instead of a happy music box it now sounded like music from a demonic fun house. The thought flashed, *I'm dreaming of a red Christmas*. The music grew louder, echoing through our house. Our haunted house.

I had seen enough. More than enough. I got my head together, turned, and ran for the front door. It was a short trip.

Standing in my way was a visitor, and it wasn't jolly old Saint Nick. Gravedigger had come to town. The dark figure stood between me and the front door, wielding the silver pick on his shoulder.

I managed to squeak out, "Who are you?"

He grinned, twisted his head like a curious dog, and spoke. "The journey can now begin," he said in the same deep voice I had heard over the phone.

It cut straight through my sanity. He moved toward me but not by taking steps. He floated. I took a step back, my shoes crunching tiny bits of wet, broken glass. I was pinned against the tree with branches poking into my back. There was nowhere to go. The ghoul locked his dead, hollow eyes on mine and reached up with his bony fingers. His face broke into a hideous grin that stretched the width of his skeletal head like a gruesome gash. That did it. I snapped. I reached behind me, grabbed a tree branch, and yanked it forward, pulling the Christmas tree down onto the floor between the ghoul and me. I jumped to my right, tripping over bloody packages, desperate to get around him.

I saw a flash of silver and realized the ghoul had swung his pick. Whatever he wanted from me, it wasn't to be friends. I grabbed at anything I could get my hands on to throw down between us. A lamp, a straight-back chair, a small table, bloody packages. Anything to stop him. Gravedigger knocked it all away with casual swings of his gleaming pick and kept on coming. I thought I heard him bellow a laugh, but it was hard to tell above the jangling, discordant notes that blasted from the music box from hell. I made a move for the front door, but Gravedigger slipped back quickly, cutting me off. He didn't even turn to look where he was going. He simply floated back and blocked my way.

"You *will* walk with me," Gravedigger growled. "Now and forever."

I wasn't going anywhere with this demonic clown. My only option was to escape up the stairs. I half stumbled, half ran up to the second floor. Gravedigger followed close behind, floating up the staircase without breaking eye contact. He was in no hurry. I wanted to scream and maybe I would have, but I didn't want to slow down. Even for that.

I got to the second floor hallway and was about to run back into my room when I realized I would be trapped in there. Instead I ran down the hall toward my father's bedroom. Glancing back over my shoulder, I saw the dark figure float casually up the stairs, turn, and follow me down the hall. I was going insane. Or maybe I was already there. Either way I had to fight to keep it together. I jumped into my dad's room and slammed the door behind me. His windows opened up onto the roof of our front porch. That was my plan. Out the window, across the roof, down the wooden porch pillar, across the yard, and straight into the nuthouse. I ran to the window and tried to pull it open.

It didn't budge.

A soft knocking came on the bedroom door. It was creepier than if Gravedigger had been wailing on it with his pick.

I strained to lift the window, but it was frozen shut, probably from the last time the house had been painted. The soft, polite knocking came again.

What was he? Why had my mind conjured the specter? Why was he coming after me? I banged on the upper frame of the window, but it was no use. The window wasn't going to open.

The doorknob turned. There were no locks in our house. The door swung open slowly to reveal the skeletal image standing in the door frame.

"Prepare yourself," he hissed as he floated toward me.

I grabbed a small potted plant from the floor and threw it through the window. It blew out and spread bits of shattered glass everywhere. A second later I was out on the slanted roof. I half scrambled, half rolled across the broken glass so quickly, I didn't realize how close to the edge I was. Before I knew it, I started to go over. I was falling off my own roof! I reached out, desperate to grab on to anything that would slow me down. What I got was the rain gutter. I grabbed it with my right hand, but it was too late to stop me from falling. The gutter bent under my weight and pulled away from the house. I lunged out with my left hand to grab one of the vertical wooden pillars that held up the roof.

That's when the gutter gave way. I let go and grabbed the pillar with my other hand, pulling myself to it. I hung there for a second, then slid down to the porch railing.

I had made it. I didn't know where to go but sure as hell didn't want to stay where I was. It was dark. The rain was pouring down hard. I started to run but spotted my bike at the bottom of the porch stairs. I scooped it up and with one quick kick I was riding. I bumped along the brick pathway that led to the sidewalk, picking up speed, desperate to be as far away from that place as quickly as possible. I shot out from between the two bushes that guarded the path and flew into the road . . .

. . . as a car came speeding along. I hadn't given a thought to traffic. Why would I? Traffic was normal and at that moment my life was anything but. The car's horn blared. I made a desperate, sharp turn to avoid getting T-boned. The car hit the brakes, but the road was rain-slicked and it kept moving forward. The squeal of locked tires on the wet road sounded like the shrieks that had come through the cell phone. I couldn't stay upright, so I bailed off the bike. The car swerved and barely missed the tumbling bike as it flew past his front grill.

"Idiot!" the driver yelled as he sped by.

I was lucky to land on the strip of grass between the sidewalk and the curb. I lay on my stomach, face pressed to the ground. Rainwater streamed down my cheeks as I fought the urge to puke. I didn't know if I was hurt. I was afraid to move. I was afraid of a lot of things. As I lay there trying to calm down, I remembered something that I hadn't thought of in years.

We were ten years old. On hot summer days after a decent rainfall, Cooper and I would ride our bikes along a small river that was normally very shallow. After a good rain the water level went up and made for some decent tubing. There was one spot along the river where a gnarly old tree stretched out over the water. Somebody had tied a thick rope to the branch with a loop at the end. It was perfect for swinging out and dropping into the cool water.

Perfect for Cooper, that is. He would put his foot in the loop, scream like Tarzan, and do a flip at the end of the arc before launching and splashing down. He loved it.

I didn't. It scared me.

"C'mon, Skeever!" he taunted. "You gotta at least try!"

It took me weeks to get up the nerve, but I finally did it. I climbed the tree and grabbed the rope.

"Uh-oh," Cooper called with a laugh. "Check this out. Next stop, Trouble Town!"

I gingerly put my foot into the loop and stood there, trying to get up the nerve to jump. I looked to Cooper. He gave me the double okay sign. That was good enough for me. I pushed off and let go before I swung too high, then plummeted down and hit the water with a perfect cannonball. It was great. In that brief moment I understood what it was like to be Cooper Foley. To be fearless. I did it again. And again. Each time I got a little higher and swung out a little farther. I wasn't graceful, but that was okay. I was doing something daring and it was flat-out awesome. All fear was gone. I couldn't get enough of it. We took turns, each trying to get higher and outdo the other. We must have been there for an hour before the final jump.

"I'm doing a flip," I boasted.

"No way!" Coop shouted.

"Yeah way!" I laughed.

"Who are you?" Coop laughed back. "What have you done with Marsh?"

"Marsh who?" I exclaimed, and pushed off from the tree, harder than I had before.

As I swung forward, I shifted my weight to prepare for the

flip and my foot slipped off the rope. I was so surprised, I did the absolute wrong thing . . . I let go. I fell straight down and when I flipped over, my foot caught in the loop like a snare. My head hit the water, but I was still hanging from the rope . . . by my foot. Gravity had me trapped. My ankle had twisted so violently, I was lucky it didn't break. Still, the pain was excruciating and I couldn't pull myself up. My head dangled in the water. I was going to drown.

Cooper dove in from shore and fought through the current and the neck-deep water to get to me. With one hand he held my head out of the water while he freed my foot with the other. He dragged me to shore, coughing and sputtering the whole way. As soon as I hit dry land, I puked. After losing lunch and most of my breakfast, I looked up to see Cooper leaning casually against a tree with his arms folded.

"You okay, Ralph?"

"Ralph?" I asked.

Cooper shrugged.

I nodded. "Yeah, thanks," I said as I spit ick.

"Don't thank me," he said. "You know I've always got your back in Trouble Town."

My nickname was set on that long-ago summer day. It wasn't like there was anything I could do about it. Whenever I was under stress, I got nauseous. Couldn't help it. From that day on, I was Ralph.

As I lay there in the rain, I knew what I had to do. I had to suck it up and find the guy who always had my back in Trouble Town.

8

"The number you are trying to reach is temporarily out of service. Please try again later."

The more I heard that voice, the more I hated it. Since I had heard it a couple dozen times, I was ready to tear the guy's head off. I sent a load of text messages too. It was like sending them into the void of deep space. I kept hoping that "temporary" meant Cooper would eventually answer.

I was sitting in an old stone bus stop a mile from my house. No way I was going back home. Ever. I was miserable. The rain wouldn't let up, and the ancient stone structure didn't do much to keep me dry. At least it was a warm night. As I sat there alone, I wished I was more like Cooper. Coop had lots of friends. I had Coop. There were plenty of guys I knew, but none that I could stop by their house in the middle of the night and declare that I was being haunted by crazy visions and needed a place to crash.

After trying Coop's number for the thirty-*fourth* time, I thought of a plan. When the Foleys went away, they always had somebody stay at their house to watch things and feed their dog. It was ten o'clock at night. Not too late to pay a visit. Chances were that whoever was house-sitting would have the phone number for Mr. and Mrs. Foley. If I could get to Coop's parents, they could get me to Coop. Once he heard how desperate I was, he would definitely convince one of his parents to come pick me up. It was a good plan and it made me feel a little better.

Cooper lived a few miles from me in a big old house at the end of a cul-de-sac. If I had a nickel for every time I had ridden my bike there, well, I'd have enough money to buy a freakin' plane ticket and get my butt to Dad in Las Vegas, where it was sunny and safe, instead of riding my bike around in the rain. When I turned onto Coop's street and saw his house, I was relieved to see lights on inside. The house sitter was there and awake. So far, so good. I dropped my bike near the front door, climbed the stairs to the porch, and rang the bell.

I hoped that whoever was staying there wouldn't be horrified by the sight of a soaked stranger paying a visit that late at night. I had a moment of panic, thinking they wouldn't let me in or give me the Foleys' phone number. I had to somehow convince them I wasn't some home-less dude and that I was Cooper's best friend and it was really important that I speak with him because I was going insane. I decided to leave out the part about going insane.

The porch light came on and a face appeared at the win-dow in the door. I don't know why I hadn't thought of this possibility before, but I hadn't. I suddenly felt totally self-conscious. Peering at me through the window was Cooper's sister, Sydney. She stared at me like I was a strange creep who had no business ringing her doorbell that late at night . . . which is exactly what I was.

"What do you want?" she said. I felt her iciness through the door.

"It's me, Sydney, Marshall Seaver."

She gave me a blank look. It was like I had said I was an alien from the planet Nimnak.

"Cooper's friend," I added.

Since Sydney and Coop didn't hang around with each other, I hardly ever saw her other than in passing. She was always on the way to somewhere more important than where I was. I didn't think much of it until we got older and Sydney started getting, what's the word . . . *hot*. I wouldn't have minded hanging around with her. Then again, I had trouble speaking in her presence, so maybe it was for the best.

"What do you want?" she repeated impatiently.

"I have to talk to Cooper."

"He's not here," she declared, and turned out the porch light.

Nice.

Ordinarily I would have skulked away, beaten and embarrassed, but there was nothing ordinary about what I was dealing with. I boldly rang the doorbell again. Two seconds later Sydney returned and glared at me. She didn't turn the light back on.

"Are you deaf?" she snarled, annoyed.

"I know Coop's not here," I said quickly. "I've been trying his cell phone, but it's out of service. Please don't walk away, Sydney. I really gotta talk to him."

I must have sounded desperate because, well, I was desperate. Sydney stared at me for another moment with those sharp blue eyes. Normally I would have melted, but I was way beyond that. Sydney unlocked the door. I was so relieved, I could have hugged her. Not that I needed an excuse to want to hug Sydney Foley. She opened the door and I gratefully jumped inside.

"Hey!" she screamed. "You're all wet!"

I looked down at my dripping sweats. "Uh, yeah. It's raining."

Sydney rolled her eyes. "Really? I wouldn't have guessed."

She reached to the floor and picked up a dirty towel that was probably there for people to wipe their shoes on. She tossed it to me like I was some leper she didn't want to get too close to. I didn't care that the towel was filthy. I took it gladly and dried off, happy for the show of kindness . . . no matter how grudging it might have been. All the while Sydney stared at me like I was an infection.

"You didn't go to the lake?" I asked.

"No," she said. "I'm up there right now."

Her sarcasm didn't bother me. I was just grateful to be able to speak. I guess my insanity was stronger than the self-consciousness I usually felt around Sydney.

She turned her back on me and went to the foot of the stairs, where she sat down and stared at me like my every move annoyed her. Her long black hair was tied back in a ponytail. She had on blue flowered pajama bottoms and a T-shirt that didn't quite reach the top of her bottoms. This was a girl who had no trouble getting boyfriends . . . which gave me a sudden, sick feeling.

"Mikey Russo isn't here, is he?" I asked.

"Why?" she shot back. "Are you checking up on me?"

"No!" I said quickly. "I don't care if he's here. That's your business, not mine. I'm not prying or checking up or anything. Really."

Actually, it *was* my business, a little. Mikey had nearly pounded me the last time I'd seen him. I had enough problems without having to deal with that creep.

"So you're running around in the rain in the middle of the night just to find a way to talk to Cooper?" she asked as if it were the most ridiculous thing she had ever heard.

I'm not sure why I answered the way I did. Maybe I was relieved to be speaking to a regular human. Maybe it was being in the familiar comfort of Cooper's house. Or maybe I was so far out of my mind, I couldn't think straight anymore. Whatever the reason, I unloaded on the last person in the world who cared.

"I'm in trouble," I began.

Sydney raised an eyebrow, which was the most interest she'd ever shown in anything having to do with me.

"Why?" she asked sarcastically. "Did you forget the secret password to your Klingon club?"

I ignored the insult.

"I'm seeing things," I said. "Impossible things."

I had her attention. The more I talked, the faster it came out of me.

"None of this is going to sound real. Believe me, that's the problem. My dad's out of town and somebody got into my house last night. I heard them. But when I searched, there was nobody around. Then today I got a call from a student teacher. Frano? You know him?"

"No."

"Well, anyway, he wanted me to pick up some unfinished artwork at school, but when I went there, I saw my cat. My cat was at school! I followed her into an old gym they use for storage, and I know this sounds impossible, but I'm not lying, I saw a character that I created. That I draw. He was there. For real. Then stuff started falling and I nearly got killed for the *first* time when these big glass windows crashed down. But I escaped, and when I saw Frano, he said he never called me, and the artwork that wasn't finished was suddenly finished! And when I went home, my cat was there. She had never left the house, but I swear it was her at school. Then the phone. I heard a strange voice tell me I had to take a journey on the Morpheus Road, and then my character . . . Gravedigger? . . . from school? . . . the guy I draw? . . . he showed up at my house! There was a Christmas tree and ornaments that exploded with blood, and Grave-digger attacked me again, so I had to get out of there and got on my bike and almost slammed into a car, which was the *second* time I was nearly killed today, and I know this is all ridiculous, but I feel like the only person who would listen to me and not think I'm crazy is Cooper . . . even though I think maybe I am crazy . . . but his phone doesn't work and I was hoping you'd call your parents, so I could talk to him."

Once I started, I couldn't stop. When I got it all out, I stood there breathing hard, facing Sydney, who sat on the stairs with no expression. I wasn't sure if she'd feel sorry for me and help me out, or call the police. She blinked once. Twice. Then her face turned hard.

"Get the hell out of here," she commanded.

"Please, Sydney, I know it's crazy but—"

"It's not crazy," she said as she stood up. "It's a joke that isn't funny."

"It's not a joke. I'm dead serious!"

"Cooper put you up to this."

"Cooper? No! I told you I can't even talk to him!" I remembered something. "Wait. There's more. It's not just about Gravedigger." I looked around and saw some junk mail near the door. I lunged for it, then grabbed a pen that was on the table near the door.

"Put that down and leave now!" she ordered. She was pretty calm, considering there was a raving lunatic in her house who was busy . . . raving.

"Wait," I begged. "There's something else. It's like a . . . a . . . symbol. It keeps appearing. In chocolate powder and on the shower door and in pieces of glass." I got down on my knees and began to draw the design with the three swirls.

"I don't know what this is or how it keeps showing up. I've never seen anything like it."

"That's it! I'm calling Mikey—"

"Call him!" I shouted. "I don't care. Don't you get it? I'm terrified. This isn't a joke or a . . . a . . . prank. I'm scared to death and I don't know what to do!"

I held the drawing of the three rings up to Sydney, hoping it was further proof that I was off my nut and needed help. I wasn't expecting the reaction she gave me. Her eyes opened and her mouth dropped. For the first time in, well, *ever* as far as I knew, Sydney Foley was thrown. She stared at the crude drawing, unable to speak.

"What?" I asked. "Does this mean something to you?"

Sydney recovered quickly. Her bewilderment turned to anger. No, rage. "Get . . . the hell . . . out!" she snarled at me.

I stumbled to my feet as she stalked toward me, backing me to the door.

"Sydney, please, I have to talk to Cooper—"

"Like you haven't already."

"I haven't, I swear! Not since he left for the lake."

I didn't know whether to be angry or to cry or to drop to my knees and beg her to call her parents.

"Please. Please, Sydney. Help me. I don't have anywhere to go."

"You can go to hell, and take my brother with you," she said as she reached past me and opened the door. Sydney was about to cut me off from the only people I thought could help me. It was the last straw. I hate to admit it, but I started to cry. That's how desperate I was. I had turned into a blubbering two-year-old.

"I'm scared, Sydney. I'm really scared. Please. Just call your parents."

"Go away!" she shouted, and gave me a shove that was surprisingly strong. Or maybe I was surprisingly weak. I stumbled out of the door and across the porch, and tumbled down the steps to the grass below. I lay there in a puddle as the rain picked up even harder. I couldn't stop crying. The only hope I had was gone. There was nowhere else for me to go. I don't know how long I lay there. Five minutes? Ten? I didn't have the strength to get up. I didn't *want* to get up. Where would I go?

I heard the sound of footsteps coming toward me. For all I knew it was Gravedigger coming to impale me with his silver pick. Oddly, the rain stopped falling. I thought maybe it had let up, but it seemed to be falling everywhere else but on me. I turned to look up and saw Sydney standing over me, holding an umbrella.

"This better not be an act," she said.

I wiped my eyes. "I wish it was," I answered.

"You swear to god you haven't been talking to my brother?"

"If I could talk to him, I wouldn't be here."

"Get up," she demanded.

I picked my pathetic self up out of the puddle and stood in front of her, too embarrassed to even look her in the eye.

"I don't think you're clever enough to be lying about this," she said coldly.

"I'm not."

"Only three people in the world have seen this."

"Seen what?" I asked, suddenly intrigued.

"Me, Cooper, and the redneck lowlife who did it."

"I, uh, what are you talking about?"

Sydney turned her back to me. She reached to the waistband of her pajama bottoms and tugged the right side down a few inches. I was too far gone to think of this as anything other than strange.

"Uh, what are you doing?" I asked.

"No, what are *you* doing? How do you know?"

"Know what?"

She looked at me over her shoulder and dropped her eyes down as if she wanted me to look. It was dark. I had to bend down to see what she was talking about. I bent at the waist and leaned in close to her. She pulled the waistband farther down on her hip to reveal a small tattoo. It was no bigger than a silver dollar, but the small size didn't make it any less dramatic. Tattooed on Sydney Foley's hip, just above her butt, was the symbol.

The triple swirl.

9

"It's an ancient Celtic symbol," Sydney explained. "There are a couple of different meanings. I see it as a sign of female power through transition and growth."

I nodded, enjoying the second cup of hot chicken soup in the Foleys' kitchen. Didn't matter that it came out of an envelope. It tasted great.

I asked, "And you believe in that stuff enough to get a tattoo?"

Sydney glared at me. "Who are you to judge? Mister 'May the Force be with you.'"

"The Force is totally plausible," I countered.

I was ready to debate the issue, but it was clear that Sydney had no interest. There was very little about me that interested Sydney . . . except for the fact that I knew about her secret tattoo, which I had no idea was a secret. Or a tattoo. Or had anything to do with her. Or why it had magically appeared to me.

I shut up and downed more soup.

Sydney let me wear some of Cooper's clothes while my sweats were in the dryer. Coop and I were pretty much the same size, except that his feet were bigger. So I kept my flip-flops but grabbed a pair of jeans and a T-shirt. Sydney was nice enough to make the soup. I guess she felt sorry for me.

"Are you calm now?" she asked.

I nodded.

"Then stop the crazy act. Cooper told you about the tattoo, right?"

"He didn't, I swear."

Sydney looked me up and down with disdain. "Right. It magically appeared in a vision."

"In Ovaltine, actually. And glass. And steam."

She gave me a withering stare. "The only reason I'm not tossing you out is I want to know why you and my dog brother are doing this."

I didn't want to get wound up again. I wanted her to believe I was being rational, even though it was all so completely irrational.

"This has nothing to do with Cooper."

"It has to," she said. "How else would you know about the tattoo?"

"I didn't," I argued. "How come Cooper knows about it anyway? You guys don't even talk."

Sydney took a tired breath. "The creep who did it probably hadn't washed his hands in a month. It got infected. It hurt so bad, I couldn't even walk. I needed help and there was no way I could tell my parents. First they'd melt down and then I'd get the lecture about how it wasn't the kind of thing you'd see on a college application. You know . . . four-four GPA, Honor Society, killer SATs . . . Celtic tat. So I told Cooper."

"Coop took care of you?"

She glared at me. "Yes," she shot back sharply. "Now he's really your hero, isn't he?"

I had to smile. Cooper and Sydney did not get along, but there was no way he wouldn't help somebody who needed it . . . even if it was his ice-cold witch of a sister.

"How come you're always giving Coop such a hard time?" I asked. I knew why Cooper didn't like Sydney. She was rotten to him. But I never heard her side of it.

"You know what?" she asked.

"What?"

"None of your damn business."

Got it. No more questions about Coop.

"How come you're not at the lake?" I asked.

"I'd rather put needles in my eyes. Stuck in a cabin with my parents and the prince? No chance. The only reason they went was to protect Cooper. That's no way to spend a summer. It's out of sight, out of mind . . . for all of us."

I kind of felt bad for Sydney. She seemed angry. At everybody. I wondered where that came from.

"C'mon, be honest," she said. "That story about the grave robber—"

"Gravedigger."

"It's a joke, right? It's something you read in one of your comic books?"

"Graphic novels."

"Whatever. I'm not mad. Just end it, all right?"

I tried to answer as calmly as possible. "I wish I could. I know you don't believe me and I don't blame you. I'm not going to try to convince you. It doesn't matter. All I want to do is talk to a friend. Cooper may not believe it either, but he'll listen."

Sydney looked at me with those steely eyes. I saw what Cooper meant about her staring you down like a cold-blooded vampire. But after all I had seen, there was no way she could get to me. I stared right back at her. Sydney stood up and went for the kitchen phone. Without a word she punched in a number.

I could breathe again. I was finally going to get through to Cooper. As she dialed, I realized that I hadn't really thought about what I'd say to him. Not exactly, anyway. Mostly I wanted somebody to drive down and pick me up so I could get away from the house until Dad came home. That was my hope. I wanted to spend the rest of the week surrounded by people who cared about me, and then when Dad got home, we could figure out what was happening. If he wanted me to see a shrink, so be it. Whatever it took. I never wanted to see Gravedigger in my house again. Or anywhere else for that matter.

"Hi, it's me," Sydney said into the phone. She listened, then added, "Sydney." (Pause.) "Your *daughter*."

She rolled her eyes.

"Put Cooper on," she commanded curtly.

Sydney listened and frowned. Whatever she was hearing, she didn't like it.

"You're kidding?" (Pause. She listened.) "No, I don't mean that literally. Did he say anything?" (Pause. More listening.) "How long?"

I was only hearing one side of the conversation, but based on her reactions, the other side wasn't good.

"Oh, please, it's not like he hasn't done this before," she said with disdain. (Pause. She listened impatiently.) "Fine. I'll call you tomorrow. No, *I'll* call *you*."

She moved to hang up the phone. I jumped up, hoping to grab it before she disconnected.

"Wait! Let me talk to them!"

Too late. She killed the call and dropped the phone on the counter.

"Forget it. Cooper took off," she said with a sneer.

"What do you mean he took off?"

"Who knows? He is such a child. If things don't go exactly the way he wants, he runs away. He always does that."

I remembered back to when we were little. A couple of times Cooper showed up at my door with his backpack full of socks and candy bars. Usually he just had a fight with Sydney and decided to run away. But that was kid stuff and he always wound up back home before dinner. Taking off at our age, and already in trouble with the police, was a whole different thing.

"When was the last time your parents saw him?" I asked.

"I don't know—sometime yesterday—who cares?"

"Did they call the police?"

"No. He's in enough trouble as it is."

"But what if something happened to him?"

"Seaver, he's done this many times before. He disappears for a day so people get all worried, then comes home as if nothing happened. It's all about the drama. He likes being the center of attention, in case you hadn't noticed."

There was nothing good about what I was hearing. Not only was my plan to get help from Cooper crumbling, Cooper himself was having his own adventure and, unlike Sydney, I was worried about him.

"Here," she said. She scribbled something on a scrap of paper and shoved it at me.

"What's this?"

"My parents' number at the lake. Call them tomorrow—he'll be back by then. Now go home."

"Home?" I repeated with surprise.

"Yeah. You know the place. You live there."

"I . . . I can't," I stammered nervously.

"Fine. But you're not staying here," she said as she strode for the back door.

I flew into a panic. "Sydney, please. Let me stay. I won't bother you. You won't even know I'm here. I'll sleep on the couch."

"Eeyew, no!" She pulled the door open and stood to the side, waiting for me to leave.

"Please! I'll call your parents in the morning and be out of here before you even wake up."

"Look, Seaver," she said coldly. "I don't know what your deal is, but you're giving me the creeps. More than usual."

I was surprised to hear that Sydney thought about me enough to have an opinion, even a bad one.

"But I'm scared!" I screamed at her.

It must have been the way I said it, because instead of firing back an insult, Sydney fell silent.

"Can't you see that?" I added, on the verge of tears again. "I'm not this good of an actor."

I could see her jaw muscles clench. She may have been a witch, but she was a smart witch. She had to know I was close to the edge.

"I can sleep on the porch," I offered.

She let the door close. "Take your pathetic self upstairs and stay in Cooper's room. If I hear a word out of you, I'll call the police myself, understand?"

"Yes, yes, thanks. You won't hear a thing. Promise."

We stood there, staring at each other.

"Go!" she yelled.

"Right! Thanks. G'night!"

I ran out of the kitchen and didn't stop until I was up the stairs and in Cooper's bedroom. For the first time in hours I felt safe. Knowing there was another person under the same roof gave me the confidence that whatever it was that had been happening, it wouldn't be happening there.

Just in case, I left the light on.

When I lay down on Cooper's bed, I stared up at the

ceiling, trying to wind down. I had been in that room a thousand times. It should have felt familiar, but oddly, it didn't. Looking around, I understood why. Like me, Cooper had lived in the same bedroom his whole life. Both of our bedroom walls were covered with posters. Batman, Hellboy, Goon. I even had an obscure, retro Green Lantern poster. Hanging from my ceiling by threads were various models I had built over the years. Some were working rockets, others were scale models of fighter jets and WWII vintage bombers. Cooper's room had always been nearly identical to mine, but not anymore. His walls were nearly bare. The colorful posters were gone. Replacing them were a few small pictures he had cut from magazines of bands I'd never heard of. From the threads that used to hold model planes he had hung a colorful tapestry that drooped down and made the place look like something out of the *Arabian Nights*.

It felt like only a few weeks before we had been sitting on that floor, playing Pokémon. How did time move so quickly? Cooper had changed and I hadn't seen it happening. What I needed was security. Instead I was surrounded by more proof that my best friend had grown up without me.

Fortunately, I fell asleep quickly. Running around in terror tends to burn one out. I don't think I had any dreams, which, given the way my mind had been working, was a really good thing.

In the morning I woke to the sounds of muffled voices. My eyes snapped open. Where was I? It was daytime. Sunlight filled the room. Hanging tapestries. Right. Cooper's room. I glanced at the bedside clock. Nine a.m. Nothing scary had happened all night. Maybe it was over. Whatever "it" was.

I heard the voices again. It sounded like an argument. I got out of bed, exchanged Cooper's clothes for my own sweats, and went to investigate. When I opened the bedroom door, I recognized Sydney's voice. It seemed like she was scolding a little child, which is pretty much how she treated most everybody.

"Stop, just stop," she commanded. "I can't stand the whining. Just sit there and don't say anything."

That was the exact kind of thing she would say to Cooper. I felt certain I knew what had happened. Coop had taken off from the lake and come home. *Yes!* I ran down the stairs and charged into the kitchen to see . . . it wasn't Cooper.

It was Mikey Russo. Oops. Russo shot me a surprised look. Freeze frame. It only took three seconds for Mikey's befuddled look to turn to one of anger.

"You gotta be kidding me," he snarled at Sydney. "The geek?"

"Oh, please," Sydney said dismissively. "He needed a place to crash."

"And he picked here?" Mikey said suspiciously. "With his little pal out of town?"

Part of me enjoyed the moment. Mikey Russo was jealous. Of course, the idea of Sydney and me hooking up was about as likely as cows dancing, but it was kind of fun to think that Mikey thought it was possible.

"You can't be serious," Sydney said, annoyed. "He's a kid."

"Hey!" I shouted indignantly. "You're only a year older than me."

Sydney gave me a sideways look. "I am a *lifetime* older than you, peewee."

I may have known there was no chance for the two of us to hook up, but it stung to know she thought so too. Unfortunately, Mikey didn't see it that way. I would have been flattered if it didn't mean I was in serious trouble.

Mikey lunged at me and grabbed my shirt. "What are

you doing here, huh?" he growled. I could feel his hot breath on my face.

"She—she told you," I stammered. "I needed a place to sleep."

"What? Your bed's no good?" he growled sarcastically.

"Let him go, idiot," Sydney ordered casually. She wasn't as concerned as I was. Why should she be? She wasn't the one about to be beaten up by Frankenstein.

Mikey obeyed her. Sort of. He shoved me. Again. I went flying backward, hit my already sore rib on the counter, and crashed into the dish drainer. Three glasses fell out and shattered on the floor.

"Mikey!" Sydney shouted angrily. She didn't care about my getting hurt, but break a few glasses and watch out!

Mikey's response was to grab the back of my neck and drag me toward the door. I struggled but wasn't strong enough to break his grip. He must have had fifty pounds on me and he was enraged. I didn't stand a chance.

"Let him go!" Sydney screamed.

Mikey was beyond hearing. "You want to mess with me?" he snarled as he kicked the door open.

Things were happening too quickly. Why wasn't Sydney telling him that nothing happened between us? Or *would* happen. I was about to get pummeled by a jealous boyfriend without having had any of the fun to deserve it. Mikey pushed me across the deck and shoved me down the steps that led to the grass of the backyard. I stumbled down the stairs, trying to get my feet under me. No go. I hit the grass with my shoulder and rolled.

"Mikey, stop!" Sydney yelled.

I looked up to see him stalking toward me. He seemed huge, with angry eyes that were locked on me. There was no time for me to get to my feet. All I could do was defend myself as best as I could.

Mikey was only a few feet away, when something got his attention. He looked up past me, his eyes focused on something. He stood there, frozen, as if not sure what to do. I took a quick glance over my shoulder to see . . . nothing. The backyard. That was it. I took the chance to get to my feet, figuring I had a better shot at defending myself upright when Mikey snapped out of it and charged again. He took two more steps and stopped again. His eyes widened.

Mikey looked scared.

"Hey, hey, no!" he mumbled as he backed away. "Sydney!"

Sydney was on the porch, looking as confused as I felt.

"What is your problem?" she called out, more confused than concerned.

Mikey took two more steps backward and fell down, flat on his back. He held his hands up as if trying to protect himself, but there was nothing coming after him.

"Stop! Help! Help me!" Mikey screamed in terror.

I looked to Sydney. She stared down at Mikey the same as me, not knowing what was happening or what to do about it.

"What's going on?" I called to him.

Mikey was beyond listening. He was crying and screaming and swiping at the air as if fending off phantom punches. As he scrambled to his feet, I saw his eyes. I don't think I'll ever forget the sight. He was out of his mind with fear.

"Get 'em away!" he screamed, then turned and ran toward the front of the house.

I gave Sydney a quick, confused look, then took off after him. The guy was running for his life. Or so it seemed. He rounded the Foleys' house and sprinted for his car, which was parked on the street. The whole way, he was crying and whimpering. When he got to the car, he grabbed the door handle while kicking back with his feet as if keeping something off him. It would have been funny, if it wasn't.

He finally yanked the door open, dove inside, and slammed it shut.

Sydney and I stood together watching as Mikey gunned his engine and peeled out, his wheels squealing. He was gone in seconds, the sound of his car fading quickly.

We were left standing there, dumbfounded for a good twenty seconds.

It was Sydney who broke the silence first. "Then there's that," she declared, stunned.

"I don't get it," I said. "He just started going nuts."

Neither of us knew what else to say. We had just witnessed Mikey Russo having a complete meltdown for no reason.

"Should we call somebody?" I asked.

"Like who?"

"I don't know. His parents?"

"And say what? Hi, Mrs. Russo. Mikey just had a mental breakdown and he's driving around like a lunatic. Have a nice day."

Not that I cared an inch about Mikey Russo, but what I'd just seen had me pretty freaked. Whatever he just saw wasn't really there. It was in his mind. I knew the feeling. Did Mikey's mind just so happen to snap around the same time mine wasn't doing so well either? As disturbing as his panic attack was, it only added to my own worries about what I had been seeing.

"I'm calling your parents," I said.

"Don't bother," she said flatly. "I spoke with them this morning. Cooper isn't back yet."

"He's been gone two nights?" I declared. "That's not right."

Sydney seemed shaken, which wasn't like her. I wasn't sure if it was because of Cooper or Mikey.

"*Now* are they worried?" I asked.

She nodded. "They called the police."

The news washed all thoughts of Mikey's strange behavior out of my head. I needed Cooper's help—only now it looked like he was having serious problems of his own.

"I'm going to the lake," I said, and started walking toward my bike.

"How? You have a car?" she asked.

"I don't even drive," I called back. "I'll take the bus."

"What bus?" she called.

"I'll find one. Or a train." I picked up my bike, which had been sitting in front of their house all night, and wheeled it toward the road.

"Wait," Sydney called.

I stopped.

"I'll drive you." She didn't even wait for a response. She turned and headed for the house.

"You don't have to," I said.

"I know," she replied. "You'll owe me."

Gotta love Sydney.

"Go home and pack," she commanded. "I'll pick you up in half an hour." That was it. She disappeared into the house and slammed the door. She didn't even wait to hear if I wanted to go with her or not.

"Okay!" I called, but it was for my benefit only. Sydney was long gone.

Things were looking up, a little. I got what I wanted . . . a ride to the lake. At the very least I'd see Coop's parents. I liked those guys. They always treated me like one of the family. Still, I wasn't feeling much relief. Where was Cooper? It wasn't odd for him to take off, but not for that long. As I wheeled my bike toward the street, a thought came to me that made me shudder.

Was something strange happening to Cooper, too? I never would have thought that way if not for Mikey Russo's fit. Were we all going off the deep end? Was something in the water making us a little unbalanced? I put the thought out of my head and focused on practical matters. I had to pack for a few days.

That meant I had to go back to my house.

Alone.

10

I stood on the street, staring up at the most normal-looking house in the world. My house. I'd lived there my entire life. It was home. It was safe.

It was haunted.

The only other explanation was that I was demented. I couldn't say which I was rooting for. Less than twelve hours earlier I had been driven from my own home by the super-natural vision of a character that sprang from my imagination. Was he still in there? Was he hiding in a back closet or in some dark recess of my brain, waiting to attack when I least expected it? Or maybe when I fully expected it. I didn't want to go in, but there were some things I had to do before leaving. Looking around at the quiet street, I tried to convince myself that scary things didn't happen on suburban streets on warm, sunny days. That kind of stuff was saved for stormy midnights in desolate mansions. That's what I told myself, anyway.

A blaring car horn made me jump. It probably saved me because if I hadn't moved, Sydney would have run me down. She pulled her silver convertible VW Beetle up to the house fast and skidded to a stop on the exact spot where I had been standing.

"Let's go," she ordered.

"I haven't gone in yet," I said sheepishly. I had been standing in front of the house for a long time.

The top was down, so I could see her look of disdain . . . even through her sunglasses. She opened her mouth, ready to tear me a new one, but chose not to. Instead she took a deep breath to control her more vicious impulses and said, "I'm leaving in ten minutes . . . with or without you."

"Would you come in with me?" I asked.

Her answer was to ignore me and focus instead on texting somebody. Enough said. I had to brave it alone and started the long walk to the house.

"What happened?" Sydney called out.

I looked back to her, not knowing what she meant.

"The rain gutter," she added. "Did the storm do that?"

I looked to the house to see the rain gutter that was torn from the porch roof and the smashed bedroom window above. Whatever had happened the night before may have been in my head, but that part was real. It had to have been if Sydney saw it too.

"Yeah" was all I could answer. I didn't have the energy to go into details.

Inside, I found more proof that what had happened the night before was real. The living room was a mess. Lamps were knocked over, along with a chair and a few small tables . . . exactly where I had thrown them. There was no Christmas tree, though. Or bloody gifts or broken ornaments or anything else that would prove I hadn't hallucinated that whole thing. Everything was normal, except for the destruction I had caused myself. Thinking that I had conjured the whole thing in my head was disturbing, but the thought of running into Gravedigger was flat-out terrifying. I had to focus on getting out of there as fast as possible.

As I moved through the house, I kept peeking around corners for fear that Gravedigger might be standing there. A couple of times I walked on a section of floor that creaked and nearly peed in my pants. The first thing I did was make sure that Winston would be okay while I was gone. Dad had gotten one of those dispensers that holds a week's worth of food and water, so I filled them both up. Winston watched me from the kitchen counter, bored. Cats don't stress. I then called Mr. Santoro to apologize for not going back to work the day before and to tell him I would be gone for a couple of days. Family emergency. It was only a small lie. Cooper was like family. Mr. Santoro told me not to worry. He said he would get Mark Dimond to come in for a few days to help out. Next I called Dad to tell him I was going to visit the Foleys at the lake. Hearing his voice made me want to break down and beg him to come home. It took all of my willpower not to tell him what was going on.

I went upstairs to my bedroom to get changed and pack. I jammed enough clothes into my backpack to last about a week. Mostly it was socks and underwear. I also packed my cell phone charger, though I wasn't sure I ever wanted to talk on that thing again. Not if I was going to be getting messages from the Twilight Zone. The last thing I did was grab some cash out of my dresser. I had to be prepared for emergencies . . . or in case Sydney pitched a fit and chucked me out of the car in the middle of nowhere.

I didn't check my watch, but I must have gotten out of there under the ten-minute deadline because Sydney was still there waiting. Her car was running and I had no doubt she would have gunned out of there if I was a second late.

As it was, she barely gave me time to get in and close the door before she hit the gas.

"Thanks for doing this, Sydney," I said. "I know I must sound like a lunatic, but—"

"Don't talk," she said.

It was a simple, straight-to-the-point command that I figured would be smart to obey. All that mattered was getting to the lake. I sat back and closed my eyes, hoping that I would fall asleep and wake up among friends.

I don't remember much about the movie we all went to see. It was the current action blockbuster that was supposed to be the "thrill ride of the summer" . . . but wasn't. It was totally forgettable. What happened that night in the theater, wasn't.

It was the night when Cooper nearly died.

A bunch of us from Stony Brook Junior High went together one Saturday night. It wasn't a group date or anything because none of us were paired up. Except for Coop, of course. He and Megan Whiteside were going out. Coop went out with most of the girls from our grade . . . and the grade ahead of us.

That afternoon Cooper complained about having stomach cramps. Mr. Foley didn't think anything of it since Coop and I had both eaten about a dozen tacos for lunch. He gave Coop some Alka-Seltzer, which took care of the problem. At least Coop said it did. There was no way he was going to give in to a little stomach pain when he could sit for two hours holding hands with Megan Whiteside.

Our group took up an entire row in the theater. Cooper and I were on opposite ends. He sat next to Megan, and I sat next to a guy named Mooch who kept whispering, "Whoa! Did you see that?" whenever there was an explosion . . . like I wasn't watching the exact same thing he was. The movie didn't hold my attention, and that's saying something for a guy who normally eats that stuff up. About halfway through I saw Cooper get up and walk to the lobby. If the movie had been better, I might not even have noticed. A few minutes later he came back and that was that.

Until he got up again to leave. I figured he had to go to the bathroom or get popcorn, but he came back the second time without any food. I focused back on the movie and the evil industrialist bad guy who nobody in the movie suspected was a villain but was so obvious that it was laughable. When the bad guy's evil self was revealed, Mooch actually whispered, "Whoa! Didn't see that coming!" Great insight.

Cooper got up again to leave. That crossed the line into being strange. This time he didn't come back. Five minutes went by. Ten minutes. I couldn't take it anymore and slipped out to go see what the deal was. It was an old-fashioned movie theater on the Ave. I loved going there because it was like stepping back in time. There was only one screen, which was framed with heavy curtains. The lobby had a dark, threadbare carpet that gave off a sour smell that probably came from decades of spilled golden popcorn topping. When I stepped out of the dark into the lobby, Cooper wasn't there. Nobody was. I checked the concession area. No Cooper. I asked the sleepy kid taking tickets at the door if a guy had just walked out. Nobody had. The only other place Cooper could have gone was the bathroom.

That's where I found him. In the last stall, on the floor, doubled over in pain.

"Are you all right?" I asked. (Why is it that you always ask somebody if they're all right when they're obviously not all right?)

"Man, I'm dying," Coop answered through clenched teeth. "Those tacos were bad. My stomach feels like it's gonna explode."

Cooper looked horrible, though I can't imagine anybody

looking good while they're writhing in pain on the floor of a dirty public bathroom. He was soaked with sweat. His eyes couldn't focus. His hair was wet and plastered to his head.

"I'll call your parents," I declared.

"No, don't," he said. "If I could just puke, I'd be okay."

"Coop! You're a mess!"

"What'll my parents do? Take me home and tuck me into bed? I'll still feel like crap and I don't want to miss the rest of the movie."

"The movie sucks!" I shouted. "You gotta get outta here."

I reached under his arms to lift him up. Cooper grunted in pain.

"This isn't from bad tacos," I said. "I ate 'em and I'm fine."

"Tacos," Cooper repeated. I think sending his mind back to those greasy treats put him over the edge. He looked at me with a blank expression and declared, "Trouble Town."

He didn't make it to the toilet and blew lunch all over the wall. The tension in Cooper's body made the pain even worse as he grunted in agony with every heave. I managed to pull him around to the toilet, where he clutched the rim and continued to hurl. It was scary. I grabbed my cell phone and punched in 9-1-1.

The sleepy ticket taker wasn't sleepy anymore. He heard the gruesome sounds coming from the bathroom and came charging in. After one look at the carnage, he nearly lost it himself.

"What's wrong with him?" the guy said, choking back his own retch.

"Bad tacos" was the only answer I could come up with.

Cooper finished and sat back against the wall. The tension in his body was gone.

"Talk to me," I said.

"I'm okay," Coop mumbled while holding up the double okay sign. "You think Megan'll still give me a good-night kiss?"

He said it with a smile and a wink. Didn't matter that Cooper felt like dirt. Anything for the joke.

I was afraid he might pass out or lose it again, so I stayed with him. The stall was a mess and it reeked, but I couldn't leave. Five minutes later the ambulance showed up and they took him to the hospital. Turned out Coop's problem had nothing to do with tacos. His appendix was on the verge of bursting. They took it out that night and he was fine.

Besides the horror of it all, one of the things that stuck with me about that night was what happened when I went back into the movie to tell the others about Coop. I knelt down at the end of the aisle next to Megan and whispered loud enough for everyone to hear, "Coop got sick. The ambulance took him to the hospital."

Everyone's eyes stayed focused on the screen like they were actually engrossed in the lousy movie. The most reaction I got was a couple of nods of acknowledgment. Even from Megan. I wanted to give them the benefit of the doubt and think that they didn't hear or register what I had said because if they had, I'm sure they would have been worried about Cooper. It's not like they were jerks. They all went to visit him in the hospital the next day. But none of them were there for Cooper that night like I was. That's what friends do.

I'm not sure why that story came back to me while I sat huddled in Sydney's car on the way to the lake. It had happened so long ago. I guess maybe it was because it gave me the assurance that when things got bad, there were certain people you could always count on. I would have been more comforted by the idea if I knew Cooper was all right. I couldn't say for sure if I was going to the lake so that he could help me or I could help him. Either way I was on my way there . . . and out of my house.

I slept for the first two hours of the drive, which was

great because I didn't have to deal with the awkward silence, and as long as I was sleeping, I couldn't see anything scary. When I started to come around, I had the fleeting hope that everything had been a dream and I'd been asleep since Dad left for Vegas.

That was blown away the moment I smelled Sydney's perfume. Reality flooded back in a mad rush.

"You awake?" Sydney asked.

"Yeah."

"Are you finished acting crazy?"

I didn't have an answer for that.

"Tell me what happened to Mikey," she commanded.

Mikey? Who cared about Mikey? Compared to everything I'd seen, Mikey flipping out was barely on my radar.

"Am I allowed to speak?" I asked.

I don't think she knew how to answer, so she ignored the question. I sat up and squinted against the bright sunshine. We were flying along a winding, two-lane highway about a half hour south of Thistledown Lake. Sydney liked to drive fast. Ordinarily it would have scared me and I would have asked her to slow down, but I was beyond caring about something as simple as careening off the road and dying in a fiery car wreck.

With her big sunglasses Sydney looked like a model. Her long black hair and perfect features probably helped the impression. The jean shorts and creatively torn T-shirt didn't hurt either.

"Was he kidding?" she asked. "I mean, he went totally off."

They were the first words she'd spoken to me that weren't some form of insult.

"I don't know" was all I could manage to say.

She gave me a quick glance. I looked straight ahead.

"You're a mess," she declared.

I guess there was no mistaking *me* for a model.

"I mean, not just the way you look," she continued. "Your whole being. You're messed up."

"Thank you," I said. I wasn't being sarcastic. Why bother? She was right. I *was* messed up.

"No offense, but what is your deal?" she asked. "How old are you now? Fourteen?"

I gave her what I hoped was a dirty look.

"Your brother and I have been in the same class since kindergarten," I said flatly.

"Oh. Right. You just seem so much, I don't know, younger than him."

"Or maybe he seems older than me."

Sydney smiled. I saw it. It wasn't huge and lasted barely a second, but it was there. I had cracked the shell of the ice queen. It felt like a huge victory, so I pressed my luck.

"So why don't you guys get along?" I asked.

All traces of the Sydney smile disappeared.

"Better question," she said. "How come you *do* get along with him? I mean, you're nothing alike. He's all popular and has girls buzzing around him like flies on . . . whatever, and you're . . . you're . . ."

"Not and don't," I said, finishing her thought.

"It's true. You two are in, like . . . different leagues. Doesn't that bug you?"

"Coop and I don't compete, so it's not a problem," I said. "But it sounds like maybe you do."

"Me? Compete with Cooper? Please."

I shrugged. "Just sayin'."

She laughed, maybe a little too hard. "Why would you say that? I'm going to be valedictorian. I'm going to Stanford. I have more people who want to be friends than I have time for. That's not a competition."

"Not for him it isn't. He doesn't care about any of that stuff."

She snapped a look to me. I didn't dare look at her. I'd said too much already.

Sydney sped up. I started to care.

"I thought I was the one who wanted to get there in a hurry," I said, trying not to let my tension show.

"What?" she replied with fake innocence. "You don't like going fast?"

I wanted to come back with something funny that would put her in her place and show that I could match wits with her.

"No" was all I could come up with.

Sydney laughed like I was an annoying little boy and eased off the gas. I almost wished she hadn't. Slowing down was further proof that I wasn't playing on her level.

We didn't say another word for the rest of the drive, which was thankfully short, because we soon hit the town of Thistledown. Driving through reminded me of the great times I'd spent there with Cooper. His family bought the house when we were in first grade, and we spent many weeks up there swimming and hiking and playing board games and basically enjoying summer. I missed those times. I hated the idea of creating new memories of the place that wouldn't be so warm and fuzzy.

We hadn't heard anything about Cooper since the call Sydney got that morning, almost six hours before. As we drove closer to the Foleys' lake house, the thought hit me that Coop might have turned up since then. I imagined pulling up to the house and seeing him standing on the dock with a fishing pole, waving to us. It wouldn't have surprised me at all.

The gravel driveway was off the main road. If you didn't know it was there, you'd miss it. The only sign that marked it was an ancient marine light that hung from a wooden post that was mostly covered by tree branches. As we approached the turn, a car was coming out of the driveway. A police car.

"Oh, great," Sydney said under her breath.

She assumed it was bad news, but I hoped the cop had brought Coop back to the house. Sydney turned into the driveway and we made the long trip to the house. It was exactly a quarter of a mile from the road to the house; Coop and I measured it once so we could time ourselves running it. Our car broke through the trees into the clearing where the yellow house sat not ten yards from the shore of Thistledown Lake. Sydney pulled up to the back door and stopped. I jumped out and looked around the side of the house to the dock.

Cooper wasn't there.

The back door opened and Mrs. Foley stepped out. One look at her face told me that Sydney was right. The cop hadn't brought good news.

11

"I am so glad you're here!" Mrs. Foley declared as she walked toward us with her arms open wide.

I thought she was talking to Sydney, but she blew past her daughter and gave me a big hug. It was awkward, but it didn't seem to bother Sydney.

"What did the cop say?" Sydney asked, bored, as if she didn't really care.

"It's been two days, so it's officially a missing-person situation," Mrs. Foley answered, sounding tired. "They'll put his picture out to the various authorities. But I'm not worried. I'm really not. He's done this before and he'll do it again."

She may have said that she wasn't worried, but her eyes were red as if she'd been crying or hadn't slept much. Or both. Mrs. Foley was one of those moms that everybody liked. I think it was because she didn't act like a typical mom. She joked around and wouldn't stress if you didn't eat all your vegetables. Actually, I don't think she cooked vegetables. Or anything else, for that matter. She mostly played tennis and volunteered at school. She seemed to like being with young people and dressed kind of like the girls in our grade. It wasn't sad or anything because she looked pretty good. In fact, she looked like an older version of Sydney, which really hit me as I looked at Sydney standing at the back door, clearly wishing she were somewhere else. They both had long dark hair and wore cutoff jeans, Ugg boots, and T-shirts. Mrs. F. was a lot nicer than Sydney, though.

Sydney opened the back door. "I'm going to my room," she announced.

"Let's give Marsh your room," Mrs. Foley called out. "He's our guest."

Sydney stopped short and turned around slowly. If looks could kill . . .

"What?" Sydney said softly but with scary intensity.

"That's okay," I declared, heading off the argument. "I'll take the lower bunk in Coop's room. Like always."

"We got rid of the bunk beds," Mrs. Foley said. "There's only Cooper's single bed now."

"Then I'll take the couch," I said quickly. There was no way I was going to put Sydney out of her bedroom. She'd probably murder me in my sleep. And I expected Coop to be back any second anyway.

Sydney didn't comment on my decision. She stormed inside, letting the screen door slam.

"Thank you, Marsh," Mrs. Foley said as if to apologize for Sydney being so obnoxious, but I could kinda get why Sydney didn't like her mom offering up her room so fast. I went to get my pack out of the car. As a peace offering I grabbed Sydney's bag too.

"What am I supposed to do with Cooper?" Mrs. Foley

asked. "The boy has got so much going for himself, but he insists on being so . . . so . . . I don't know, self-destructive."

I shrugged. I wondered the same thing.

"What happened before he took off?" I asked. "Did you guys have a fight or anything?"

"No! There was nothing like that. After all his complaints he actually seemed happy to be here. I think that has as much to do with the girl down at the marina as anything."

"Oh, yeah," I said. "Britt."

"Yes, Brittany. He was looking forward to spending time with her."

Britt Lukas lived in Vermont but spent her summers in Thistledown. She and Coop had had a summer thing every year since we were eleven. Coop was a fast starter.

"Does she have any idea where he might have gone?" I asked.

Mrs. Foley shook her head. "I haven't spoken to her. But you know what? I'm not going to stress. I know he's going to come waltzing back here any second with some story about how he fell asleep on a train and woke up three states away with no money to get home. Or something else just as ridiculous."

"I think that's exactly what's going to happen," I said optimistically, though I wasn't sure why.

"I'm glad you're here, Marsh," she said sincerely. "You're such a stable influence in his life right now."

I couldn't argue with that. I was a stable guy. At least until I started having hallucinations about being attacked by imaginary demons.

"You look tired, though," she added. "Is everything okay?"

I thought about spilling it all and saying how I was being haunted by impossible visions and had barely escaped my house because I was being chased by a creature from my imagination, but decided to hold off on that particular purge until Coop showed up.

"I'm fine" was my answer.

"Good. Let's have some lunch!" she declared cheerily, putting on a happy face.

I was starved but didn't realize it until that very second. Being at the lake had already gotten me to relax a little about my own issues. As much as I was worried about Cooper, thinking about him got my mind off my own craziness. I felt safe at that house. It was a familiar place with great memories, and it was away from home. Home had gotten scary. In my mind I had left behind whatever it was that had caused me to see those frightening things. The only other possibility was that it had all happened in my head, but since I couldn't leave my head behind, I preferred my first theory.

The Foleys' cabin had two stories and three bedrooms. Mr. and Mrs. Foley slept in the downstairs bedroom; Coop and Sydney were upstairs. It was an old house that had been spruced up with some paint but still had the feel of a rustic cabin. The floorboards squeaked if you so much as breathed on them. The furniture was all secondhand. There was nothing fancy about the place. It was awesome. I dumped my pack behind the couch and went upstairs to deliver Sydney's bag.

She was in her room, sitting on her bed with her back to me, talking on her cell phone. I couldn't tell what she was saying because she was barely speaking above a whisper, but I could tell that she was angry with somebody. She hunched over the bed, resting her elbows on her knees. She cupped the phone as if to make sure nobody could hear what she was saying. I didn't want to eavesdrop, so I knocked on the door to let her know I was there. She whipped around suddenly. Her eyes were red. She was almost crying. Almost. I don't think Sydney knew how to cry. Still, it was awkward. I held up the bag to show her why I was there. She got up quickly, rounded the bed toward me, grabbed the bag, and slammed the door in my face.

"You're welcome," I said to the door.

After I found a place to put my things and went to the bathroom, I went into the kitchen, where Mrs. Foley had a bologna sandwich and some chips waiting for me. That was pretty much the outer edge of her cooking ability. It was fine by me. I inhaled it. Bologna is awesome, especially when you're starving. The kitchen was on the lake side of the house. I looked outside to see Mr. Foley walk out onto the dock. He was on his cell phone, speaking quickly and gesturing with his free hand for emphasis, which was lost on whoever was on the other end of the conversation. For as long as I'd known. Mr. Foley, he was always on the phone doing business. He must have been successful, seeing as they had a house on a lake. He worked at some big Wall Street company in the city. He commuted from Stony Brook on the train, which meant he left early in the morning and didn't get home until late at night. I don't think the rest of the family saw him much. I know I didn't. I barely knew him. He was friendly enough, but he wasn't the kind of dad who got involved with his kids' stuff, at least as far as I knew. We never went camping or played ball or anything. Though whenever I saw him, he always greeted me with a big, boisterous "Seaverino! How the heck are you!" and shook my hand so hard, I thought bones would snap. I guess you'd call him a preppy type. He wore suits to work, but on the weekend he'd wear ridiculous yellow pants and pink shirts. He was kind of a cartoon, but I never said that to Coop. He was pretty nice to me when Mom died. Same with Mrs. Foley. I'll always remember that.

Mrs. Foley sat on a deck chair on the dock. I wasn't sure

if she was there to listen to her husband's conversation or to get a tan. I hoped that whoever Mr. Foley was talking to, it was about trying to find Cooper and not working his next business deal.

"I've got to buy some groceries in town," Sydney yelled into the kitchen. "You can help."

It was more of a command than a request. I figured I'd better obey, so I dumped my plates into the sink and hurried after her. We drove into the town of Thistledown, though to call it a town is exaggerating. It was a single block of shops and restaurants on the shore of the lake that pretty much existed for tourists. Most of the places only opened during the summer. There was a mini golf course, a drive-in movie, and far more T-shirt shops than customers who wanted to buy T-shirts. I don't know how they stayed in business. Most of the businesses closed after Labor Day, when all the tourists went home.

But this was still June, peak season, and the street was humming. People were everywhere; Top 40 music blared from restaurants and cars, and the ice cream store had a huge line. It was your basic summer day.

The town was at the foot of Thistledown Lake, which was about seven miles long. You could rent most any kind of watercraft from the marina at the end of Main Street, so that's where all the tourists launched. The lake around the marina was always packed with a mess of people in canoes and Jet Skis and ski boats. You took your life in your hands if you tried to compete with that bunch because most of them had no idea of what they were doing. Cooper and I never took his fishing boat near town during prime tourist time. It was way too dangerous.

"This is on my mother," Sydney said as she locked up her car. "You want me to buy you an ice cream?"

I didn't know if that was her way of apologizing for

slamming the door in my face, but I didn't appreciate it.

"Thanks. I can buy my own ice cream," I replied.

"Just asking," she said with a shrug.

We headed for the General Store, which served as a combination grocery, hardware, and sporting goods store. You could also buy live worms for fishing there, which grossed me out. Selling worms and milk in the same place was just wrong.

"I'll meet you back here," I said. "I want to see somebody at the marina."

Sydney didn't even acknowledge that she heard me and kept walking toward the store. I had to make sure to be back by the time she finished her shopping or I'd be walking the three miles back to the house.

Cooper's summertime girlfriend, Britt Lukas, worked at the marina. The place was only about a hundred yards from the center of town, right on the lake. The salesroom was built on pilings out over the water. Stretching out behind it was a spiderweb of floating docks that held the various rental boats and watercraft. There was also a gas dock, a repair dock, and a slip to launch private boats. Looming over the small store, tied to its own dock, was a huge, Mississippi-style stern-wheeler riverboat that did tours of the lake. People rented it out for parties, too. Cooper and I used to buzz the boat as it slowly made its way to the top of the lake and back. I'd be at the wheel of the Foleys' speedy fishing boat while Cooper would stand on a wakeboard, trying to moon the partiers on board. It was totally embarrassing and a full-on crack-up.

I entered the small shop and was happy to see Britt behind the counter. She was a petite, cute girl with blond hair and freckles. She lived most of the year in a Vermont town called High Pine, but her family owned the marina in Thistledown, so she and her brother spent summers working there. I walked past the displays of outboard motors and

Jet Skis until Britt saw me. I expected her to break out in a big smile and say, "Marsh! How are you?"

She didn't.

"Oh, great," she snarled. "What is this? Good cop, bad cop?"

"What?" I asked, dumbfounded.

"Tell him it's not going to work," she said.

"Uh . . . do you know who I am?" I asked, thinking she was mistaking me for somebody who might know what the heck she was talking about.

"I know exactly who you are, Marsh, and if Cooper thinks he can send you in here to apologize for him, he's wasting his time."

A big guy stepped into the store through the back door. "This guy giving you a hard time?" he asked gruffly. It was Ron, Britt's older brother.

"What? No! I just came in to say hi!" I assured him.

"I'm fine," Britt said to her brother. Good thing, too. Ron was scary. During the winter he worked at a ski area in Vermont, grooming the snow. For all I know he did it with his bare hands. The guy was built, with huge arms and a ruddy face from working outside in the sun too much. You wouldn't want to mess with the little sister of a guy like that. I don't know how Cooper survived.

Something hit the window behind the counter, making us all jump.

"What the . . . ?" Ron barked and glared out of the window.

Standing on one of the floating docks outside was a guy who looked to be around my age. He had messy, sun-bleached blond hair and was wearing baggy shorts and a bright green T-shirt. He stood there looking impatient with his arms out and palms up as if to ask, "So?" Obviously, he had just thrown something at the window to get attention.

"Who's that?" Britt asked.

"Some rich weenie from the camp. He wants me to repair the hull on his newest toy. Yesterday," Ron groused. "Like I live to serve him."

"He can't come in to talk?" Britt said.

"Why would he do that? He's special," Ron said with sarcasm. He then added, "But we need the business."

Ron left to handle the impatient guy.

Britt looked at me and scowled. "Are you still here?" She turned away and busied herself doing paperwork.

"Cooper didn't send me here, Britt."

"Bull."

"But I did want to talk to you about him."

"See! Here it comes! What's his excuse this time?"

"I don't know what you're talking about. Haven't you heard?"

"Heard what?"

"Coop is missing. He took off a couple days ago and nobody's seen him since. The police put out a missing-person report on him."

Britt's expression froze. It was like she was trying to process the information and it wasn't sinking in.

"But . . . oh, man." She sat down on a stool behind the counter as if her legs wouldn't hold her.

"Have you seen him?" I asked.

"He came in here a couple nights ago. He was all cute, as usual, like it wasn't ten months since we'd seen each other and he hadn't even bothered to text."

I was beginning to get the picture as to why Britt was less than thrilled with Cooper. I wasn't surprised that he hadn't contacted her. Coop was always on to new things. He's an "out of sight, out of mind" kind of guy. His girlfriends didn't see things the same way.

"How was he?" I asked. "I mean, did it seem like there

was a problem? Did he say anything about taking off?"

"No!" she said quickly. "He wanted to take me out on the lake to watch the stars . . . like he was really interested in stars and wouldn't be all over me the second we left shore."

"So you didn't go?" I asked.

"No way!" she shot back. "He didn't call me all winter. What did he expect? Like I was going to just pick up like no time had gone by?"

I was sure that was *exactly* what Coop expected, but that's Coop.

"So what did he do?" I asked. "Was he upset you didn't want to go?"

"Cooper?" Britt said with a sarcastic laugh. "You're kidding, right? I'm sure he went out and found some other girl to go with him. He's a dog, you know."

I knew. Though Britt was being kind of harsh. Going out on the lake at night to watch stars is actually fun. We used to do it all the time. We'd power to the center of the lake and kill the lights so it was totally dark, then lie on our backs and drift. It was awesome. The only thing you could hear was the lapping of the lake water against the hull. Best of all, you could see billions of stars. Maybe that was all Coop wanted to do with Britt. Yeah, right.

"So that was it?" I asked. "He just left?"

"Yeah. He said he was spending the summer at the house and hoped we could hang out. He wasn't mad or anything, but does he ever get mad?"

I'd seen him get mad, but not after getting turned down by a girl. Probably because that didn't happen much.

"Where do you think he went?" Britt asked, showing genuine concern.

"I don't know. Nobody knows. That's why I came in. I was hoping you might have an idea."

Britt shook her head and shrugged.

The sound of a car horn blared from outside. Sydney had arrived. Small miracle.

"Is there anything I can do?" Britt asked.

"I have no idea," I replied. "Everybody's hoping he'll just turn up with some dumb excuse."

"What do *you* think?" she asked.

I didn't answer. I wasn't sure what I thought.

Sydney strode into the shop. She had only been waiting a grand total of ten seconds and was already annoyed. "Do you seriously want to walk back?" she asked.

"Sydney, this is Britt. She saw Cooper the night he disappeared."

Sydney looked Britt up and down as if appraising her. Britt was the opposite of Sydney. Where Sydney was tall and thin with long dark hair, Britt couldn't have been much more than five feet tall with a sparkling, friendly smile. Sydney's cold assessment of Britt bordered on being rude.

"Sydney's Cooper's sister," I said, trying to fill the dead air.

"I know," Britt said. "Hi. I hope he's okay."

"Of course you do," Sydney said, and turned for the door.

I gave Britt an apologetic shrug and followed Sydney. I really didn't want to walk back to the house.

Britt called, "Let me know when you hear something, okay?"

"Absolutely," I said, and ran after Sydney.

Outside the marina Sydney strode for her car but stopped short when she saw that somebody was in her way. It was the guy in the green shirt who needed the boat repair. He was leaning against her car like he owned it. Draped casually over his shoulders was a sweatshirt.

"This your ride?" he asked, trying to sound all casual and cool. "Cute. Who makes it? Matchbox?"

He laughed at his own joke.

"Who are you?" Sydney asked, surprisingly friendly . . . for Sydney.

"Cayden Reilly," he said as if it was some big announcement that would make everybody gasp. "And who might you be, sweet thing?" he asked without unfolding his arms.

Sydney held out her hand for Cayden to shake.

"My name's Brittany!" she declared with a big smile and a bright giggle.

Uh-oh. That wasn't good.

Cayden snickered as if he thought it was silly to have to shake her hand. He shrugged, but he took it. Wrong move. Sydney gripped his hand and took a step forward until her nose was inches from his. When she spoke, it was with a cool, sinister whisper that made my own blood run cold . . . and I was nowhere near her.

"And I step on turds like you," she said while squeezing his hand so hard, I could swear I heard his knuckles crack.

"Heeey," he squealed in agony.

Sydney kept her eyes locked on his and continued to squeeze until she felt as if he'd had just a little bit more than enough. She let him go, yanked his sweatshirt off his shoulders, and used it to wipe the spot on the car where Cayden had been leaning. She checked her work, dropped the sweatshirt onto the ground, and yanked the door open to get in.

"What is your problem?" Cayden whined, trying to recover. Too late. His cool was destroyed.

Sydney didn't bother to answer. She gunned the engine and took off. I was so stunned by the scene that it didn't hit me for a few seconds that she'd left without me and I was going to have to walk back to the house. The guy named Cayden looked at me sheepishly. Not only was he totally humiliated, but there had been an audience. Me.

He scoffed as if trying to save face. "Witch," he muttered, and jogged back to the docks.

The guy deserved it. Ron was right. Cayden was a weenie and probably used to getting his way. I knew guys like that. I'd engraved a lot of sailing and tennis trophies for them. He learned that messing with Sydney was a very big mistake. Part of me hoped that she would circle back and pick me up, but to be honest, I was just as happy not to have to be in the same car as her just then.

I heard the sound of a loud engine whine to life. Looking down at the water, I saw Cayden on a Jet Ski, flying away from the dock. Since he was still in the marina and close to shore, he was breaking all sorts of water rules by opening the throttle like that, but he probably needed to show some macho after having been totally humiliated.

I didn't mind that Sydney had ditched me. I wanted time to think. I tried to put myself into Cooper's brain. If he were upset about something, where would he go? What would he do? Was he trying to get away from something? Or run to something else? It bothered me that I didn't have a clue. I thought I knew Cooper better than that. It was one more indication that the two of us were going in different directions.

The long walk back began along the row of stores that lined Main Street. I got maybe halfway along the crowded block when I saw something that made me stop short. A small, unpaved alley ran between two buildings that was barely wide enough for a single car to get through. Standing alone, beyond the buildings near a green Dumpster, was a man with long, unkempt gray hair and several days' growth of beard. He caught my eye because everybody else in this bustling little tourist trap was hurrying somewhere, but he stood stock-still. He was maybe thirty yards from me, but even from that distance I could see that he was staring at me. I looked around, thinking that there was something else he might be focused on, but there was nothing. This guy was locked in on me. My first instinct was to keep walking. After all that I had been through at home, the last thing I wanted was to have some strange old homeless-looking river rat staring me down. I would have kept going if not for one thing. As grungy as this guy looked, he was wearing a clean, bright red jacket. The logo on the front was unmistakable. It was an intertwined *D* and *G* over a football. It was the logo of the Davis Gregory football team. I knew that jacket. It was Cooper's.

"Hey!" I screamed.

The guy instantly took off running, and I sprinted after him.

12

The guy may have been old, but he was fast.

I ran up the alley to the back of the building and only caught a brief glimpse of the red jacket as he skirted around a parked SUV and disa————ed into the sea of cars and vans.

"Stop!" I yelled, ——————————————————helped. What did I think he would say, "Sorry, I didn't ——— If I had known, I wo—— What can I do for yo——

Needless to say, —— got around the SUV —— of stores facing a me—— guy in a red jacket—— chasing him, I reac——— What would I do i——— intimidate him int———

Another thought crept up that was more disturbing. What if the guy was a hallucination? Was it possible that I so desperately wanted to find Cooper that my mind had created a character in Coop's jacket? If I caught him, would it turn out to be Gravedigger? I didn't want to go there. In fact, I didn't want to *be* there. A short block away there were dozens of people with ice-cream cones and crying kids, but back there I was feeling very alone. I took one last paranoid glance around, then turned and sprinted back for the alley. I kept looking over my shoulder, hoping the guy in the red jacket wasn't following me. I made it back to Main Street with nothing more to show for my efforts than a stitch in my side and another piece of a confused puzzle.

It was a long, hot walk back to the Foleys' house. I kept expecting to see Sydney pull up in her VW to rescue me. Didn't happen. The next time I saw her was back at the house. She was lying on a lounge chair on the dock, reading a book. In a red bikini. Actually, it was only the top half of a bikini. She still had on her jean shorts and I knew why . . . if she had worn the bikini bottom, she would have revealed her swirly tattoo. Too bad.

I dragged myself down to the dock and stood behind her chair. "Thanks for the ride," I said, trying to drip sarcasm.

She didn't look up from her book. "You were supposed to help me with the groceries."

"You didn't give me the chance."

"You took off to meet the freckle girl. You're lucky I tried to find you."

"It wasn't my fault that obnoxious guy leaned on your car," I countered.

"If I didn't have to come looking for you, I wouldn't have had to deal with him."

It was a battle that couldn't be won, so I gave up.

"Where are your parents?"

Sydney shrugged. I was getting frustrated. I wanted to tell somebody about what had happened, but the only person available was Sydney. She would have to do.

"I saw a guy in town wearing Cooper's football jacket."

She finally looked up from her book. "How do you know it was Cooper's?"

"What are the odds of a homeless-looking guy wearing a Davis Gregory football jacket up here?"

"Everybody around here looks homeless to me," she said caustically. "And people come up here from Stony Brook all the time."

"It was Coop's," I insisted.

"So tell the police," she said dismissively.

She put the book down, pulled off her sunglasses, and strode to the end of the dock. I have to admit, I watched. She didn't break stride and dove into the water gracefully, still wearing her jean shorts. She surfaced and swam straight out until she reached the wooden float that was anchored about twenty yards beyond the end of the dock. She climbed the ladder and lay down on her back to let the sun dry her. It was an impressive display. Why did she have to be such a witch? I saw that she had been reading a thick SAT study guide. She may have been a witch, but she was a driven witch. The summer had barely begun and she was already prepping for next year's SATs . . . and from what Cooper told me, she had already taken them once and killed them. I guess you don't qualify for valedictorian without working at it.

I, on the other hand, was done with studying for the summer. I went back to the house and grabbed a Batman graphic novel from my pack. Getting lost in Gotham seemed pretty appealing while I waited for the Foleys to get home. I took a beach towel from the porch and brought it down to the water's edge. It was a beautiful day. I didn't want to spend it inside. Besides, I didn't mind checking out Sydney every once in a while. So long as we didn't have to speak to each other, we got along just fine. I laid the dark blue towel out on the grass and sat down to begin pretending all was right with the world. My plan was to immerse myself in the world of the Bat. I'd already read that volume a few times, but for me that was, like, nothing. I don't just read graphic novels. I study them. Every nuance. Every twist. I want to understand the choices that were made by the artist as to what story elements should be told through pictures or through words. Some people think it's a waste of time. Okay, *most* people think it's a waste of time. They aren't me. I've liked comics and graphic novels since before I could read. I saw no reason to stop just because I wasn't a little kid anymore.

I don't know if it was the sun or the fact that I had been going pretty much nonstop, but I started getting drowsy. I put the book down and rested on my elbows. Looking around, I saw Sydney still on the float, dragging her fingers lazily through the water. I really wished she didn't have such an attitude. I wanted to like her.

I felt a slight wind kick up. It was so soft that it didn't even move the branches of the trees that hung over the lake. It was like the breeze had floated in just for my benefit. It was only strong enough to kick up some dandelion seeds. The spores floated through the air in a soft, dancing storm of gray that bounced and fluttered around me. I lay down on my back to watch the show. It was hypnotic. I let my mind wander to another time. Another place.

It was called the National Felt Company and it had been around since the Civil War. The sprawling brick factory looked like a medieval fortress. I passed it twice a day on my way to school and back. In third grade we went there on a school field trip and got a tour. That's how we found "the bales."

Behind the factory was a warehouse they used to store left-over felt. They rolled it up and tied it together in bundles that were about the size of a bale of hay.

The place was huge. It had to be three stories high with hundreds of the colorful bales stacked everywhere, filling the massive space. The building was ancient, and so was the door to get in. Cooper had no trouble figuring out how to get past the crack security lock (a cotter pin) and gain entry. There were no guards. Who was going to steal leftover felt? Each bale probably weighed a hundred pounds. But they were soft, which made playing on them a blast. We'd climb the mountain of bales and move them around to create slides, tunnels, and cliffs. It didn't occur to us that we were trespassing. We were only eleven and we weren't breaking anything. How could we? It was felt.

"Let's make an igloo," Coop would say, and we'd struggle to move the bales into position. He was full of creative ideas of how to play with the giant, soft toys. "Let's pretend we're racing time to get to the top of Everest before the weather turns" was one of his games. Another was "We're in the center of the Earth and an earthquake is knocking down boulders and blocking our way out . . . ," after which he'd start pushing the bales over and I'd have to duck and jump to dodge them. Where Cooper's imagination was endless, I looked at the bales of felt and saw . . . bales of felt. Cooper was more like my mom. He didn't just see what was in front of him—he saw potential.

"There's more to everything than what's obvious," he always said. "You just have to look for it."

I credit Cooper with opening up my own imagination and allowing me to begin to develop my art. He also made me more daring, which didn't always work out for the better. One day while playing "Acapulco Cliff Diver," Cooper stacked up a number of bales. More than ever before. He climbed to the top, ready to leap.

"Don't," I called.

"Why not?" he called back.

"Uh, maybe because you'll kill yourself."

"Impossible!" he declared. "Cliff divers laugh in the face of danger. Ahahaha!"

"But you're not a—"

Too late. He stepped off the pile and plummeted down, landing safely on his back with a huge WHOOSH as the felt compressed under his weight.

"Your turn," Coop said, flush with the rush of having survived the stunt.

"No way," I said quickly.

"Okay."

I was shocked because he didn't try to talk me into it.

"That's it?" I declared. "No argument?"

"Nah," he said with a shrug. "I really didn't think you'd go for it."

That was the worst thing he could have said. Whenever he tried to talk me into doing something risky, it was to get me out of my comfort zone and take a chance. Clearly he thought it wasn't worth his effort anymore, and that ticked me off.

"I'm climbing the cliff," I declared.

Coop's eyes went wide. "Really? You sure?"

My answer was to scramble to the top as quickly as possible. I crept out onto the tower Coop had built, gazing out over the warehouse. It felt like I was a mile in the air. It was exhilarating . . . and terrifying.

"Vaya con Dios, mi amigo!" Coop called.

I put my arms out in front of me like I had seen the cliff divers do on TV. I then held them out to the side, as if I were about to fly. I inched my toes over the edge. My heart raced. I was on top of the world . . . and decided I didn't want to be there anymore. I shifted my weight, ready to turn and slink away. Bad move. The weight shift caused the bale I was standing on to *move, which threw my balance off, which threw the balance of the entire stack off . . . which caused the avalanche.*

"Jump!" Cooper yelled.

I never got the chance. I was standing on a giant Jenga game that was on its way down. The bales toppled and I toppled with them. I remember seeing nothing but a jumble of color as the bales bounced down around me. I had enough sense to cover my head with my arms. I landed on my butt, twisted, got rocked one way and then the other as the heavy bales bounced over me and knocked me around. I finally came to rest flat on my back, looking up at a bright shaft of sunlight that came through a window near the ceiling. The air was filled with felt particles. The light hit them in such a way that they looked electric, like phosphorous. It was magical. Bottom line was, I had broken my foot and Cooper had to carry me home. But at that moment I wasn't in pain. All I felt was the exhilaration of having taken a ridiculous chance, and survived.

Cooper looked down on me with big, scared eyes.

"Hey, you okay?" he asked.

"No mas, señor. Por favor," I said, and laughed. My ribs ached and my foot started to throb, but I laughed.

Cooper did too. "Excelente, mi amigo!" he exclaimed. "The first cliff diver to destroy the cliff!"

He collapsed, laughing.

It was a good day.

I still remember the sight of the billions of felt particles dancing in the air.

It was the dandelion spores.

That's what sent me back to that warehouse. I lay on my back on the towel near the lake, watching them float over me. I had to laugh. It was a good memory.

That is, until I was hit with a blast of cold water. I jumped up fast to see Sydney holding an empty bucket.

"What was that for?" I screamed, sputtering and wiping my eyes.

"You were creeping me out, lying there laughing like that," she said. "I thought you were having a freak seizure."

"That's idiotic," I shot back. Not only had she ruined my perfect dream, she'd nearly drowned me.

"Idiotic? Me?" She reached down and picked up my Batman book, *The Dark Knight Returns.* "You're lying here reading comic books and laughing like a lunatic and *I'm* the idiot?"

"It's a graphic novel," I corrected indignantly. I tried to grab it back, but she held it away.

"Seriously? Batman?" she asked. "Isn't that for kids? Pow! Bam! Crunch!"

"If you looked closer, you'd see it's a much edgier, multi-faceted version of the legend of the Bat than the comedic version you're referring to."

Sydney lowered the book and looked me square in the eye. "I'd laugh if I thought you were kidding." She unceremoniously dropped the book onto the towel and headed for the house, clutching her four-pound SAT study guide.

I'm sure there were times when I'd felt more foolish, but I couldn't remember any. People always made fun of me for keeping one foot in the fantasy world of sci-fi and super-heroes. Cooper loved to give me a hard time about it. But Sydney was the first person who actually made me feel stupid. I don't know if it was because of what she said, or the way she looked at me like I was somehow developmentally stunted, but it made me wonder if maybe she was right.

I stood on the grass, not sure what to do next. Should I pick up the book and continue reading? Or throw it in the lake? As I stood there, I became aware of more dandelion spores flying around me. I felt the same soft breeze that didn't touch the trees or any of the bushes near the house. It was like I was in the center of my own personal, benign tornado. There were more spores than before. They blew all around me, got caught in my hair, and tickled my nose. It was like an attack of dandelion locust. I lifted my hands to let them tickle the hair on my arms. I wondered where they could be coming from. There must have been a field of dandelions upwind from the house.

The breeze stopped. Just like that, as if a fan had been turned off. It was the first clue I had that whatever was happening wasn't normal. The second clue came quickly. Instead of drifting off randomly, the spores seemed to hang in the air. They hovered for an instant, then fell together to the ground. It was about as unnatural as an act of nature could be. My eyes drifted down to where they fell. At my feet was the dark blue beach towel I had been lying on. Most of the dandelion spores had fallen on it. Looking down, I caught my breath.

The spores had formed a pattern on the towel. It was nothing I recognized, but it was definitely not random. Some fell in small, tight groups, forming a pattern that looked like a twisted rectangle. Other patterns appeared. Some snaked through others in shapes that meant nothing to me other than the fact that they were definite shapes. I didn't know what any of the patterns signified, but I knew what they meant.

Whatever it was that had happened to me back at home, whether it was in my head or something more sinister, it was there.

My demons had followed me to the lake.

13

After what I had seen on that towel, it was clear that whatever was happening, it wasn't about a specific place. My house wasn't haunted. I guess that was one silver lining, though maybe it would have been better if my house *was* haunted. You can always get away from a place. You can't get away from your head.

I had to be imagining things. What else could I think? It was a grim possibility but a logical one. The only thing that gave me hope that I wasn't a total lunatic was that I couldn't come up with any reason why I had suddenly gone out of my mind. As far as I knew, those things don't happen without warning. Or reason. I hadn't had an accident. I hadn't banged my head. I hadn't had a traumatic emotional experience that would have sent me into bozo-ville. Sure, I was ticked about Coop messing up the summer, but that's not the kind of thing that lands you in an asylum.

I thought back to when it began. What was the first bizarre thing that happened? Was it the banging on the walls at my house? The absence of all sound? The message in Ovaltine? When had it begun?

I remembered.

The blood.

I had smashed that curious golden ball out of anger and splattered blood all over my bedroom wall . . . that magically disappeared. That was it. That was the first. As far as I could remember, nothing traumatic had happened before that incident that would have made my brain suddenly snap. I had an argument with Dad. He said I needed to get out more and make friends. Had that been enough to push me off the deep end? Not likely. I was upset, but c'mon. Crazy?

Was the illusion of the blood the result . . . or the cause? Did I unearth some deep-rooted fear or phobia that was buried in my subconscious, lying in wait until I gave it an excuse to spring out? That golden orb had belonged to my mom and I destroyed it. Was it a guilt thing? Or by break-ing that glass ball had I triggered something more sinister? Something that had nothing to do with me. Was there really something supernatural going on? Was I being haunted? Could I possibly come up with any more questions?

The ideas and fears and possibilities kept running around my head, but there were no solid answers. Or relief. All I knew for certain was that even if it was manufactured in my head, it was real. The only way I could deal was to stay focused on something more pressing. Cooper. That made sense. Sort of. After we found him . . . I'd still be crazy. Once Coop reappeared, I'd go home and lay all my nuttiness out for Dad. We'd find a doctor or psychiatrist or witch doctor or something to help me figure out why I sud-denly had gone out of my mind and then do what we could to get me back in.

I guess my plan to go to the lake for help wasn't a total failure. Worrying about Cooper was keeping me together while I waited for Dad to get home. What made it so tough was that I couldn't talk to anybody about it. I didn't want to lay it on the Foleys. They had enough to worry about. And when I told Sydney about what I'd been seeing, she didn't believe me. I didn't blame her. I wouldn't have believed me either. Besides, she wasn't exactly the sympathetic type. I felt very much alone . . . and that was the exact thing I had to avoid. Things happened when I was alone. I had to make sure I was always around people. It was the only way to keep my brain from spinning off into the abyss of lunacy.

When the Foleys got back to the cabin, I told them about the grungy guy in the Davis Gregory jacket. They took it more seriously than Sydney did. Mrs. Foley did a quick check of the clothes in Cooper's room and couldn't find the jacket.

While Mr. Foley called the police to report the possible lead, Mrs. Foley and I decided to drive around looking for the mystery man. It was a long shot, but why not? What else were we going to do? Night was coming . . . the third night Cooper would be gone. Mrs. Foley was too antsy to sit in the house, so driving around made her feel like she was doing something positive. For me, it ensured that I would be with somebody for a while and keep my own demons at bay.

"Do you want to drive?" Mrs. Foley asked as we walked for the car.

"I don't drive."

She gave me a surprised look that said, "Are you kidding?"

I shrugged. What could I say? My bike got me around just fine.

We drove to town and methodically turned onto every

street we came to. I don't think either of us expected to see the guy hanging out eating an ice-cream cone or playing mini golf, but it felt good to be doing something.

"I don't understand Cooper," Mrs. Foley said. "He was always a wild kid, but it was harmless. The things he's been getting into lately . . ." She didn't finish the sentence. She didn't have to.

"I hate to say this," I said. "Does anybody think that Cooper being MIA might have something to do with the counterfeit ticket thing?"

Mrs. Foley shot me a quick, dark look. "I don't want to believe that. The names he gave to the police were just kids. They aren't dangerous criminals."

I nodded. I wanted to believe that the dumb ticket scam wasn't serious enough to push somebody into doing something even dumber . . . like hurting Cooper.

"Besides," she added, "the police already checked. They know where all those characters are."

"Yeah," I added. "All of them except for Cooper."

Her eyes started to tear up. I wanted to hit myself on the head. It was a pretty insensitive comment.

"Sorry," I said quickly.

"It doesn't make sense," she said. "Cooper's life is about as normal as can be, yet he's always acting out. Then there's you."

"Me?"

"You're a good kid, Marsh. I mean a really good kid. You've had to deal with some life-changing problems and you've handled it so well. If anybody has an excuse to act a little crazy, it's you. But you don't."

I wasn't sure how to tell her how wrong she was.

"I have such respect for you," she added. "And for your father. What d'ya think? Maybe he can give me a few pointers on raising a guy."

Part of me wanted to say "Thanks" and let it go. But I was desperate to tell somebody the truth.

"Things aren't always what they seem," I said.

"What do you mean?"

I chose my words carefully. "I think everybody's different and they're affected by things differently. Coop is who he is. I thought I would always be the same too. That is, until . . ."

I couldn't finish the sentence.

"Until what?"

I wanted to tell her everything, to spill it all. To unload. But I couldn't make it about me. Not with Cooper still missing.

"Well, until Mom died," I said. "It made me appreciate what I've got."

Mrs. Foley gave me a warm smile. "Like I said, you're a good kid, Marsh."

I didn't want to talk anymore and I don't think Mrs. Foley did either.

She was right. I had gone through something traumatic with the death of my mother, but I couldn't imagine why I would suddenly start seeing demons two years later. That didn't make sense, though I did make a mental note to bring it up with the psychiatrist . . . when I got a psychiatrist.

We drove around for another hour and, big surprise, we never saw the guy with the red jacket. I think we probably would have continued the search for a while longer, but it was getting dark, so we gave up and went back to the lake house.

Mrs. Foley made dinner for everyone. Her specialty. Frozen pizza. I didn't care what it was—I wasn't hungry. Sydney didn't care either because she never came down to eat. She stayed in her room doing whatever girls do when they don't want to talk to anybody. Just as well—things were tense enough without adding Sydney to the mix. The three of us ate at a picnic table on the lawn between the house and the lake. Several tiki torches were burning to give us light and to roast mosquitoes. The whole conversation was about trying to avoid the one thing that was on all of our minds. Cooper.

At one point the table started shaking. I mean, it was like an earthquake was building up. I heard a low rumble that slowly grew like some infernal engine was digging up from below. At first I thought it was another hallucination, but the soda cans chattering across the table made me realize there was more to it than that.

"Does anybody else feel that?" I asked hopefully.

"It's kids with more money than brains," Mr. Foley said with disgust.

"What does that mean?" I asked.

"Wait," Mrs. Foley answered.

The rumbling continued to build. I could feel it in the pit of my stomach. As it grew even louder, I realized it wasn't coming from underground. The sound was rolling toward us from the lake. Looking out onto the water, I saw the running lights of a big speedboat halfway across to the other side.

"Kids from the camp across the way," Mrs. Foley said.

Mr. Foley added, "It's one of those highfalutin camps for the privileged. You see parents dropping off their kids in seaplanes all the time."

"Really?" I said. "Seaplanes on the lake?"

"It's ridiculous," Mr. Foley said with a sneer. "That's not a camp, it's a country club."

Mrs. Foley chuckled. "Don't get all righteous. If we could afford it, we'd send our kids there."

"We absolutely would not!" Mr. Foley countered. "Those kids have no perspective on reality."

I couldn't argue with him. The speedboat pulled even with us. From the low configuration of the lights and the throaty sound of the powerful engine, I figured it was one of those high-speed cigarette boats. The thing was flying, too. In seconds it was gone, the rumbling subsided, and my soda can stopped jumping.

Mrs. Foley said, "I wouldn't mind seeing things from that perspective for a while."

"You wouldn't like it," Mr. Foley shot back.

"Wanna bet?" Mrs. Foley countered.

The two continued arguing over whether or not it was good to be rich as they cleared their plates and brought them inside. I didn't want to be alone, so I followed close behind. Once everything was cleaned up and put away, Mr. Foley announced, "It's been a long day. I'm done. G'night, Marsh."

"Uh, wait!" I said. "Don't you want to hang out and . . . and . . . watch some TV? You've got some great DVDs here."

The truth was, I didn't like any of their movies, but I would have sat through a Hugh Grant flick if it meant I didn't have to be alone.

"Sorry, maybe Mrs. Foley wants to watch something."

"Not me," she said quickly. "I can't keep my eyes open."

I tried to head them off from going into their bedroom. "But what if Coop calls? Or comes back?"

"It's a small house, Marsh. I think we'll know," Mrs. Foley said. "G'night. I'm glad you're here."

And that was that. The Foleys went to bed, Sydney was up in her room, and I was alone . . . exactly what I wanted to avoid. I thought about watching TV or reading or doing any of the things you would normally do when you're on your own, but none of them appealed to me as much as sleep. If my mind started messing with me again, unconscious was a good place to be. I kicked off my shoes, grabbed an extra blanket, and stretched out on the couch. I even turned the lights out. Why not? Most of what I'd seen showed up in broad daylight.

I wasn't awake for long. My mind may have been dealing with a million dilemmas, but for some reason that didn't stop me from powering down. I guess exhaustion beats worry. I fell into a deep sleep. I know that because when I woke up I was groggy and disoriented. It was still nighttime, but I had definitely been out for a while. What pulled me out of dreamland was a sound. It was gentle but incessant. It started as part of a dream. Somebody was playing a steady rhythm on a drum. Whoever it was, wasn't very good. It was nothing more than a steady *tap . . . tap . . . tap . . .*

I gradually came around to realize the sound wasn't a dream. I was really hearing it.

Tap . . . tap . . . tap . . .

I opened my eyes to see movement on the ceiling. There was a big picture window over the couch where I was lying. Moonlight flooded in, creating shadows from the branches of a tree. It was windy, because the shadow swayed back and forth on the ceiling. I figured this had to be the culprit.

Tap . . . tap . . . tap . . .

The branch was knocking against the picture window. I rolled over and closed my eyes to try to get back to sleep, but the annoying noise wouldn't let me.

Tap . . . tap . . . tap . . .

I couldn't ignore it. I figured my only hope of getting to sleep was to go outside and break off the branch. I sat up, rubbed my eyes, looked to the picture window . . .

. . . to see Cooper standing there with a big smile on his face. He was outside on the porch, looking in at me through the glass, tapping on the frame. I think I squealed like a little girl. I definitely lurched back with a start and fell off the couch. I was about to scream out "Coop!" but he put his finger to his lips as if to say "Shhh." He winked and waved for me to come outside.

I was in shock. I guess I should have screamed for everybody to wake up, but for whatever reason he didn't want anybody else to know he was there. I stumbled around in the dark to get to my feet. I didn't even bother putting on shoes. I had a million questions for him and a million more things to tell him. I couldn't get outside fast enough. I jumped out of the door and looked to the window, but Coop was gone. For a brief instant I worried that it had been a dream. Or another hallucination and Cooper wasn't really there.

"Marsh!" I heard Coop call to me.

He was standing on the far end of the dock, facing the water. How did he get out there so fast? And why? Maybe he was afraid that his family would hear once we started talking. That had to be it. Coop was being very mysterious. I walked quickly across the lawn and onto the dock. I didn't call out to him. I wanted to keep things quiet, just as he had asked. Coop was standing with his hands in the pockets of his red jacket. Since he was looking out onto the water, I saw A>SFP DOB LOV spelled out across the back of his jacket in white on top of a big football.

When I got to within a few yards and safely out of earshot from the house, I called out, "I can't wait to hear the story."

Coop didn't turn around. He kept staring out over the dark water as he said, "The story has only begun."

I stopped walking. Something about his voice bothered me. He sounded strangely intense, which wasn't like him.

"Are you okay?" I asked. "Where have you been?"

"It's not about the past, it's about the journey we're about to take."

Journey. The hair went up on the back of my neck. Gravedigger had talked about a journey.

"What are you saying, Coop?" I asked tentatively.

"We will walk the road together," he answered.

Coop was freaking me out. What had happened to him while he was missing?

"Hey, are you okay?"

"I will be," he answered. "Once the poleax is returned."

"The what?"

"It is mine. It will be returned," he said flatly. "And the journey can finally begin."

I had had enough. Cooper was jerking me around and it wasn't funny.

"Stop with the riddles. What journey are you talking about?"

I stepped forward, grabbed his shoulder, and turned him around. What I saw made my heart freeze. It wasn't Cooper. Everything about the guy who stood inches from me looked exactly like my friend, except for his face. It was the face of Gravedigger.

"The journey along the Morpheus Road, of course," he said, his mouth breaking into a ghoulish grin. I could see the cracks in his bone-white teeth. His voice had already changed from that of Cooper's to the deep growl I had heard earlier. I stumbled backward but couldn't take my eyes off the hideous creature. It was Cooper's hair and body and clothes, but the face was the pale, skeletal ghoul of my imagination. Though his eyes were empty sockets, I knew they were focused directly on my soul.

I opened my mouth to say something, but nothing came out. I turned to run back along the dock, but when I whipped around, I was confronted by Gravedigger again. He was now behind me. Or in front of me. I didn't know how he was able to do that and I didn't care, because all I could see was that he had also changed his appearance. He wore the long black cloak and wide-brimmed black hat, which was pulled low over his empty eyes. I glanced quickly back over my shoulder. The Cooper-Digger wasn't there anymore.

One other thing: Gravedigger was holding his silver pick.

"We will walk the road together," he bellowed in that inhuman voice.

I backed away. "I . . . I'm not going anywhere with you."

Gravedigger pulled the silver pick off his shoulder and swung it like a batter in the on-deck circle. "But you will," he hissed. "There will be no other road to take . . . once you die." He punctuated his words with a swing of his pick.

That was all I needed to hear. Hallucination or not, I had crossed a line into a place I didn't want to be. I was rocked out of panic mode straight into survival gear. I turned and took off running toward the end of the dock. Without hesitation I dove headfirst into the water and swam with everything I had, straight for the wooden float. My hope was that imaginary ghouls couldn't swim. I reached the float in seconds and pulled myself onto the deck. Looking back, I saw the dock was empty. The thing was gone. It wasn't onshore, either. Where did he go? Based on how quickly he had moved away from the house and around me on the dock, he could be anywhere.

I fought to catch my breath and calm down. Was it over? I was prepared to spend the entire night on that float and not set foot back onshore until the sun was up and the Foleys were out in the yard, yelling at me to stop acting crazy and swim back for breakfast. I held my breath and listened. Nothing was in the water. The only sound I heard was the wind in the trees and the lapping of the water against the float. I relaxed. The episode was over. I turned to move to the center of the raft . . . and came face-to-face with Gravedigger.

"You are the source," he said, and swung his pick at me. "You must walk the road."

This time he wasn't warming up. He was trying to kill me. I flung myself backward without looking and felt the sharp breeze of the pick as it barely missed me. I hit the water head-first. It was dark and I was totally disoriented. I scrambled to get my head above water while pushing away from the float, though I wasn't sure if I was swimming up or down. Seconds later my head broke the surface and I spun around to get my bearings. I was too close to the float. One swing of that pick and he'd get me. I kicked and stroked backward to get some distance. After a few desperate seconds I looked back to see the float was empty. Gravedigger was gone. But to where? I stopped and treaded water, constantly glancing around for fear that Gravedigger would swim up to me. I had to get out of there. I scanned the shore, thinking I should swim away from the house to a place in the woods where I could hide. I decided to swim left, though it really didn't matter. I was reaching out of the water to begin pulling myself along, when I felt it. A tug on my ankle. Something was under the water.

"No!" I cried in a panic, and kicked to get away.

The first tug was a warning. The second was serious. A bony hand grabbed my ankle and pulled me under. I barely had time to hold my breath before I was jerked below the surface and back into the dark. I kicked desperately with my free leg to get my foot loose. I got a solid shot on the arm and the hand released. Quickly I shot back to the surface and swam like mad. As scary as it was facing this ghost onshore, dealing with him in dark water was absolutely terrifying. I had to get to shore . . . or drown. I took one stroke when something surfaced directly in front of me. Something white. My first ridiculous thought was that it was a soccer ball. It wasn't. The skull-like head of Grave-digger broke the surface and stared me down.

I stopped moving. It was useless. I felt a strong hand grab the front of my sweatshirt.

"We will travel the road together," he screeched, and pulled me under.

I was surrounded by nothing. And water. I struggled to free myself from the force that was pulling me down, but Gravedigger was ready for me this time. His grip was strong. I opened my eyes to see his hideous white face, inches from mine. Even in the murky water I could see that he was smiling. I pulled at his bony hands to loosen his grip, but he was too strong. It was like trying to pry open a visc. I kicked up with my knee, hoping to score a shot on something critical . . . assuming ghouls had critical things. It didn't matter. My legs got tangled in his and I couldn't put any force behind it.

My lungs hurt. I don't know how long I was down there, but I knew I couldn't last much longer. Fighting only got me closer to the end. All I wanted to do was breathe in. The pain was so intense that I was ready to end it by sucking in water. At least there would be relief and it would be over. I grew dizzy and was seconds from opening my mouth to let my lungs fill with water, when Gravedigger released his grip and flew away from me. He actually shot backward in the water as if being pulled from behind. He didn't kick or stroke, he just floated away . . . and disappeared.

I felt the collar of my shirt being grabbed, and my nanosecond of relief ended. I figured Gravedigger had somehow whipped around behind me again and was going to pull me backward and down to my death. I relaxed. There was no more fight in me. I was pulled by my collar but not deeper. My head broke the surface and though I was nearly unconscious, I instinctively gulped air. I didn't know what was happening and didn't care. I lifted my chin and sucked in oxygen. My head cleared quickly and I realized I was still being held by the collar. I spun around, breaking the ghoul's grasp, and was ready to fight him off . . . when I saw that it wasn't him. It was Sydney.

"Relax," she ordered, breathing hard herself as she treaded water.

I wasn't sure it was even her after what had happened with Cooper. Or what I thought was Cooper. I pushed back and kicked away to keep my distance from her.

"What are you doing?" she yelled. "Calm down!"

"Stay away from me," I commanded.

"Okay, okay," she said calmly. "I'm not moving."

The two of us treaded water a few yards apart. My brain was scrambled. I guess a near-death experience will do that.

"Let's swim in, okay?" Sydney said calmly. "Can you swim?"

"Is it you?" I asked.

"Who else would it be?"

I didn't answer that.

"It's Sydney," she added. "Don't you recognize me?"

My head had cleared enough to realize she was talking to me slowly as if I was an unbalanced, crazy person, which was smart because I was an unbalanced, crazy person.

"Is it really you?" I asked.

"Yes, and I'm getting tired and cold. Can we swim in?"

That sounded exactly like Sydney. She was no illusion. I nodded and the two of us went for shore. A few seconds later I crawled up out of the water and collapsed onto the grass. It took a couple of minutes for me to catch my breath. When I opened my eyes, I saw Sydney sitting next to me, dripping wet in her plaid pajama bottoms and T-shirt. She looked at me with wide eyes like she didn't know what was going to happen next.

"Are you all right?" she asked. (There was that idiotic question again.)

I was far from all right, but I think she was asking

specifically if I would survive the next minute. I nodded.

She seemed shaken. It took a lot to shake Sydney.

"Did you see?" I asked softly.

"I saw you splashing around in the water," she said. "What's the deal?"

I had my answer. All she saw was a guy in the water, drowning. One guy. Me. It was more proof that everything I'd seen was happening inside my head.

"Doesn't matter," I answered. "I was in trouble and you saved me. Thank you."

"You weren't, like, trying to hurt yourself, were you?"

Sydney was trying to understand. I'll give her that much.

"No."

"You were thrashing around like . . . like Mikey did this morning. Like you were fighting something."

I'd almost forgotten about Mikey. I shrugged. I couldn't speak for him. I didn't know why he flipped. I sat up and looked out onto the water, which now looked calm and serene.

"Did you see that guy again?" she asked. "Gravedigger?"

I shot Sydney a look. She remembered what I had told her the night before. She was listening.

"Yes," I said. Why lie? She didn't believe me anyway. "I know it's stupid. I don't believe a character I created has somehow come to life and is trying to kill me. It may not be real, but to me it is, and maybe that's as bad as if it were really happening. I could have drowned. If you hadn't saved me, I would have. So . . . thank you."

Sydney nodded.

"There's something seriously wrong with me," I added. "I fought it for a while, but there's nothing I can do. When my dad gets home, I'm going to tell him everything and get help. I just hope I don't hurt myself before then."

I waited for Sydney to take me apart. Showing vulner-ability to somebody like her was like throwing chum into shark-infested waters. She stared at the ground, picking at grass. I thought she was trying to come up with the perfect, skewering insult that would finish the job Gravedigger had started.

"I think you're wrong," she finally said.

"About what?"

"About what you've been seeing."

"Really?" I said skeptically and with a little anger. "How do *you* explain it?"

I couldn't wait to hear her theory. I knew she would somehow turn it around so that it was all some game that Cooper had a hand in. That's how her mind worked. It ticked me off. Here I had opened myself up and she was more than willing to ridicule me.

"I can't," she said. "But I saw what happened to Mikey. That wasn't normal. And I still don't know how you knew about my tattoo."

"You think this is some prank conspiracy thing, don't you?" I said with impatience.

She kept her eyes on the ground and shook her head. As hard as it was to believe, she seemed truly upset. Seeing Sydney Foley like that was almost as strange as seeing a fig-ment of my imagination come to life. Almost.

She said, "You didn't ask how I knew you were in trouble."

"You must have heard me splashing around."

She shook her head. "I didn't. I was asleep."

"So then—"

"Somebody woke me up," she said quickly. "Or some-*thing*. It felt like a breeze. It rustled the sheets on my bed and tickled my cheek. I thought it was my mother trying to get me up. It pissed me off and I sat up ready to tell her so, but nobody was in the room."

My palms started to sweat. "Maybe it *was* a breeze," I said.

"My windows were closed," she declared as she looked at me. I saw something in her eyes that was totally alien for Sydney Foley. Uncertainty. Maybe even fear. "But they weren't closed for long. When I sat up, the front window blew open. That window opens out. There was nothing inside that could have done that."

The hair went up on the back of my neck. I was having trouble breathing.

She continued, "I sat there trying to understand, when a piece of paper on the desk was blown into the air. At least I think it was blown. It fluttered across the room like a feather bouncing on the breeze. Suddenly it changed direction and blew out of the window. I sat there stunned. Then the window slammed shut! It was so fast, it made me jump. A second later it opened again. Slowly. It was like . . . like . . . I was being called to it. I forced myself to get out of bed and went over to lock it. When I got there, I looked out onto the lake . . . and saw you struggling."

My mouth was so dry, I couldn't swallow.

"I don't know what happened in that room," she said. "But it got me out of bed to go to the window and see you. I don't know anything about hallucinations or mental disorders or anything else that could cause somebody to see something that isn't really there, but it doesn't take a psychiatrist to know that the chances of it happening to three people at the same time are probably longer than can be measured. There's something strange going on, Marsh, and I don't think it's happening in your head because you are not alone. What Mikey saw was real, or at least he thought it was. The same with me."

I don't know what scared me more. The idea that I had some brain dysfunction that created dangerous visions, or the possibility that they weren't products of my imagination at all. At least being crazy was disturbing but explainable. The other possibility was far more frightening because it meant that Gravedigger really existed.

And he wanted me dead.

14

Sydney and I spent the rest of the night on the porch.

After changing into dry clothes, we sat on opposite ends of the couch, trying not to fall asleep. Either she felt sorry for me and didn't want to leave me alone, or she was scared and didn't want to be alone herself. She had seen something in her bedroom that she couldn't explain and it disturbed her. I knew the feeling . . . a few times over. Whatever her reasons, I was glad for the company.

As much as I tried to stay awake, I eventually nodded off and had a dream that was both great and disturbing. It was about my mother. She was sitting in a big easy chair and I was lying next to her with my cheek resting on her shoulder. That's the way she used to read books to me when I was little, and that's exactly what she was doing in my dream. I could hear her voice clearly as she softly read one of my favorite books from when I was a kid, *The Wind in the*

Willows. I felt comfortable and safe. It was a good dream. At least for a while.

At one point I looked up to see . . . it wasn't my mother anymore. It was Sydney. And I wasn't asleep. Somehow I had rolled over and was lying with my head against her shoulder. I sat up so fast, I nearly gave myself whiplash. Luckily, I didn't wake Sydney. She had no idea of what had happened, thankfully. There was a little wet spot on her sleeve where my mouth had been. How embarrassing was that? If she had woken up, I wouldn't have to worry about Gravedigger anymore. Sydney would have killed me right then and there.

I crawled back to my side of the couch, feeling hollow. With all that had been going on, I hadn't thought much about my mother. Having that dream was yet another cruel trick my mind had played on me. It made me feel more alone than before, if that was possible.

The sky was starting to lighten. We had made it through the night without any more excitement . . . except for the drool-on-the-sleeve incident. The back door opened and Mr. Foley came out onto the porch. The strain was starting to show on his face. He looked older than the day before, with dark bags under his eyes. It was the morning of the fourth day that Cooper was missing.

"Did you two sleep out here?" Mr. Foley asked, confused.

No way he suspected that Sydney and I had hooked up. It was more likely that fish could sing.

"Sydney couldn't sleep, so she came down here," I whispered so as not to disturb her. It wasn't a total lie.

"Oh," he said, accepting the logic easily. "I'm taking the fishing boat out while the lake's calm. Want to come?"

"No, thanks, I'm not awake yet," I answered.

"Okay. I'll be back for breakfast," he said as he walked off the porch, headed for the boathouse.

There was a small wooden shack about forty yards from

the house that was built half on land, half over the water. It's where the Foleys kept a wooden fishing boat as well as their dock and wooden float during the winter. Cooper and I used it as our clubhouse when we wanted to get away from Sydney. In another life.

"So?" Sydney asked, groggy. "Was it a dream?"

I hoped she wasn't asking about my sleeping on her arm. And the drooling.

"I wish" was my answer. It was an answer that worked either way.

She sat up, rubbing sleep from her eyes.

"You okay?" she asked.

"I guess," I muttered. It wouldn't have done any good to be brutally honest.

"Do you have any idea what's going on?" she asked as she spotted the wet mark on her sleeve. She looked at it with a scowl and tried to rub it off.

I answered quickly to distract her. "I'm thinking there are two possible explanations. One is I'm crazy and the other is I'm being haunted by a ghoul that's trying to kill me. I think I'd rather be crazy."

Sydney thought about my answer and said, "What about Mikey? And the window upstairs?"

"I don't know," I said softly.

Sydney added, "We can't all be going crazy."

"Is it any more likely that a supernatural being from my imagination somehow came to life?"

Sydney frowned. "There better be a third explanation."

I shrugged.

"Did he say anything?" she asked. "I mean, did he give you any idea why he wanted to drown you?"

I thought back to the times I had encountered the apparition. "He said I was going on a journey with him after I was dead."

"Nice."

"And he talked about some things that made no sense, like he wanted the poleax and we'd be traveling along the Morpheus Road."

"Morpheus Road," Sydney repeated, trying the words on for size.

It felt good talking to somebody about it all, though strange that it was Sydney. On the other hand, discussing it made it feel more real and that wasn't so great.

"Oh," I added. "And he brought you and me together."

Sydney's eyes went wide. "What do you mean?"

"The symbol. He showed me your tattoo."

"No way," she said in protest. "Just because the boogeyman drew some swirls in sugar doesn't mean—"

"Ovaltine."

"Whatever. This is your problem, not mine."

I didn't argue. She was right.

"We can't tell them," she added.

"Tell who what?"

"My parents. About whatever it is that's happening. They're already on edge about Cooper." She looked at me through sleepy eyes to see if I agreed. Even in that sorry state, Sydney was a knockout.

"I won't," I assured her. "I'm kind of surprised you don't want to tell them, though."

Sydney shot me a cold glare. "Why? Because I'm incapable of worrying about anybody else's problems?"

It was like I had waved a red flag in front of a bull.

"I didn't mean that. It's just . . . I mean . . . you haven't seemed all that worried about Cooper."

Sydney started to say something quickly, but stopped and gave her words some thought.

"It's hard to have a whole lot of sympathy for him."

"Why?"

"Oh, c'mon, you know how it works. Whenever he wants attention, he runs away and my parents welcome him back like a returning war hero. If I tried that, they'd treat me more like a war *criminal* . . . assuming they even knew I was gone. The stuff he gets away with is incredible."

"But . . . so what? Why do you care? You're like . . . a star."

"A star?" she repeated, scoffing.

"Seriously. You're the most popular girl in this hemisphere and you're, I don't know, okay-looking, and you're gonna be class valedictorian. I don't see you getting a whole lot of competition from Cooper."

I'd never been so blunt with Sydney. I guess her honesty had taken me by surprise and I was too tired to filter my thoughts.

"Sorry," I said. "It's none of my business."

"I don't resent Cooper for who he is," she said seriously. "I resent that he doesn't have to work at it. You don't get points for effort . . . especially from my parents."

I didn't know what to say. The incredible Sydney Foley was admitting to me that it was hard work to be Sydney Foley. She was a girl who seemed to glide through life effortlessly as she looked down on all those mere mortals who didn't live up to her high ideals. Turned out she was just as worried about what people thought of her as anybody else was. She was just better at hiding it. Sydney Foley was actually showing, dare I say it, vulnerability.

"You're right," I said, trying to sympathize. "Cooper doesn't care about what people think about him. I guess that gives him a certain, I don't know, power."

"Yeah, that's one word for it," she said with a shrug. "I don't blame my parents. Much. We are who we are. But if anything happened to him, I mean *really* happened, they couldn't handle it. So let's not make things worse by telling them we're dealing with a mass hallucination. At least not yet. Okay?"

I'd had a crush on Sydney since I was five years old. It had everything to do with her looks and total confidence. Superficial stuff, to be honest. It was a crush that had lasted for eleven years . . . and ended on the spot. I no longer had a crush on Sydney. I actually started to like her.

"Sydney!" Mr. Foley called. He was walking back quickly from the direction of the boathouse. "Where's the fishing boat?"

"You're asking me like I've been fishing in the last decade," Sydney answered, back to her sarcastic self.

Mr. Foley bounded up the porch stairs. "It's not in the boathouse."

"Maybe it drifted away," I offered.

"Doubt it" was his answer. "When was the last time you saw it?" he asked Sydney.

Sydney stood and strode for the house. "I've been here less than twenty-four hours. I promise you I didn't go to the boathouse to do inventory. When was the last time *you* saw it?"

She didn't wait for an answer and went into the house.

"Did you see it yesterday, Marsh?" he asked.

"I didn't go anywhere near the boathouse," I answered without sarcasm.

Mr. Foley stood looking out at the water, rubbing his chin thoughtfully. "I guess it was stolen," he said.

"Or maybe Coop took it," I offered.

Mr. Foley shot me a worried look. "I'll let the police know," he said, and hurried into the house.

My first reaction was to go to the boathouse and look for any sign that Cooper might have taken the boat. If he had, it raised all sorts of possibilities as to what had happened to him. Not all of them were good. I bounded off the porch and was halfway across the lawn toward the structure when

I stopped. I was alone. I looked ahead to the small, wooden shack and imagined being cornered in there by Grave-digger. I immediately turned around and ran back into the house. That particular mission would have to wait until I had backup.

Mr. Foley didn't bother making the call. He went directly to the police station to tell them about the missing boat. I hitched a ride with him into town but not to go to the police. I wanted to see Britt Lukas. I hoped she might be able to put a few pieces into the puzzle of what happened the night Cooper went missing.

When I walked up to the marina, I saw Britt's brother, Ron, on one of the floating docks. He was arguing with the obnoxious kid from the camp that Sydney had humiliated the day before. Cayden was his name. I couldn't hear what they were arguing about, but Cayden looked ticked. He seemed like the kind of kid who always got his way, and whatever Ron was telling him, it wasn't what he wanted to hear. He was all red-faced and ranting as he paced back and forth, waving his arms like a spoiled two-year-old. Ron stood there with his arms folded, looking bored. He wasn't intimidated by Cayden.

I went inside to see Britt talking with a customer. He was a tall guy with graying hair that was cut short and neat. He wore khaki shorts, a bright green sweatshirt, and shiny leather loafers . . . definitely not the look of somebody who was used to being around boats. He looked more like a guy who wore a suit most of the time. I figured he was a tour-ist who was going to rent a Jet Ski and become an instant hazard to anybody within buzzing distance. I kept busy by checking out the new water skis they had for sale.

The guy had a booming voice, like he was speaking in front of a crowd. I couldn't help but overhear what they were talking about.

"Four hours," he said sternly. "Not three and a half. Not three forty-five. Four. Understand?"

"We won't come in a minute early," Britt assured him.

"And the clock doesn't start until we cast off. I don't want to be charged for any finagling with engines or ropes. That's on your time."

"You'll get your full four hours, Mr. Reilly, I promise," Britt said sweetly. "No finagling."

"And I want the DJ to play right up until we dock," he demanded.

"That's his call," Britt answered.

"Make it your call," the guy snapped at her. "I'm paying you, not him."

"All right," Britt said with patience, though I could tell she was gritting her teeth. "I'll talk to him."

"I'll pay you the balance once the party's over," he said.

"Uh, it's our policy to receive payment in full prior to the event, so—"

"That's your policy. Not mine."

I peeked through a rack of boat bumpers to see the guy towering over poor Britt. She looked like a tiny little girl next to the domineering guy. She didn't back off, though— I'll give her credit for that.

"Fine," she said, trying not to sound as ticked as I'm sure she was. "I'll be here on the dock waiting when you get in."

The guy snickered. "Why? Don't you trust me?"

Britt gave him a big smile that looked about as genuine as a four-dollar bill. "Of course we trust you, Mr. Reilly—I just want to make things convenient for you."

The big guy stared down at her. Britt didn't break eye contact. I liked Britt. Before Mr. Reilly had the chance to say anything, the kid named Cayden blasted in through the back door.

"Are we done here?" he snarled at the tall guy impatiently.

The man looked to Britt. "Are we?"

Britt smiled. "There's nothing left to do but enjoy the birthday party."

"Yeah," Cayden said sarcastically. "Happy birthday to me . . . rednecks."

Reilly. Cayden Reilly. The tall guy was Cayden's father. It suddenly made sense why the kid was so obnoxious. He had learned it from a master.

"We'll see you tonight," Mr. Reilly said to Britt as he followed his son out of the front door.

"Looking forward to it!" Britt called after them with a big smile . . . that dropped off her face the instant the door closed behind them. "Rednecks," she grumbled to herself. "Jeez."

"Hi, Britt," I said as I stepped out from behind the display.

Britt looked at me with confusion for a second, then recognized me and relaxed. "Welcome to my life," she said, rolling her eyes.

"Planning a party?" I asked.

Britt continued doing her paperwork. "We rented out the *Nellie Bell* for that kid's sixteenth birthday party."

"Oh. That's cool. They seem kind of like, I don't know, what's the right word? Jerks."

Britt looked at me as if wondering how she should react. She decided to laugh.

"You could say that. But they're paying customers and we haven't been renting out that big old party boat much, so it's best to smile and cash the check."

"I guess," I said.

"What's the good word, Marsh? When did Cooper show up?"

"He didn't."

Britt's face fell. "Oh."

"Yeah. We just found out his fishing boat is gone. When he was here the other night, did he come by boat?"

Britt thought back. "I don't know. He could have, but I was stuck in here closing up. I didn't hear anything."

"What time was that?"

"I don't know exactly. It was still light out. Maybe seven thirty? Eight?"

"Was he wearing shoes?"

Britt chuckled. "I didn't notice. Why?"

"Coop has this thing about being barefoot on a boat. He says he can feel the rhythm of the water better or something dumb like that, like he's some old sea captain. I figured if he wasn't wearing shoes, it meant he came by boat."

"And you're thinking if he was on the boat, there might have been an accident?"

"I'm trying not to go there, but yeah. Mr. Foley is talking to the police about it now. I thought I'd ask you about it first."

"Sorry, I don't know. Should I tell the police about Cooper wanting to go out on the water?"

"Yeah, probably."

The two of us stood there for a second, feeling awkward.

"This is scary," Britt finally said. "Do you think something happened to him?"

"Not necessarily. He could have motored to the top of the lake and gone somewhere from there. It's the kind of thing he'd do."

Britt nodded. She knew.

"You guys have been friends for a long time."

"Since kindergarten," I said.

"It's weird. The two of you are so different."

"Yeah, I get that a lot. I can't tell you why he hangs out

with a geek. It's one of those uncanny mysteries that will never be solved."

"That's not what I meant," she said quickly. "I was wondering why a sweet guy like you hangs out with a flake like Cooper."

Britt gave me an absolutely sparkling smile. I think that was the nicest thing that anybody ever said to me . . . who wasn't a parent of mine. If I hadn't been so worried about Cooper and being haunted by supernatural demons, it would have made my day.

The best reply I could give was a shrug. I could feel my face turn red.

"I didn't mean to embarrass you," she said with a flirty chuckle.

"You didn't," I said. "Okay, I lied, you did. But thanks. I better go."

"Do me a favor?" she asked. "Let me know as soon as you hear something?"

"Sure."

"Promise?"

"I promise."

I left the shop feeling confused. I felt like Britt was flirting with me, which was weird because she and Cooper were together. Sort of. Or maybe they weren't. She definitely wasn't happy with him. But none of it really mattered, because Cooper was missing. I left the marina and walked toward town. My plan was to go to the police station and let them know about how Cooper had gone to see Britt on the night he disappeared. I hoped he hadn't taken the boat. That raised all sorts of possibilities, and too many of them were scary.

As I walked along the side of the road, my brain was definitely somewhere else . . . and I didn't see it coming as two strong hands grabbed my shoulders from behind. A single thought shot to mind . . . Gravedigger.

"I know," came a frightened voice close to my ear. "I've seen."

I tried to pull away, but the guy was strong and held me tight. I didn't want to turn around and come face-to-face with the skeletal apparition . . . so I tried to pull away without turning.

"Help!" I called out as a cold hand clamped over my mouth to keep me from screaming again. I looked around, desperate for help, but the street was empty. It was too early for the tourists to be out. I fought to get away, but it was no use. I was pulled into a small alley, where I was roughly spun around and pinned against a wall to see . . .

. . . the old guy who had Cooper's football jacket. He wasn't wearing the red Davis Gregory jacket anymore, but it was definitely him. I didn't scream. I think seeing him made my brain lock. His gray hair was an uncombed tangle. His breath was putrid. Or maybe it was his body odor. Whatever. The guy reeked. What made me freeze more than anything was his eyes. They were wild and darting every which way. He seemed more scared than I was.

"I know," he mumbled, breathing hard. "I saw."

"Wh-what?" I managed to stammer out. He was gripping my shoulders, pressing me against the wall. He didn't need to. I was pushing against the wall just as hard to try and get away from the crazy old dude.

He got right in my face. I could feel his hot, sour breath and the spittle that came from his mouth as he spoke. "Don't listen," he begged, half crying, half laughing. "Don't do what he says."

"Listen to who?" I asked.

"And don't tell," the guy continued. "Oh no. Don't tell. Anyone. The more people who know, the more will be in danger."

"In danger from what?"

He laughed. "What am I saying? We'll all know soon enough and none of it will matter."

The guy was out of his mind, and I was dangerously close to joining him. "D-do you know what happened to Cooper Foley?" I asked.

The guy shot me an intense look and nodded. "I do," he whispered. "He's on the road."

"What road? Where did he go?"

He took his hands off my shoulders and dug into the pocket of his worn, plaid shirt. I thought of running but couldn't. Not if he had information about Cooper. The guy pulled something out of the pocket, grabbed my hand, and pressed it into my palm.

"Take this. You'll find answers. But don't follow him. Please, don't follow. For your own sake, and everyone else's."

He snapped a look to his left. His eyes widened in fear. I looked too, but there was nothing there except an empty alley.

"No," he gasped, backing away. "I didn't tell. I didn't."

"Who are you talking to?" I asked. It was like watching Mikey Russo all over again. This guy was seeing something that wasn't there. Or maybe something was there and only he could see it. Add one more person to the list of the insane . . . or the haunted.

"Leave me be!" he screamed, and ran off . . . straight for the street.

"Hey!" I screamed. "Tell me where Cooper went!"

The guy glanced once over his shoulder as if to see if he was being chased. He was. By me. But I wasn't the one scaring him. He let out a terrified yelp and ran out onto Main Street.

"Whoa! Stop!" I shouted.

A black SUV was bearing down on him.

"Look out!" I screamed at the driver while waving my

arms, hoping he would see the crazy old man before running him down.

The SUV swerved. The old guy saw it at the last instant and leaped out of the way. The car didn't slow down but missed him by inches and sped by, blaring the horn. The old guy was safe . . .

. . . for about half a second. He jumped out of one lane, right into another. A horn sounded. A big horn. It was on the cab of a bloodred eighteen-wheeler that was coming up fast from the other direction. The old guy landed off balance, directly in front of the oncoming monster. The driver leaned on the horn. The big truck was too close to stop and too big to swerve. It hit him dead-on. The sound of screaming brakes was deafening, but I still heard the dull sound of the old man's body as it hit the chrome grill. He grunted once and was thrown across the road like a puppet with its strings cut. Somebody screamed somewhere. It must have been a tourist coming to town for their daily ice cream fix. Or a shopkeeper opening up their T-shirt store. Whoever it was wasn't expecting to see a gruesome accident play out in front of them on this quiet street in Thistledown Lake. The old guy hit the pavement and rolled, his arms and legs flopping wildly. I'd never seen anything like it before and hope I never will again.

I reacted without thinking and ran to the guy. The truck was skidding to a stop and the SUV had stopped a block away, so I was the first to reach him. I didn't know what I would do, but I knew for sure that I wasn't going to ask: "Are you all right?" I already knew the answer. His body was twisted into an unnatural, grotesque sculpture. His mouth was open, with a line of blood dribbling out. He was hanging on, though. His eyes had life and his chest heaved with labored breathing. Looking up, I saw the guy from the SUV running toward us while talking on the cell phone. I hoped he was calling 9-1-1.

I knelt down in front of the broken old man and said, "Help is coming. Hang on."

The guy didn't move, but his eyes caught sight of something and his breathing grew faster. Whatever the nightmare vision was that caused him to run into the street, it was still there. I slowly turned to look and this time, I saw it too. We were across the street from the line of tourist shops of Thistledown. The store directly opposite us had a second-floor balcony with a white railing. Standing on the balcony, watching over the scene was Gravedigger. Even from as far away as we were, I could see that he was grinning.

I turned back to the old man and said, "Do you see that guy?"

It was too late. The light had left his eyes. His breathing had stopped. I feared that the last sight of his life had been of a demonic ghoul of my creation. I looked down at my hand, to the thing the doomed man had given me in his last act of life. It was a tarnished brass key on a chain. Sharing the chain was a brass circle that was engraved: "Rolls-Royce." I didn't think for a second that this guy owned a Rolls-Royce. I flipped the circle over to see writing on a piece of white tape.

George O. Long Pine Road.

"I'm sorry, George," I whispered to the guy.

There was no longer any doubt. These weren't hallucinations. At least not entirely. Whatever this monster was, it was real and it had claimed a victim.

It meant that I wasn't insane.

At least not yet.

15

"He knew about Cooper," I said, trying to get the sheriff to understand how important that was. "He said he was on the road."

"What road?" the sheriff asked.

"I don't know, he didn't get the chance to tell me."

We were sitting in the small sheriff's office in Thistledown. The department consisted of exactly two people: an older lady who was the receptionist . . . and Sheriff Vrtiak. I guess there wasn't much crime in Thistledown.

"So he grabbed you to tell you that Cooper Foley was on a road somewhere?" Vrtiak asked.

"No," I said, and stopped talking. I wasn't exactly sure why he had grabbed me, other than to blabber some insanity about seeing something and knowing the truth. Trouble was, I kind of knew what he was talking about, but how was I supposed to explain that to the sheriff? I had to choose my words carefully so I wouldn't sound like a lunatic.

"He grabbed me because he wanted to warn me about something. But I saw him wearing Cooper's jacket yesterday, so I asked him about it and he told me that Cooper was on the road."

"You sure it was Foley's jacket?"

"Well, no. But if it wasn't, it sure is a coincidence."

"Coincidence," Sheriff Vrtiak repeated, thinking out loud. He sniffed, then continued. "What did he warn you about?"

We were now stepping into lunatic territory.

"It was crazy talk, mostly. He told me that he knew. That he saw. And he told me not to follow somebody."

"Foley?"

"I don't know. Maybe. Then he saw something that scared him and he ran to get away from it and . . . you know what happened next."

Sheriff Vrtiak pulled at his eyebrow nervously. I didn't think he was used to dealing with such drama. Or tragedy.

"George O. was a local fixture," he explained. "He's lived here longer than anybody I know. He may be a little . . . eccentric, but he's not crazy. At least not by my standards."

"Well, he sure was acting crazy before he . . ." I couldn't finish the sentence. What had the guy done? Committed suicide? Had a terrible accident? Been frightened to death? All the above?

"You say he was scared," Vrtiak said. "What do you s'pose he was scared of?"

That was the big question and I knew the answer. Sort of. Up until that moment I had only discussed Gravedigger with Sydney. I wasn't sure if she believed me or not, but I was tired of being alone in this.

"There was a guy," I said tentatively. "He was standing

on the second-floor balcony of the ice cream shop. I think that's the guy George was afraid of."

"Who was he?" Vrtiak asked.

There was a yellow legal pad on Vrtiak's desk. I grabbed it along with a pencil and did a quick sketch of Gravedigger, complete with his sunken eyes and broad hat. Vrtiak waited patiently, then took the pad when I offered it to him. I wasn't surprised at his reaction. He looked at the sketch, then at me, then back to the sketch. He pulled at his eyebrow so hard, I thought he might pluck out every hair.

"What the hell is this?" he asked.

"It's the guy I saw on the balcony. I think he scared George into running into the street."

Vrtiak scoffed. "Well, he's plenty scary, but I've never seen anybody like that around Thistledown."

"I saw him," I stated flatly.

Vrtiak tossed the sketch onto the table dismissively. I had gone from a credible witness to a wiseass kid who was pulling his chain.

"So you're telling me that some guy wearing a Halloween costume scared George O. into jumping out in front of that semi?"

How the heck was I supposed to tell him that it wasn't some guy in a mask, it was an apparition that could appear at will and scare you into seeing things that weren't there? It was pretty clear that I wasn't going to be getting any help from Sheriff Vrtiak. I reached into my pocket and felt the rough edges of the key that George had given me. I should have given it to the sheriff, but I figured he probably would shove it into his desk and forget about it. The key stayed in my pocket.

"Yes" was my simple answer.

"Thank you, Mr. Seaver. If we have any more questions, we'll be in touch."

I wasn't sure who the "we" was, since he was the only guy around.

"What about Cooper?" I asked.

"We've got his picture out all over the state," he said. "He'll turn up."

Sheriff Vrtiak didn't seem all that concerned about Cooper.

"What about the missing boat?" I asked. "What if Cooper took it out and there was an accident?"

Sheriff Vrtiak stood up. The questioning was over and he wanted me to leave.

"We'll be on the lookout for the boat, too," he said.

"Who is we?" I asked, getting frustrated. "Is there another sheriff hanging around someplace?"

Vrtiak took a deep breath like he was trying to hold back from saying what he really felt. I didn't think he liked being challenged by a kid from out of town.

"You're right, young fella. I'm the only sheriff and there's only so much I can do. Right now I've got to deal with what happened to poor George. I can't go scouring the lake for a single boat."

"What about the fire department? Or the State Police? Or anybody?" I asked.

"Listen," the sheriff said. "Let's not kid ourselves. Your friend is in serious trouble down south. I've seen his record. From what I've read, he's taken off plenty of times when there wasn't any kind of heat on him. Now that he's under a little pressure, it wouldn't surprise me if he went somewhere to get away from it."

"You can't say that!" I shouted, jumping to my feet. "You don't know him."

"I know enough," he shot back. "We're doing everything we can to hunt him down, but between you and me, I think when we find him, he's going to have some explaining to do because he's made a lot of people jump through hoops looking for him."

There was nothing more I could say. This guy wasn't taking Cooper's disappearance as seriously as he should be, and nothing I was going to say would change that.

"I hope you're right," I said.

Outside of the sheriff's office, Mr. Foley was waiting for me behind the wheel of his SUV.

"You okay?" he asked.

I nodded.

"Let's call your dad."

"Nah," I said quickly. "What can he do?"

"Marsh, you just went through something pretty traumatic. You should be with your father."

Mr. Foley had no idea of the traumatic things I had been through. George was only the latest.

"It's okay," I said. "He's coming home the day after tomorrow anyway."

"I don't know . . . ," he said, thinking out loud. Mr. Foley was a good guy. A little stiff but okay. He wanted to do what was right with me, but his mind was definitely more on Cooper.

"Seriously," I added. "I'm good."

He thought about it for a second, then said, "Okay. Your call."

"Thanks," I said, then added, "You know they're not going to search for the boat."

"Yeah. At least not yet. Let's hope they won't ever have to. Hop in."

"No, I want to hang out for a while and walk back. You know, to clear my head."

"You sure?" he asked.

I wasn't sure at all. I wanted help from anybody who could offer it. But George O.'s words haunted me.

The more people who know, the more will be in danger.

"Yeah, I'm sure," I said.

"Okay. Call if you want me to pick you up."

"I will."

Mr. Foley spun the car into a U-turn and headed back for the lake house, leaving me on the side of the road feeling very much alone.

My encounter with George O. had changed things. He knew something about Cooper. I didn't know if he had anything to do with his disappearance or not, but George had seen Gravedigger. Up until that moment, Cooper's disappearance and my hallucinations were two different stories. That strange man brought them together, which made me worry all the more about Cooper. I reached into my pocket and pulled out the tarnished key. It looked like a house key and since his name was on it, it was probably the key to George's home. The guy was trying to tell me something. Was it about Cooper or Gravedigger? Either way he wanted me to have the key and paid a horrible price to make sure I did.

Over the past few years I'd been spending a lot of time getting lost in the world of fantasy books and art. Those stories spoke to me. The battle lines between the forces of good and evil were always so clearly drawn, and whether the good guys won or lost, it was a safe place to go because escape was as easy as putting the book down. As much as I aspired to create characters and stories of my own, I feared that I didn't have what it took. Frano was right. I didn't have the inspiration. I only copied other people's work. The only original idea I came up with was a ghoul named Grave-digger. I couldn't even write a story about him.

Not anymore. My creation had come to life. But how? Did I want to create something so badly that I somehow conjured him into actual existence? If so, was it my fault that George O. was dead? And Mikey Russo was going insane? And Sydney was seeing the impossible? What did this character want from me? What had I done to deserve this? And what did any of it have to do with Cooper's disappearance?

Again, more questions than answers were flying around. The idea that I could be responsible for so much fear and suffering was beyond anything I knew how to deal with. But I couldn't run and hide anymore because no place was safe. Only one person could break this insane chain, and that was me. I had to find answers and I felt certain that the key given to me by a doomed man was my best chance of doing it.

I walked back toward the center of town, figuring I could ask somebody where George O. lived. If he was a local yokel, people would know. It was close to noon on a hot, sunny day, which meant tourists were crawling all over Main Street. The accident had to be the talk of the town, but as I walked along, I saw no sign that it had happened. I guess news of a violent, gruesome death was bad for ice-cream sales, so everyone was pretending like it didn't happen. I wished I could do that. I was about to go into the General Store to begin my investigation when I spotted Sydney's silver Beetle parked in front of an arcade.

Sydney. She'd seen things. She'd understand. I figured at the very least she wouldn't treat me like the sheriff had. I needed an ally. Somebody I could tell about George O. who wouldn't completely dismiss me. I turned away from the General Store to look for her.

Not far beyond the building was the parking lot for the mini golf course. I rounded the corner to see Sydney sitting on a picnic bench next to a line of coin-operated kiddie rides. Standing in front of her, pacing back and forth nervously, was Mikey Russo. What the heck was he doing up there? And what was he so worked up about? Sydney kept her eyes on the ground, listening to him rant. I was too far away to hear what he was saying, but he was definitely upset. I stayed where I was, leaning against the wall.

Without warning, Sydney lashed out and slapped Mikey across the face. The big guy took a step back in surprise as Sydney glared at him with those steely eyes. I saw the tension in Mikey's body. There was no telling how he'd react. The guy was a creep. A bully. Sydney might have been in trouble, so I had no choice but to head over there.

"Hey! What's up?" I called out, friendly, trying to sound like I had no idea that Sydney had just whacked him solid across the lips.

Mikey spun toward me. The moment he registered who I was, his expression fell. His anger turned to fear.

"Back off, Seaver!" he said, holding his hand up as if to fend me off.

I stopped.

"Don't come near me," he said, his voice shaky.

Mikey was scared. I mean, really scared. He backed away like I had a flamethrower or something.

"What's your problem?" I asked.

"Leave me alone," he whimpered.

I looked to Sydney. She didn't look as confused as I thought she'd be.

"What's going on?" I asked her.

"He's afraid of you," she said matter-of-factly.

"Me? Why?"

Mikey circled away from us and backed toward the road . . . the same road where George O. had been run down.

"Watch where you're going!" I shouted.

Mikey pointed a finger at Sydney and said, "Be careful! You hear me?"

Careful? Mikey was worried about Sydney being careful? She'd just smacked him!

"Mikey," I called out. "What are you so scared of?"

"Freak," he hissed, then turned and ran.

I held my breath and watched as he sprinted to the sidewalk, took a right turn, and disappeared. There were no screeching brakes and no accident. Only questions. Sydney and I didn't move for several seconds.

"Uh . . . what just happened?" I finally asked.

Sydney grabbed her shoulder bag and hurried away. "Come with me," she ordered.

I followed without question. Sydney walked past the closed mini golf course and through the bushes, where a break in the chain-link fence led to the drive-in theater. It was daytime, so the place was empty. The giant white screen loomed over the barren lot, waiting for darkness and the night's show. At the base of the screen was a playground where kids could burn off energy while they waited for the movie. That was empty too. Sydney went straight for a bench, threw her shoulder bag down on it, and spun back toward me.

"What the hell is going on?" she demanded.

"You're asking me?" I shot back.

"How did you scare him like that?"

I was dumbfounded. "Scare him? I didn't do anything. You saw, you were there."

"I'm talking about back at my house in Stony Brook. Mikey told me what he saw."

"Really? What did he see?"

"He said there were wild dogs. Vicious dogs that bit at his legs."

"What! There weren't any dogs."

"That's not what he thinks." Sydney looked me square in the eye. She may have been coming after me aggressively, but she looked scared. "He said they were protecting you. One came after him, but the others stood at your side like guard dogs."

"Sydney, I swear. I have no idea what he's talking about. C'mon! You were there. You didn't see any dogs, did you?"

Sydney broke down and started to cry. Whoa. Her hands were shaking. She had to sit on the bench. "What is happening?" she asked.

"Whatever it is, it's getting worse. A guy was killed this morning."

"I heard," she whispered.

I sat down next to her. "What were you arguing with Mikey about? Why did you slap him?"

Sydney gave me a red-eyed look. "I hit him because he doesn't have a clue."

"Really?" I said with a chuckle. "You'd have to get in a long line to take a whack at Mikey Russo for that."

Sydney glared at me. She didn't see the humor. I stopped chuckling.

"The only person Mikey worries about is Mikey. He couldn't care less that it's partly his fault Cooper is missing."

My ears rang. Did I hear right?

"Mikey?" I asked tentatively. "And who else?"

Sydney took a labored breath. "Me."

I didn't know what I expected her to say, but it definitely wasn't that. I couldn't form a coherent thought.

"I . . . I . . . don't get it," I mumbled. "You know what happened to Cooper?"

"No."

"Then how are you responsible?"

Tears ran down Sydney's cheeks. She couldn't look me in the eye. "Marsh, I'm the one who gave him the counterfeit tickets."

It was a good thing I was sitting down. I couldn't line up

enough thoughts to say anything more than, "But . . . how? Why? For money?"

"It's way more complicated than that," she said.

"Tell me."

Sydney took a while to answer. I think she was trying to figure out what to say. She wasn't used to defending herself or justifying anything she'd done. She had to work hard to speak calmly, as if saying the words physically hurt her.

"This isn't an excuse, it's just what happened. My parents expect a lot from me. Always have. Since I can remember. If I become vice president of a club, they say I should have been president. If I make a team, I should be a starter. If I'm a starter, I should be an All-Star. All-County. All-State. Why take a regular course when I can take AP? Every A should be an A-plus. Every test the top end of the curve. There's no winning with them."

"Why do they push so hard?" I asked.

Sydney gave the question a long moment's thought. "I don't know. Maybe because I'm the oldest. Or because I'm a girl and supposed to try harder. Who knows? The thing is, I let them."

"And Cooper doesn't," I added.

"Yeah. Cooper doesn't and it pisses me off. He deflects their criticism and I take it to heart. I know it's juvenile to resent Cooper for that, but I do. Call it another failure."

"What's that got to do with the tickets?"

"I told my parents I was going to get the tattoo. I don't know why. I wasn't serious. I don't even like tattoos. I think I just wanted to piss them off. Of course, they hated the idea."

"You told me," I said.

"No, I told you they'd be angry if they found out I got one. This was before. We got in a huge argument. I told them I was going to get one no matter what they thought about it and they'd just have to deal. They went ballistic. There was no good cop, bad cop. They came at me like two very bad cops. I really got to them. I loved it. For a few seconds it was like a victory. I'd won because I was finally able to take a little control. To be honest, I wasn't even going to get the stupid tattoo. Why bother? I made my point. But then they threatened me."

"Threatened? How?"

"They said they'd refuse to help pay my college tuition. Can you believe that? They wouldn't even discuss it. They didn't want to know why I wanted the tattoo or how I might feel about it or even try to talk me down by telling me I could always do whatever I wanted after I was out of school or any of those things that parents are supposed to say. Their word was law, end of story, which meant I only had one option."

"You got the tattoo."

"Exactly. I mean, c'mon! Their biggest threat was to hold back money for college? Think about that. It's not like I was some loser they were ashamed of. My whole life I did everything I was supposed to so I'd get into a good college, exactly what they wanted, and their threat was to stop me from going? How wrong is that!"

"It is," I agreed.

"So I did it. I went out and got inked as my big in-your-face statement. It wasn't even a big tattoo. You can only see it when I'm wearing a bathing suit, but I had to do it. And what happened? It got infected and I got sick. It was horrible. No way I could tell my parents. I didn't want them to know that they were absolutely right about it being a bad idea. I went to a doctor but couldn't put it on my parents' insurance without them finding out. I had to pay cash. It was a couple hundred bucks I didn't have, so I asked Mikey for a loan. Can you believe that? How desperate can you get? He said he'd help, but I had to earn it. Great boyfriend, right? He said he knew some guys who could get him tickets to scalp. Whatever profit we made, we'd split. But I didn't know how to scalp tickets. Give me a break. I told him I couldn't do it and he said he didn't expect me to. He had other ideas."

"Cooper."

She nodded sadly. "He said Coop had connections. He could sell the tickets, no problem. So I sucked it up and asked my brother for help. It was one of the toughest things I'd ever done. But you know what? Cooper didn't think twice or give me a hard time. He told me to step out of it and he'd deal with Mikey. Two days later I had the cash to pay the doctor. I got better and my parents didn't know a thing. It all seemed so simple."

"Except the tickets were counterfeit," I said.

Sydney started crying again. "I didn't know. Honest to god I didn't."

"Did Mikey?"

"He says he didn't, but I'm not so sure. The guy's a low-life. He set it up so Cooper took all the risk . . . and the blame. Now Cooper is missing and all Mikey cares about is that he might turn up and give his name to the police. That's why I slapped him. For the record, Cooper didn't tell any-body about Mikey. He hasn't given them my name either. Cooper only gave up the guys who Mikey got the tickets from. Cooper knew who they were. He's way more con-nected than even Mikey realized. But Cooper didn't know the tickets were fake either. I truly believe that."

"Do you think those guys have something to do with him disappearing?"

"I don't know. I wouldn't be surprised. Counterfeiting tickets isn't small-time. Those guys may be kids, but they're like . . . criminals. That's what's eating me up. Even if they had nothing to do with Cooper being gone, it's why he came up here to the lake. Whatever happened to him, it all started with me doing something stupid and then asking him to bail me out. I do nothing but give him a hard time, yet he took a huge risk for me. And this is what happened. I hope he's just being typical Cooper and having fun somewhere, because if anything bad happens to him, I don't know what I'll do."

We sat in silence for a good long while. Things had suddenly gotten a whole lot more complicated.

"I don't know if this will make you feel better or worse," I said. "But I'm afraid there's more to Cooper being gone. It might not have anything to do with the counterfeit tickets."

"What do you mean?"

"I don't know," I said. "I thought the stuff I've been seeing and Cooper's disappearance had nothing to do with each other, but the guy who jumped out into traffic changed that. He saw Gravedigger. I know it. He was terrified, just like Mikey was. And now you say Mikey saw vicious dogs that weren't there. And then there's the stuff you saw in your room last night. We can't all be hallucinating."

"What's that got to do with Cooper?" she asked.

"The guy who died, George, was trying to warn me about something. He said he knew the truth. He told me not to listen or follow."

"Follow who? Coop?"

"Maybe. When I asked him if he knew where Cooper was, he said he was on the road, which is what Gravedigger has been saying to me."

"So there's a connection between Cooper and the things you've been seeing?"

"I think so."

Sydney let that idea settle in, then said, "And that George guy won't be talking anymore."

"I'm not so sure about that." I reached into my pocket

and pulled out the key. "He gave this to me. He said it would help me find answers."

Sydney examined the key. "His house key?"

"That's what I'm thinking."

"Shouldn't you give it to the sheriff?"

"No. I tried to tell him about Gravedigger. He didn't come close to believing me."

"But if that guy had some information about Cooper, the police should know," she argued.

I stood up and paced.

"George told me something else. He said the more people who know, the more will be in danger. After what happened to him and after the couple of close calls I had, I believe it. The fewer people who are involved, the better."

"So you're not gonna tell anybody about this?"

"How can I? First off, they wouldn't believe me. You should have seen the look on that sheriff's face when I showed him a sketch of Gravedigger."

"Marshall, you have to try and convince them."

"The only way anybody's going to be convinced is if they see the same things I've been seeing. But if what George said is true, that'll put them in danger. Only five people have been touched by this. One is missing. One is dead. That leaves me, Mikey . . . and you."

She shot me a surprised look.

"You've seen things, Sydney."

She looked like she wanted to argue, but stopped.

I added, "I don't think this is just about a guy who's gone missing. Something bigger is going on. Something bad. I don't want to be part of it any more than you do, but I don't have a choice. Not with Gravedigger coming after me. I've got to see this through and I'm afraid to do it on my own. I don't want you to be involved, Sydney, but I think you already are. I need your help."

She kept staring at me. I tried not to break eye contact. I wanted to show strength, even though I wasn't feeling all that strong.

She said, "A couple of days ago you were ready to argue about *the Force* like every other good little geek."

"That's before a guy died at my feet. I thought I was going out of my mind, and I might be, but whatever's happening is real. It's not just in my head, but my head is where it came from. I'm the center of this thing and I have to deal with it or I might end up like George O. . . . And then we may never find out what happened to Cooper."

I was ready for Sydney to flip me off, run for her car, and drive as far away as possible. I wouldn't have blamed her if she had.

Instead she stood up, tossed me the key, and declared, "Then let's go search the house of a dead man."

16

It wasn't hard to find George O.'s house.

If you could call it that. The guy lived in a trailer that had been jacked up and put on cement blocks. It was a mobile home that was no longer mobile. It sat at the end of Long Pine Road, which really should have been called Long Pine Double-Rutted Path Through the Trees. We got directions from the guy who worked at the pizza place on Main Street. One look from Sydney and the guy melted like hot mozzarella. It wasn't like George O.'s house was a secret or anything, but I believe that guy would have carried us there on his back if Sydney had asked.

The road wasn't far from the center of town, but once we turned onto it, it felt like we were out in the boonies. Branches scraped at Sydney's car from both sides. She didn't complain, but I saw her wince every time she heard the screech of another branch sliding along her doors.

"Not exactly a popular route," she commented after a particularly nasty branch battered her window.

Thankfully, the trees opened up and we drove into a clearing that looked more like a junkyard than somebody's front yard. The mobile home was barn red, though most of the paint had either been chipped off or bleached white by the sun. It was surrounded by more weeds than grass, along with a collection of odd machine parts, ancient cars, and old road signs. I saw a rusted baby carriage; outboard engines on blocks; a wooden dinghy loaded with moldy life preservers; more tires than I could count; and a huge plastic ice-cream cone that looked as if it had once crowned a snack stand. It was a collection that probably took decades to gather.

The two of us stood surveying the odd mess.

"Some people would look at this and see junk," I said. "Others see history."

"But most wouldn't be caught dead here," she replied coldly. "I'm not sure what category we're in."

I led her through the odd maze toward the house. As I was about to step onto the cement stairs that led to the front door, my eye caught something that stood out amid the clutter. Next to the house were two sawhorses with long wooden planks between them. Lined up on the planks were at least twenty pots of healthy flowers. I didn't know the names of most of them, though I think one was a red geranium. They were brilliant splashes of color that stood out against the rust and decay. It would be easy to think of George O. as a nutcase hermit who lived to collect odds and ends that others threw away. Seeing those flowers made me realize that there was more to him than that. I didn't know if he had a family or kids or anything else, but he had created something beautiful and took the time to make sure it stayed that way. I felt bad for him and bad for the flowers, knowing that in a few days they'd be dead.

I glanced at Sydney. She was staring at the flowers too. I was glad she didn't make any snide comments. I dug the key out of my pocket, pulled open the rusty screen door, and tried to put it into the lock. It fit. It turned. We had come to the right place. I was about to step in when Sydney grabbed my arm.

"You don't think Cooper is in here, do you?" she asked.

I hadn't even thought of the possibility. I was holding on to the hope that Cooper was on his own and safe somewhere. If he was in that nasty old house, well, there was no good scenario there.

"Nah," I said. I gave her a quick, reassuring smile and stepped into the house.

The first thing that hit me was the smell. It reminded me of the locker room at school. Most guys didn't bring their gym stuff home to wash very often, so the place always reeked of dry sweat. The only difference with George's place was that there was nobody coming in to swab the floors with disinfectant. Whatever else I could say about George O., one thing was for sure: He was a lousy housekeeper. He definitely spent more time with his flowers than he did with a mop. The cramped home was a mini version of the junkyard outside. There looked to be three rooms. We stepped into what I guessed was the living room. There was a ratty old couch with the stuffing coming out of the arms and a leather recliner chair that I'd bet a nickel wasn't real leather. Both faced a pretty big old-fashioned tube TV that had a bent wire hanger for an antenna. To the right of the front door was a tiny kitchen where you could stand in the middle and reach everything. Far to the left, beyond the living room, I saw a door that probably led to the bedroom.

It wasn't exactly luxurious, but it wouldn't have been a horrible place to live if not for the fact that almost every square inch was filled with some kind of junk. I'm not talking about the typical cheesy stuff that people sometimes have around their house—I'm talking junk. The living room looked more like a workroom than a place to hang out and watch TV. There were old tools scattered across a low table; fishing gear hanging from the walls; and wooden bins full of screws and washers and pieces of machinery that could have gone to anything and probably fit nothing. Glancing into the kitchen, I saw more of the same. Among the few cooking pots and cans of food were more machine parts and tools.

Sydney said, "Wouldn't it be funny if we went into the bedroom and it was, like . . . really nice?"

I'm not sure if funny was the right word, but I knew what she meant. Seeing any kind of homey touch in this mess would be totally out of left field.

She added, "Then again, let's not look in the bathroom. That could be ugly."

I gingerly stepped into the living room to take it all in.

"What are we looking for?" she asked.

"No idea," I said. "I was kind of hoping we'd know it when we saw it."

"He didn't give you any kind of clue?"

"All he said was that I'd find answers," I said. "So look for answers."

"I'm not even sure what the question is," Sydney said. "Unless . . ."

She didn't finish her sentence.

"Unless what?" I asked.

"You don't suppose this George character did something to Cooper? I mean, this is right out of some bad movie. You know, strange loner lives in the woods and lures unsuspecting victims into—"

"I get it," I said, cutting her off. "I don't think it's like that."

"Because you're an expert on human behavior?"

"No, I just think George was as much of a victim as Cooper was."

Sydney looked me right in the eye. "So you think Cooper is a victim."

"I don't know what to think," I said quickly. "That's why we're here."

Sydney raised her hands as if to say, "Fine. I'll back off."

I stood in the center of the living room and did a slow three-sixty to try and see anything that might jump out as being important.

"What about the jacket?" Sydney offered.

I nodded and walked toward the bedroom. I didn't see any clothes in the living room and figured that whatever clothes George had would probably be in there. The bedroom door was closed. I didn't like that. I wanted to know exactly what I was headed for. The closer I got, the more nervous I became. I thought about Sydney's concern that George had somehow done something to Coop. With each step I grew more afraid of what I might find in there. It took a lot of willpower to reach for the doorknob. Looking back, I saw that Sydney was hanging back by the front door. Fine. I would have to go in on my own. I twisted the knob and pushed the door open slowly. I actually squinted, just in case there was something horrifying in there. Squinting made me feel as if I had control over how much of it I would see at first. The door was halfway open when . . .

Crash. Something fell down inside. I jumped back.

"What was that?" Sydney shouted.

"I don't know."

My heart was pounding. I reached back for the door and pushed it farther open.

Something fell out of the room and hit the floor at my

feet. I jumped back again, but quickly saw that it was only a gray, wooden board. Nothing sinister at all.

"It's just a piece of wood," I called back to Sydney.

I waited a few seconds in case something else might come tumbling out, but nothing happened. I reached forward and pushed the door open the rest of the way. The room was dark . . . far too dark for that time of day. My first thought was that the blinds were down and curtains covered the windows, but there was no way that blinds and curtains could make a room so dark. I took a step closer to the doorway and allowed my eyes to adjust. Once I could make out details, I realized why the board had fallen at my feet.

The bed was empty, with only a threadbare blanket lying in a heap next to a stained pillow. There was a dresser, on top of which was a tray with some plates and silverware that were left over from a meal. Clothes were strewn everywhere. There was nothing out of the ordinary about the contents. What was strange was that the room was boarded up from the inside. Long lengths of wood of all shapes and types looked to have been hammered into the walls on either side of the windows, blocking out the light.

"You gotta see this," I called to Sydney.

She came forward cautiously and peered over my shoulder. I picked up the board that had fallen onto the floor. There were several others like it leaning against the wall inside the door.

"Is this a prison?" she said. "Was he keeping somebody in here?"

"No," I said. "You don't keep somebody in by hammering boards from the inside." I showed her the board that had fallen. "Looks like he used these to close off the door. He wasn't trying to keep somebody in, he was trying to keep something out."

"Like what?" Sydney asked.

"He said he saw things. If he was seeing the same things I am, he might have hidden in here for protection. I'd do the same thing if I thought it would work."

"Look for the jacket," Sydney said.

It wasn't as if George O. had an extensive wardrobe, but I no sooner wanted to go through his dirty clothes than I wanted to pick up plutonium. I used the board to dig through what was lying around. Mostly it was jeans and flannel shirts. George wasn't a fashionable guy. I opened up each of the drawers in his dresser but just saw socks and underwear.

"Help me flip the mattress," I said.

Sydney gave me a dirty look but didn't argue. We lifted up the mattress to see that there was nothing under the bed but dust . . . and a hammer and nails. Cooper's jacket was nowhere to be found.

Sydney picked up the hammer, feeling its weight. "So he barricaded himself in here to hide from whatever, but then pried himself out to tell you that Cooper was on the road and not to listen to anything or to follow. You think he could have been any more mysterious?"

"Let's check the kitchen," I said.

On the way out of the bedroom I saw a narrow door to my left. I kicked it open to see the tiny bathroom. Sydney was right. We didn't want to go in there. It wasn't exactly spotless. Still, I stuck my head in long enough to see that there was nothing out of the ordinary, if ordinary was sad and disgusting. I didn't go in. The bacteria could have it.

The kitchen wasn't much better. The white sink was stained yellow. There wasn't anything in the fridge besides moldy bread, which was just as well because it wasn't working anyway. It looked like George O. ate his meals right out of the can.

We spent nearly twenty minutes in that sad home, and all we did was confirm that George O. lived like an eccentric slob . . . and boarded himself into his bedroom. We didn't find anything to do with Cooper.

"Now what?" Sydney asked.

We had hit a dead end. A creepy, sad dead end. My mind shot forward to what might be next. Dad was coming home in two days. That was good. I would tell him everything and hope he didn't send me to a shrink. At least not right away. We still had to find Cooper.

"I'm going to ask my dad to come up to the lake," I said. "Maybe then we can tell all three of our parents what's been happening."

Sydney frowned.

"I know," I said. "Your parents are having it tough enough as it is, I just think that—"

Suddenly a bright light hit me in the eye. It was so blinding, I had to put my hand up to block it. At first I figured it was sunlight that had crept through a kitchen window, but neither of the kitchen windows had any sun coming in.

"Where's that coming from?" Sydney asked.

We both looked down the length of the trailer to see a pin spot of light coming from the darkness of George O.'s bedroom.

"The sun must be leaking through cracks in the wood," I offered.

The light left my eyes. I looked to Sydney and saw her face fall as she looked toward the floor.

"What's the matter?" I asked.

"Look!" she exclaimed, pointing down.

The spot of light that had hit me in the eye was moving. It traveled the length of my body, down my leg, and onto the floor.

"What the hell?" she exclaimed.

Whatever it was we were seeing, it wasn't natural. Sunlight didn't move that quickly, or that deliberately.

"I hope you're seeing this too," I said, my voice shaking.

"I'm the one who told *you!*" Sydney answered.

It wasn't a hallucination. Two separate people were watching a beam of light travel along the threadbare carpet of the mobile home, headed for the bedroom. There was only one thing to do. I took a step to follow it, but Sydney threw her arm out to stop me.

"Don't!" she warned. "What if it's the grave-guy?"

"Then it is," I said flatly without taking my eyes off the moving light.

I pushed past her and slowly followed the light. Sydney ran up behind me. I didn't think she wanted to come, but she wanted to be alone even less. She kept her hands on my back.

"This isn't happening," she muttered.

For the record, it was. But I wasn't about to stop and convince her of that. The light brought us to the threshold of the bedroom door. I could see the exact place where it was coming from. There was a crack between two of the parallel boards that George had nailed up over the window. It seemed like there was an intense light shining through from outside. Ordinarily I would say it was the sun, but the sun didn't move like that. I stood in the doorway with Sydney peering over my shoulder. The light had stopped on the floor just inside the doorway.

"Whatever's doing that," I said, "it wants us in here."

We stared at the bright spot of light. It didn't move.

"I want to leave, Marsh," Sydney said nervously.

The light began moving again, slowly drifting across the floor. I can't speak for Sydney, but I don't think I was breathing. Both of us were locked on to the light, following its journey. The light made it to the base of the opposite wall from the window and began climbing. It soon reached the bottom of another series of boards that had been nailed up to cover the other bedroom window. It traveled higher and higher and then suddenly stopped. We stood there, waiting for it to continue.

"Is that it?" Sydney asked.

The light had come to rest on a unique piece of wood. Most every board ran all the way from one side of the window to the other. Not this piece. It wasn't long enough. It was wider than the others too. And blue. Where all the other boards were a weathered gray, this board was painted. It wasn't a uniform plank but more of an oddly shaped piece of a jigsaw puzzle with rough, splintered edges. The light came to rest on this unique blue board. Sydney and I watched for a solid minute, but the light didn't move.

"Yeah?" she said. "And?"

Something hit the board from the outside, making the wood rattle. Sydney yelped in surprise. Up until that second it had been deathly quiet in that claustrophobic bedroom. The knock wasn't dramatic, but coming as it did, when the two of us were already on edge, was like shooting off a cannon. Whatever hand we were following, it had brought us into that bedroom and to that board specifically. I stepped forward to check it out. Sydney was right behind me. I could hear her breathing hard, trying to suppress a frightened whimper. I wasn't much better off. I was afraid to touch the piece of wood but didn't want it to start banging again. That would have driven me off the deep end. I leaned in closer to the rack of boards, staring at the light, trying to understand what we were seeing. I was a raw nerve. If the board banged again, I would have turned and run for sure.

As I got closer, I saw that the light was hitting a spot on the blue board that had writing on it. The words were crudely drawn, faded black lettering. It looked like gibberish, until I realized that the letters, and therefore the board, were upside down. I tried to imagine what the letters would spell out if they were right side up . . . and gasped.

"Oh my god."

"What? What?" Sydney implored.

"Galileo."

"Galileo? Like the astronomer?" she asked.

"No, like the shuttle craft of the USS *Enterprise*."

"You're kidding me, right?" she said coldly. "You're geeking out on me now?"

"No. The name was my idea, but Cooper went along with it."

"What are you talking about?"

I turned to Sydney. "Didn't you know? I painted the letters myself."

Sydney looked to the piece of wood that was nailed to the window. Skepticism was written all over her face, until she recognized it too. Her expression dropped.

"It's a piece of our fishing boat," she croaked.

At that instant the light disappeared. It was as if the message had been delivered and the light was no longer needed. I reached up for the board, wrapped my fingers around one end, and yanked it off the wall. Bright light flooded in, making the sad little room come alive. The piece of wood was no more than two feet long and maybe a foot wide. It was only a partial chunk of the stern. I flipped it upright and examined the lettering.

"Are you sure?" Sydney asked.

"Yeah. That's my lettering."

"So our fishing boat was destroyed and George O. has a piece of it. How is that possible?"

"I don't know," I said. "But it's all the more reason why we've got to find out if Coop took it out that night."

"Okay. Sure. How?"

"I think I know," I said. "But I'm not doing it alone."

We left George O.'s house quickly, taking the piece of boat with us. Neither of us was sorry to go. We had gotten what we came for. I was sure of that. How George had gotten hold of a piece of the fishing boat was still a mystery, but I was certain that it was what he wanted me to find. It may not have explained what had happened to Cooper, but it got us a step closer. Of course, neither Sydney nor I could explain the mysterious light that led us to the piece. We had searched the room and missed the clue George wanted us to find. The light made sure we went back for a closer look. It was further proof that there were forces at work that weren't normal.

As we drove back to the Foleys' house, I gave a silent thanks to George for whatever role he had played in getting us to find that piece of boat. I didn't think for a second that George had anything to do with Cooper's disappearance. I can't explain why, but my gut told me that George was being swept up in this craziness as much as anybody else was. He probably found the piece of boat somewhere. Same with Cooper's jacket. Finding them may have sealed his fate. It was a crazy way to think, but rational thinking wasn't getting me anywhere, so why not?

Much more disturbing was the fact that the Foleys' fishing boat was destroyed. I couldn't think of any good news that could come from that.

When we got back to the Foleys' cabin, I was happy to see that Mr. and Mrs. Foley weren't there. I still had to go by what George had said. The more people who got involved, the more would be in danger. I didn't want the Foleys involved. At least not yet. It was too late for Sydney and me.

"Are you going to talk to me now?" Sydney asked impatiently.

I hadn't said a word the whole drive back. I was too busy running possibilities around in my head.

"I'm afraid Cooper went out on that boat," I said. "Let's find out for sure and then I'll tell you what I'm thinking. And let's hope I'm wrong, because you won't like it."

"Swell," Sydney said.

I followed her around to the back of the house.

Toward the lake.

Toward the boathouse. The garage-size shack was built partly on land, with much of the structure out over the water. There were two ways in. In a boat on the water through the big double doors in front, or through the door on land. There was a combination lock on the walk-in door that used the highly secure code of 0000 to open. I spun the wheels, released the lock, and yanked the door open wide.

The boathouse was exactly as I remembered it. It probably hadn't changed in the thirty years since it was built. Stepping in through the door led to a dock that started on land and reached out over the water, forming a square U shape that traveled along the inside walls. At the mouth of the U, directly opposite us, were the double boat doors that led out to the lake. Both were closed and probably padlocked. Light came from windows set high near the ceiling. There were shelves and cabinets for boating gear like life vests, water skis, and fishing tackle. Mr. Foley also used the place to store paint and tools.

"What do you expect to find?" Sydney asked.

"I'm hoping *not* to find something" was my answer. "If Cooper went out on that boat, something bad happened. I really hope he didn't and it was just stolen and vandalized."

"How are you going to figure that out in here?" she asked.

I walked along the dock to a shelf that had a couple of blue coolers on it.

"Cooper never wears shoes on a boat," I explained. "He

says he can feel the movement of the boat and the water through the soles of his feet."

"That's ridiculous," Sydney sniffed.

"Maybe, but he believed it. The last thing he always did before shoving off was . . ." I reached behind the coolers and felt something. My heart sank. Hidden back there was a pair of nearly new, classic Pumas. I lifted them out and held them up for Sydney to see.

"His?" Sydney asked softly.

I nodded.

"So he took the boat out," she said flatly. "And never came back for his shoes."

I nodded again.

She asked, "What were those ideas you said I wasn't going to like?"

It took me a second to pull my thoughts together. I had hoped I wouldn't find the shoes. Now it was time to face the reality of what it might mean.

"I don't believe in fantasy," I said. "I know I draw comics and can quote every *Dr. Who* episode, but it's just for fun. I never took it seriously. Until now. I've been seeing things I can't explain. Whether they're coming out of my head or not, they're real because other people are seeing them too."

"Yeah, I'm real thrilled about that part," Sydney said sarcastically.

"George O. was killed. I nearly drowned and narrowly missed getting hurt a few other times. This is no joke."

"So you think there's some kind of evil force going after people?" She stopped herself and added, "I can't believe I just said that . . . and meant it."

"I don't think it's that simple because not everything we've seen has been dangerous. That light today. It wasn't trying to hurt us—it was guiding us to the piece of boat.

And the swirls I saw that led me to you. There was nothing dangerous about that."

"Maybe not to you! That's what got me involved in the first place!"

"Cooper's disappearance got you involved," I corrected.

Sydney nodded. "I know. What about that piece of paper that was flying around my room? It got my attention to the window when I saw you in the water."

"Exactly. It's like there are two forces at work. One is trying to hurt and the other is trying to help."

Sydney gave me a sober look. "If you had said that to me yesterday, I would have handed you your head."

"But now it sounds kind of possible, doesn't it?" I asked.

"No, it doesn't!" Sydney barked. "Do you hear yourself? You think you're being haunted! Let's just say it. Ghosts. Ghouls. Demons. Boogeymen. Whatever. You're saying the things that go bump in the night really do go bump in the night."

"Yeah, I guess I am."

"And whatever it is, it's trying to lead us to Cooper?"

"Or stop us from finding him," I added.

"That's insane," Sydney said. She backed toward the door but didn't leave. Her common sense was telling her that my theories were impossible, but her eyes were telling her something else.

"Okay, mighty oracle," she announced. "What do you think happened to Cooper?"

This was the tough part. The part she wasn't going to like. I knew because I didn't like it either.

"I think he's hurt, or at least in serious trouble. At worst . . ." I let that thought dangle. I couldn't say the words out loud. I didn't have to. She knew what I meant.

She swallowed hard and said, "Okay, why?"

"Because he took the boat out the night he disappeared

and now it's in pieces. There was something else I didn't tell you about. When I was lying on the grass here yesterday, I had a dream. Dandelion seeds were flying everywhere. That's why I was laughing. Remember?"

"Yeah. It was creepy."

"And it was real. Suddenly all the seeds fell down onto the blanket. They formed a pattern, Sydney. I didn't recognize it at first, but now I realize what it was. They formed stars. Constellations."

"And that means . . . ?"

"Cooper wanted to take Britt out onto the water to watch the stars. We used to do that all the time."

"I know, I've done it too."

"I think it was another clue. I was being told something, about watching the stars."

"That's it? A bunch of seeds fell onto a blanket and you think you're getting a message from the great beyond?"

"That. And the boat fragments. And Cooper's jacket turning up. And his shoes. And oh, by the way, Coop's been missing for four days. Sydney, it's hard not to put this all together and think that something really bad happened to him."

"So then why the threats? Why is that George guy dead? And why is some ghoul that you created trying to do the same to you?"

My shoulders dropped. "I don't know."

"I'm sorry, Marsh," Sydney said. "The boat piece is scary. I'll give you that. And I don't know why we're seeing these strange things. But let's try to stick with reality instead of tripping off into fantasyland."

I nodded. "Okay. There's enough solid evidence to try and—"

"Whoa, what is that?" Sydney interrupted. She was looking over my shoulder to the double boat doors beyond.

I turned to see something on the unpainted pine doors. I hadn't noticed it when we first came in. Or maybe it wasn't there. Either way, when I saw it, my head went light and my knees buckled.

"You see it?" I asked, my voice wavering.

"Yeah. Who would have splashed paint on the doors?"

"It isn't paint," I said, barely above a whisper.

It looked exactly like the same splash of blood that had covered my bedroom wall when I smashed the golden ball. Red liquid ran down the length of the door, spreading the stain before hitting the water with a steady *plip . . . plip . . . plip*.

I hated that sound.

"Then what is it?" Sydney squealed, ramping up. "Where did it come from?"

It had suddenly gotten dark. But when I looked up to the windows above the double doors, I saw that the sky was as bright and blue as before.

"Do you hear that?" Sydney asked.

She listened. I listened too. What I heard was . . . nothing. All sound had disappeared except for the drops of blood on the water.

. . . plip . . . plip . . . plip . . .

"We gotta get out of here," I said, and went for the door. I yanked it, but the door wouldn't open. I pulled harder. No go. I was able to open the door a crack . . . enough to look out at the lock. It was back on the latch and clicked shut.

"We're locked in!" I exclaimed.

"That's impossible!"

"We gotta go out through the boat doors," I said, and turned for the water.

One look and I realized why it had gotten dark. Normally the water level didn't reach up to the bottom of the large double boat doors. There was a gap of about a foot between the water and the bottom of the door. The gap was gone. The water level had risen impossibly high, blocking off the light that came from below. It was like the tide had come in.

Lakes didn't have tides.

"How is that possible?" Sydney asked.

She didn't expect an answer. Water lapped up onto the dock. Within seconds we were standing in an inch of water.

"This . . . this is wrong," I said.

There was something odd about the water. Not only was it rising fast, but it was dark. Too dark. Sydney bent down and ran her fingers through it. When she raised her hand back up, her fingers were bright red. Bloodred.

"This can't be real," she said softly.

The windows over the boat doors went dark. The wooden doors squeaked and groaned as if straining to hold back a tremendous weight.

"Can it?" Sydney added.

As if in answer, the double doors were blown open by the force from a massive wave of blood.

17

We were about to get hit by the dark, warm wave.

The moment before impact, I reached out to grab Sydney's arm. I don't know if it was to help her or to help myself. Either way I thought we'd have a better chance of surviving together. The last thing I remember before getting swamped was that I smelled meat. It was revolting but the least of our problems. Drowning in water or drowning in blood was still drowning.

The force of the wave threw us against the back wall of the boathouse. I hit my shoulder against a shelf, then slammed my back against the wall. It didn't hurt, or maybe my mind was too busy to register pain as we were tumbled around in the turbulent, thick liquid. We were underwater. Or under blood. My instinct told me to kick for the surface, but I didn't know which way was up. Sydney grabbed at me, making it that much harder to swim. I couldn't see her—that's how thick and dark the blood was. I've always heard that when you get disoriented underwater, you should watch for bubbles because they always drift to the surface, but it was too dark to see any bubbles.

It was like being stuck in a gruesome washing machine. Trying to get my bearings was nearly impossible, but we had to do something. We needed to breathe. I chose a direction to swim. If we hit the lake bottom, we'd know which way was up. If we hit a wall, maybe we could follow it to a window and break it open. Or find the open boat doors. That was the most logical escape route. The big doors had to be open, that's how the blood came in. But if they were still open, why didn't the blood rush back out? The level wasn't going down, which meant whatever force had sent this sickening wave at us had thought to close the doors. Whatever the case, we had to find a way out. I pulled my right arm free from Sydney, kept a grip on hers, and started kicking.

Something hit me in the head, probably one of the plastic coolers. That meant there were obstructions floating in the blood. I kept pulling until we hit a wall, but there was no way to tell which wall it was. Sydney shot forward and put her hands on the wall too. She felt her way along and nudged me to go to my right. It was as good a choice as any. My lungs were aching. I didn't know how much longer I could hold my breath. I had no thoughts about the impossibility of what was happening, only that we were both about to drown.

A light appeared through the thick liquid. It was faint, but it was there. It seemed like the beam of a flashlight. There was nothing in the boathouse that could be making that. Whatever it was, it was part of the supernatural event we were experiencing. Was it there to help us? Or drive us deeper to our deaths? I made a snap decision. We had only seconds left anyway. We had to grab at any lifeline.

Sydney was still nudging me to move to my right. I could feel her urgency. She must have been near panic too. I grabbed her shirt, put my feet on the wall, and kicked toward the light. She fought me, but I was not about to let her go. She must have sensed my conviction and made the same choice as me: We were about to drown anyway, so why not go down kicking? She quickly pulled in the same direction. I hoped she could see the light too.

The faint light was moving. It was definitely leading us somewhere. I thought of the moving light in George O.'s bedroom. That hadn't meant us any harm. That is, unless it meant to show us the piece of boat that would lead us into this boathouse so we'd drown in a sea of meat-smelling blood.

My hand scraped the bottom. The light had brought us down. Was that its evil plan? Bring us down so low that there was no chance for us to get to the surface? The water, or rather the blood, started getting lighter. And colder. My hopes jumped. We were leaving the blood and entering the water of the lake. I knew then that the light was definitely trying to help us. It was showing us the way out of the bloody death trap.

Sydney pulled away from me and I knew why. She sensed that we were close to freedom. The light directed us under the boat doors and out into the lake. The closed boat doors. I was right. Whatever had done this to us wanted us trapped in there. Visibility got better, which led to orientation. I grabbed Sydney and motioned for her to swim up, since I could finally tell where up was. She responded instantly and kicked for the surface. I did the same and seconds later we broke up and out into fresh air. We both took huge breaths. It was the second time in less than a day that I had nearly drowned. I didn't like swimming all that much to begin with—I was thinking that I never wanted to get wet again.

"My god," Sydney said between gulps of air. She was looking at the boathouse.

I looked, expecting to see blood oozing out of every crack. It wasn't. There was no blood, and the water level was below the boat doors, just like always. It was as if nothing had happened, other than two near drownings.

"C'mon," I said, and swam for shore.

We crawled out of the water and fell down on the grass near Sydney's house, exhausted. As the panic from almost drowning wore off, the panic from having been through a supernatural event set in.

"Where did it go?" Sydney said through deep breaths. "How could it just disappear?"

"It didn't go anywhere," I answered. "It was never there."

"But we were swimming in it. It was in my nose, my hair! It was blood, Marshall. I could smell it. It was so . . . real."

"I didn't say it wasn't real." I touched my sore shoulder and winced. "It nearly killed us. That's real enough for me. But it wasn't physically there. Did you see the wave of blood throw the boat doors open?"

"Yeah."

"Those doors don't open in. They swing out. But we saw them thrown in because it fit the illusion. Then they somehow magically closed to trap us inside. That isn't physically possible."

"So then how did it happen?" she cried in frustration.

"I . . . I don't know."

We were both spinning out of control. I forced myself to calm down and breathe. Sydney was in worse shape than I was. She sat huddled on the grass next to me, nervously pulling at her wet hair.

"This is . . . this is . . . impossible," she mumbled.

"But it isn't. This thing has been coming after me and

now it's after you. It's like George O. said. The more people who know, the more will be in danger."

"Know what?" Sydney cried. "I don't know anything!"

"Not yet, but we're getting closer," I said.

"To what!" she screamed with frustration.

"To Cooper."

Sydney stared at me blankly. "That makes no sense."

"I think maybe it does," I said. "This has been about him as much as me. I started seeing the strange things about the time Cooper disappeared. The night he went out on the boat. It could be a coincidence, but what if it isn't? Every time I try to get in touch with him, something happens. It's like I'm being prevented from trying to find him."

"By who? Or *what*?"

"I don't know, but I've seen things that have helped, too . . . the tattoo swirls, the dandelion stars, the light in George's bedroom, and the light underwater. That light saved us, Sydney."

"So you think two cosmic forces are battling to either kill you or help you? Is that what you're saying?"

I gave that a few seconds' thought and said, "Yeah, I guess I am."

Sydney's eyes flared. "You're warped," she said, and jumped to her feet, ready to run off.

"Then you are too," I called.

She stopped.

"I think Coop is in trouble, Sydney. He went out on that boat and something bad happened. He may be holed up somewhere, hurt. I never believed in mediums or cosmic connections or anything like that, but it seems like Cooper is somehow reaching out to me so I can find him."

"You can't be serious," she said with the kind of cold disdain she had been perfecting her entire life.

"But I am. It's the only thing that makes sense."

"Sense?" she screamed. "None of this makes sense. You think Cooper is out there somewhere channeling his thoughts to lead you to him?"

I nodded. It was exactly what I was saying.

She added, "But then some evil force wants to stop you so badly, it's trying to kill you? Am I getting this right, Yoda?"

"What else can I think!" I screamed, jumping to my feet. I was tired of Sydney shooting down everything I had to say. "I'm not making this up. You've seen it. You almost drowned too. What do *you* think is happening?"

Sydney backed down. She wasn't used to being confronted like that, especially by me. But I wasn't the same guy who built rockets and read comics with Cooper. Not anymore.

"I don't know," she answered, suddenly meek. "But we're in trouble and I wish to hell I knew how to get out of it."

"We have to find Cooper," I said. "Now. Right away. For him, and for us."

"And you think that'll end it?" she asked.

I shrugged. "I can hope."

Sydney looked out onto the water. Her eyes were red and swollen.

"So what do you want to do?" she asked.

"There's something in town that might explain why the boat was in pieces. If we can prove that, the sheriff will have to listen and start a real search for Cooper. Are you with me?"

We stood facing each other. Sydney didn't answer right away. I saw her uncertainty. I wished there was something more I could say to convince her.

"No, I'm staying here," she finally said. "When my parents get back, I'll tell them what's happening."

"But Coop's been out there for days! Who knows how much time he has left?"

"I'm sorry, I don't buy it, Marsh. I heard what you said and I don't have any better explanation, but I can't believe Cooper is out there injured and somehow using his will to create lights and make patterns in powder."

"I know. It seems impossible, but what if I'm right?" I asked.

Sydney thought and then said, "I really hope you're not."

"Why?" I asked, surprised.

"I don't know if I believe in cosmic forces, but if you're right and Cooper is somehow reaching out to you, there could be another explanation."

"Tell me. Please."

Her eyes filled with tears. "Cooper might be dead."

I felt as if I'd been punched in the head. "No," I said quickly. "I'm not going there."

"You think I want to? It's your own logic, Marsh. I mean, let's just say it. You're talking about being contacted by spiritual forces. That's a ghost story."

"He's alive," I said with finality. "And I'm going to find him."

"I'm sorry, Marsh. I can't help you. I'm too scared. After what happened in that boathouse, I think you're only headed for more trouble."

"What makes you think you'll be any safer here?"

She gave me a sad smile and said, "Because you won't be with me. This is about you, Marsh. I'm just along for the ride."

It was a cold thing to say but absolutely true.

"Do whatever you have to do," she added. "Just be careful."

She turned and ran back into the cottage. With a quick slam of the screen door she was gone and I was alone, again. I thought about staying there and waiting until the Foleys came back, but I didn't see how they could help. They were already doing all they could to get the local authorities to focus on finding Cooper. There needed to be more reason for a serious search to begin, and I had an idea of how to find it.

Without a driver's license I couldn't take Sydney's car, so the only way I had to get into town was to ride one of the cruiser bikes that the Foleys kept at the cabin. After changing into dry clothes, I found the bikes near the front door and grabbed the one with tires that didn't look too dried and cracked. It was a barely roadworthy junker with three, count 'em, three gears. Didn't matter. As long as I didn't get a flat, it would be better and faster than walking. I wheeled it quickly along the gravel driveway to the road, then jumped on and peddled for town.

It was late in the day. Shadows were getting long. Since there were no lights on the road, I wanted to make town before it got dangerously dark. The bike didn't have any reflectors. Riding at dusk was probably the most dangerous time of day. Drivers didn't always put their headlights on, which made it tricky for a rider to know if a car was coming up from behind until it got close. I kept glancing over my shoulder to make sure I wasn't being crept up on. By anything.

I got maybe halfway to town when I heard a siren blare behind me. It was so fast and so loud, I nearly lost my balance. Looking back, I saw the sheriff's car speeding up with its lights flashing. I figured he had gotten a call and was headed to the scene of some heinous lake crime.

I was wrong. He drove up right behind me, washing me with the flashing lights.

"Stop right there, Mr. Seaver," came the sheriff's voice over his loudspeaker.

I pulled to the side of the road and got off the bike with no idea why I was being stopped. The sheriff should have been out looking for Cooper, not chasing down some kid on a bike for . . . what? No reflectors? No lights? Was he serious?

Vrtiak stopped the car several yards behind the bike and got out. He was still wearing sunglasses even though it was nearly dark out. Dork. He walked up to me with his thumbs in his belt like some kind of badass trooper. Part of me was happy to see him. It would save me the trouble of looking for him later.

"I'm glad to see you, Sheriff," I said. "I'm going to the—"

"Shut it," Vrtiak snapped abruptly.

The guy was all business.

"You broke into George O.'s place, didn't ya?" he asked with a sneer.

Uh-oh.

"Why do you think that?" I asked innocently.

"Don't be a smart-ass," he growled. "I know everything that happens in this town."

His boast wasn't even close to the truth or he would have known what had happened to Cooper. I decided not to point that out to him.

He added, "It makes me think that you might know a little bit more about poor old George than you let on."

"Whoa, hold on," I said quickly. "I didn't know the guy before—"

Vrtiak poked me in the chest with two fingers. "I can book you on suspicion of trespassing," he said.

"Trespassing! I was just—" I stopped myself. It wouldn't have been smart to admit to anything, even though the idea of getting in trouble for trespassing in the old guy's mobile home seemed like a pretty small problem compared to what I was dealing with.

"Get in the car," he ordered.

"Sheriff, I think I figured out what—"

"Get . . . in . . . the . . . CAR!" he shouted angrily.

When I had met him earlier that day, he came across like a laidback kind of guy. Not anymore. Something had happened that set him off. I figured he was under pressure about George's death. I hoped he didn't think that I was responsible in any way.

"What about my bike?"

"Leave it," he barked as he opened the rear door of his car.

I picked up the bike and put it behind some trees off to the side of the road. I didn't have a lock. I figured it would be gone by morning and I'd owe the Foleys for a new cruiser, but it wasn't like I had a choice. I walked slowly to the sheriff's car and crawled into the backseat. He slammed the door, making the whole car rattle. I had never been in the backseat of a police car. It was a chilling experience. A metal cage separated the front from the backseat. There were no door locks. At least no locks that I had control over. I wouldn't be getting out of there until he wanted me out.

Sheriff Vrtiak got into the driver's seat, killed the flashing lights, and hit the gas. The tires spun and got traction, and we lurched onto the road.

"I have an idea of what happened to Cooper," I said.

Vrtiak didn't react.

"I think he might have had an accident in the boat. He could be lying in the woods somewhere, hurt."

Vrtiak still didn't respond.

"Sheriff?"

I heard him sniff. And whimper. "Why?" he said, his voice cracking with emotion.

"Why what?" I asked.

"Why didn't you listen?"

"What are you talking about?"

Sheriff Vrtiak spun the wheel hard. With a squeal of

tires he made a sharp right, turning off the main road onto a windy country lane. He hit the gas again and we took off . . . way too fast for the narrow roadway.

"Where are you going?" I asked.

"He warned you, didn't he?" the sheriff said. "But you just kept looking. Kept poking around."

Alarms went off in my head.

"Sheriff, stop the car."

Sheriff Vrtiak whipped off his sunglasses. He was crying.

"I don't want to do this," he whimpered.

"Do what? Sheriff, slow down!"

He took a curve way too fast. The car skidded to the side, kicked up gravel on the shoulder, then continued on. The trees surrounding the road were getting thicker. The road was getting darker.

"Do what he says, all right?" the sheriff said. He was begging me, like a guy at the end of his rope. "If you don't, he'll just keep coming. And the more people who know, the more will be in danger."

My stomach sank. It was then that I knew whatever had gotten to George had gotten to the sheriff, too. His hands were white-knuckled on the wheel as if he were fighting with the car to keep it on the road. We veered into the oncoming lane, and the sheriff had to grunt and struggle to bring us back. We slid all the way across to the opposite side. The wheels rumbled onto the gravel shoulder, but Vrtiak kept control and moved back into the lane.

The headlights of an oncoming car appeared in the distance.

"Who told you that, Sheriff? Who is he?"

"Give him what he wants," the sheriff whined. "Let him take the road wherever he wants to."

The oncoming car grew closer. The sheriff was gripping the wheel so tightly, I expected it to snap.

"What road?" I asked.

"You know," Vrtiak said.

We drifted into the lane of the oncoming car. It blew its horn. Vrtiak yanked our car back into our lane.

"What road?" I demanded again.

Vrtiak took one hand off the wheel. He used his left hand to steer while reaching for the rearview mirror.

The oncoming car was nearly on us.

Vrtiak gripped the mirror and turned it so I could see his reflection. It wasn't the reflection of Vrtiak that glared back at me. It was the dead gaze of Gravedigger.

"The Morpheus Road."

Vrtiak, or somebody, jerked the wheel, sending us directly in front of the oncoming car. It never stopped blowing its horn as it skidded off the road to the far side. Vrtiak pulled his right hand off the rearview mirror, gripped the steering wheel with both hands, and jerked our car back into our lane. We turned hard, missing the oncoming car by no more than a few inches. I saw the face of the driver as it flashed past. I could have been wrong and maybe I was, but it looked like the guy behind the wheel was George O.

Our car flew across the road and kept going . . . into the woods. Vrtiak let out a scream as he spun the wheel to avoid hitting trees. He jammed on the brakes and I flew forward, smashing my head into the metal bars.

The next thing I felt was a vicious jolt, and everything went black.

18

My ears rang and my head felt like it was spinning.

I don't know if I was knocked out cold or just seriously dazed. When I opened my eyes, it took a while to understand what I was seeing. The world had turned upside down. In truth, it had turned ninety degrees. The car had flipped onto the driver's side and I was lying on the door. My face was pressed against the metal cage that separated the front and backseat, inches from Sheriff Vrtiak's face. Whoa. I pulled away quickly.

The sheriff lay crumpled behind the wheel.

"Are . . . are you okay?" I asked.

His eyes stayed focused straight ahead, looking at nothing. At first I thought he might be dead, but then I heard him take short breaths.

"Sheriff?"

He turned his head to look at me but couldn't focus.

He muttered, "Won't stop. Won't. So many people. So many lives."

He was delirious. There was no way to know how badly he was hurt, if at all. At least physically. His brain was a whole 'nother issue.

"I'll get help," I said.

I struggled to roll onto my feet so I could stand on the door. Nothing hurt too badly, which meant I wasn't injured. I reached up to the far door that was now the ceiling and gave it a shove. I expected it to be locked, but it wasn't, though it was tricky to push open. I had to wedge my feet against the back of the seat and the cage to get enough leverage to push the heavy door up. I managed to scramble out and up until I was sitting on the side of the car.

I wasn't sure why we had flipped over. Maybe we hit a low rock and the car kicked up. Whatever it was, it had saved us from an even worse fate. The nose of the car had come to rest only a few feet from a couple of thick, solid trees. As it was, the car was a goner. The front end was caved in, but the cab was intact, which is why Vrtiak and I were still alive.

Vrtiak. What had happened to him? It was like he was possessed. Or somehow under the control of Gravedigger. Whatever it was that made him do what he'd done, I didn't think it was his choice. Not after seeing the image of Gravedigger in the mirror. The question was, was he still going to come after me?

"Can you move?" I called down to him.

The sheriff didn't answer. At least in any way that I could understand. He was awake but out of it. There was no way I was going to try and move him. I knew enough from Boy Scout first aid that you shouldn't move an accident victim without a fracture board in case he had a spinal injury. Just as well. I didn't want to get anywhere near him in case Gravedigger was still at work. Still, the guy needed help. I remembered that I had my cell phone. I dug it out and flipped it open to find . . . it didn't work. Either the battery was dead or my swim through the bloody lake had killed it.

"I'll go into town and send help," I said to Vrtiak. "Don't move, all right?"

He answered with gibberish. I had to trust that he understood. It didn't look like he could move anyway. I pulled my legs out, swung them over the side of the car, and slid to the ground. The car had landed in a field about thirty yards off the road. The car coming the other way, the one we nearly hit, hadn't stopped. Either the guy driving didn't realize what had happened, or there was something more sinister about it. Was that really George O. behind the wheel? At that point I was willing to believe anything. The only thing I could do was get back to the main road, find the bike, and get to town as quickly as possible. Nothing had changed, other than the fact that after I verified my theory about Cooper's accident, I wouldn't be sharing the information with Sheriff Vrtiak.

Another theory had already been verified. I was moving closer to solving the mystery of what had happened to Cooper . . . and Gravedigger tried to stop me. It gave me confidence that I was on the right track.

My legs were wobbly, but I was able to jog back through the field toward the winding country road. I had only gone a few steps when my cell phone rang. Huh? A minute before it had been dead. I grabbed it and flipped it open.

"Hello?"

I was answered by a shrill screech that was so loud, I had to pull the phone away from my ear. I figured it had to do with water damage. That is, until the sound turned into something familiar. The sharp squeals took on life. And a voice.

"There is nowhere to hide. You *will* travel the road."

"Who the hell are you?" I screamed into the phone. "Why are you haunting me?"

"The choice was not mine," the horrid guy answered.

"No? Then whose was it?"

"Why . . . it was *yours*, of course."

"What? What's that supposed to mean?"

The phone went dead. I snapped it shut and threw it as far as I could. I didn't think for a second that Gravedigger was calling me through Verizon. The phone was useless, except for demons who wanted to taunt me with riddles. I didn't need that.

I started to run. I hit the winding road we had flown off of and turned toward the main road that led into town. How far had we come? A half mile? A mile? Didn't matter. I had to stay focused. I had to find Cooper. I believed that more than ever. He was out there somewhere and needed my help. But I needed his, too. I held on to the hope that once I found him, the haunting would stop.

I must have been unconscious in that car for pretty long because it was nearly dark. Luckily, the moon was bright, so I had no trouble getting back to the main road and finding my bike. I was grateful that no other cars came along. I didn't want to see who might be driving. Once on the bike I peddled toward town and made it with no problem. It was a Monday night, the one night of the week when the shops and restaurants were closed. Same with the mini golf course and the drive-in. The town was empty. That was bad luck. I wanted to be around people. I rode along Main Street without seeing a soul. My destination was the marina. I didn't expect anybody to be there, but I was happy to see the light on in the salesroom. I hoped that it was Britt inside and not somebody spooky who was lying in wait for me. I dumped my bike on the side of the road and sprinted along the walkway to the salesroom. When I jumped inside, I saw two people. One was Britt. Yes! The other was the older guy I had seen the day before. Reilly. It was the last guy I wanted to see. Okay, maybe not the *last* guy, but I wasn't too thrilled about his being there.

"Marsh!" Britt called out brightly when she saw me. "What's up?"

"You almost done?" I asked.

She stood on the opposite side of the counter from Reilly. The guy looked to be filling out paperwork.

"Mr. Reilly is finishing up the forms for the party. You should see the *Nellie Bell*—it looks awesome! We did it all up with lights and streamers and balloons."

I remembered that this guy had booked the party boat for his son's birthday party. I didn't care. "Britt, you gotta make a call—"

"Excuse me," Reilly said, cutting me off curtly. "I'm not finished here." He looked to Britt and smiled. "Don't want to miss the plane. It's costing me enough."

I looked to Britt, confused.

"It's the finale to the party," she explained. "A seaplane is going to land and take Cayden and some friends back home. Nice way to finish up camp, huh?"

"A plane is coming?" I asked. "Here? To take him back home? Tonight?"

"Yup," Britt answered. "It'll pick him up out on the lake."

"If you don't mind—," Reilly said, annoyed at my presence.

"Yeah, I do mind," I shot back at him.

The guy gave me a look like I had just peed on his foot.

"There's been an accident," I said. "Out toward the Foleys' house. I'm not sure of the road, but it's off the main highway. A car flipped."

Reilly looked like he wanted to cut me off again, but even he wouldn't go that far.

Britt clicked into fix-it mode and went for the phone. "I'll call the sheriff."

"No! He's the one who flipped! He's trapped in his own car."

"Oh my god!" Britt exclaimed.

"Is he all right?" Reilly asked.

How was I supposed to answer that? "I think, but he needs help. We gotta send an ambulance." I decided against saying that he was being possessed and influenced by an evil spirit. That would have taken a little bit too much explaining.

"I'll call 9-1-1," Britt said efficiently. "It's the road between here and the Foleys' place?"

"Yeah, I don't know the name. It's about a mile and a half out."

"There's only one," Britt said as she grabbed the phone.

"The car is about a mile up that road," I added.

Britt called 9-1-1 and gave them the information. I stood there watching Reilly. He kept his head down and finished his paperwork. A few times he looked up at me as if he was nervous about something. Or maybe I just imagined that.

Britt finished her call and came back to us. "Emergency services are on the way, but they're miles from here. Maybe we should go out there and—"

"No!" I shouted, maybe a bit too quickly. "There's nothing we can do. He can't be moved without a fracture board."

"How scary," Britt said.

She had no idea how true that was.

"Done," Reilly exclaimed. He arranged the stack of contracts on the counter and dropped a check on top. "I'd best be going. I want to see the look on those kids' faces when the plane shows up."

He didn't seem worried about Sheriff Vrtiak in the least.

"Fine, bye," I said, and grabbed Britt's hand, pulling her from behind the counter toward the door. "I want you to show me something."

"Uh, sure." She turned back to Reilly as I dragged her out. "I'm glad everything worked out, Mr. Reilly. Maybe next year we can—"

"G'night!" I called back, and pulled Britt out of the door.

Outside I kept moving along the walkway that ringed the showroom toward the maze of floating docks that stretched out onto the lake.

"Marsh!" Britt exclaimed. "What are you doing?"

I didn't answer until I thought we were out of earshot of the building.

"The boat that kid brought in for repairs. I gotta see it."

Britt frowned. I was throwing too much at her.

"What? Why?"

"Because I think it has something to do with Cooper's disappearance."

Britt's eyes grew wide. Her mouth moved as if to ask a question, but her brain hadn't formed any yet.

"Please, Britt. We've gotta do this fast. Take me to that boat."

She didn't question. She saw how serious I was.

"We'll take a Jet Ski. It's faster," she said, and led me to a row of sleek blue Jet Skis they had for rent.

There were probably ten of them all lined up in a row, looking like floating snowmobiles. I had always wanted to try one out but never had the chance. Or the guts. Britt boarded the Jet Ski on the far end, throwing her leg over the seat and settling in like she had been doing it for years. Which she probably had. The key was under the seat. Not exactly crack security. She put it in the ignition and fired the engine. It wasn't as loud as I expected. It was more like a steady, deep whine.

"Hop on," she commanded.

I got on behind her awkwardly, rocking the craft from side to side.

"Just sit," she instructed.

I did what I was told and the wobbling stopped. Britt backed the craft away from the dock, then turned and throttled up. I wanted her to gun it, but there were laws about going too fast that close to shore, especially if you were in a marina. The wake could cause damage when it bounced boats around.

"This is faster than walking along the floats," she explained. "The Reillys' boat is so big, we docked it the farthest out."

There were lights on all the floats, making it easy to see all the boats that were tied up. I saw plenty of fiberglass ski boats with big outboard engines, wooden fishing boats with much smaller engines, and lots of sailboats that could carry three or four people. None of them were like the big, sleek white boat that appeared when we reached the final float. This monster had to be at least thirty-eight feet long. It had a low aerodynamic profile and an enormous V-shaped hull. I had no doubt that there was a powerful inboard engine in back. Or two. I'd heard that they were called cigarette boats because they went incredibly fast and smugglers used them to move cigarettes. Bottom line was, it was a monstrous boat that was built for speed.

"That's a lot of boat for this lake," I said.

"You think? But you don't tell people like the Reillys what to do. Money talks."

"What is their deal?" I asked.

"I think they pretty much fund the camp up there. It's loaded with rich kids from New York. It's not exactly rustic.

They have maid service to make their bunks and clean their cabins . . . all of which have Wi-Fi, of course."

"What repairs are you guys doing on their boat?" I asked.

"Cayden hit some rocks in the shallows. He knew he wasn't supposed to go there, but like I said, you don't tell the Reillys what to do. He freaked, though. He wanted my brother to fix it before his dad found out."

"Did Ron fix it?"

"Nah, he could have done it fast, but you don't tell Ron what to do either." She chuckled. "Money may talk, but Ron doesn't always listen. What's this got to do with Cooper?"

"I want to see the damage," I said.

Britt slowed down. We drifted forward along the length of the boat, headed for the bow.

"I think Cayden's lying," she said.

"About what?" I asked, very interested.

"I don't think he hit any rocks."

"Why not?"

Britt expertly maneuvered the Jet Ski around the bow of the enormous boat.

"Because rocks don't cause that kind of damage," she answered. "And rocks aren't blue."

There was a crack in the fiberglass bow just above the waterline. Deep scrapes were dug along the hull, headed to the water. It was exactly what I expected and dreaded to see. Whatever Cayden had hit with that boat, it was blue. The same color as the *Galileo*.

"Cooper went out on his boat that night," I said. "His blue boat. I think Cayden ran him down."

Britt gasped. She looked back at the boat, appraising the damage. "Oh my god, that's exactly what it looks like. Marsh, if Cooper was in a small boat and got hit with this monster at full speed—"

"I think he's out there somewhere, hurt," I said. "The boat hasn't turned up. He could have floated all night holding on to the wreckage."

"Maybe," she said. She didn't seem convinced. I think her mind immediately went to a much worse scenario . . . a scenario I refused to accept.

"We can't let the Reillys go home tonight," I said. "Not before somebody in authority sees this."

"I can call the State Police, but that might take a while."

"Call them," I said. "I'll stay here with the boat. I don't want anything happening to it."

"What could happen?" Britt asked.

What I wanted to say was, "I don't want Gravedigger possessing anybody else and taking away the evidence." Instead I said, "Just in case."

"What about Cayden?" Britt asked. "The seaplane is on the way. Once it picks him up, he's gone."

"Can you call off the plane?" I asked.

"Too late for that."

"What about the *Nellie Bell*? Can you contact the captain?"

She gave me a sheepish look. "The radio hasn't worked for weeks."

There weren't a whole lot of options.

"Then get the State Police," I ordered. "Tell them what we think happened. Maybe they can stop the boat or the plane somehow."

Britt maneuvered the Jet Ski to the floating dock. I jumped off with no more grace than when I had jumped on. Britt rolled with the wake.

"One more thing," I said. "Call Sydney Foley. Tell her I found what I was looking for."

"You got it," answered Britt. Before taking off, Britt gave me a serious look. "I hate to say this, Marsh, but if you're right, I don't know how Cooper could have survived."

"He's alive," I said with absolute conviction. "And we're going to find him."

Britt nodded, gunned the engine, and took off. She wasn't worried about breaking any powerboat rules anymore. She flew over the water as fast as she could safely go. She was soon out of sight and the whine of the Jet Ski faded. I leaned over the powerful boat to examine the damage. I thought back to the night when the Foleys and I had heard the sound of the cigarette boat on the lake. It was crazy to have such a powerful boat on a lake like Thistledown with all the speedboats and Jet Skis and kayaks. At night it would be worse. The lake wasn't more than seven or eight miles long. This kind of boat could hit a hundred miles per hour. Driving at night was suicide.

Or murder.

I pushed that thought away. Cooper was alive. I was sure of it. He could have been lying on the shore only a couple of miles from the house and we wouldn't know it. I can't explain the cosmic stuff, but I believed Cooper was somehow trying to contact me. Not his ghost . . . Cooper. What I didn't know was why some other force was trying just as hard to stop me. Whatever the answers were, I felt certain that it would all end when we found him.

"She's a beauty, isn't she?" came a voice from behind me.

I stood up quickly to see Mr. Reilly strolling toward me along the floats. Did he know what had happened? Had Cayden fessed up?

"My boy can be reckless, but he's a good kid," Reilly said. "He isn't afraid to take chances. I applaud that. It's why he'll succeed in life. He never looks back."

"He didn't look back, all right," I said. "He didn't stop to see what he hit."

"I heard it was a rock," Reilly said.

"Rocks aren't blue."

Reilly looked me square in the eye without flinching. He knew exactly what had happened. He strolled along the float to the stern of the speedboat.

"That's true," he said casually. "Things happen."

"How can you say that?" I yelled. "My friend has been missing for days. I think your kid hit him and he's out there somewhere, hurt. Maybe it was an accident, but he should have reported it."

Reilly chuckled. I couldn't believe he was being so casual.

"You think it's funny?" I yelled.

"I do," he said. "You're right about one thing. Cayden *did* hit your friend, but you are very wrong about something else."

I stared at the guy, not sure of what to say.

He smiled and added, "Why do you assume it was an accident?"

The force of his words nearly knocked me over. Seriously. I had to move my feet apart or I would have lost my balance.

"Cayden *tried* to hit Cooper?" I said, barely above a whisper.

Reilly reached into the stern of the boat and pulled out a length of rope. "Perhaps. Perhaps not. However, I do find it amusing that you believe there's only one life at stake here."

"What?" I gasped.

Reilly smiled. "I've seen. I know. Soon we'll all be on the road, and what happened to your friend will be nothing more than an inconsequential memory."

Uh-oh.

He whipped the rope out of the boat. In his other hand was the sharp, metal boat anchor. I was frozen, not believing what I was seeing.

"Enjoy the journey," he said, then raised the anchor . . . and attacked.

He threw the heavy anchor as if it were plastic. I ducked to my right as the anchor whipped past me and crashed onto the deck, gouging out a chunk of wood.

We were on the last float of the marina. There was only one way off. I ran for the next float back, but Reilly cut me off, blocking the way. His eyes were wild. He was breathing hard. It was like George O. and Sheriff Vrtiak. This guy wasn't just out to protect his son. He was being controlled. The guy rubbed his hands nervously. He looked confused, just like Vrtiak had. When he looked at me, I saw fear and even confusion.

"I don't want to do this," he said in a strained whine. It was as if for that brief moment he was trying to fight the demons that were forcing him to attack me. "I'm sorry." He rubbed his eyes. He was crying. He looked to the sky and screamed, "Don't make me do this!"

He turned and started to run off the float but suddenly stopped. I saw why. Standing in his way on the far end of the next float was Gravedigger. The demon hovered a few inches off the dock, floating our way. His silver pick sparkled in the moonlight. Reilly let out a pained cry as if it physically hurt to resist. Or maybe his fear was complete and he had lost his mind.

I wasn't far behind.

Reilly spun toward me. The anguish in his face was replaced by a look that I can only describe as one of rage.

"This will end now!" he screamed . . . and charged at me.

I took a few steps back, but to go where? He was on me in a second. Both his hands wrapped around my throat and squeezed. He was trying to strangle me! The guy was insane. He was crying and laughing and growling in agony as he fought with himself. And with me. Reilly didn't want to kill me. Whatever had taken control of him did.

I couldn't breathe. He was crushing my windpipe. I felt the pressure build up in my head like blood was rushing to my brain. I tried to pry his hands away, but the guy was much bigger than me, and strong. I think his insanity made him even more powerful. I tried to knee him where it counts, but he was ready for that. His body was twisted away, so all I did was jam my knee into his leg. If it hurt, he didn't show it.

Gravedigger stood on the float behind him. He didn't move. He didn't react. I had no doubt that he was driving Reilly to do what he was doing. To kill me.

I had never hit anybody in my life, but this was survival. I gave up trying to pry his hands from my neck. Instead I went for the throat. Literally. I made a fist and shot my arm straight out, hitting him square in the Adam's apple. The pressure from his hands released instantly. He made a pained, choking sound and lost focus. I didn't wait to see how long it would last. I drove both my hands between his and thrust them out, breaking his grip. I had bought myself a few seconds.

I couldn't run off the float. Even if I got by Reilly, I'd be running straight into Gravedigger. There was only one place for me to go . . . into the water. Again. I whipped around, ran the few steps to the edge of the float, and dove in headfirst. After what had happened to me back at the Foleys', the water was the last place I wanted to be. I take that back. The last place I wanted to be was on the float, being choked by Reilly. The water was a close second. I surfaced and swam for my life. I didn't even think about the terrifying images that Gravedigger might throw at me. It was all about getting away from Reilly.

The splash behind me said that the guy wasn't giving

up. A quick look back showed me that he had recovered and jumped in after me, swimming hard. All I could do was put my head down and swim as fast as I could. I ripped through the water, fueled by terror, only looking up long enough to find a place to pull myself out. I didn't even look back to see if Reilly was closing. Seconds counted. I heard the splash of his frantic strokes. The longer I was in the water, the better chance he had to catch me.

I churned past rows of boats that were tied up to floats, making only one turn to try and lose him. It didn't work. He was right after me. I was getting tired. I didn't want to have to swim all the way to shore, which was still about fifty yards away. I didn't think I could stay ahead of him for that long. I had to find a length of dock where I could pull myself up, but every place I passed was crammed with boats.

Finally, I spotted the gas dock. No boats were tied up there. I pushed hard and hit the empty float within seconds. I grabbed on to the edge with both hands and popped out of the water in one quick move. My arms were tired, but the adrenaline pumping through my system did the job. I took one look over my shoulder to see that Reilly was headed my way. He was only twenty yards out and closing fast. It was time to get lost.

I sprinted off the float, hit the shore, and ran. I had no plan other than to get away from the crazed guy. Once I lost him, I'd figure out how to get back to Britt. The only smart choice was to run toward Main Street. There were places to hide there. I didn't need to turn around to know that Reilly was out of the water and chasing me. I didn't hear him splashing anymore. He was definitely on foot. I hit the row of stores and turned into the parking lot of the mini golf course. Everything was dark and quiet.

I ran into the closed course, winding my way past windmills, open-mouth whales, and mermaids. Sydney had shown me a break in the fence behind the golf course earlier. Hopefully Reilly didn't know about it. I jumped behind a miniature lighthouse and looked back toward the parking lot. Everything was closed, which meant it was deathly quiet. I didn't see Reilly. Had he kept running straight along Main Street? I waited a few minutes to see if he was creeping up through the kiddie rides but didn't see him. Moving quickly but quietly, I worked my way to the far side of the golf course and into the trees. The break in the fence was right where Sydney had showed me. I snuck through and came out on the edge of the giant parking lot of the drive-in movie. I had to stay near the fence and the trees because there was nowhere to hide in that wide-open field. That was okay. If somebody was creeping up on me, I'd see them.

My neck was sore. For sure there would be black and blue marks where Reilly's fingers had dug into my skin as he tried to crush the life out of me. I needed to rest but didn't want to waste too much time. Cooper's life could depend on it. Who knew what kind of shape he was in? His boat was smashed days before. I knew that for certain now. How long could he survive? And what did Reilly mean when he said it wasn't an accident? Was Cayden being controlled by Gravedigger the same as the people who were after me? It was possible, I guess, but the question then became . . . why? Why would this figment of my imagination, this evil spirit or whatever it was, want to hurt Cooper? It added a whole 'nother level of confusion to a situation that had plenty going on already. The only thing I could do was to stay focused on finding my friend. I'd deal with the rest after that.

I figured my best hope was to get to Cayden and force him to say where the accident happened. From there the search could begin. The State Police would make sure of that. No more dealing with Sheriff Nutburger. The damage to the cigarette boat would be all the proof they would need to search the lakefront. All I had to do was stay alive long enough to make sure it all happened. My wind was back. I felt better. I was about to start making my way along the fence toward town and the marina when I saw a flicker of light come from the projection hut in the center of the parking lot. That was strange. The drive-in was closed. There wasn't a single car around. I thought maybe the owner was doing maintenance on the projector.

The giant screen came to life with a movie that showed a nighttime shot of a beautiful lake. The sky was loaded with stars. There was no music, just a wide shot that slowly panned across the water. The shot continued to move until it showed a small boat floating in the dead center of the serene lake. That's where the shot stopped. It was such a wide view that the boat looked tiny. It bobbed on the water peacefully. I actually thought that whoever the character in this movie was, he was an idiot for being out on the lake with no running lights.

That's when I heard the sound. It was the same sound I'd heard on the lake the night before. It was the deep growl of an oncoming boat engine. A big engine.

I stood up straight.

The camera slowly zoomed in on the small boat. The blue boat. It didn't take long for me to recognize it.

"Oh god, no," I whispered.

The movie cut to an overhead view, looking straight down on the little boat. With a quick move-in the blue boat filled the screen, along with its passenger. Lying flat on his back, gazing up at the stars, was Cooper. His head was on a red pillow . . . his Davis Gregory football jacket. He didn't have on shoes.

The rumble of the approaching boat grew. I realized

with horror that I was being shown the shadows of events that had happened several nights before. I didn't want to watch, but I knew I had to. Gravedigger was no longer content with simply trying to kill me. He wanted to torture me.

The sound of the cigarette boat grew louder. I didn't have to see it to know it was moving fast. Seeing Cooper looking up at the stars with a smile on his face, oblivious to the danger that was speeding toward him, made my gut twist. I realized why he didn't know something was headed his way. He was listening to his iPod and tapping his feet to the rhythm of a song. Knowing Cooper, the volume was cranked.

The sound of the oncoming boat grew deafening. It filled the space of the empty parking lot. I thought for sure that people would hear it and come running to see what was happening at the drive-in. Or maybe it was an illusion and I was the only one who could hear it. I wanted to turn away. I didn't want to see the impact. I forced myself to stay focused. I braced myself as if the boat was going to hit me. The event lasted barely a second. The giant white boat entered the frame, obliterated the smaller craft, and was gone. It happened so quickly, so violently, that I wasn't sure if I saw exactly what happened. For that I was grateful. My eyes had been on Cooper's face, but I hadn't seen him register a thing. He truly didn't know what hit him. The roar of the engine was so loud that there wasn't any sound of the crash itself. The monster boat had completely overwhelmed the pitifully small fishing boat in every way. It flew through the frame and was gone instantly, leaving nothing but wake on the water.

The *Galileo* was gone. Cooper was gone. I expected the shot to move out wider to let me see the aftermath. I wanted to see Cooper clinging to a piece of the shattered boat and drifting away. It didn't happen. All I could see was the turbulent water as the roar of the cigarette boat faded.

I stared at the screen, willing it to show me more. Willing *Gravedigger* to show me more. Instead I heard another sound. Another engine. My heart leaped. Was it Cooper's outboard motor? Was there enough of the blue boat left for him to fire up the engine and get to shore?

"Show me!" I shouted at the screen.

The engine sound grew louder, but the screen went dark. The show was over. Still, the sound continued to grow. What was I hearing? Another illusion? Was I going to be treated to another macabre movie that Gravedigger wanted me to see?

The screen stayed dark. Above it, a plane appeared in the sky, headed for the lake. A seaplane. It was the plane that would pick Cayden Reilly up and take him away. I couldn't let that happen. At least not before he told me where he had hit Cooper's boat. It wasn't about revenge. Or justice. It was about finding my friend and unraveling the whole story.

I had to stop running away, and start running toward the truth.

19

I had to find a way to stop Cayden Reilly.

A seaplane was on the way in to swoop him up and take him away from Thistledown for good, along with everything he knew about the accident. He was out on the lake somewhere, partying it up. There was no way the State Police would arrive in time to stop him from leaving. It was going to be up to me. I needed to find a small, fast boat, and the only place I knew of to get one was the marina. The trick was to get there without running into Cayden's father because the guy was trying to kill me.

Sneaking back through the fence to the mini golf course, I stayed alert for any sound that might mean the deranged preppy dad was about to attack me again. It was total bad luck that all this was happening on the one night of the week that the tourist businesses of Thistledown were closed. Having tons of people around would have made everything so much easier. Or maybe not. Who knew what damage Gravedigger would do if there were more potential victims around?

I had to move quickly but with caution because Reilly was hunting me. I ran from hiding place to hiding place, each time stopping to see if I'd been spotted. I had no idea if it was the right strategy, but that's what they did in the movies, so why not? It was like playing army when I was a little kid. It seemed like only yesterday that Cooper and I had played those games.

I made it all the way back to Main Street, where I could see the marina. Reilly was nowhere around, so I focused on what I would do once I got there. I needed Britt to find me a boat. She was definitely more experienced on the water than I was, but there was no way she was going with me. She was already too involved in this lunacy. I didn't want Gravedigger to turn his sights on her.

I snuck along Main Street until I reached the gangway that led from land to the salesroom of the marina. I sprinted along the wooden walkway and blasted into the building without breaking stride.

"Britt?" I called out.

No answer.

"Britt?" I called again, not as loud. I didn't want my voice carrying to other, less friendly ears. Still no answer. I did a quick search of the salesroom. No Britt. I jumped behind the counter to the window that looked out to the sea of floats and docked boats. From there I could see if Britt had gone back to the Reillys' cigarette boat to meet me. Gazing out over the floats, I didn't see a soul. Where was she? No way she would have gone home. She was supposed to have called the State Police to come examine the damage to the boat. The evidence. I wondered if Britt had seen what happened with Reilly. Did she know the guy nearly squeezed my head off? Could she have taken off in fear? No. She had more guts than that. Under normal circumstances she probably would have called the sheriff. But Vrtiak was trapped in the wreck of his own car, drooling and babbling about walking the Morpheus Road.

My confusion was instantly replaced with worry.

The more people who know, the more will be in danger.

Britt definitely knew some stuff. Was she now on Gravedigger's hit list? Did Reilly come back looking for her? I had to fight the panic that was trying to control me. This night was getting more complicated and dangerous by the second.

Bang!

Something fell down on the wooden walkway outside. Somebody was out there. The door was closed, so I couldn't see. Was it Britt? Reilly? Gravedigger? Whoever it was knew I was inside. As far as I knew, there was only one way out and that was the door that led to the walkway. I looked around for something to defend myself with and found an orange flare pistol behind the counter. It was part of a marine emergency kit and this was definitely an emergency. I pulled the orange pistol out of the display, cracked open the barrel, and inserted the single shotgun-like shell. I'd done this before as part of a Power Squadrons safety course I had taken at sailing camp back home. The instructor had fired one of the flares to show us how to use it, but also to demonstrate how dangerous it was and why it should never be aimed at anyone. The gun had fired off a burning projectile that arced about five hundred feet into the air, trailing smoke. The instructor explained how somebody could get burned pretty badly if they were hit by the burning flare. I wondered how badly a demon would be hurt if I nailed him with it, point-blank. Part of me really wanted to find out.

I listened for any movement outside. Boards creaked and cracked. Was that the normal sound that came from the movement of the floats on the water? Or was Reilly circling the small building, looking for a way to get in and corner me? I ran to the wall and turned out the lights. I didn't want anybody seeing me inside. I waited another minute, then decided I couldn't take it anymore. I crept to the door, reached for the knob, and raised the flare gun. I held my breath and with one quick move, yanked the door open.

Nobody was there. I poked my head out and looked to the right and left. Nobody. The walkway to the street was empty too. I decided I must have been hearing the natural sounds of the floats on the water. I had to get a grip and get out of there. Since Britt was nowhere around, I was going to have to find a boat on my own to get out on the lake and . . .

"Seaver!"

I spun around so fast, I nearly fell off the walkway into the water. I lifted the flare gun, but the barrel hit the railing and it was knocked out of my hand. It clattered to the walkway, out of reach. At that moment I cursed myself for being such a bumbler. A second later I realized it was the best thing that could have happened. If I had lifted the gun, I would have fired it for sure and nailed . . . Sydney. She had rounded the corner of the building and was walking toward me like nothing was wrong.

"What are you doing?" she asked, annoyed. "Why did you turn the lights out?"

For about three seconds I felt like a dumb little kid who was caught doing something embarrassing by the intimidating hot girl. I started to offer excuses, then realized she had no idea what I had been through. I clicked out of defensive mode, swept up the flare gun, and walked past Sydney toward the floating docks.

"What are you doing here?" I asked as I moved past her.

Sydney followed. "The freckle girl called to say you

found what you were looking for. Tell me it's Cooper."

"It isn't. But I know what happened to him. More or less."

Sydney grabbed my shoulder and stopped me. "What?" she cried. "Where is he? Is he all right?"

"The *Galileo* was smashed by a speedboat while he was out on the lake looking at stars. I don't think he even knew what hit him."

Sydney took a wobbly step backward and leaned on the rail, stunned. "But . . . how do you know?"

"A guy brought a cigarette boat here for repairs the other day . . . it was the kid who was leaning on your car and flirting with you."

"The kid . . . ? Oh, right." It took a second for her to remember. Guys flirted with Sydney all the time.

I continued, "Britt and I checked out the damage. The hull is full of gouges and deep blue streaks . . . the same blue as the *Galileo*."

"Is that proof?"

"It's a start."

I chose not to go into all the details of what had happened with Reilly. There would be time for that later.

Sydney looked dazed. "What about Cooper?"

"Britt called the State Police, but who knows how long it'll take for them to show up. I've got to get to that kid. Now. Right now. He's the only one who knows where the accident happened. But he's out on a party boat somewhere and about to be picked up by a seaplane."

Sydney gave me a skeptical look. "Are you serious? A seaplane? On this lake?"

"If he leaves Thistledown, it'll take days to get to him and I don't think Cooper has days."

I looked around at the floats to see if there was a likely candidate of a boat to borrow. It didn't take long. I took off running onto the floats. Sydney followed right behind me.

"Marsh!" she called as we ran. "What are you going to do? Steal a boat?"

"Not steal, borrow. And not a boat." I stopped in front of the line of Jet Skis.

"You're kidding. Do you know how to handle one of those?" Sydney asked.

I jumped onto the nearest Jet Ski, pulled the seat up, and grabbed the key. "How hard can it be?"

I went to put the key into the ignition . . . and couldn't find it.

"I just rode one with Britt," I explained as I searched for a place to put the key. "It's simple. Like riding a motorcycle."

"You know how to ride a motorcycle?" Sydney asked skeptically.

"Well . . . no. But that's like riding a bike. And I know how to ride a bike, in case you were wondering. If I can just find the . . . the . . . where the hell is the stupid ignition?"

Sydney leaned over and yanked the key out of my hand. "Back up," she commanded.

I slid back. Sydney lifted her long leg over the seat, sat down in front of me, and had no trouble finding the ignition. A second later she powered the engine to life.

"Thank you," I said sheepishly. "Now go away."

"What are you going to do?"

"Find Cayden and stop him from leaving."

"How?"

"I don't know. One thing at a time. Go home!"

"I'm going with you."

"No, you're not."

Sydney turned around to face me. "I'm sorry I bailed on you, Marsh. I was scared. You can't blame me for that."

"I don't, but—"

"I realized if there was any chance of finding Cooper

alive and we didn't take it, I'd hate myself for the rest of my life."

"It's not about you."

"But it is. It's about me, and Cooper and everybody else that's been touched by this madness . . . especially you. I don't know why you're in the middle of this, Marsh, but what you've done to find Cooper has been amazing. I can't let you face this on your own anymore."

I leaned forward and hugged her. "Are you sure?" I asked. Sydney nodded. For the first time since the nightmare began, I felt as if I wasn't alone.

"He's alive, Sydney. I know it."

She pulled away from me, gave me a dazzling smile, and said, "Then let's go get him."

I wanted to cheer, but that wouldn't have been cool. Sydney turned back around to the Jet Ski controls.

"Besides," she said, all business, "you have no idea how to drive this. You need me."

The ice queen was back. Didn't bother me at all. We kicked away from the dock and drifted backward. Once we cleared the other Jet Skis, Sydney grabbed the handles and let out a simple command.

"Hang on."

She didn't wait for me to obey. Sydney gunned the throttle and we rocketed forward. If I hadn't grabbed her, I would have somersaulted off the back. Sydney wasn't concerned about safe boating rules and I was right there with her. If anything, I hoped somebody saw us flying out of the marina and called the State Police. Or the Coast Guard. Or the Marines. Or anybody else who would show up and help bring this nightmare to a close.

"Where's the party boat?" she called back.

"Keep heading north," I yelled above the whine of the powerful engine. "It'll be hard to miss."

Sydney made sure to put on the headlight. The last thing we wanted to do was run into anything, or have something run into us. The lake was glassy. With no boat traffic and little wind, it made skimming over the water like sailing on ice. Sydney kept the throttle wide open. I looked at the speedometer and saw that we were hovering around fifty-five miles an hour. That may not be all that fast in a car, but when you're on top of a hurtling projectile with no seat belts, it was like flying. I didn't complain. If anything, I wanted to go faster.

We were traveling for maybe ten minutes when I looked ahead to see an odd, bright light flickering in the distance. The closer we got, the bigger it grew. The one light became two, then four, then many.

"That's it!" I yelled.

The *Nellie Bell* was the only party boat that size on the lake. If there was any doubt that we had found it, we knew for sure when fireworks started shooting from the stern. They weren't your basic home-style bottle rockets either. These were full bust-out boomers that flew into the sky and exploded into huge, cascading colorful displays.

"It's good to be rich," Sydney called back.

It looked like it was a heck of a party. Too bad we were going to have to spoil it.

"Don't slow down," I called. "If they're shooting off fireworks, the party is probably going to end soon. We've got to get there before he boards the plane."

"Are you sure about this plane thing?" Sydney asked.

I looked ahead, scanning the waterline.

"Look," I said, pointing.

Sure enough, there was a dark silhouette of a seaplane floating on the surface about fifty yards off the *Nellie Bell*'s port bow. It looked to be a four-seater . . . the same plane I had seen flying over the drive-in theater. Its tail and wing lights were on as it silently bobbed on the water, waiting to take on passengers. It was time to figure out our next step. I hoped that Britt had gotten through to the State Police and that they would be headed our way quickly, because no matter what we did, I didn't think we could keep Cayden on that boat for long.

As if reading my mind, Sydney asked, "Now what?"

"Bring us up to the port side. We'll tie up there."

"Port?" she asked.

"Left."

"Then say left."

The *Nellie Bell* was an old-fashioned stern-wheel paddle-boat. Britt was right—they had really done it up. Thousands of Christmas lights hung from the upper deck. Helium-filled balloons rose in colorful clusters on both decks, looking ready to lift the boat up out of the water and float away with it. The fireworks continued to explode. Everyone would be looking skyward, which meant nobody would see us coming. Sydney throttled back as we drew near. No sooner had we drifted up to the port (left) side than the skyrocket display stopped and a cheer went up. When Sydney killed the engine, I heard music. A DJ was set up in the bow on the boat's upper level. Kids were dancing in front of the wheel-house and on either side of the deck. The party may have been nearly over, but nobody looked ready to leave. I saw at least a hundred people. I wondered how many had come from the camp and how many the Reillys had imported from their home in New York.

As the Jet Ski kissed the side of the *Nellie Bell*, I spotted a coil of rope that was used to tie the big boat up to the dock. I climbed up onto the deck, unwrapped several feet, and threw it down to Sydney, who wrapped it around the handlebars of the Jet Ski. My end was tied to a cleat, so we were secure. It wasn't the most shipshape work, but it would do the job. Sydney reached up, I grabbed her hand, and with a quick pull we were both on board the floating party.

"I don't remember what this guy looks like," Sydney said.

"I do."

"What do we do when we find him?"

"Ask me again when we do," I answered honestly.

"Are you sure the State Police are coming?"

"No."

"Great. We're all set!"

I hadn't even considered the possibility that Britt hadn't gotten through to the police, but what if she hadn't? Or they didn't believe her? Or what if Reilly had stopped her? Or worse, Gravedigger.

"You have your phone?" I asked.

"Dead," she said. "Our bloody swim, remember?"

Right. That.

"Let's just hope the police will be here," I said, and started walking.

It seemed like most of the action was on the upper deck, so that's where we headed. We climbed a staircase that led up top and emerged in the middle of a floating rave. The DJ was playing techno dance music while colored lights flashed, creating a strobe effect. Speakers were positioned everywhere, enveloping the boat in sound. Many of the kids danced with Day-Glo sticks. It was crowded. Kids were either dancing or hanging on the rails, bouncing to the music.

Sydney gave me a look as if to say, "Where to?"

I shrugged and made my way through the dancers toward the DJ at the bow. It was as good a place as any to try and find Cayden. I took a good look at every kid I passed but didn't see him. Sydney was getting the same kind of attention right back. Compared to most everyone there who was in logo camp gear, Sydney looked like a model in her jean shorts and tiny T-shirt. The guys stared. The girls were surprised at first, then shot dagger looks at her. A group of guys danced toward Sydney, forming a tight cluster around her. She stopped short and gave them a look that would have melted steel. They got the message and danced away.

We were halfway to the bow when the music stopped and the strobes burned white. Everyone let out a collective disappointed "Awwww!" After a speaker feedback screech a guy's voice boomed through the sound system.

"Testing, testing. Can you guys hear me?"

Everybody cheered.

"All right!" he exclaimed enthusiastically. "Is this the best party ever or what?"

Another cheer went up. The pilothouse blocked our view of the DJ setup, but I figured that's where the guy was.

"C'mon," I said to Sydney, and grabbed her hand to pull her forward.

"I think I gotta have more birthdays!" the guy exclaimed.

Another cheer went up. Sydney and I exchanged looks.

"That's him," I said as we pushed our way forward. Everyone else had the same idea and crowded toward the bow. I had to be aggressive to get through. I didn't make any friends.

"Thanks for coming, everybody," Cayden continued. "Next year we'll do something even bigger like, I don't know, maybe I'll get a submarine or something! Yeah!"

I rounded the pilothouse in time to see him standing in front of the DJ, who was set up on top of a locker. Cayden punched the air for exclamation.

The crowd loved it and shouted, "Woo! Yeah!"

A chant started: "Cay-den, Cay-den, Cay-den!"

Cayden was eating it up. He punched the air each time

his name was shouted, whipping them up. Seeing him acting all cocky and arrogant made me hate him even more. This was the guy who had nearly killed my best friend. I wanted to jump up on that locker and pound him.

Sydney must have sensed my tension. She put a hand on my shoulder and whispered, "Don't do anything stupid."

I knew I wouldn't attack the guy. That wasn't me. But I couldn't promise not to do something else that was equally stupid.

"And now!" Cayden announced, holding up his hand to quiet the crowd. "My two weeks at camp are over."

Everybody let out disappointed "Awwww"s again. For whatever reason, Cayden was a popular guy. I guess putting on huge, floating parties helped with that.

"I know, I know," he said. "I'll miss you guys too, but I've got big plans for the rest of the summer. Gonna do a little river rafting on the Colorado!"

This guy really *was* rich.

"Yeah, isn't that awesome?" he said. "I'd take you all with me, but . . . I don't want to!"

Most everybody laughed. I wanted to punch his arrogant face.

"But now I gotta fly," he said, gesturing out to the plane that was floating off the boat's bow. "Literally. You can all stay here and party until I take off, and then the boat'll take you back. In other words, when I'm done, so is the party."

"Don't move!" I yelled.

I don't know why I shouted that. I had no plan. It just came out. The crowd went dead silent. Every head turned to me. There was a moment of confusion, waiting for what I would do next. I wished I knew myself.

"Good luck," Sydney whispered. I didn't know if she was being sincere or sarcastic.

"Dude? Who are you?" Cayden asked through the speakers.

I pushed my way to the front of the crowd and stood next to the locker, looking back at a sea of confused faces. I didn't know what words I was going to say until they came out of my mouth.

"There was an accident," I announced. "Somebody is hurt."

A concerned murmur went through the crowd. I had enough sense not to start shouting out accusations at Cayden, though I sure wanted to. All I wanted was to keep him on that boat until the State Police arrived.

"It happened a couple of nights ago!" I shouted, loud enough for everybody to hear. "Right here on the lake!"

I glanced up at Cayden. His cockiness was definitely gone, though I can't say for sure what replaced it. Fear? Anger? Nausea?

I continued, "Right now the State Police are headed here to ask some questions. Of everybody."

A nervous murmur went through the crowd.

"So . . . so . . . nobody can leave the boat until they get here. But that's good! It means the party keeps going!" I said this with enthusiasm, hoping everybody would shout out "Yeah!" and start dancing again.

They didn't. There was more confusion than anything else. I saw a guy who was probably the captain of the *Nellie Bell* leaning out of the pilothouse window. He didn't look too happy.

"Captain!" I shouted. "Let's help the police out and get this boat back to the marina!"

The guy looked confused. It didn't look like he wanted to take orders from some kid who had suddenly decided to start shouting out commands. Me. The boat didn't move.

Cayden turned to the DJ and commanded, "Play. Now."

After a second of fumbling the DJ kicked back in with some techno dance thing. The lights went out and the colored strobes flashed. Some people started dancing, while others milled around, not sure of what to do. I only cared about one of them. Cayden. He jumped off the locker and pushed his way through the crowd, headed toward the back of the boat. I had no doubt that he was headed for the plane. I pushed my way after him. A couple of his friends tried to stop me to ask about the accident. I stayed focused on Cayden and kept moving. He was having just as much trouble getting through the crowd as I was. His friends were clapping him on the back and trying to chest-bump him. Cayden didn't acknowledge any of them. He pushed a couple guys away, violently. He wanted off that boat.

I finally caught up to him as he was about to climb down the stairs to the lower deck. I grabbed his arm and forced him to stop.

"You can't leave," I commanded.

The music was so loud that I had to get close to him to hear.

"The hell I can't. Who are you?" he asked with a snarl.

I should have played dumb, but I was too angry. "I know what you did," I said, inches from his ear. "I saw your bashed-up boat. You better hope my friend is okay."

Cayden gave me a confused look. Or maybe it was disbelief. He thought he had gotten away with it, the way he probably got away with everything.

"You're wrong. I . . . I hit some rocks," he said weakly.

"Yeah?" I shot back. "Tell that to the State Troopers. I don't think they'll believe you either."

Cayden's eyes flashed around, looking for help or a way out. He spotted something over my shoulder and smiled. He relaxed. His arrogance had returned.

"I hope you can swim," he said with a sneer.

"Why?" was all I had time to say.

"Marsh!" Sydney called out to warn me, too late.

Cayden gave me a shove. I had been so focused on him that I hadn't realized someone had crept up behind me and opened the railing. One second I was standing facing Cayden, the next I was plummeting through the air, headed for the water. I was vaguely aware of the screams and laughter as I fell. I pinwheeled my arms and tried to twist around so I wouldn't hit at a bad angle. It didn't help much. My head went in first, which gave me an instant, painful, nasal brain-rinse. It took more than a few seconds for me to get oriented and back to the surface. I wasn't hurt, but I was angry. I looked up to the boat to see a few dozen of Cayden's obnoxious friends hanging over the railing looking down at me, laughing.

"Come on!" Sydney yelled. She had already made it down to the lower deck and was reaching out to me through the railing to help me back on board.

"Are you all right?" she asked.

I hated that question.

"Where is he?" I demanded.

We both looked around to see Cayden hurrying for the stern of the boat.

"Stop him!" I shouted to anybody who would listen.

Nobody did. Sydney and I ran after him, but we were too late. Waiting in the water near the stern was a Zodiac boat. It was all part of his grand plan for a big exit. He jumped into the inflatable raft and pushed away from the *Nellie Bell* just as we arrived. He gave us a cocky salute as the boat pilot hit the throttle on the outboard engine and sped away.

"He's going for the plane," Sydney said.

I ran for the Jet Ski. It was our last hope to stop him. Once he got on that plane, there would be nothing we could do. I pushed my way through the mass of people, knocking over a few as I went. It wasn't as crowded belowdecks, so I made it to the Jet Ski quickly. Sydney was right behind me.

"Cast off!" she commanded as she leaped onto the craft, straddling the seat.

I unwrapped the line as Sydney powered up the engine. We had one chance. The Zodiac wasn't fast. The Jet Ski was. We had a shot at catching him on the water and Sydney knew it. I jumped on the seat behind her and barely had time to grab her waist when she hit the throttle. We shot forward, headed toward the bow of the *Nellie Bell* and a race to the floating plane.

"We'll get him," she said with confidence.

We cleared the bow and saw the Zodiac motoring toward the seaplane. Cayden was crouched in the stern, watching for us.

"Cut him off," I said.

Sydney pushed the Jet Ski faster. We were going to catch him. I was sure of it.

I was wrong.

I heard it before I saw it. It was the low rumble of a powerful engine. It was a new sound. At first I thought it was the *Nellie Bell*.

It wasn't.

We were closing in on the Zodiac. I envisioned leaping off the Jet Ski and jumping into the inflatable raft to grab Cayden and force him to confess. That was my plan, anyway.

"What is that sound?" Sydney asked, her eyes focused on the Zodiac.

The deep rumble grew louder. It wasn't the *Nellie Bell*. I turned around to see the white hull of a monstrous cigarette boat bearing down on us at full throttle.

Reilly was at the wheel.

Standing next to him was a copilot.

Gravedigger.

20

"Go! Go! Get out of here!" I screamed.

"No! We've almost got him!" Sydney yelled back.

"Forget him!"

Sydney didn't know what was happening. She hadn't been attacked by Cayden's father.

"He's going to run us down!" I shouted. "Move!"

The cigarette boat charged closer.

Sydney froze. Things were happening too quickly for her to comprehend. Instead of speeding up she took her hands off the throttle. The Jet Ski lurched to a stop. Her eyes were wide and focused on the boat. I guess you'd call it a deer in the headlights. We were seconds away from being run down by a 1,000-horsepower monster. There wasn't time to convince her that we were about to be shredded. I lunged forward, my arms wrapping around either side of her, and grabbed the handlebars myself. I cranked the throttle and spun the Jet Ski hard to the right. We launched just as the behemoth boat cut across our stern. The surge from its wake propelled us forward.

I stood behind Sydney, leaning over her shoulder, riding the wave and pushing the craft as fast as it could go. A quick look back showed me that Reilly was making a wide turn to come around and take another shot at us. There was no way we could outrun that big boat. Our best hope was to outmaneuver it.

"Who the hell is that?" Sydney screamed.

"Turn off the light," I ordered.

"What? No, that's dangerous!" she shouted back.

I ignored her. Sydney wasn't an idiot. It only took her a second to realize what a dumb comment that was. She reached forward and killed the running light.

"We'll head toward shore," I said. "Maybe we can lose it in the shallows."

I turned the Jet Ski toward the closest shore. We were in a spot on the lake where there were no cabins or camps. The shore was dark and thick with foliage. I felt sure we could hide there, that is, if we could get there before Reilly got us.

"It's an illusion, right?" Sydney said. "Like the blood. It's not really there."

I glanced back. The speedboat was coming up fast.

"It's real," I said. "It's Cayden's father. That's the boat Cayden used to run down Cooper."

I had my chin resting on Sydney's shoulder. She made no attempt to take control of the Jet Ski.

"Why is he coming after us?" she asked, confused.

"How many people do you see on that boat?" I asked.

Sydney ducked under my arm and looked back. "Two."

Her answer actually came as a relief.

"That means you see him," I said.

"Who?"

"Gravedigger. He's somehow possessed Reilly. Maybe he's scaring him into coming after me. Or maybe Reilly just wants to protect his son. Either way Reilly wants me dead. He tried to strangle me before."

"And you didn't tell me that because . . . ?"

"Because there was already too much to tell you."

"This can't be happening," Sydney muttered, and looked behind us again.

We were several hundred yards from the safety of the shallow water. Though we were moving fast, it wasn't fast enough to get there before the cigarette boat would catch us.

"We won't make it," Sydney said. Her cool had returned. "We gotta do something."

She put her hands back on the handlebars, but I wasn't ready to give up control.

"It's okay," she said calmly. "I got it."

"This is real, Sydney," I warned. "It's no illusion. They want to kill us."

"I get it," she said. I believed her. Sydney was Sydney again. She was cool, even though the boat from hell was gaining fast. "Let go, Marsh."

I did. Reluctantly. Sydney was back in command.

The cigarette boat was nearly on us. If we maintained our speed for only a few seconds more, the boat would hit and shatter the Jet Ski . . . along with us.

"Hang on," Sydney cautioned.

She turned hard to the right without letting up on the throttle. The Jet Ski slid into the turn, moving sideways across the water's surface. We both leaned hard to the left to counterbalance the turn. For a second I thought we might flip, but the Jet Ski kept moving. It wasn't as sharp a turn as I would have liked, but it was tighter than what the cigarette boat could do. I looked back to see Reilly make the same turn, but his speed forced him to make a much wider circle.

"We're going to cross the wake!" she yelled.

I knew enough to lift my butt slightly off the seat and keep my knees soft to handle the shock. It was rocky. We bounced over the small sharp waves that had been created by the speedboat, our engine whining each time we rose up out of the water. With each wave we got air, then crashed back down. It was teeth-rattling. Once we had done a three-sixty, Sydney accelerated toward shore. I looked back to see that the cigarette boat was making the same circle, though much wider. Sydney's maneuver bought us enough time to reach the shallows.

"Nice," I said.

"What do you mean Reilly's possessed?" Sydney asked. "You mean like *Invasion of the Body Snatchers* or something?"

I was impressed that Sydney knew that reference. Maybe there was a little bit more geek to her than she let on.

"No," I answered. "It's more like Gravedigger is frightening people into doing things. Like George O. committing suicide. Sheriff Vrtiak went nuts too."

"My god," Sydney whispered as she glanced quickly back over her shoulder. "We can't outrun that boat . . ."

"Go close to shore," I instructed. "Find a dark spot and kill the engine."

Sydney didn't question me. She drove us to within ten yards of the shore and brought us to a stop. We drifted under the branches of a tree that hung out over the water. Once the Jet Ski's engines were quiet, all I could hear was the roar of the cigarette boat. It was coming up fast.

"How shallow can that boat go?" she asked.

"I don't know, but he'd have to be crazy to speed that fast close to shore." As soon as I said that, I realized what a dumb comment it was. Reilly *was* crazy, thanks to whatever Gravedigger was doing to him. The guy was a jerk, but I didn't believe he was a killer. Not normally, anyway. But this was all about Gravedigger.

"He's still coming," Sydney whispered, as if her words might carry over the water to Reilly.

"Get ready to start up," I said. "If he sees us, we'll beach it and hit the woods."

The small stretch of rocky beach led to thick forest. I didn't know which was worse, dueling Reilly in his killer boat on the lake, or facing Gravedigger in the middle of a dark, desolate forest.

The cigarette boat was headed directly toward us.

"Does he see us?" Sydney asked.

I didn't answer. I didn't know. I wanted to wait as long as possible before abandoning ship.

The cigarette boat kept coming, but it slowed. Reilly made a course correction and turned left until he was traveling parallel to the shore.

"He's searching," Sydney whispered. "He doesn't know where we are."

The cigarette boat slowed even further. Reilly was definitely hunting for us. Alone. Gravedigger wasn't next to him.

"We'll wait a few minutes, then head back for the party boat," I whispered.

Reilly drove his boat farther away, going south toward town.

"What if he circles back?" Sydney asked.

"Then we'll—"

I stopped talking.

"Did you feel that?" I asked.

"No, what?" Sydney replied.

"I don't know. It was a wave or something."

"It's not the wake from the cigarette boat," Sydney said. "That hasn't hit yet."

"There!" I exclaimed in a hoarse whisper. "You had to feel that."

Sydney tensed up. She felt it too. "It's like . . . like . . . something swam underneath us."

The Jet Ski rocked on the water, and it wasn't from the oncoming wake.

"There's something down there," she said in a frightened whisper. "It must be a fish."

I shook my head. "There's no fish in this lake that's big enough to do that."

The Jet Ski was bumped from underneath. Sydney yelped. I looked ahead to see the cigarette boat moving further away from us.

Where was Gravedigger?

I heard something slap the water behind us. Sydney and I both turned to look in time to see the rings of a big ripple that was growing larger.

"I don't want to know what made that," I said.

"Let's go, Marsh," Sydney whined.

I looked at the cigarette boat. It was still too close. If we started the engine, Reilly would hear it.

"It could be a turtle," I whispered. "Or . . . or . . . maybe there really is some freak big fish. Every lake has one of those, right? You know, the big old bass that everybody has stories about and—"

Sydney gasped. Not five feet from the bow of the Jet Ski, a dark, reptilian shape lifted out of the water, then sunk down and disappeared. For that brief moment the dark scales on its back glistened in the moonlight, and then it was gone. The thing was moving fast. There was no way to tell how long it was, or how wide, or what kind of creature it was, but there was no question about its size. It was big.

"That's not normal," Sydney cried.

The water bubbled behind us. We looked toward the stern to see the scaly back rise up once more.

"Look!" Sydney shouted, pointing forward.

Another black, scaly spine broke the surface. Or maybe it was part of the same creature.

"It's circling us," I said, unbelieving.

"Is this an illusion?" Sydney whimpered.

"Who cares? Let's get the hell out of here."

Sydney didn't need convincing. She fired the engine and twisted the throttle just as the creature rose up directly in front of us. I caught a quick glimpse of a black eye the size of a tennis ball. It was sunken into a scaly reptilian head that could have been a snake or an alligator or the Loch Freakin' Ness Monster for all I cared. The head had barely broken the surface when the Jet Ski hit it and skimmed over the top. I felt the back of the Jet Ski kick up as the creature rose out of the water. For a second I thought we'd do an end-o and somersault forward, Jet Ski and all. Luckily, we had gotten too far ahead for that to happen and instead came crashing back down to the water as the head of the creature continued to rise. I looked back to see a dark, dragonlike head lift out of the water and open its mouth to reveal an impossible number of sharp teeth set into alligator jaws.

My brain told me it was an illusion. There was nothing like that in Thistledown Lake. There was nothing like that anywhere. That was small consolation. We had both nearly been killed by an illusion before.

"What is it?" Sydney called back while keeping her eyes forward.

"Nothing," I lied. "It's nothing."

I watched as the giant reptile splashed back down into the water and twisted its snakelike body our way.

"But don't slow down," I added.

Looking to my right, I saw exactly what I feared. Reilly

had heard us power up and was coming around to chase us. He was a couple hundred yards away, but the speedboat could cover that distance in seconds. We were headed toward the party boat, but it was at least a half a mile away. Behind us I saw the dark shadow of the reptile sliding through the water, right on our tail. I didn't think our situation could get any worse.

I was wrong.

Sydney was focused on the *Nellie Bell*, pushing the Jet Ski to move as fast as possible. "Do you hear that?" she asked.

I listened. It sounded like another engine.

"Maybe it's the police," I said hopefully.

I looked to our left and saw another cigarette boat closing in on us. It wasn't the police. It was an exact duplicate of Reilly's boat and we were seconds from crashing bows.

"Look out!" I shouted.

Sydney made a quick glance left and reacted instantly, throttling back. The Jet Ski slowed as the big boat crossed our bow, barely missing us. At the controls of this new threat was Gravedigger. Mystery solved. He turned and smiled at me as he flashed past.

"Go!" I shouted.

Sydney throttled up and continued our dash back to civilization.

"Where did that come from?" she screamed.

Before I could answer, I saw another flash of white headed our way. A third boat was speeding toward us from the right.

"Two o'clock!" I shouted.

"What?" Sydney shot back.

"Turn!" I commanded, grabbed the right handlebar, and yanked it.

The Jet Ski made a sharp turn to the right as the third boat flashed by on our left. This new threat was identical to

the other two boats. At the wheel was Gravedigger. Again. There were three boats in the water, all hunting us down. Gravedigger was at the controls of two of them. Who knew how many more would show up?

"Are they real?" Sydney asked, breathless.

I looked ahead. Another boat was bearing down on us, head on.

"That one is!" I yelled.

It was Reilly's boat. The other two had maneuvered us into a collision course. Sydney turned hard to the left, making a sweeping turn. Too soon. Reilly's boat hadn't arrived yet. Instead of letting it pass behind us, we were about to collide.

But Reilly didn't react fast enough. He had too much speed to make the slight adjustment that would have killed us. Instead he crossed our bow.

The water was churning from the wake of three huge boats. The little Jet Ski bounced like a toy in a turbulent ocean. Sydney hit the throttle, the engine whined, we lurched forward . . . directly toward the open mouth of the reptilian monster that had been shadowing us. The beast rose out of the water, its mouth gaping wide. Sydney screamed but stayed focused and turned hard to her right . . . to see that the first Gravedigger boat had made a huge, looping circle to make another run at us.

"Keep turning!" I screamed.

Sydney kept the Jet Ski in a tight right turn. The maneuverability of that little craft was keeping us alive. The Gravedigger boat rocketed by on our left, kicking up a wake that buffeted us so hard, I feared we would capsize.

"Now left!" I screamed. "Hard!"

Sydney reversed the turn and brought us around so we were once again headed toward the party boat.

"What is that?" Sydney yelled, looking ahead.

I didn't want to know if it was another impossible villain headed our way. But of course, I had to. Far ahead, near the party boat, I saw a flashing red light. It was a rescue craft.

"The police!" I shouted. "Go, go, go!"

Sydney gunned the engine and set course for the party boat and help. The moment of relief didn't last. I looked back to see all three boats were circling around to make another run at us. The serpent was nowhere in sight. A quick calculation made me realize that no matter what we did, at least one of the cigarette boats would reach us before we got to the police. All we could do was move as quickly as the Jet Ski could take us.

"Fast is good," I cautioned.

"We're wide open," Sydney shot back.

We were moving closer to the party boat, but not fast enough. The cigarette boats were closing in on us from three different angles. There would be no maneuvering out of danger this time. Whichever way we turned, we'd end up right in the path of one of the boats.

"What do I do?" Sydney asked, her voice finally showing the strain.

"I don't know."

The boats were converging. All three looked to be at full throttle with plumes of white spray flying from behind. We had no hope of outrunning them.

"The other two boats," Sydney said. "Do you believe they're illusions?"

"Does it matter?" I yelled back.

"Yes! If they're not real, I mean physically real, all they can do is make us do something dumb. Like the blood in the boathouse."

"You don't think the other two boats can hurt us?" I asked.

"Not unless we do something stupid, like turning into Reilly's boat to get away from them."

It made sense. Was anything we had seen real? Or were they just shadows that were there to push us toward danger? If so, there was no giant lake serpent ready to eat us and Gravedigger wasn't behind the wheel of two different boats. That left only one very dangerous guy trying to run us down.

Reilly.

I glanced around to see the three boats converging. Left, right, and from behind. I had a quick hope that somehow they would all slam into one another, but if the illusion theory was correct, that wasn't going to happen.

"We have nowhere to go," Sydney cautioned.

I heard the far-off sound of an amplified voice. The roar of the four engines made it impossible to understand what was being said, but it had to be a warning from the police. I didn't think for a second that it would help. Reilly's boat had taken the lead. We couldn't outrun it.

"Seaver? What do we do?" Sydney asked on the verge of panic.

Reilly was nearly on us.

"Turn! Now! Do it!" I screamed.

Sydney made a sharp left, turning us square into the path of a Gravedigger boat. Reilly flashed by behind us, but I barely noticed. We were on a collision course. I hugged Sydney hard around the waist and tensed up, as if that would have helped in a head-on collision. The boat loomed over us . . .

. . . and we passed right through. It was like moving through a cold cloud of vapor.

"Yeah!" Sydney shouted.

"Head for the party boat!" I screamed.

We had won a battle, but the war wasn't done. Reilly was still after us. Sydney turned hard to the right and accelerated toward the *Nellie Bell*. We were still at least a quarter of a mile away . . . and in trouble. Reilly had come around and was now lining himself up for another run at us. We were in open water with nowhere to hide. Sydney slowed. Reilly adjusted. We sped up. Reilly adjusted back.

He had us.

"What do I do?" Sydney cried.

I felt something move near my stomach. It was a twitch, as if somebody had poked me. Whatever it was, wasn't natural. My hand went to my belt instinctively and felt something in the pocket of my hoodie. I knew instantly what it was, though I had no idea how it had moved on its own to poke me. That was a question for another time. I reached into my pocket and grabbed it.

"The flare gun," I said.

"Use it!" she screamed back without hesitation.

I had completely forgotten about the orange pistol that I had shoved into my pocket at the marina. It was a weapon, sort of. I had never fired any kind of gun before, let alone at another person. I wasn't sure if I could do it.

"Shoot it in front of him!" Sydney yelled. "It might throw him off."

"He's gotta be closer," I said. "This thing isn't that accurate."

I had only one shot. If I fired too soon, there was no chance of getting the flare anywhere near him. If I waited too long, we'd crash.

"Keep it steady," I said.

I held the pistol in my right hand with my arm out straight. With my left hand I grabbed my right wrist to steady the gun. The Jet Ski bounced every time we hit a ripple. No matter how good my aim was, if we bounced at the wrong time, I'd end up firing the flare into the water. Or the sky. We were going to have to get very lucky for it to work.

"Now, Marsh!" Sydney yelled.

I didn't fire. I wanted Reilly closer. Both crafts were racing toward the same imaginary point. If we both reached it, we'd be dead. Reilly's boat probably wouldn't feel more than a bump . . . just like when Cayden destroyed Cooper's boat.

"Turn on your lights," I said. "The police should see this."

Sydney toggled the light switch, and the running lights of the Jet Ski flared to life, along with the headlight.

We were close enough that I could see inside Reilly's boat. He was alone. Gravedigger was going to let him finish the job himself.

"Shoot him!" Sydney bellowed.

"Not yet . . . ," I said while taking careful aim. I focused on a spot out in front of the cigarette boat. I had to try and calculate the speed of the flare and how fast the boat was going so that it would pass as close to Reilly as possible. It was guesswork at best.

"Marsh!" Sydney screamed. "Shoot!"

We were seconds away from a collision.

I squeezed the trigger and felt the kick from the charge as the flare rocketed from the barrel. With a sharp crack and the smell of burning chemicals, the flare lit up the water. I knew instantly that I had miscalculated. The burning missile sped on a dead-straight line, trailing smoke, on a course that would take it behind Reilly. I had blown our one and only chance.

I want to say that what happened next was impossible, but after all we had been through, I have to reset my ideas of what's possible. The flare was moving in the wrong direction but not for long. The burning projectile made a sharp course correction. I saw the trail of smoke it left behind. It shot straight on its natural course, then suddenly took a left-hand turn and curved toward Reilly. The flare seemed to speed up as it headed directly for the guy. It flashed no more than a foot in front of his face, and when it passed him, it lit up even brighter and exploded like a fireworks display. That wasn't how flares worked, but I wasn't about to complain.

Reilly reacted by throwing his arms up to block his eyes. He recoiled from the light and fell back into the boat. Nobody was at the controls. The boat swerved to its right, away from the line that would have crashed it into us.

"Turn right!" I shouted.

Sydney turned hard, but it wasn't enough. The Jet Ski clipped the back end of the cigarette boat and spun our craft around. We were both nearly thrown into the water but managed to hang on. The cigarette boat charged on with nobody at the wheel. Sydney brought the Jet Ski around so we could see what happened next.

"Oh my god," she whispered.

We were much closer to the party boat than I thought. Kids lined the railings, watching the drama play out. The boat with the flashing lights could now be seen for what it was. A fire rescue boat. It was tied up to the party boat at the same spot where we had tied up the Jet Ski.

The cigarette boat was out of control. Reilly struggled to get to his feet, but his hands were over his eyes. He had no chance of taking back control of the speeding craft. At least not before it was too late. The boat was still moving at full throttle, which for that beast meant close to a hundred miles per hour. At that speed, hitting even a small rock would be disaster.

It was headed for something much bigger than that.

The seaplane that was waiting to fly Cayden away in a dramatic, ego-driven show was bobbing lazily on the lake . . . directly in the path of the charging speedboat. We were close enough to see people frantically diving off. I wondered if Cayden was one of them. Reilly had no idea of what was happening, until the last second. He stood up, facing us. He must have sensed the danger because he suddenly turned forward. He dove for the controls, which meant he saw his fate . . . too late. The cigarette boat slammed square into the floating plane. There was the sound of screaming metal. At least, that was what I thought was screaming. That was followed by a monstrous explosion that had to have been the gas tank of the plane. The cigarette boat blew up into the air in flames. A moment later, its own gas tank caught the flame and another eruption followed. Sydney and I had to duck as flaming bits of boat and plane and I-didn't-want-to-know-what-else flew past us, sizzling as they hit the water.

The hulk of the burning boat splashed back down into the water, its engines still whining. There was nothing left of the seaplane but burning debris on the water. It only lasted a moment, but as the ball of flame erupted from the doomed boat, I saw the giant shimmering face of a smiling demon peering out of the inferno.

Gravedigger had claimed another victim.

21

I don't know why they call funerals a "celebration of life." When my mother died, nobody felt much like celebrating. It all happened so fast that it was hard to get my head around it, let alone accept that I'd never see her again. My father was in even worse shape. To everybody else he looked like a guy who was being strong and doing his best to make sure everybody else was okay, but I knew better. At night, when each day's painful festivities were over, I heard him crying in his room. It tore my heart out. I, on the other hand, didn't cry. Not even when I was by myself. I think I was in denial. The two of us went along, doing our best not to talk about how we really felt.

The one person who didn't treat me like a crystal glass that would break if you breathed on me was Cooper. We were all back at our house after the funeral, trying to talk about anything but Mom. Relatives and neighbors were everywhere, mostly eating food they had brought themselves. Every once in a while an older lady or some guy would walk by and give me a sad nod. They were being nice, but they didn't know what to say.

I was sitting alone in the living room when Cooper plopped down on the couch next to me.

"Well," he said. "This sucks."

That said it all. It sucked on so many levels, I couldn't begin to count them. I laughed. It felt good. I still didn't feel like celebrating, but some of the pressure had been relieved.

"You want to get outta here?" Coop asked.

"Absolutely" was my answer.

The two of us snuck out the back of my house and went for a walk in the neighborhood. There was no destination—it was just about getting away from the intensity.

"Your mom was pretty cool," he said.

I shrugged. I knew.

"She gave me this for my birthday last year," he said as he pulled a framed photo out of his pack. I recognized it immediately. It was one that Mom had taken in Africa when she was on assignment there. It was a shot of a prehistoric-looking guy from some primitive tribe. He looked like he was a hundred years old. His face was full of deep lines that Mom had caught perfectly by getting the sun to hit them at an angle that made them look bottomless. In his arms was a little girl, probably a year old. She was beautiful. Her unlined face was a real contrast to the face of the ancient-looking guy. What made the picture was that they both wore the exact same beaded necklace and colorful wrap. It was a stunning picture that was published in National Geographic.

"She gave you this?" I asked, a little surprised.

"Yeah. I was kind of hoping for Madden NFL."

I laughed.

Coop continued, "I saw it in the magazine and told her I thought it was really cool. She asked me why. I had to think about it, but told her it was because it showed the two ends of life. She got that, but said it wasn't what she saw."

"What did she see?" I asked.

"Eternity."

"Uh . . . what?"

"Yeah, I didn't get it either. She said that the beads and the clothes showed that the old guy was passing down a piece of himself to the little girl. She said that when he died, and to me it looked like he might not make it to the end of the day, the girl would still have his spirit. So even after the guy died, he wouldn't really be gone. Then someday the girl would pass down a piece of herself to somebody else and on and on. You know, eternity. It was all a little cosmic for me, but I liked the picture. When my birthday came around, your mom made a print for me."

He held out the framed photo for me to look at. Cooper's story made me appreciate her photos in a new way. I realized that even though it was a photo meant for everybody, it was her vision. I was seeing something exactly the way she had seen it. Literally. It was like looking through her eyes.

Cooper said, "I think we all get stuff from everybody else. Some of it's good, some isn't so hot. We're all just pinballs bouncing off each other. People may leave, but the stuff we get from them stays. Which means they never really leave. Not entirely. You're pretty lucky. Your mom left you some pretty good stuff."

That's when I cried.

Cooper didn't feel all sorry for me either. What he did was take the photo back. "But this one is mine, Ralph," he said. "You got plenty."

Once again, Cooper made me laugh.

•   •   •

Mr. Reilly was dead.

Nobody blamed Sydney or me for shooting the flare at him. There were hundreds of witnesses who watched in horror as Mr. Reilly did his best to chase us down on the lake. There was no question that I had fired the flare in self-defense. They all knew we were seconds from disaster ourselves. It had played out right in front of them. What they didn't see were any other boats on the lake, or a dark spirit riding shotgun next to Reilly, or a sea serpent rising up to eat us. Those visions were for Sydney and me alone. All they saw was a deranged guy trying to run us down . . . and the horrific end to his life.

Reilly's death was a tragedy, but I don't regret what we did. If I hadn't fired the flare, it would be Sydney and I who would be gone. There was no question—Reilly would have killed us. But was it his fault? He was trying to protect his son, but I didn't believe for a second he'd go that far to do it. No, there were forces beyond his control that put him behind the wheel of that boat. It wasn't Reilly who was after us. It was Gravedigger.

Though Reilly paid the price.

Then there was Cayden. When the cigarette boat showed up, he went back to the *Nellie Bell* and was nowhere near the plane when it exploded. As much as I hated the guy, I knew what he was going through. His father was taken away from him suddenly and with violence. I felt bad for him, but his story wasn't complete. There were questions that had to be answered. Cooper was still out there.

The captain of the *Nellie Bell* brought the party boat back to the marina, where all the stunned kids were transferred to buses and brought back to camp. Waiting at the marina for them was a handful of State Troopers, along with Britt. I found out afterward that Britt hadn't been at the marina earlier because when she tried to call the State

Police, the phone didn't work . . . probably thanks to Grave-digger. Britt was smart. She drove to the firehouse to tell them about the cigarette boat and our theory that it had run down Cooper's boat. The fire rescue team responded by calling in the State Police and taking their own boat out to the *Nellie Bell* to try and stop Cayden from leaving.

Instead of a simple pickup, they were treated to a fiery disaster.

Sydney and I got a ride back to the marina with the firefighters. They tied up the Jet Ski to their boat and towed it behind us. Sydney and I sat huddled together in the back, wrapped together in a blanket. Once the firefighters were confident that we weren't hurt, they didn't ask us another question for the entire trip back to town. I guess they figured it was best to leave that up to the police.

When we landed, Sydney and I were put into a State Trooper's car and driven thirty miles to their closest station. We were told that Mr. and Mrs. Foley would meet us there. Sydney and I didn't say much to each other. I can't speak for her, but I was trying to process all that had happened. There were forces at work that I couldn't begin to understand or explain. I think the only thing that kept me focused was the fact that there was still a very real, very understandable problem to deal with.

We had to find Cooper. My hope was that with Cayden in the hands of the authorities, we'd get some answers and a real search could begin. I had to hang on to that fragile silver lining.

When we arrived at the State Police barracks, the Foleys were there waiting in the parking lot. They looked about as bad as I felt. When Sydney saw them, she stiffened. There was a lot of tension in that family. Sydney stood there like she didn't know what to do.

Her mom took one look at her and burst into tears.

"Sweetheart, are you all right?" she cried as she ran to her daughter with her arms open to hug her. She wrapped her arms around Sydney, holding her tight. Sydney was hesitant at first, but then she hugged her mom back. Both were crying.

"I'm okay, Mom," she said.

Mr. Foley came over and gave his daughter a kiss on top of her head. If there is anything positive I can find about that night, it was that moment. Sydney and her parents may have had issues, but they were still a family.

"How are you doing, Marsh?" Mr. Foley said. (At least he didn't ask if I was all right. Score one for Mr. Foley.)

"I'm okay," I answered.

We were brought inside and gathered in a lounge, where Sydney and I were given dry coveralls and hot chocolate. It was there that I explained to everyone, including the State Police, what Britt and I feared had happened to Cooper. I explained about the broken pieces of dinghy with the *Galileo* markings. I told them how Cooper had planned to go out on the lake with Britt to look at the stars . . . something we always did with the running lights turned off, like idiots. I told them about the key that George O. had given me that led us on a trail to find the broken piece of boat; Cooper's shoes in the boathouse; and the damage to Reilly's cigarette boat. I also told them about how Mr. Reilly had attacked me on the dock after admitting his son had done something wrong. I thought it would help to explain why he was chasing us down with the cigarette boat.

What I avoided was any mention of visions and sea serpents and drive-in movie previews. I didn't want to cloud the waters. There were plenty of real, concrete clues that would lead us to the truth about what had happened to Cooper.

Sydney sat between her parents, holding her mom's hand. She added a few comments, confirming about Cooper's shoes in the boathouse and how we found the piece of the dinghy at George O.'s place.

There were three State Troopers there, but only one spoke. His name was Captain Hoffkins.

"So you broke into George O.'s house?" he asked.

"No," I said quickly. "He gave me the key. I think he wanted me to go there and find the piece of the boat."

"How would George O. know about your friendship with Cooper?" Hoffkins asked.

Sydney answered for me. "That guy knows everything about everybody. You can't sneeze around here without George O. knowing it. At least that's what everybody says about him. Right?"

Hoffkins nodded as he took notes. That answer seemed to satisfy him.

"How's Sheriff Vrtiak?" I asked.

Hoffkins frowned. "It's not for me to say."

"Hey, I was nearly killed in that car wreck," I shot back. "I deserve something."

Hoffkins hesitated, then said, "I don't know what's wrong with him. Physically he's fine. Just a couple of bruises. But the guy has gone off the deep end. I've never seen anything like it."

"My god," Mrs. Foley said with a gasp.

I told them how Vrtiak had picked me up for having broken into George O.'s house, but then he started acting all crazy and lost control of the car. I didn't tell them about how we were run off the road by a ghost car driven by George O.

"You're both lucky to be alive," Hoffkins said.

He didn't challenge my story. Any of it. Vrtiak's condition must have been so bad that it made perfect sense. He may not have been dead, but it was looking as if another victim had fallen to Gravedigger.

"Captain Hoffkins," Mr. Foley said. "I've been trying to get an organized search started for my son for days now. I believe we now know where to start."

Captain Hoffkins had been writing on a clipboard. He took out a sheet of paper that was beneath the one he had been taking notes on and did a quick read. The Foleys and I exchanged nervous looks.

"Mr. and Mrs. Foley," Hoffkins began in a low voice. "I'm afraid to say that it's looking like things happened exactly as these kids have said. The young lady from the marina verified the damage to the Reillys' boat."

"Finally!" I shouted.

I looked to Mr. and Mrs. Foley, expecting to see them just as relieved. If anything, they looked sicker. I was being an idiot. They were hearing confirmation that their son had been run over by a speedboat. To me it was old news. To them it was a devastating shock.

Hoffkins continued, "Cayden Reilly has confessed. He did run over a fishing boat the night your son disappeared."

Mrs. Foley broke out in tears. Sydney hugged her, but she didn't look any better than her mom.

Mr. Foley turned white before my eyes. "And he left Cooper out there to die."

"We don't know that!" I shouted. "I mean, we don't know that he's dead. Did Cayden say where it happened?"

Hoffkins checked the sheet. "Emerald Cove. About two miles north of town."

"Perfect. That's where we start to search. Right, Captain?"

Hoffkins looked glum.

"You *are* going to search now, right?" I yelled.

"Of course," he said. "But we can't begin until daylight."

"Right. Makes sense," I said, my mind racing. "What are you bringing in? A helicopter? What about tracking dogs? We can get Coop's clothes for a scent. Right?"

Nobody seemed to be as excited about this news as I was. Not even the Foleys. I didn't understand.

"What's wrong? We've been looking for this break for days. We're going to find him."

"Marshall," Captain Hoffkins said. "The search will begin at daybreak, I promise you that. Mr. and Mrs. Foley, we will find your son. However . . ."

He didn't finish the sentence. He didn't have to. Mr. and Mrs. Foley looked pained. Sydney couldn't open her eyes. I knew what they were all thinking.

"He's out there," I said. "Alive."

"We'll find him" was all Hoffkins said.

Mr. Foley drove us all back to the cabin. There was nothing to do until the next morning. The gathering point for the search would be the Thistledown firehouse. Search teams would be dispatched from there. It was past midnight. Once the adrenaline wore off, I realized how exhausted I was. I figured the best thing to do was sleep for a few hours and get ready for a long day.

Mr. and Mrs. Foley gave me a hug and went right to bed. I saw defeat in the way they spoke and moved. I wanted to tell them that I knew Cooper was alive because he was calling out to me, but it would only have made it worse.

Before knocking off I called Dad to tell him what was going on. I didn't go into a huge amount of detail, or mention anything about Gravedigger or supernatural doings, but I did tell him about Cooper's accident and the destruction of Reilly's cigarette boat. Dad was stunned, obviously. He was ready to charter a plane and fly right home, but I told him there was nothing he could do and to stay on the flight he had scheduled. It was good to talk to him. It would be even better when he got back.

When I got off the phone, I looked out to the porch to see Sydney sitting alone. I sat down next to her and for the longest time the two of us just looked out onto the lake.

"Coop would be proud of you," she finally said.

"Are you kidding? He's gonna owe me. Big-time."

Sydney smiled, though she looked horrible. Her shoulders were hunched over, her eyes red.

"You don't believe he's alive," I said.

Sydney wiped her eyes. "You saw the power of that speedboat. If that thing hit us, we wouldn't be here. How can you possibly believe Cooper survived that?"

"Because he's been calling out to me for help," I shot back quickly, then lowered my voice. I didn't want the Foleys to hear.

"That makes no sense, Marsh."

"Like anything else has?"

Sydney argued, "But it's been four days—"

"I don't care if it's been four months. He's been with us every step of the way, Sydney. He's been with *me*! He wants us to find him. How else do you explain what's been happening?"

Sydney thought for a moment, then said, "I agree with you. I believe. He *has* been helping us. He's been protecting us too. I saw what happened with that flare you shot. It should have missed Reilly by a mile."

I nodded. I thought the same thing.

"But something more is going on here, Marsh. Something wrong. It can't just be about a kid who ran down my brother in a big-ass boat. That's way too easy."

"I know," I said softly.

Sydney took a breath. There was something on her mind and I wasn't sure I wanted to hear what it was.

"What if we've been looking at this through the wrong end of the telescope?" she said. "We've been fixated on finding Cooper, obviously, but he isn't the only victim here. Reilly's dead. George O. is dead. Vrtiak is out of his mind and Mikey Russo isn't far behind. What's the one thing they all have in common?"

"Gravedigger."

"No," Sydney said gravely. "You."

"Me? I didn't try to hurt any of those people!"

"No, but Gravedigger did. And you created Gravedigger."

I stood up and paced nervously. "No, no way. I didn't conjure a monster that could do those things. He's a cartoon. A drawing."

"But he came out of your head and that's the image everybody is seeing. There's no such person, except in your imagination."

"So you think I somehow created an avenging spirit who is going around scaring people to death? It's all my fault?"

"It's not your fault. You're in as much danger as anybody else. But whatever force is at work here, you're the center of it."

I wanted to tell her she was wrong. I couldn't.

Sydney added, "I don't think finding Cooper is going to end this. He may just be another piece in the puzzle. You're a good friend, Marsh. The best. But you're going to have to start worrying about yourself."

I searched for a comeback . . . something that would prove her theory wrong. I came up empty. Sydney stood up and gave me a hug. It was the kindest gesture she ever made toward me.

"I'm going to try to sleep," she said. "You want to share the couch again?"

"No. Go to bed. I'll be fine."

"I don't think you'll be fine. What if—"

"Nothing's going to happen."

"You don't know that," she said.

"Yeah, I think I do." I couldn't explain why, but I felt as if a line had been crossed. Knowing the truth about Cooper's accident had somehow defused things. At least for the time being.

I added, "Believe me, if anything strange starts, I'll scream."

She squeezed me tighter and said, "Whatever happens tomorrow, and beyond, I want to help you. I'm in this too." With that she left me and went upstairs to bed.

I didn't want to be anywhere near the lake, so I went inside and lay down on the living room couch with my eyes wide open. No chance I was going to sleep, not after everything Sydney had said.

Ever since I had gotten to the lake, I had been focused on finding Cooper. Of course that was important, but it was also a good excuse for me to avoid dealing with the other disturbing problem. I was being haunted. There was no other way to say it. Something was coming after me. Was it a spirit? A demon? The boogeyman? Whatever it was, it had the power to make people see things that weren't really there. There *was* no Gravedigger. He was just another illusion. But many people saw it. George O. Sydney. Even Sheriff Vrtiak and Reilly. They weren't faced by an image that was special to them—they saw Gravedigger, my creation. Sydney was right. This was about me. For reasons I couldn't begin to understand, I was being hunted by a powerful spirit. Everybody else just so happened to be in the way.

Including Cooper.

I felt a breeze. An impossible breeze. I'd felt it many times before. It moved over my face and through the room. I wasn't scared. There was nothing sinister about it. I heard something fall with a sharp slap that made me sit up with a start. At the far end of the couch was a table with a lamp and a few framed pictures. One of the pictures had fallen over. Only one. The breeze had been selective. I crawled to the end of the couch and reached for it. The other pictures were family shots of the Foleys when the kids were little. There was one each of Cooper and Sydney, and one with all four. I lifted up the one that had fallen . . . and my throat clutched.

That was the moment. That's when I knew.

It was a familiar picture. I didn't know why I hadn't noticed it before. It was the photo that my mother had given to Cooper for his birthday . . . the photo of the ancient African man and the baby. Eternity. Seeing it made me realize I had been kidding myself. I wanted there to be a happy ending and so I created a scenario where that was possible . . . even though logic had been screaming at me to face the truth. I couldn't begin to understand why everything had been happening, but I could no longer deny the fact that there were spirits at work. They surrounded us. They surrounded me. They could appear at my house, in a long-abandoned gym . . . or in a locked boathouse. Basically, anywhere.

Whether it was one spirit or many, I was a target. The mystery of why they were after me had yet to be solved, but there was one thing I felt certain of: Not all of them were bad. There was one spirit who was looking out for me, and there was only one possible way that could be.

A moment before I couldn't wait until morning. Now I didn't want the night to end because when it did, my fears would become reality and everyone else would learn what I then knew for certain.

Cooper Foley was dead.

22

The search began at daybreak, as promised.

For several hours before, police from around the area gathered at the Thistledown firehouse. I was there along with the Foleys to offer any help they might need. It wasn't a small operation. I expected there to be a couple of locals with walking sticks and maybe a bloodhound or two to start tromping through the woods. Instead rescue units came in from everywhere. From Boston, Hartford, and Providence. I didn't know what half the uniforms stood for. It was all very organized. The plan was to turn one team loose near Emerald Cove, which was where Cayden Reilly said he hit Cooper's boat, and fan out from there. The other half of the team would search the opposite bank in case Cooper drifted that way. The woods were thick on both sides of the lake. They expected it to be slow going.

The Foleys looked better than they had the night before.

Seeing the efficient operation gave them hope that Cooper would be found quickly. The fact that they were calling it a "rescue" operation and not a "recovery" operation buoyed their spirits. Rescue meant saving somebody. Recovery meant finding a body. Mrs. Foley busied herself making coffee and offering encouragement. Mr. Foley studied topographical maps of the area, searching for any hidden place where Cooper might have holed up.

Sydney sat by herself in a far corner with her arms folded. She didn't have the same enthusiasm for the search as her parents did. Every so often her father walked over to her and gave her a hug and a quick "It's going to be okay." Sydney would smile for him, but her heart wasn't in it. She was dreading what she thought was the inevitable.

For me, the experience was strangely calming. I knew they would find Cooper. It was only a matter of time. After Cooper's picture had been blown over the night before, nothing else strange had happened the rest of the night. For nearly a week I had been a raw nerve. Even when nothing spooky was going on, I always felt like it might . . . at any moment and with no warning. There had been a kind of electric charge in the air. Not anymore. I no longer expected to round a corner and come face-to-face with Gravedigger . . . or any other illusion. I wondered how long that would last.

There was no luck finding Cooper that morning. The Foleys stayed optimistic, but I could tell they were getting nervous. Around noontime the operation took an ominous turn. While searchers continued to move through the woods, rescue boats took to the water. The scuba divers had arrived from Woods Hole. Four divers splashed down to search the lake bottom for my best friend. Nobody wished them luck.

The first thing they found was an engine . . . an 85 horsepower Mercury outboard. The same kind of engine that was on the *Galileo*. We heard the news of the discovery through a radio the rescue workers had set up in the firehouse. Up until that moment the place had been alive with activity. Many people were on phones coordinating rescue workers and equipment. A news crew arrived from Hartford. People buzzed in and out. When we heard the words over the speaker, "We've recovered an engine," the room fell silent.

The radio voice crackled, "Looks fairly new. Eighty-five Merc. Hasn't been down there long."

Captain Hoffkins looked to Mr. Foley. Mr. Foley nodded. It was probably the engine from the *Galileo*. From that moment on, the room was like a library. People continued to work, but they spoke in whispers. The Foleys stopped their busywork and sat together for support. All three of them. I didn't join them. I didn't want to intrude.

A half hour later we heard the radio voice over the speaker again. The rescue guy was all business. "They've brought up some debris," he said matter-of-factly. "Looks like pieces of a wooden seat. Blue. A splintered piece of rail and . . ." The voice trailed off. Nobody spoke. Everyone looked at the radio as if willing the guy to speak. Or not.

"Uh," he continued. I sensed the tension in his voice. "We, uh, we've got an iPod."

I heard Mrs. Foley whimper ever so slightly. Sydney gripped her arm.

I had to sit down. It wouldn't be much longer.

Work stopped. Every so often a phone rang, but nobody answered it. Even the news crews put down their cameras.

The sound of the radio mike being keyed a few times came through the speakers. Each time there was a crackle, I saw Mrs. Foley flinch as if needles were stinging her. She stared straight ahead vacantly. Sydney looked to me and gave me a small smile. It was going to be rough for her. For her family. For all of us.

"Uh," the voice crackled. "We, uh . . ." The guy was

searching for the right words. Even through the small speaker I sensed his emotion. "We've recovered a body."

That announcement brought the mystery to a close, along with the life of my best friend, Cooper Foley.

The next few days passed by in a blur.

The Foleys went right to the local hospital. They had the horrible task of identifying Cooper. I went back to the lake house to wait for them. Alone. Only a day before I had been terrified of being alone. Not anymore. I was numb. And angry. I almost would have welcomed an appearance by Gravedigger because I wanted answers. Now that the mystery was solved and we knew the horrible truth, so many questions still remained. Was it just an accident? Or did the entity that was Gravedigger have a hand in it? That was a disturbing road to go down, not only because of the impossible nature of the illusions, but the fact that if it were true, Cooper's death had something to do with me.

I had no doubt that Cooper's spirit was trying to protect me. The haunting began on the night of the accident. It could have been at the exact moment, for all I knew. But why did I need protection? Why was this spirit, or whatever it was, trying to hurt me? Because I smashed a glass ball full of disappearing blood? One mystery was solved, leaving me with another that I couldn't even begin to try and understand.

A big part of me hoped it was over, but that meant I would have to live with the horror of what happened for the rest of my life without ever knowing why. I didn't want it to end like that. Learning that spirits really existed and could terrorize people isn't something you take lightly. I wanted answers, but as I sat alone in the Foleys' lake house, I feared I'd never get them.

The Foleys got back late that afternoon. Mr. and Mrs. Foley looked shaken. Especially Mrs. Foley. She leaned on Sydney, who helped her inside the house and into her bedroom to lie down. She didn't see me when she came in, and I didn't say anything. What was there to say? Mr. Foley sat down with me in the living room. He looked horrible.

He gave me a quick hug and said, "If not for you, we might never have found him."

"I'm sorry" was all I could get out while trying hard to choke back tears.

"I am too," he said. "For you, Marsh. I know this is hard for you. You're like our third kid. I'm glad you're here."

I nodded.

Mr. Foley took a deep breath to try and control his emotions and said, "For what it's worth, they determined that Cooper didn't drown. There was no water in his lungs. It meant he died quickly. Probably before he even went in the water. His body was . . ."

He couldn't finish the sentence and I didn't want him to. If Coop had died from injuries he got from being run down by that monster boat, his body must have been in rough shape. I couldn't imagine how tough it must have been for the Foleys to see their son like that.

Mr. Foley continued, "They say he probably didn't even know what hit him. That's something, right?"

I remembered the grisly illusion that Gravedigger had shown me on the movie screen. If that was how the accident had happened, I believed Cooper died instantly.

"Yeah, that's something," I said softly.

"Dad?" Sydney said as she walked into the room. "She wants you to go in."

Mr. Foley wiped his eyes and patted me on the knee as he got to his feet. "Right!" he bellowed, trying to sound like his usual, jovial self. It wasn't convincing. He went to

Sydney and kissed the top of her head. "We'll take this one day at a time. I love you, sweetheart."

"I love you too, Dad." Sydney hugged her father and he disappeared into the bedroom to comfort his wife.

Sydney looked at me, shrugged, and said, "Well, this sucks."

A classic Cooper understatement. I wasn't sure whether to laugh or cry.

"How are you doing?" I asked.

Sydney took Mr. Foley's place next to me on the couch. She seemed to be struggling between her usual cool act . . . and breaking down.

"I don't know," she replied. "I'm dazed. I think it'll take a while for this to feel real."

That pretty much said it all. None of this felt real.

"What are we going to do, Marsh?" she asked. "I mean, about the things we saw."

"I don't know. I want everything to come out, you know? I want people to know that something caused this and it wasn't just an obnoxious kid. But who would believe us?"

"It's not just about Coop," she said. "Two other people are dead and one guy is nuts. *Three* guys if you count Mikey and Cayden. And Gravedigger is still out there. Doesn't that scare you?"

"I guess" was my answer.

"You guess?" she replied. "He could show up again. Anytime. Anywhere. If you're not scared, then you're as crazy as the sheriff."

"Or maybe it's over," I said. "Nothing strange has happened since the lake. Now that we've found Cooper, it might be done."

"*What* might be done?" Sydney cried. "There was no purpose to any of this."

She sat back and started to cry. Sydney Foley looked so incredibly vulnerable, it made me want to lean over and hold her to try and make her feel better, not that it would have helped.

"My brother's dead and I need to know why," she said through her tears. "If not for me, he never would have been here in the first place."

"Cooper never did anything he didn't want to," I said. "You know that better than anybody. You didn't put him out on the lake that night, or turn out his running lights, or put Cayden Reilly behind the wheel of that boat."

"But if he hadn't sold those tickets for me, he'd still be alive."

"Or something else might have happened to him."

She gave me a confused look. "What's that supposed to mean?"

"It means if anybody's responsible for Cooper's death, it's me. You said it yourself. Gravedigger is my creation. If he caused Cayden to run down Cooper . . . " I couldn't finish the thought. The idea that I was somehow responsible for the death of my best friend was too hard to even imagine, but it was something I had to accept.

Sydney said, "I don't believe for a second that you did anything to hurt Cooper."

I fought to stay calm. Losing it wouldn't have helped anybody. "I've been terrorized for a week by an image that was pulled out of my head. It wasn't random. It wants something from me. It wants me to take a journey."

"The Morpheus Road," Sydney said.

"Yeah. It called me the source and said the journey would begin once the poleax was returned."

"Do you know what any of that means?" she asked.

"No, and I have the sick feeling I never will. Part of me doesn't want to know. I want this to be done. I want my life back. But I'm not sure which is worse . . . being targeted by a supernatural being or never knowing why my best friend was killed."

I took a deep breath and added, "I don't have answers to any of this. I don't even know the right questions to ask."

Sydney rubbed her forehead. It didn't matter that her eyes were red and swollen, she was the most beautiful girl I'd ever seen. "Do you hate me, Marsh?"

"What? Why would I hate you?"

"I haven't exactly been civil to you for, oh, your whole life."

I shrugged. "We're two different people."

"Maybe, but you're not the same person you were."

I thought about what that could mean and said, "I know you meant that as a compliment, but I'm not so sure it's a good thing. I kind of liked who I was."

Sydney leaned over, held my chin with her hand, pulled me closer, and kissed me. A real kiss. It was such a surprise that I didn't have time to enjoy it. It was over before I even registered what had happened. She pulled away from me and, while still holding my chin, she said, "As long as you're around, we'll never lose Cooper entirely. So don't go anywhere, okay?"

"Okay" was all I could croak out.

I glanced to the picture on the table. The one Mom had given Cooper. Eternity. Mom had told him that as long as we leave things behind, we never truly die. Cooper may have been gone, but he'd never die.

As it turned out, my dad didn't listen to me. He found a flight out of Las Vegas to Hartford, rented a car, and drove directly to the lake that same night. As glad as I was to see him, it made things awkward. Up until he arrived, I felt like part of the Foley family. Once Dad got there, it made me realize I wasn't. Not really. Or maybe it was because Dad was the outsider. He spent some time with the Foleys, offering his support and listening to whatever they had to say. The Foleys were going to have to hear and say the same things over and over again, but at that moment it was all new and it seemed like talking to Dad helped them a little. After some teary good-byes, we got into his rental car and headed home.

On the drive I was happy that Dad didn't pump me for information. If anything, he offered some.

"I went to the State Police barracks first," he said. "They pretty much filled me in on what happened. They had some nice things to say about you."

That was a relief. I didn't feel like telling him the story because I didn't even know what story to tell.

Dad said, "Apparently, the kid who was driving the boat is a mess. He was racing another boat when the accident happened, but the police don't know of any other boat like that on the lake."

My stomach twisted. Was this mystery boat an illusion created by Gravedigger? If so, it was further proof that Gravedigger had orchestrated Cooper's death.

Dad said, "They told me you were the one who put it together and figured out what happened."

"Sort of," I answered. "Me and Sydney."

"I'm proud of you, Marsh."

I shrugged. Dad wanted me to talk, but I wasn't in the mood.

He said, "I want to be a wise parent and give you the wisdom I gained from going through a tragedy and losing somebody close to me, but you've got as much experience along those lines as I do. I'm sorry."

"For what?"

"For not being here, for one. But more because you've had to deal with such tragedy, twice. Jeez, you're so young. It's not fair."

Dad didn't know the half of it. I wanted to tell him everything. I wanted to explain about Gravedigger and the illusions and the violent deaths of Reilly and George O. and about how Sydney and I had nearly bought it a couple of times . . . but I couldn't find the words. It all sounded so incredibly, well, incredible. And George O.'s words kept running through my head.

The more people who know, the more will be in danger.

I told him everything else, though . . . about Cooper's almost-date with Britt, and the Reillys, and George O. giving me his key before he got hit, and finding the pieces of the *Galileo* in his house. I explained that Sheriff Vrtiak had picked me up for having gone into George O.'s house, and the accident that followed. I told him how Reilly had attacked me to protect his son because I was getting close to the truth, then tried to run Sydney and me down on the lake. I even told him about firing the flare gun that made Reilly lose control of the boat and slam into the seaplane. I told him everything . . . except about the supernatural force that guided it all.

After I finished the story, Dad didn't say a word. I think he was in shock.

"Dad?" I said. "What are you thinking?"

"Uhh," he muttered, dumbfounded. "I'm thinking my biggest worry in Vegas was that you'd have enough to eat."

Having Dad home was a huge relief but awkward. I had been on my own, more or less, for the past week. I had had to deal with a lot of stuff and didn't have to answer to anyone. With Dad back in the picture, I wasn't sure what my role was supposed to be. How was he going to react to it all? Was he going to be all guilty for leaving me alone and start hovering over me like a protective parent?

My answer came when we got back to the house and he saw the smashed window and damaged gutter. He could easily have gone crazy and grounded me and demanded to know what I had been doing.

"What happened?" he asked.

"It was an accident," I said. "My fault. I'll get it fixed."

"Okay," he said.

And that was it. He didn't press for details. He didn't lecture. Maybe it was because after all that had happened, a little fixable damage was small potatoes. Or maybe he trusted me to do the right thing.

It was good to have him home.

There were so many thoughts and emotions running through my head that I had trouble sorting it all out. There was grief over Cooper, sadness for the Foleys, guilt over the deaths of those people at the lake, and most of all, the fear that I might have somehow caused it all. Oddly enough, even with all that confusion bouncing around, I had the first full night's sleep I'd had in a week. It helped that there were no visions, no visits from evil demons, no fear that something was out there waiting to pounce on me. When I woke up, the sun was shining and life seemed close to normal.

The funeral was the following day because the Foleys didn't want to stretch things out. The big old gray stone church on the Ave was packed. It looked like all of Stony Brook had shown up. I think most of our class from Davis Gregory was there along with their parents. The guys Coop played football with sat together, wearing their red jackets. It reminded me that we hadn't recovered Coop's jacket. That was a shame. The Foleys had many relatives who had flown in from I-didn't-know-where. I had no idea that Cooper knew so many people. Maybe he didn't, but they sure knew him and came by the hundreds to say good-bye.

Dad and I took seats a few rows behind Coop's family. When Mrs. Foley saw us, she marched back, grabbed me by the hand, and brought us both up to sit with them. I really appreciated it. As Mr. Foley said, I was like their third kid. I was positioned between Dad and Sydney, who had on a black dress that looked fantastic. She never took off her sunglasses. I had on an old blue blazer and a tie I had borrowed from Dad.

The coffin sat in the center aisle, covered with flowers. I couldn't take my eyes off the thing. It was hard to believe that Cooper was in there. I had to keep telling myself that it wasn't him. It was only his body. The spirit that was Cooper was someplace else. I knew that for sure because he had been looking out for me. I wondered if he was in that church somewhere, checking things out. I knew what he'd be thinking: "Decent turnout. Cool." One guy who didn't turn up was Mikey Russo. With Cooper gone, he was probably off the hook for his part in the counterfeit ticket fiasco. I'd put money on the fact that it was the first thing he thought of when he heard that Cooper was killed. I hoped Sydney was finished with that loser.

A lot of people got up to speak. Coaches, teachers, even a couple of kids. They tried their best to put on the whole "celebration of life" show, but it was strained. Up near the altar was a big picture of Coop that showed him at his best. He had a big, beaming smile after having just won a race for the school track team. I remembered the moment. I was there. It was the best thing about the service, and the saddest.

The hardest part of the event was when I got up to speak. I wanted to bail on giving a speech, but that would have been wrong. I don't think anybody would have blamed me, except for Cooper maybe. Since he was probably watching, I didn't want to let him down. Once everybody had said what they had to say, I got up and walked to the podium. I hadn't written anything down. As soon as I got up there, I wished I had. It would have been a lot easier to read from a piece of paper than to keep my head together and actually think.

Looking over the sea of sad faces was tough. There had to be hundreds of people there, all with the same pained expression.

As I looked over the crowd, trying to collect my thoughts, I saw something unexpected. In the back of the church, standing among all the others who couldn't find a seat, was Ennis Mobley, my mom's old assistant. What was he doing there? He didn't know Cooper. Besides, he was supposed to be in Pakistan. I figured he was there to support me and Dad, but why would he fly back from Pakistan for that? Can you get from Pakistan to Connecticut that fast? How would he even have known about Cooper?

I couldn't worry about it just then—I had too many people waiting for me to say something. My fear was that I was going to start crying and make an ass of myself, but once I launched, it all came pretty easy.

"Coop and I have been friends since forever," I began. "I can't remember life without him. I'm going to miss him. We all are. But the thing is, Cooper isn't really gone. Right now he lives on in our memories. I know, that sounds nice and it's a good thing to say at times like this, but the truth is, memories don't last. It's harsh but true. I lost my mother not too long ago and I'm already having trouble remembering little things about her."

I looked to Dad, who gave me a sad smile.

"But that's okay. What she left for me, and what Cooper left for us, is more important than that. Cooper taught me how to have fun. He made me laugh at things that most people wouldn't find funny. He taught me to take chances and not be afraid to fail. He taught me not to stress over details but to never accept second best. We visited Trouble Town more times than I can count, and I wouldn't have had it any other way. Does any of this sound familiar?"

There was a general murmur of agreement throughout

the church. I looked to Sydney. She actually had a small smile on her face.

"I'm a better person for having known Cooper Foley, and that's something that won't change when memories fade. I'm going to make sure of it."

I looked up toward the ceiling and called out, "And Coop, wherever you are, I'll bet you're listening to all this and thinking you're something special after hearing all the nice things these people have said about you. Right? I don't blame you. And I want to say one more thing. I owe you."

I meant that in more ways than anybody in that church could understand. I'm sure they thought it was a nice, sentimental touch. What they didn't know was that I was actually talking to Cooper. For real. I was absolutely sure of that. When I sat back down next to Sydney, she grabbed my hand.

"We both owe him," she whispered. She understood.

The service ended shortly after and it was a crush to get out of the church. It was time to go to the cemetery, and the Foleys asked Dad and me to sit with them at the final service there. It was an honor we gladly accepted. Dad ducked out the side door of the church to get the car, but I went with the flow toward the front doors. I stepped out into the sun, where most everyone from the service was gathered in the front courtyard, talking and saying good-byes. Everyone but Ennis, that is. I looked everywhere, but he wasn't around. It was so odd. Dad and I had to be the only two people there he knew. Why wouldn't he stick around to talk with us? I figured I'd ask him about it eventually. I couldn't hang out any longer. I had to join Cooper on his final journey. At least in this life.

Cooper was headed for the same cemetery where we had buried Mom. I hated the place and not just for the obvious reason. It was old. Like Revolutionary War–old. There were tombstones that were so worn with age, you couldn't read the inscriptions. Some were broken in two and repaired with cement. Others were so beaten down by years of sun, rain, and snow that they looked like white, gnarly bones reaching up out of the ground. Why were cemeteries made to look so creepy? I mean, yeah, it's where you bury dead people, but why do people make it so much worse by erecting sorrowful statues of winged angels and mausoleums right out of a horror movie? The fact that so many of the gravestones and statues were ancient and dirty and covered with moss only added to the eerie feel. There wasn't a whole lot of "celebrating life" going on in this place. It was more like: "Let's remind everybody that they're walking over buried dead people." Cemeteries should be a little more inviting, like a park. I mean, the residents didn't care one way or the other, but lots of people visited graves. You'd think they'd want to remember the person for who they were, not be reminded that they're stuck in a creep show. Forever. But that's just me.

I hadn't been to Mom's grave since the day of her funeral. I couldn't do it, and not because the place gave me the creeps. I didn't go because it made me sad. I had better ways to remember her than staring at a piece of marble with her name carved in it and thinking of her being under the dirt.

The part of the cemetery with the new graves wasn't anywhere near as creepy, but it was just as sad. The long line of cars that made up Cooper's funeral procession drove over a hill that held the older, spooky section and continued down the other side until we reached an area where the tombstones were new and the flowers were fresh. I guess there weren't a lot of people left to put flowers on graves that were two hundred years old.

Cooper's casket was already there. Somebody rolled out some fake grass around it to make it a little more attractive, and to cover the dirt that would soon fill the hole that Cooper would be lowered into. All the flowers from the church were there, along with several rows of folding chairs. Not everybody from the church showed up and that was just as well. I did a quick look around to see if maybe Ennis had come, but didn't see him.

Dad and I sat in the front row with the Foleys. The priest said some prayers that were all sorts of somber. It was torture. At least at the church they had talked about Cooper as an individual. Here the ceremony felt pretty generic, which made it all the more sad. I tried not to listen. I just wanted it to be over. Thankfully, it didn't last long. The priest made an announcement that everybody was invited back to the Foleys' house for some food. Not knowing what else to do, the crowd slowly dispersed.

Mr. and Mrs. Foley looked lost. They had to be directed to their limousine by a guy in a dark suit who I figured was the funeral home dude. (Why do they call funeral places "homes"? It's not like anybody's living there.) Sydney went up to her mom and gave her a big hug. I know this is a small consolation, but it was looking like this tragedy might actually have mended some fences. I sure hoped so. Mr. Foley nodded to Sydney as if agreeing to something. Sydney gave him a kiss on the cheek, then walked directly over to me.

"Ride back with me?" she asked.

I looked to Dad. He shrugged. "F-B-M," he said.

Sydney looked confused.

"That means 'fine by me,'" I said.

Sydney gave Dad a curious look.

"Sorry," Dad said with a shrug. "Habit."

"Odd habit," Sydney said.

"I'll see you guys back at the Foleys'," Dad said, and made his escape.

"Don't you want to ride with your parents?" I asked Sydney.

"I drove myself. The whole ceremony of this thing makes it even worse."

I knew how she felt.

"Besides," she added, "if I'm riding in a limo, I want to be going someplace cool."

That made me laugh. There was more of Cooper in her than I had realized.

"Let's go for a walk," she said, and moved quickly away from the grave site. I followed without looking back. I wasn't about to stand over the casket and say good-bye. That was way too . . . final. Though going for a walk in a cemetery wasn't much more appealing.

"I wanted to talk to you alone," she said. "It's going to be crazy back at my house."

"Well, we're in the right place. To be alone, I mean."

I was happy to see that Sydney wasn't walking toward Mom's grave. I didn't want to go anywhere near there.

"How are you doing?" I asked.

"Okay," she said. "It's all a party now. A really strange party. I think once it's over, we're going to get slammed."

"That's exactly what's going to happen," I said. "I've been there."

Sydney gave me a sad smile. She knew.

I added, "But you're talking with your parents. That's something."

"Yeah, there's that," she said, keeping her eyes on the ground. "I'm gonna tell 'em about the tattoo."

"Ooh, risky."

"Yeah, but they should know what Cooper did for me."

I chuckled. "Careful. You're going to lose your reputation for being an ice witch."

"Is that what he called me?" she asked with exaggerated indignation.

"That was one of the nicer things."

"Such a brat," she said, shaking her head. She wasn't angry at all.

We walked along in silence. I didn't mind it, in spite of the fact we were in the middle of a freakin' huge graveyard. After a while we found ourselves on the edge of the older part of the cemetery. We rounded an ancient mausoleum to see a small courtyard with a reflecting pool. There were marble benches built around the stone floor and urns filled with colorful, living flowers. It was set at the bottom of a hill that was dotted with graves. On top of the hill was a thick weeping willow tree.

"Now, this is more like it," I said. "If you gotta hang around this place for eternity, you might as well do it in style."

Sydney led me to a stone bench and we sat directly across the reflecting pool from the mausoleum.

"Have you thought about what you're going to tell people?" she asked.

"Only every waking moment."

"And?"

"And I still don't know."

Sydney kicked at the stone walkway. She seemed nervous.

"This is your call," she said. "Whatever you want to do is cool. But I think we should let it go."

I didn't say anything. I wanted her to finish.

"You said yourself that it might be over. If it is, the worst thing that can happen is we'll never know all that really happened. If it starts again, we'll have to deal, but if it's over, we might cause a lot of people grief by what we have to say."

"Maybe," I said.

"My parents are destroyed, Marsh. You of all people

should understand that. I'm the only kid they've got left and we finally started to talk. If I tell them about illusions and evil spirits, how do you think they'll react?"

The sky grew darker. I looked up to see a large gray cloud drifting over the sun. It was the perfect ominous change, given our conversation.

"I want to believe it's over," I said. "But if it is, for the rest of my life I'm going to wonder why it happened, and if I had something to do with Cooper's death."

"I know," she said. "I feel the same way. But there's nothing we can do to bring him back."

I heard a far-off rumble. The wind picked up. Was a storm coming in?

"I hear you, Sydney, but I have to know. What if I could have prevented it from happening? We wouldn't be sitting here right now."

"Do you really want to know that?" she asked. "What would it change?"

The cloud moved on, but strangely the day had turned from sunny and bright to dark gray.

"It might stop it from happening again," I answered.

"Okay, sure. You're right. We should try to figure it out. All I'm saying is, I don't want to lay this on my parents. Not right now. Maybe in a few months, after—"

"What was that?" I asked. I heard something unnatural. Like a scraping sound.

Sydney shrugged.

"Listen," I said.

I heard it again. It sounded like a stick was being drawn across cement. It was faint but growing louder. Sydney heard it.

"Where's it coming from?" she asked.

"The wind's kicking up. It must be knocking some branches around."

The sound stopped and we both relaxed.

I said, "Look, I don't know the right thing to do. I hear what you're saying about your parents and maybe now isn't the time to tell them. But at some point we're going to have to face—"

"There it is again," she said.

It was louder this time. The instant I realized where it was coming from, the hair stood up on the back of my neck. The electric feeling was back. Sydney looked to the mausoleum on the far side of the reflecting pool.

"Tell me it's not coming from in there," she said, her voice quivering.

The scraping got louder. It was joined by another sound. It was a dry shuffling that sounded as if someone was dragging their feet across the ground. Or through the mausoleum. The wind grew stronger. On top of the hill the weeping willow tree swayed violently. Sydney slid closer to me. The scraping and shuffling grew louder, as if whatever was making the sound was coming closer to the door of the mausoleum. From the inside.

"Is this real?" she said in a hoarse whisper.

Before I could answer, the sound stopped. All sound. Everything. The scraping. The shuffling. The wind. The rumble. An impossible void had descended on the cemetery. The only sound was a steady *drip . . . drip . . . drip* from the pool in front of us. At least I thought it was from the pool.

A moment passed. Two moments. I could hear Sydney swallow—that's how quiet it had become. She squeezed my hand.

"It's not over, is it?"

Boom! The double doors of the mausoleum blew open, tearing them from their hinges and throwing them across the courtyard. All sound returned. A howling wind blew from the dark crypt. It smelled old. And dead.

"Out of here!" I yelled, and pulled Sydney to her feet.

We jumped off the bench and turned toward the hill. The hill with the weeping willow. We both looked up to see we weren't alone anymore. Standing beneath the swaying tree . . . was Gravedigger.

The nightmare wasn't over.

It had barely begun.

23

"My car," Sydney said breathlessly as we ran together, dodging our way past ancient graves.

The sky had become impossibly dark, making it look more like night than day. There was no rain, but the swirling wind made it seem as if we were in the middle of a storm. Or would be soon. We ran around the base of the hill, trying to move fast and not trip on a gnarled root or a sharp stone hidden by long grass.

"Is he coming?" Sydney asked.

"Don't know. Don't care. Don't want to be here."

We rounded the hill and got a view of the new section of the cemetery below us. Sitting on the road by itself, not far from Cooper's already covered-over grave, was Sydney's Beetle. Every last person from the funeral was long gone. People didn't hang out in cemeteries after the show was over. I wished *we* hadn't. The car was a few hundred yards away. Still, it was in sight. The only thing that stood between us and our escape was a sea of tombstones, statues, and mausoleums.

"Keep moving," I said, and we began winding our way across the grass and the graves.

We had only gone a few steps when the ground shuddered.

"Did you feel that?" Sydney called while still running.

"Earthquake?" I replied. I'd never been in an earthquake, but it was the only thing I could think of. Another jolt hit that was so strong, I was nearly thrown off my feet. I stumbled toward Sydney and she caught me before I went down.

"Don't stop!" I commanded.

We tried to run, but the ground was shaking so violently, it made it impossible to move. Sydney and I held on to each other and dropped to our knees.

"Gravedigger must be doing this," I said. "They don't have earthquakes around here."

"So it's an illusion," Sydney shot back.

We were both nearly knocked down by another strong jolt.

"A really good illusion," she added.

There was a cracking sound, like rocks grinding together.

"Look!" Sydney shouted.

She was pointing to a large mausoleum about five yards from us. A jagged crack made its way up the cement wall, like an egg breaking in two. The crack ran up toward the marble roof. When it hit, a section of the wall fell away, revealing two wooden coffins inside. The rumbling knocked them off their shelves and they tumbled out.

Sydney screamed.

I would have too, but I was too horrified to open my mouth. We both turned away before seeing what happened when the coffins hit the ground.

"We gotta keep moving," I said. We helped each other to our feet and struggled to move forward. The earthquake, or whatever it was, intensified. We held on to each other for support and managed to stumble closer to the car. All around us, tombstones and statues were falling over and smashing. I heard a sharp crack and looked up.

"Move!" I shouted, and pushed Sydney forward just as a marble cherub fell from the top of a tomb and smashed to the ground, barely missing us.

Sydney was crying, but that didn't stop her from moving. We were both focused on getting to the car. It was our only way out of danger. We were maybe fifty feet away from it when the ground shook so violently that we both fell down. I hit the ground first. Sydney landed on top of me. We rolled and got back to our feet to continue our dash for the car . . . when the car moved. It shook, rocked on its wheels, and rolled forward slowly.

"Nobody's driving," Sydney cried.

For a second we both feared some demonic force had gotten behind the wheel and was about to drive away. What *did* happen was far worse.

"It's not the car," I declared. "It's the ground."

The roadway beneath the car was cracking apart. A huge gash appeared that ran directly under the silver Beetle, front to back.

"Hurry!" Sydney shouted, and ran for it.

I grabbed her.

"No, it's too late," I said.

She was desperate to get to the car and fought to pull away, but I held her tight. We both watched the ground beneath the car being torn apart by some horrific force. The gash in the road grew very wide, very quickly. The Beetle tilted to its side, then tumbled into the chasm with a metallic screech of metal against cement.

"No!" Sydney screamed, and pulled away from me.

I didn't know what she expected to do. The car was a goner. I followed and we made it to the edge of the deep, wide gash that had been ripped into the ground. Wedged near the bottom was Sydney's car. Useless. We would have to get out of the cemetery on foot.

The wrecked car wasn't the worst of what we saw down in that rift. When the ground pulled apart, it revealed the remains of dozens of coffins. Some looked ancient, others could have been buried last week. All were rudely disrupted from their resting places and thrown into the rift. Not all of them stayed closed. Bodies tumbled out as the coffins rolled down the side. One silver coffin flipped and sprung open to reveal an occupant that hadn't seen the light of day in a century. There was nothing left but a brown skeleton dressed in the shreds of what was once a suit.

Sydney clutched at me but didn't take her eyes off the chilling scene. A few dozen coffins had been flung into the pit and half of them had sprung open, leaving a trail of bodies in various stages of decay and mummification.

The ground stopped moving. The rumbling stopped. The only sound was the shrill whistle of the wind and Sydney's sobs.

"I'm going out of my mind," she whispered.

"It . . . it must be an illusion," I said shakily. "It has to be. Like the speedboats. And the blood. This isn't happening."

I didn't think it could get any worse.

I was wrong.

One of the bodies moved.

Sydney yelped in surprise.

I saw the movement but thought maybe the body was still settling after having been so rudely pulled from its not-so-final resting place. No such luck. A man's body that had been flung from its coffin turned its head and looked up at us through empty eyes. I couldn't tell if the shreds that hung from its bones were rotted clothes or flesh. Or both. It was dead, yet it was alive. And it wasn't alone. All around it the other disturbed corpses began to stir as if they had been awakened from a nap. A long, dead nap. So much for resting in peace. One after another the corpses pushed to their feet and began to claw their way up the side of the ravine . . . toward us. They all opened their skeletal mouths to let out a sorrowful moan, joining together in a macabre chorus that pushed me closer to the edge of sanity.

"These aren't evil people," I reasoned aloud, my voice shaking. "They're just . . . people."

"Dead people," Sydney mumbled. "Woken up by Gravedigger."

That's all I needed to hear.

"C'mon," I said, and pulled her away from the edge.

The only choice we had was to run for the gates of the cemetery. I didn't know if that would get us away from Gravedigger, but it was a good start. The sky was still dark and the wind hadn't let up. I tried to remember how deep we were into the huge graveyard and feared that we had at least a half mile to go. That was a long way on foot. I glanced back over my shoulder to see skeletal hands reaching up from below the lip of the crevice, grabbing the edge to pull themselves up. Would they keep coming after us? Could corpses run? What would they do if they caught us? Would they blame us for disturbing their final resting place? I didn't want the answers to any of those questions.

"We're okay," I said between breaths. "We just gotta get out of the cemetery. It's a busy road outside. We'll get a ride. We'll . . ."

The rumbling returned. It was like trying to run on top of a volcano that was gathering the energy to erupt. Sydney and I held on to each other to keep from falling over, but we kept moving.

"There!" I shouted.

The iron gates that marked the entrance to the cemetery were only a couple hundred yards away. Unfortunately, the road made several sweeping S turns between us and escape. The fastest way to get there would be to forget the road and run . . . straight through a labyrinth of tombstones and mausoleums.

"Straight through," I announced.

Sydney stopped. "I can't. Not over those graves."

I looked back to see the dozen corpses that had climbed out of the rift in the road and were shuffling forward on brittle legs, their moans calling to us. I flashed on *Night of the Living Dead*. It was a bad flash. Sydney looked back and saw them. It was all the convincing she needed.

"Straight through," she echoed.

She grabbed my hand and ran forward, plunging into the sea of tombs.

The ground continued to move. I feared that it might open up and swallow us the way it had the car. Why not? If Gravedigger was calling the shots, he could make us see whatever he wanted. That is, if this were actually an illusion. We couldn't take the chance. We had to get out of there.

We stayed together, dodging around the marble monuments, moving closer to what I hoped was safety. We skirted one large tomb and came upon a stunning monument. It was a white marble statue of a pure white angel that was kneeling with its arms on a tomb. Its head was resting on its crossed arms as if it were weeping. The thing was bigger than life-size, with huge wings that were held tight against its body. It was stunning.

And it was alive.

The marble angel lifted its head and turned to us with a lifeless gaze as if upset we had dared disturb its mourning. Sydney and I stopped short. The rumbling intensified. With a roar the doors blew open to a mausoleum, spewing out brilliant light and a musty wind. A second mausoleum across from it blew open, hitting us with light and dust from another side. Between the dust in my eyes and the wind and bright light, I was nearly blinded. Sydney and I stumbled to get away, but we had lost all sense of direction. The marble tomb that the angel had been weeping over exploded. The cement cover shattered as light and wind blew up from below. Through the dust and light I caught a glimpse of the angel. Its wings were spread wide. It was coming for us.

"No!" Sydney screamed, and pulled away from me.

"Sydney!" I shouted, too late.

The angel pounced on her, wrapping its wings around her body.

"Marsh!" I heard her call as her scream faded to oblivion.

I ran to her, too late. She was gone. The stone angel was gone. I heard a cracking sound and looked up to see a tall obelisk toppling over . . . toward me. I jumped away quickly as the marble pillar crashed across the top of the tomb, sealing it off. I stumbled over a gravestone and hit the ground. The moment I landed, the demon wind and light stopped. Both mausoleum doors were closed and the marble tomb was sealed off by the fallen obelisk.

Sydney was nowhere to be seen.

"Sydney!" I yelled. "Sydney!"

No answer. The angel, or whatever it was, had taken her. But to where? How could an illusion make a living person disappear? I ran to each of the mausoleums and yanked on the doors, but they were sealed tight. I tried to lift the marble obelisk off the broken tomb, but it was far too heavy. Wherever Sydney was, I couldn't get to her. I heard the moaning of the corpses. I'd almost forgotten about them. They were getting closer. The only thing I could do was escape from the cemetery and get help. That's what I decided. I'd find somebody, anybody, and bring them back. We'd pry open the mausoleums. We'd find Sydney. No more secrets. I didn't care if they thought I was crazy. There was another life at stake. I didn't want Gravedigger claiming another victim. Especially not Sydney.

I ran for the gates. After leaping over several toppled tombstones, I broke out onto the twisting cemetery roadway and stopped to plot my course. The cemetery was surrounded by a black metal fence that was too high to climb. It was in a residential area in a remote part of Stony Brook that had mostly big homes on giant, tree-covered properties. Directly across from the cemetery was a huge stone mansion from the nineteenth century. Farther up the road to the right was an ivy-covered all-girls school. To the left of the mansion was a giant tank that held the town's drinking water. It was a familiar part of town for me. I'd ridden my bike along that road many times. I knew the neighborhood.

But the neighborhood was gone.

Beyond the tall metal fence was nothing. I should have seen trees blowing in the wind and the big stone mansion and the water tank. Instead I saw a dark, swirling soup that had no beginning and no end. The cemetery had become an island that floated in a murky, supernatural sea. There was no road, no sky, no life. The world beyond the fence looked like an artist's canvas that was dripping with colorful paint but with no recognizable image.

"He's trying to keep me here," I muttered to myself.

I ran for the gates, convinced that it was one of Gravedigger's illusions. I was sure that as soon as I got out of the cemetery, the world would return to normal. We had made that gamble with the speedboats and won. I was ready to go for it again.

That is, until the cemetery erupted. The sudden, earthquakelike rumblings were so fierce that I could barely keep my balance, let alone run. I stumbled and fell on the roadway, then had trouble getting back to my feet. But I was almost there and kept going on my hands and knees. I had to get out of there and if it meant crawling, that was fine by me. Sydney's life depended on it. On the far side of the road, tombstones tumbled and statues fell. Gravedigger was throwing down obstacles in my way. I had to duck and roll and look everywhere for fear that something heavy would land on my head.

I made it to the last paved road before the final stretch of graves. The ground in front of me was littered with the remains of shattered marble and broken statues. I stopped to look ahead and plan a route through the rubble . . . and saw the ground move. Something was under the grass. Something alive. Not five feet in front of me, the grass was being pushed up from below. Whatever was down there was coming up. I couldn't move. My eyes were fixed on the spot. The grass tore apart as . . .

. . . a mummified head poked up from below. A head! Its hands pushed up through the dirt, tearing at the sod as if making a desperate escape from the world below. Behind it, another skeletal hand reached out of the ground, followed by another.

The rumbling continued. I backed away on the paved road and looked around to see the same thing happening everywhere. It was like this demonic earthquake had shaken awake the dead. Hundreds upon hundreds of corpses in various stages of decay were pulling themselves up and out of their graves.

The cemetery had come alive with the dead.

It was mind-numbing. There were thousands of them. Multiple thousands. Stony Brook was four centuries old. The cemetery was loaded. They pulled themselves up from below, shook off the dirt from the ages, and began to move . . . toward me.

The only undisturbed ground was the roadway. Though I was close to the gate, there was no way I was going to plunge into a mass of living corpses to get there. I had to stick to the road. I put my head down and ran. I didn't want to see. It was beyond a nightmare. Their moans grew. I heard the wails of men and women and probably even some children. There were no words, just the sad cry of thousands of people who shouldn't have been disturbed.

"It's not real," I kept saying to myself. "This can't be happening."

When somebody dies, their spirit dies with them. Or goes somewhere else. The idea that their personalities had returned to their dead bodies and somehow been reanimated was too horrific to imagine. I had to keep telling myself it was an illusion, like the speedboats and the lake serpent . . . or even my cat at the school. I kept moving with my eyes on the ground, though I sensed their presence all around me. None of them stepped onto the roadway. They were crowding the edges of the pavement, reaching out to me. I feared their cold touch, so I kept to the middle of the road. The wailing grew along with the crowd. I put my hands over my ears, but that only muffled it. Tears ran down my cheeks. I was growing closer to the gate and to the edge of sanity. There was no telling which I'd hit first. The only thing that kept me going was the belief that as soon as I stepped through the gate, the illusion would end and everything would be fine.

I rounded the final curve in the road and dared to look up. What I hoped to see was a clear path open through the metal fence. Instead I saw an old-fashioned horse-drawn hearse blocking the way. The black wagon had smoky glass sides, through which I saw the outline of a wooden coffin. The two horses that were lashed to the vehicle looked every bit as dead as the thousands of corpses that lined the walkway. Dry flesh hung from their bones, revealing rotted muscles covering yellowed bones. Did they bury horses in this cemetery too? Sitting up high in front, holding the reins, was a corpse that looked like an undertaker from two hundred years ago. He wasn't much more than a skeleton with a tall, worm-eaten top hat. He turned to me with a sly smile and tipped his rotten hat.

I didn't return the greeting.

Suddenly, as if the undertaker's tip of the cap was a signal, the moaning of the gathered corpses stopped. How did they all know to do that? It wasn't like this was rehearsed. At least I didn't think it was. The cemetery grew silent. The wind stopped. The rumbling was finished. The dark clouds still made the place feel like night, but the force that had pulled these people from the graves was at rest. All I wanted to do was get past the hearse and out of the cemetery. Sydney's life depended on it. Mine too. The undertaker propped his hat back on his head and snapped the reins. With the squeal of rusted wheels the dead horses pulled the hearse forward, away from the gate.

I kept my eyes on the ground but could sense when the hearse had cleared the gate. When I was confident that the way was clear, I continued toward the gate, only to see that the swinging doors were closed. I tried not to panic. I reached up and wrapped my fingers around the metal bars, though I think I knew what was going to happen before I even tried. I pulled, but the gates wouldn't budge. I looked up, thinking I might be able to climb out, but the bars were too high and were topped off with sharp, spikelike points. There was no room under the gate for me to squeeze out. I shook them hard, thinking they might only be stuck. It was a waste of energy. Gravedigger wasn't going to make it that easy.

I glanced to the hearse. It had stopped in the middle of the road. The undertaker was looking back at me, waiting for me to realize and accept that I wouldn't be leaving. He lifted his hand and crooked his bony finger, beckoning me to follow. Going after that guy was the absolute last thing in the world I wanted to do. I looked out through the bars of the gate to the world beyond. There was no up or down out there. There were flashes of colorful light and large shadows that drifted past. I didn't want to know what they were shadows of. Even if the gates were open, I might have thought twice about stepping into that void. But it wasn't like I had a choice. There was only one thing I could do. I had to follow the hearse. Sydney was still back there somewhere—maybe he would lead me to her.

The undertaker turned forward and the hearse began to move again. This time I followed. My one hope was that wherever he was taking me, I would find answers there. And Sydney. The hearse moved slowly. I kept my eyes to the ground and followed the sound of the dead horse's hooves and the steady squeak from the wooden wheels . . . or was it the grinding of the horse's dead bones? I couldn't bring myself to look up and see what was surrounding me, though I could sense it. The entire roadway was lined with corpses who crowded together, watching silently. Though I wouldn't look at them, I knew they were glaring at me. Every last one of them. What did they want? Did they think it was my fault that their eternal rest had been disturbed?

I made the mistake of looking back. Though the roadway was completely clear in front of the hearse, the mass of dead filled in the road behind me, shuffling forward. Following.

I quickly looked forward and wished that the hearse would move faster.

As we wound our way along the twisting roadway, I figured there must have been a destination. A thought so horrifying came to me that I almost dropped to my knees and stopped walking right then and there. From what I saw, every last person who was buried in that cemetery had come to life. We had just buried Cooper. Would I look up and catch a glimpse of my friend's mutilated body? As awful as that thought was, there was another that was even worse. My mother was buried in that cemetery. If I saw her, it would be the last sane moment of my life.

We walked for around ten minutes. I think. I'd lost all track of time. I sensed that the road was growing steeper. We were going up a hill. That could only mean that the undertaker was leading me back to the oldest part of the cemetery. We walked for another few minutes when I heard the hearse squeak to a stop. Had we arrived? I squinted so I wouldn't have to see much detail and looked around. I was still standing in the middle of the roadway, surrounded by walking corpses on three sides and the hearse in front. I looked up to the undertaker, who raised his hand and pointed a bony finger off to the left. With that gesture the corpses on that side of the road obediently cleared a path. That was where I was supposed to go.

I was too numb to fight it. Not that I would have known how. With my head still down I shuffled off the road onto the grass and through the gauntlet that the cadavers cleared for me, stepping over bits of crumbled tombstones and shattered coffins. The bodies hadn't cleared back far enough for comfort. The pathway was only a few feet wide. They could easily have reached out and touched me. I forced back my revulsion and kept walking with my eyes on the ground. The hope of finding answers, and Sydney, was all that mattered. I walked maybe forty yards until I sensed that I had left my escort of corpses. Wherever I was being led to, I had arrived. When I summoned the nerve to look up, I knew it for certain.

I was back in front of the reflecting pool where Sydney and I had been sitting when this latest nightmare began. The thousands of corpses that had pulled themselves from their graves were still there but kept their distance. They had formed a ring around the ancient memorial garden that looked to be several hundred bodies deep. I felt like a boxer in the ring, ready to do battle, while thousands of fans were gathered to witness the fight.

And my opponent had arrived.

Standing on the opposite side of the reflecting pool, in front of the open doors of the mausoleum, was Gravedigger. The two of us faced each other like gunslingers. The only problem was, I had no guns to sling. He also had a couple thousand backups that surrounded us. I was totally at his mercy.

"So?" I called out. "I'm here."

Gravedigger responded by lifting his silver pick onto his shoulder. At that moment I wasn't scared. Not that I had suddenly gotten all brave. It was just the opposite. I was done. I had lost and I didn't even know what the game was.

"Where is Sydney Foley?" I called out to him.

Gravedigger smiled. That made me angry.

"Who are you?" I shouted. "Why are you haunting me? Did I do something wrong? Have I somehow disrupted some cosmic force to deserve this? Please tell me. At least give me that much."

Gravedigger barely reacted. He kept staring at me through hollow eyes from under the brim of his dark hat.

"You killed my best friend," I cried. "And others, too. Why? What was the point?"

Gravedigger lifted the pick over his head as if ready to strike. I heard the far-off rumble of thunder. He clutched the pick with one bony hand and brought it down to the ground, hard. The sharp pick stuck in the dirt. At that exact moment the wind picked up again, but not from any storm. It blew from out of the open door of the mausoleum behind Grave-digger making his dark cloak billow. I wanted to turn and run, but to where? I was trapped by thousands of dead bodies.

I sensed movement inside the mausoleum. We weren't alone.

"Sydney?" I called out.

A shadow appeared at the door. Whoever it was, it wasn't Sydney. This new guy was big. And a guy. Even though he was a shadow, I could see that he was built like a defensive end. He had to duck down to clear the doorway of the tomb. I was surrounded by thousands of walking corpses, yet the sight of this brute stepping across the threshold and stand-ing up to his full height made my stomach turn. Not out of disgust . . . but from fear.

He looked like a spirit from another time. And place. He wore leather sandals and a white tunic that seemed like something they wore in ancient Greece or Rome. His legs and arms were muscular. This was no mummified corpse. The seams of his white clothing were trimmed with gold thread, making it seem like he might have been a ruler of some kind. Or a warrior. Or another freakin' illusion. I was hoping for that.

All those details were window dressing. I couldn't take my eyes off his face. He had short dark hair and coal black eyes. Ruthless eyes. I had no doubt that he had been in more than one battle—his face was crisscrossed with dozens of scars that cut him up like a confused roadmap. This guy had suffered, and I'd bet anything he'd caused just as much suffering right back.

He stepped out of the mausoleum and walked up behind Gravedigger. He towered over my tormentor by at least a foot. Gravedigger didn't react. The big spirit raised a clenched fist into the air and brought it down hard . . . on Gravedigger's head. Gravedigger crumbled like chalk dust. The black hat and cloak fluttered to the ground next to the pick, coming to rest on a pile of dried bone. The spirit had literally crushed the demon. Gravedigger was no more. Maybe he never was.

With that one violent act I realized that like everything else I had seen, Gravedigger was an illusion. He had no power. I never had anything to fear from him.

The spirit who was to be feared had finally made himself known and was standing across from me.

24

I stood across the reflecting pool from this imposing spirit, fighting the urge to drop to my knees and beg for mercy.

"Are you the one who's been haunting me?" I called out.

The giant kept his dead doll-eyes on me. He nodded.

"Are you real or an illusion?" I asked.

He cocked his head as if it were a question he had never been asked. He thought about it, then twisted his lips into a smile. He wanted to keep me guessing.

"Did you kill my friend?" I asked.

"His journey has begun," he growled. His voice was the same low rumble that came from Gravedigger. It sounded like bones rattling in the bottom of a grave.

"On the Morpheus Road?" I asked.

He nodded.

"What is the Morpheus Road?" I asked.

"It is the way of life and death," he replied. "A road that all must travel."

"Not me," I said quickly.

The giant bent down and grabbed Gravedigger's pick. He admired it and let out a low, guttural laugh. He was enjoying himself. "All must travel," he repeated.

"Do you have a name?"

"I am Damon," he replied.

"Are you a spirit?"

"I know of spirits."

"Why are you haunting me?" I asked. "What do you want?"

"The poleax" was his answer.

"The what?"

"Bring it to me," he said.

I felt as if he had just revealed the reason for this entire nightmare. I'd heard the word before, but it still meant nothing to me.

"Hey, I don't even know what a poleax is, so if all this was to try to get me to bring one to you, you've been wasting your time because I'm the wrong guy to . . . whoa!"

Damon reared back and flung the pick at me. I ducked, but I wasn't the target. The sharp pick spun through the air and nailed a corpse standing behind me. The corpse practically exploded, sending shattered body parts flying. None of the other corpses even flinched. I sure did. I didn't want to get hit by any gore. I covered my head and waited until the sound of falling body parts ended.

"You possessed a crucible," he said.

"Crucible? I don't know what that is either."

"You destroyed it."

My mind raced. What was he talking about? Then I remembered. "You mean that ball with the blood? Was it yours? Look, I'm sorry. I didn't mean to break it."

"The search has brought me to you," he said as he stepped onto the cloak that used to belong to Gravedigger. He started to make his way around the reflecting pool toward me. "You are the source," he added.

"Me? Why me? Look, I'm sorry I broke the blood-ball thing, but I don't know anything about a poleax."

He continued to round the reflecting pool. I moved the opposite way. No way I wanted this creep getting any closer to me.

"You will find it and bring it to me," he said.

"Why? You've made my life a nightmare. You killed my friend! You could haunt me forever and I still wouldn't help you."

"There is no forever," he said. "When you walk the road, you will see."

"No, I won't because I'm not going anywhere," I said stubbornly.

"You do not have a choice."

All around us the ring of corpses had been slowly tightening.

"There are many routes to take along the Morpheus Road," he said. "Your journey could be peaceful or filled with grief."

He lashed out, grabbed one of the walking dead by the throat, and pulled it toward him. With a mighty snap of his arm he shook the corpse violently, flicking off bones that clattered to the ground. He was left holding the spinal cord. The only bone still attached was the skull. He held it up like a trophy.

"I have haunted your thoughts," he said with a proud smile. "I know what frightens you."

He snapped the spine like a whip. The skull flew off and I had to duck or it would have nailed me in the chest. My stomach twisted, but I managed to keep it together.

"Why scare me?" I asked. "And why did you kill my friend?"

"To reach you."

My knees buckled. It was true. Cooper's death *was* about me. But why? Why did this ghost think I could help him find his pole thing?

"Then you made a mistake," I said. "If you think I'm going to help you, you're wrong."

"And what of the girl?" he asked with a superior sneer.

I felt dizzy but kept moving away from him.

"Where is she?" I asked.

"All must travel the road."

"Is she . . . dead?"

"Find the poleax," he demanded. "It is here. In the Light. If you wish to remain, you will find it and bring it to me."

"What light? You mean the sun?"

"The Light is the beginning of the road."

"And what happens if I find this poleax thing?" I asked. "Will you leave me alone? And Sydney?"

Damon laughed. It was hideous. I had been thinking that he was a mindless ghost warrior from another time, but he had more going on than that. He was crafty. He knew how to work me and others. That had been proven over the last week. He had pulled Gravedigger out of my head to haunt me. He twisted my familiar life into a grisly house of horrors. He had driven people to insanity and death. This guy was smart and he had plans. Bad plans.

"So many questions," he said, sounding bored.

"I want to understand," I replied.

"You do not matter!" he bellowed, suddenly losing his patience.

"Really? Then you're spending an awful lot of energy on somebody who doesn't matter. I think maybe I'm pretty important or you'd get somebody else to help you."

Damon leaned back and let out an angry howl that shook the ground.

I was frustrating him, which may have been a really bad move. But at that point there was nothing to lose, so I added, "I think maybe you need me or you'll never find this poleax thing."

Damon stopped moving and fixed his eyes on me. I shuddered. Looking into them was like gazing into the depths of a grave. My grave.

"You will bring me the weapon," he said through clenched teeth.

"Weapon? The poleax is a weapon?"

"It is *my* weapon. I created it."

"So create another one," I said.

"There is no other. I will not be denied again."

"Again? You've been through this before?"

"Find it!" he shouted.

"Sorry, but I have no idea where it is."

Damon looked out over the sea of corpses. What was he thinking? Was he going to lash out and grab me the way he had that corpse? I didn't move. Where would I go? This was his show.

"I believe you," he said, regaining control.

I could breathe again. Was it going to be that easy?

He added, "But you can find it."

No, it wasn't.

"I don't know where to look," I said.

"The poleax is in the Light, but the answer is in the Black."

He started moving again. This time when he looked at me, I sensed something different. Something sinister. He wasn't trying to scare me anymore. He was stalking me. I backed off but couldn't go far because of the snare of corpses.

"The answer has always been in the Black," he muttered.

"What is the Black? What does that mean?"

Damon reached out and grabbed another corpse. He took its skeletal arm and wrenched it from the body like he was snapping the leg off a roast turkey. He stripped the finger and hand bones away until he was left with one solid bone, which he clutched like a weapon. My stomach lurched again, both from the gruesome image and the realization that he now had a weapon . . . and was coming after me. I looked around for an escape route but saw only a sea of the living dead.

"You will walk the road and enter the Black," Damon said. "You will find the poleax."

I was starting to panic. "Tell me what the Black is," I said, groping for something, anything, trying to buy time for I-didn't-know-what. "Where is it? How do I get there?"

"There is only one way to enter the Black," Damon said.

"Okay, how?"

He picked up the pace.

"You must die."

It had come to this. All that had gone on before meant nothing. I was going to die. If there was anything I'd learned in the last week, it was that spirits existed. Maybe that was good because I was about to become one. My back hit the mausoleum. I had nowhere to go. Damon rounded the reflecting pool. He wasn't in a hurry. I think he enjoyed watching his prey sweat.

"This will be painful," he said with a hint of glee as he tapped the brown bone in his outstretched hand. The guy was a monster in more ways than one. He was about to add to the body count and that excited him. He stood opposite me, his legs apart, staring me down through dead eyes.

I glanced around for something I could use to defend myself. What a waste. Even if I found a stick or a brick, I was no match for this giant of a ghost. There was only one chance for me. I had to make a run for it . . . straight through the crowd of bodies. They were gruesome but frail. What was the worst that would happen? They'd grab me and throw me back at Damon's feet? If they didn't, getting lost in the thousands of bones might slow the ghost enough for me to get away. Or hide. Or do anything other than accept death without a fight.

"This is your choice," Damon said as he took a step closer. "I will allow you to stay in the Light if you bring me the poleax."

That was my lifeline. If I agreed to help him find his precious weapon, I would live. I didn't know what a poleax was or why I was the one who had to find it, but as I stood there seconds from death, I was ready to agree to anything. My mind flew back to what had happened over the past week. I had been tortured by this guy. Worse than that, he had killed Cooper. And George O. And Reilly. Who knew if Cayden and Vrtiak would ever be the same? I didn't know who this ghost was or how he came to be, but he had frightening powers. Would getting the poleax make him even stronger? What then? Who else would he terrorize? How many other lives would he destroy?

Damon stalked closer, clutching the sharp bone that would end my life. I wondered how badly it would hurt.

"Answer me," Damon growled. "Do you live in the Light? Or die in the Black?"

I didn't want to die, but how could I help this guy after what he'd done? How could I live with that? It would be like trading my soul for my life, and that wasn't a swap I was prepared to make. I stood there, paralyzed, unable to make a decision. I couldn't stand looking at the demon anymore, so I made an incredibly feeble gesture and turned away from him. He could do whatever he wanted. I didn't care anymore. I was done.

What I saw when I turned around changed my mind about that.

Of all the things I had seen . . . all the illusions, all the incredible images that haunted me, nothing could have prepared me for what I was confronted with after I made that turn. It made me believe that in spite of the corner I had been backed into, I might not be done after all.

Standing on the rim of the reflecting pool, leaning against a shattered statue with his arms folded casually, was my best friend.

Cooper Foley was back.

25

Cooper didn't look anything like the other corpses.

There were no signs of injury. He was wearing jeans and a T-shirt, not the jacket and tie his parents had buried him in. He looked pretty much exactly as he did in life with one small difference: I could see through him. He seemed solid enough until one of the corpses behind him moved . . . and I saw the movement through Coop's body. It wasn't Cooper's body standing there—it was his spirit. He had come back to help me this one last time.

Whatever he was going to do, he would have to do it fast because Damon was almost on me. The ghost warrior saw that I·was focused on something other than him and looked up to see Cooper.

Cooper gave him the finger.

Damon looked shaken, or about as shaken as a spirit

warrior from another time could look. He glanced quickly to me, then back to Cooper.

"Is this what you wish?" he called to Cooper. "For him to join you?"

Damon was surprised to see Cooper, which meant it wasn't an illusion he had created for me. Cooper was really there. Or at least his spirit was. He didn't speak, which wasn't like him. He looked to me and held up both his hands and patted the air as if to say, "Don't move."

Not moving was the last thing I wanted to do. Cooper or no Cooper, I had to do something or this giant ghost would skewer me with a cadaver bone.

"You can save him," Damon bellowed at Cooper. "End this now. Make him see."

I didn't need Cooper to save me. I could do it myself. All I had to do was agree to help Damon. I looked to Cooper. He held his hands up again and slowly shook his head "no." His movement made his image become more transparent, as if the act was using up his energy, but his intent was clear. He didn't want me to help Damon. Damon whipped back toward me and lifted the bone weapon high over his head.

"I will let you live," he snarled at me. "If you bring me the poleax."

I looked to Cooper. Cooper didn't look nervous at all, but Cooper never looked nervous. He took a few steps toward me, smiled, and gave me the sign. The double okay that meant everything was going to be fine. If he could speak, I knew what he would say: "Trust me, Ralph." That effort was his last. Cooper's image faded. He was gone and I was alone.

I looked up at the spirit warrior, who had the bone held high, ready to bash my head in. His body was shaking with rage. The scars that slashed across his face were angry and red. He was loaded and ready to strike.

"What is your answer?" he shouted.

All I had to do was agree to help this monster find his poleax thing and my life would be saved. A simple "yes" and I'd be spared the pain. But a horrible death might be easy compared to what would come after. If there really was a Morpheus Road, and many different paths to take on it, giving in to this monster might send me down a route that was far worse than anything I could imagine. In the end, the answer wasn't easy, but it was obvious.

I stood up defiantly, looked straight into the dead eyes of my tormentor, and said, "I'm not helping you."

The demon raised the bone higher. I didn't flinch. I trusted Cooper.

Damon shook with rage. He took a step backward and with a ghastly, anguished scream he went ballistic and brought the bone down . . . smashing it onto the ground.

"Raaaaaa!" he screamed, the horrific bellow echoing off the marble tombs.

The bone shattered, sending sharp white splinters everywhere. The pieces multiplied, spread out, and flew away from the impact point. The wave of bone material grew like ripples on a lake. Several hit me but passed through harmlessly.

They were shadows.

Illusions.

Cooper knew what he was doing.

The storm of bone matter hit the circle of cadavers and cut through them like an acid-laced buzz saw, vaporizing everything it touched. Row after row of the living corpses disappeared. The bone matter acted like an eraser, spreading wider, wiping them out of existence. The corpses didn't react. They had no feelings. They weren't real. In seconds every last body was gone, leaving only the destroyed remnants of the cemetery . . . and Damon.

The demon spirit was down on one knee, breathing hard, still clutching the remaining fragment of bone in his big hand.

"You have no physical power, do you?" I said. "Cooper knew that."

"There are worse things than physical pain," Damon said between breaths. "I gave you a choice. Now you must live with the consequences. How much are you willing to endure before giving me what I seek?"

Damon raised his fist into the air and looked to me one last time.

"You will walk the road with me," he said. "And you will suffer."

He brought his fist down, punching the ground so hard that the earthquake returned. There was a rumbling sound that could have been thunder, or the final destruction of the cemetery. I stumbled forward, tripped over the edge of the reflecting pool, and fell into the water. The pool was maybe six inches deep, but my head hit the bottom as water stung my eyes. I fought to stay conscious. If I had been knocked out with my head in the water, Damon would have gotten me to the Black after all.

The Black. What the hell was that? And why did you have to die to get there?

I raised up on my hands and knees, my head spinning. I kept my eyes on the water until my head cleared, watching the water ripple between my outstretched arms. As the water grew still, a bright light appeared and reflected off the surface. I thought of the light that had guided us out of the boathouse. Had Cooper come back? The water settled and the light came into focus. It was unmistakable. It was real. I lifted my head to see it and my heart sank. It wasn't Cooper. It was the sun. Whatever force or illusion Damon had used to darken the skies was no longer in play. Puffy white clouds drifted across a deep blue sky. It was a beautiful day. The same kind of day that we had buried Cooper. I looked around to see that the cemetery had returned to normal. There wasn't a bit of damage. It had all been an illusion. Cooper knew that, which was why he didn't want me to run . . . or to agree to help Damon. He knew that Damon couldn't hurt me. At least not directly. If I had done something stupid like run out into traffic or drive a boat into a floating plane, that would be different. Once again, Cooper had saved me.

"Man, I thought for sure you were going to take off," came a familiar voice from behind me.

I thought it was another illusion. Or my mind was playing tricks. Or anything other than what I hoped it would be.

"Kinda creepy to be swimming in a cemetery, Ralph," the voice said.

I whipped around to see Cooper standing by the mausoleum. He was barely visible. It was more like seeing a faint echo of Cooper. I stared at my friend's spirit, stunned, unable to speak.

"Close your mouth, you look like a trout," he said.

Cooper's image disappeared, only to appear again a few feet away. I stepped out of the pool and stood across from him.

"I . . . I don't understand . . . Cooper? What's happening?"

"Very cool, Ralph. That took guts."

"Not really. I trusted you."

"I'm trying my best," he said. "It's hard. I don't have much control."

Every time he spoke, his image disappeared, only to appear somewhere else. It was like the wind was blowing him around.

"Are you okay?" I asked.

"Well, no. I'm kind of dead, Ralph," he said. "But it's cool in the Black. Sort of."

"What is the Black?"

Cooper disappeared. I glanced around quickly, desperate to find him.

"Cooper!"

He appeared again on the far side of the memorial garden. "You're in Trouble Town, Ralph."

"Yeah, tell me about it. Who is Damon?" I asked.

Cooper disappeared again and reappeared on the exact opposite side of the garden. "A total foul ball, but you know that. Don't help him. Whatever happens, whatever you see, don't help him."

"What is the poleax?" I asked.

"I don't know for sure, but he wants it bad. It's why he killed me, Ralph. To get to you, to get the poleax."

My head spun. It really was true. This whole thing was about me.

"But why?" I cried. "I . . . I don't know anything about a polcax."

Cooper disappeared. This time he reappeared directly in front of me. I took a surprised step back.

"I'm doing what I can to help you. You know that, right?"

I nodded. "Yeah. Thanks."

"Keep your head on straight. Don't believe the impossible. Damon can do stuff I can't. He's had a lot more practice than me. But remember, it's all an illusion."

"So what happens if he gets the poleax?" I asked.

"Then it won't be an illusion anymore."

I had no comeback for that. It was too frightening a concept to even imagine.

"I got your back," Cooper said as he winked out, then came back. "Just like always."

"I miss you, Coop."

"Me too. Those things I said? I'm sorry. I was mad."

"I know."

"And tell Sydney I think she's cool for what she's doing."

"She really cares about you," I said.

Cooper smiled. It didn't matter that he was barely visible. His cocky smile came through. "Of course she does. She's not a total Agnes."

He may have been dead, but he was still Coop. How strange is that?

"Don't be sad for me, Marsh. I'm okay. There's a lot going on. Some of it is pretty sweet. Then again . . ."

"Yeah. Then again." I reached out to Cooper, but he disappeared. As his image faded, I heard him say, "Be cool. I'm around." But it was like whispers on a far-off wind.

I waited a few seconds for him to reappear.

"Coop?" I called out.

There was no answer. I felt like I had lost my best friend for a second time. But he had said he would be around and I believed him. I believed in ghosts. And why not? My best friend happened to be one.

Things had changed so much over the course of one week. My toes had been over the edge of the abyss between life and death and I had no idea why.

The sound of two sharp beeps of a car horn echoed across the cemetery. I ran for the sound without even thinking. I sprinted past the now peaceful mausoleum, up the hill of ancient graves, and beyond the weeping willow tree on top, where I could look down the far side . . . to see Sydney's silver Beetle, right where she had parked it. The door opened and Sydney stepped out. I sprinted down the hill, weaving my way through tombstones, and didn't stop until I reached her. If I hadn't been so overcome with emotion, I wouldn't have done what I then did. I grabbed her in a bear hug and held her close. I didn't care that I had crossed a line. I wanted to hold her and know for certain that she was real.

She was definitely real . . . and she hugged back.

"I thought you were dead," I said.

"I thought so too," she replied.

"What happened?"

"It was that statue. The angel. He closed his wings around me and everything went dark. I must have blacked out or something because the next thing I knew I woke up next to my car."

I held her at arm's length, looking into her beautiful eyes.

"None of it was real," I said.

"Yeah, I got that," she said. "But still, when I was in the dark, I heard a voice. It sounded like Cooper's."

"What did he say?"

Sydney snickered and shook her head. "It's wild what your mind can do when you're under stress. I could have sworn he said: "Keep the tattoo. It's you.""

I laughed. "I'll bet that's exactly what he said."

Sydney gave me a curious look. "What happened, Marsh? Was it Gravedigger?"

I took one more look around the cemetery and at the fresh grave where my friend, her brother, was laid to rest. Where his human body was laid to rest.

"Gravedigger is gone. For good. But it's not over, Sydney."

Sydney nodded. "Didn't think so."

"I don't know what's going to happen next, but there's one thing we can rely on."

"What's that?"

"Cooper's going to be there for us. And I think you should keep the tattoo too."

"That's two things," she said with a wink.

"Marsh," I heard someone call.

We both turned quickly to see a guy standing alone on the far side of Cooper's grave. It was Ennis Mobley.

"Now what?" Sydney said, worried.

"It's okay, he's a friend," I said, though seeing him standing there alone in that cemetery didn't feel right.

"Ennis!" I called out. "What are you doing here?"

He didn't move.

"Is this another illusion?" Sydney asked.

I walked toward him, making a wide circle around Cooper's grave. Ennis kept his eyes on me the whole way. Sydney followed close behind.

"What's the story, Ennis?" I said. "I thought you went to Pakistan."

"I had no choice but to return," he said.

I walked right up to my mom's old friend and reached out to touch his arm. I didn't think he was an illusion, but I wanted to be sure. I was relieved to find that he was solid.

"You came back just for the funeral?" I asked. "That's nice, but you didn't even know Cooper."

Ennis scowled. I saw beads of sweat growing on his forehead.

"What's going on, Ennis?"

"Did you break the crucible?" he asked.

Once again, my stomach twisted.

"How did you know about that?" I asked.

"About what?" Sydney asked, confused.

"Tell me," Ennis insisted. "Did you break it?"

My mind raced with a hundred questions and possibilities. None of them made sense.

"I asked you to call me," he said, his voice rising to a shrill whine. "Why didn't you call?"

"I tried," I said. "The call didn't go through."

Ennis's breathing grew quicker.

"What's he talking about, Marsh?" Sydney asked.

"Let's go home, Ennis," I said. "We'll talk with Dad and—"

"Tell me!" Ennis yelled. That wasn't like him. Not one bit. He was definitely on edge.

"Okay! I broke it," I said quickly. "I threw it against the wall."

Ennis's eyes grew wide as if I had just said the sky was falling.

"Broke," he repeated in a thin whisper as if trying to understand the word. It wasn't what he wanted to hear. He swayed like the news had a physical effect on him. For a second I thought he was going to faint.

I added, "It was full of blood, Ennis. It was all over my wall and then . . . it wasn't. What was that thing? How do you know about it?"

"It was your protection," he said, reaching into his pocket. "And this is how I know."

He pulled out . . . another golden ball. Another crucible. It was identical to the one I had smashed.

"This is mine," he said. "Here, take it."

He tried to force it into my hands, but I didn't want it. Things were happening too fast. It was my turn to sweat. I forced myself to focus and think logically. To try and understand. There were connections being drawn that I didn't like.

"What are they, Ennis? Where did they come from and how did that one get in my house?"

"Marsh," he said with tears in his eyes. "The crucible you destroyed . . . the one in your house . . . it belonged to your mother."

His words hit me like a punch to the gut.

He said, "When she no longer needed it, it was passed to you. I made a promise to your mother to keep you safe and I will do nothing less. She didn't want you to suffer for her mistakes and neither do I. Please take this one. Without it I cannot guarantee your safety, or the safety of your very soul."

I was beyond fighting. It was like I had entered a dream

state. I held out my hand and let Ennis place the golden orb in my palm.

"God help you, Marshall Seaver," Ennis said. "And those you love, here and beyond."

With all that had happened the past week, with all I learned that had challenged my understanding of how the world worked, nothing could have prepared me for that. I had come to accept that I was the target of a spirit who was hunting for an ancient weapon. For reasons I didn't understand, he chose me to find it for him. And now, after wondering in frustration for so long why I was at the center of the storm, the truth was more difficult to accept than anything I could have imagined.

It wasn't about me. Or Cooper. Or Gravedigger or any of the people who had been swept up in the mystery. I was being hunted, and haunted . . . because of my mother. My dead mother.

My journey was only beginning, but at least I no longer felt alone. Cooper's spirit was with me. So was Sydney. I had no idea where we were all headed, but I had no doubt about how we would get there.

We were all about to set foot on a supernatural highway known as the Morpheus Road.

Epilogue

I believe in ghosts.

It's not like I have a choice. After all that's happened over the last week, I pretty much have to come down on the "ghosts are real" side of the debate. To be honest, I never thought about it before. I do now. A lot.

Week? Did I say a week? I think that's how long it's been, but there's no way to know for sure. Time doesn't have much meaning when you're dealing with the supernatural. Though I guess I can't call it supernatural anymore. There's nothing *super* about it. It's just . . . natural. I've seen so much and had experiences that I never thought possible. Some of it's okay. Great, even. I mean, the idea that after you die, it doesn't mean that your story is over is pretty cool.

But it's not like what most people think. It's definitely not what I thought, not that I thought much about it. Dwelling on death isn't something I planned on doing for another seventy years. At least.

From what I can tell so far, and I'm still trying to figure it all out, your destiny isn't necessarily set in stone after you stop living. There are still choices to be made and paths to choose. That much was made pretty clear to me by a nasty spirit named Damon, among others.

The guy has caused a lot of people grief. I don't even know why. Not exactly, anyway. He's on a mission and it isn't a good one. Like I said, even after death there are choices to be made, and Damon is choosing to cause trouble.

With the living.

I want to ignore him. I wish I could. It's not like I want to be a hero and stop him from whatever vicious quest he's on. That's not me. But he's making that impossible. The guy is trying to get hold of some kind of weapon. If he finds it, things are going to get vicious. If I had a choice, I'd avoid the guy like the plague and let him do whatever he wants. I don't want to have to care, but that's not how it's working out. The thing is, for some reason his plan involves me. And people I care about. The guy has already caused a lot of deaths and he's barely gotten started. I can't let that go, as much as I'd like to.

I can try to stop him. Or not. That's the choice I'm faced with. Like I said, your destiny isn't complete when you die. Your story continues and I think I know where mine is headed. I can't let him continue down the road he's on because he's already caused too much trouble. People died. Lives were changed. That's a reality I can't ignore. After what I saw and experienced, there's one other bit of reality that can't be ignored.

I now believe in ghosts.

I have to, because I'm one of them.

My name is Cooper Foley and after you hear my story, you'll believe too.

To be continued . . .